The Elementals—a unique environmental fantasy from the legends of our ancestors and the fears of our children.

"A roaring good read . . . no mere modern retelling of ancient saga. This time, indeed, a truly remarkable author has ambushed us. Profoundly."

—Turlogh O Faolain

"Reading *The Elementals* is an intensely rewarding, startling experience . . . startling because at first it 'just' seems to be an engrossing, yet essentially familiar fantasy adventure, but soon the reader is hurled into a mighty odyssey crafted as skillfully as a Chopin etude and culminating in a powerful ecologic warning."

—Marvin Kaye

"Never does Llywelyn neglect her storytelling in order to make her point. Each novella is compelling, and as they came to an end I found myself wishing that she had lingered and told more; and yet the headlong rush through time and across the generations is part of the effect she was trying for, and it works. This is fantasy at its best. The societies and characters are real; the magic does not take over the story, but rather underlies it like a living foundation that every now and then shrugs, shaking all that is built upon it. This is the first of Llywelyn's fiction that I have read; I was astonished and faintly embarrassed that somebody this good could have escaped my attention for so long. . . . Reading *The Elementals* was, for me, a wonderful introduction to Llywelyn's work. Go thou and do likewise."

—*The Magazine of Fantasy & Science Fiction*

"As in much environmental fantasy, there are overtones of Gaian mysticism in the book . . . [but] Llywelyn draws less on current political issues than on her demonstrably superior talents as a historical novelist. When there is a past or exotic world to be conjured up, she does it with great skill."

—*Booklist*

"Compelling reading about the powers of the earth with a contemporary environmental message."

—*VOYA*

THE ELEMENTALS

Morgan Llywelyn

TOR

A TOM DOHERTY ASSOCIATES BOOK NEW YORK

THE ELEMENTALS

Copyright © 1993 by Morgan Llywelyn

A Tor Book
Published by Tom Doherty Associates, LLC
175 Fifth Avenue
New York, NY 10010

www.tor.com

Tor® is a registered trademark of Tom Doherty Associates, LLC.

Book design by Maura Fadden Rosenthal

Library of Congress Cataloging-in-Publication Data

Llywelyn, Morgan.
        The elementals / Morgan Llywelyn.
              p. cm.
        ISBN 0-312-85568-0 (hc)
        ISBN 0-765-30697-2 (pbk)
        I. Title.

    PS3562.L94E4 1993   93-12760
    813'.54—dc20   CIP

First Hardcover Edition: June 1993
First Trade Paperback Edition: June 2003

Printed in the United States of America

0 9 8 7 6 5 4 3 2 1

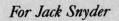

For Jack Snyder

The earth does not belong to Man.
We are merely tolerated.
For now.

We are the sea.

We are the planet's dual-purpose organ of reproduction and reverence. The trinity of sun, moon, and earth exchange their sacred energies through the linkage we provide.

We acknowledge no limits, merely impediments that we continually whittle away. We are a prism through whose liquid lens the colorful diversity of the planet is refracted. We contain the images of Atlantis and Lemuria and Mu, of transoceanic Pheonician trading vessels and the Titanic and the five lost planes of Flight 19.

Aswarm with life, we think trillions of versions of thought. Our sentience is in your blood, in everything that contains water.

We are the sea.

We do not see humans as humans perceive themselves. The creature called Man appears to us as a core of heat giving off radiance in the warm spectrum. Man is a seeker of solid surface, a self-replenishing organism capable of creating toxic wastes.

Man is a cancer that crawled from our womb.

We are watching. We are aware. We are the sea.

1

As the ice cap melted, the seas rose.

When they realized the land mass would be

inundated, people reacted in various ways. Some

planned, some panicked. Some did nothing, retreat-

ing into apathy until it was too late.

A colony of craftspeople that had established itself on the western shore of a forested peninsula built a boat. They equipped it with oars and a square sail, and painted it a defiant crimson. They worked night and day on their project while the sea crept higher with each incoming tide.

Soon they found themselves having to fight to defend their boat from others who had not been wise enough to build one. The attacks grew progressively more desperate and savage. By the time the boat was completed only three men of the colony survived. Three men, and fifty females.

The woman called Kesair was big-boned and tawny-colored, with angry eyes. When the others gave way to despair, she climbed onto a stump left by the timbering and shouted at them. "Get ready to board and set sail! We must leave here before we are attacked again and lose the boat!"

"How can we," asked a grieving widow, "with no men?"

"We still have three," Kesair reminded her, "and our own strong backs. Don't just sit there! Let's get going!"

The surviving men, exhausted by their labors and battered by battle, gazed numbly at Kesair.

Fintan had broad shoulders and a noble head, but his face was grey with fatigue and blood was seeping from his bandaged arm. "She makes sense," he said hoarsely. "Let's do as she says."

"I don't like taking orders from a woman," Ladra growled.

"Then why didn't you get up on the stump and give the orders yourself?" asked Byth, the third man, who was slumped on the earth as if he had grown to it.

Ladra said defensively, "I was busy tarring the ropes."

"That's an excuse."

"Take the livestock from their pens and get them into the boat," Kesair ordered. After a brief hesitation, the others began complying. Fintan and Byth joined the women in the work, but Ladra stood off to one side, scowling, until so many people glanced at him contemptuously that he was forced to join them, muttering to himself.

They loaded a few small black cattle, a few long-legged sheep, a trio of yellow-eyed goats. The animals resisted but not very much. They could sense the sea, waiting to swallow them. They clambered up the ramp into the boat and stood shivering, with no control over their fate.

The humans felt the same.

When the moment arrived, they were sick with fear.

"We can go inland and wait a while longer," Ladra urged. "Perhaps the water will stop rising. We'd feel like fools then, if we had panicked unnecessarily. It would be better to be safe on dry land than on that boat somewhere. What if it leaks? What if it sinks?"

Kesair looked at the sea, heaving and muscular and alive. Then she looked down at her feet, where the first wavelets of the inrushing tide were already lapping her toes. "The peninsula will be inundated today," she predicted, "and I had rather be on the boat when that happens."

Turning her back on the others, she marched up the ramp.

They followed her. Timorously, casting anxious glances at the water and the land as if there was a choice, they followed her. Even Ladra, in the end, boarded the boat.

They pulled up the ramp, secured their vessel, and settled down to wait for the sea to float the boat.

The water hissed around its timbers as the tide swept in, rising past all previous high-tide marks. Rising and rising. There was a gentle bump; the boat shifted slightly. Its occupants tensed but nothing happened. Then it rocked again and they heard a grating sound down below.

At that moment men came over the horizon, running hard, yelling, waving weapons.

"We're trapped here!" Ladra cried. "They'll kill us and take the boat!"

The running men drew closer, shouting threats and demands. Byth, who was a grandfather, regretted his age. Fintan regretted his wound. Ladra shook his fist at Kesair. The women drew together in the center of the boat as the sea, testing, tentative, gave a tug at the vessel.

Then it wrenched the boat free from its blocks and swung it into the tide with a creak and a groan and a mighty rolling motion.

Kesair gasped and caught hold of the nearest support. A cow bellowed, a goat bleated. The waves pounded in, devouring the shore, hurling the boat forward like a battering ram. Its attackers broke ranks and ran, making for the rapidly shrinking surface of the dry land. The sea pursued them, driven by a power beyond all understanding. Reclaiming the earth.

The boat was hurled across a shallow sand spit and into deeper, roiling water that swept it away like a leaf on a river.

At first its occupants were too dazed to do more than hang on and stare back at the land as it fell away from them. They were dazed by the rapidity with which they were launched. The square sail was still furled at the mast, the oars lay untouched in their oarlocks. No one was doing anything, except the sea with its unexpected tidal surge.

"Can't we steer this thing?" Kesair cried.

Fintan shook off his shock and hurled himself toward the tiller. His wounded arm was the left; his right arm was undamaged, and strong enough to grasp the tiller and begin trying to bring some direction to the boat's gyrations. When she saw what he was doing, Kesair made her way to him and crouched down beside him, adding her strength to his on the tiller.

Through the wooden shaft and up into their straining arms came a sense of the boat and the water beneath it. Their efforts seemed hopelessly minuscule, compared to the forces with which they struggled, yet a faint response shuddered through the boat timbers. Out of sight, the rudder moved, making a statement against the tide.

The prow of the boat edged northward.

"Yes," Kesair said. "Yes!"

"We can't do anything with the tiller alone," Fintan told her. "We need the oars and the sail."

She repeated his words in a shout of command, addressing them to whoever would respond. Byth and Ladra were the first. It was hard work and they were awkward, being carpenters rather than sailors. Those who knew how to manage the boat had died defending it.

Some of the women began trying to help them. Confusion mounted. Men and women got in each other's way, stumbled, lost their tempers. An oar was somehow broken, snapped like a twig.

Fintan groaned in despair. "We have to do something," he said through clenched teeth. But he did not say what.

Kesair knew no more about boats than the rest of them. She was a weaver. But she was familiar with lines, leverage, spatial relationships. They were part of her craft. She squinted at the sail, which was now half-raised and flapping. "Take hold of that rope, that one there, and pull it toward you hard! No, toward *you!*" she shouted at Byth. Then, to one of the women, "And you there, take an oar and sit there, And you, next to her . . ."

They gaped at her, but did as she commanded. Hers was the only commanding voice in a great din of sea and snapping sail.

The sail tautened, the boat bounded forward.

Then the wind failed. The boat hung in the water. The inexperienced rowers flailed the oars to no purpose.

"Someone needs to set a beat for the oarsmen to follow, I think," said Fintan.

Kesair caught the eye of the oldest woman, Nanno, who had no useful strength, but had always been musical. "Nanno!" she shouted. "Pick up that broken oar and beat it against one of the kegs in a steady rhythm. The rest of you, follow the beat, row together!"

After a bit of trial and error and some ludicrous mistakes, the amateur crew began a rough approximation of rowing. The boat moved forward, slowly but with a sense of purpose.

"You don't know any more about boats than I do," Ladra said resentfully to Kesair. He was among the rowers, but had soon learned he did not enjoy the feeling of blistered hands.

She did not bother to answer him. The intensity of the task at hand—molding a crew out of people with no training, when she had no training in seamanship herself—took all her concentration. She paid no more attention to Ladra than to the bleating of the goats.

When the wind filled the sail, Kesair let the crew rest on their oars. When the wind fell off, they rowed again at her command. She began to feel an unfamiliar, and pleasant, sensation of power, as if the boat itself were consciously obeying her order.

The vessel was not easy to handle. It had been hastily built, wide in the beam to carry livestock, but with a draft too shallow and a rudder inadequate for the size of the boat. A rough sea would have swamped them.

But the sea was not rough. Once they passed beyond sight of land it subsided into vast grey-blue swells that heaved slowly, almost titanically, carrying the boat gently along. Toward sunset it grew even calmer, a huge beast settling itself for the night.

Fewer people were vomiting over the rails.

Byth leaned on his forearms on one of the barrels lashed to the deck, watching as the sail was lowered at Kesair's command. He felt shrunken by the immensity of sea and sky. "What will happen to us?"

"Did you say something?" Her task finished, Kesair turned toward him. She was hoarse from shouting orders.

"Just talking to myself. I . . . did you ever really believe the ice was melting?" he asked abruptly.

"I didn't pay much attention one way or the other, not for a long time. We were always being threatened with something, weren't we? Failing economy, disease, war; one after the other. That's why we moved to the peninsula. At least, that's why I did. To escape all the gloom and doom and live a constructive life in some sort of peace."

"Once it began, the disaster came upon us so fast," Byth said wonderingly.

She nodded. "What do you suppose has happened to the others?"

"Which others?"

"Everyone."

Byth drew a deep breath. "I don't know. It depends on where they were, I suppose. And how soon they realized the danger and began preparing for it."

"We didn't start soon enough, ourselves."

"No," Kesair agreed, "but at least we started. We didn't sit around waiting for someone else to save us. Those who waited are—"

"—probably dead now."

"Yes," she said sadly. "When I was a child, there were always strange men who wandered around prophesying the end of the world. My mother said we should feel sorry for them because they were mad."

"When I was a boy we threw stones at such men," said Byth. "If I had one of them here now, I would apologize to him."

"So would I."

Byth looked at Kesair out of the corner of his eye. He liked her. He wondered what she thought of him. He ran his fingers through the tight curls of his close-cropped, grizzled hair. You are an old man, he reminded himself.

Aloud, he said, "We have fifty females and only three men."

"What of it? There were always more women than men in the group anyway."

"But not such a disparity. Wherever we land, if we do land, it could be a problem."

"What are you talking about?"

"I am saying there is a possibility we may be the only people left alive. We haven't seen any other boats, not one. If you are going to be the leader, you have to think about these things."

"I never said I wanted to be the leader."

"No, but no one has challenged you for it."

"That's because they're dazed by everything that's happened."

"You were less dazed than the rest of us, it seems," Byth pointed out. "You could still think and act when action was most needed. That's what leadership is, I suppose. You have the title whether you sought it or not, and I suspect it will be very hard to put down."

Nightfall necessitated assigning people to stand watch. Kesair chose the most alert to take turns. Ladra was among them, grumbling, but he served his time when it came.

Kesair the leader had been created where only a weaver existed before.

When the last light faded from the sky it seemed to linger in the sea, a dark green luminosity lurking in the depths. Then it too faded. A velvety darkness, more intense and tangible than they had ever known, clamped down on the occupants of the red boat. Its weight pressed them into their weariness and they fell asleep thankfully, except for the few who had duties, or tried to stay awake long enough to search for familiar stars in the sky.

There were no stars. The night was overcast.

The wind ceased. The air was still.

The ocean surrounded them like a dark universe, oily-smooth, boundless. The brooding, merciless, destroying sea.

Empty except for themselves.

The boat drifted on the surface of the sea like a child's forgotten toy.

Trying to follow her mental image of a leader's behavior, Kesair had taken a place in the prow. There she spread her blankets for the night. She meant to sleep but lightly, just enough to restore a measure of energy.

The sail was lowered, the oars were in their locks. She had decided there was no point in trying to make more headway. They might as well drift during the night.

Tomorrow would be soon enough to decide on a course and begin a serious search for land.

But in which direction?

Kesair closed her eyes, but she could not sleep. Her eyeballs felt grainy against her lids. She opened them again and stared into the darkness.

The sides of the prow rose, curving, above her, like walls looming over her. Like waves about to crash down on top of her. She felt suffocated. She sat up abruptly and bunched her blankets behind her back, so she could lean against them without lying down.

Time passed without definition. Kesair tried to fight back the fears that kept surfacing in her mind. Her fists clenched with the effort.

A delicate, questing touch drifted across her face.

"What?" She glanced around, startled. She could make out only faint shapes in the darkness, but no one was anywhere near her.

There was no wind to have blown a strand of hair across her face.

Her mouth went dry. Don't panic! she told herself sharply. You're tired, that's all. You're imagining things.

She was touched again. This time the pressure was more pronounced.

Gooseflesh rose on her arms. Her frantically groping fingers found nothing in the air around her face.

She started to get up and was touched a third time. She froze, knees bent, one hand outstretched. The touch trailed lingeringly down her cheek, explored her lips, cupped her chin, then circled around below her ear, crawled up her hair, across the top of her head, down over her forehead, pressed her eyelids closed.

The thudding of Kesair's heart shook her entire body.

The pressure on her eyelids eased; she opened them. She was aware of a presence, unseen but palpable, beside her. The nearest human lay sleeping several paces away.

Something else was with Kesair in the night.

The night seemed endless. Byth's

years weighed heavily on him. He stayed awake

during his turn at watch with the greatest difficulty,

and gladly surrendered his post to Kerish when she

came to relieve him.

"What should I watch for?" she asked him.

"I don't know," he replied honestly. He shot a look in the direction of Kesair but she was only a shadowy shape in the prow, unmoving and unspeaking.

Byth was asleep before his head was pillowed on his arm.

Kerish shivered in the night and wrapped her cape more snugly around herself. She wished Kesair would come back and talk to her. Kesair was always so practical, so reassuringly full of common sense. But she seemed oblivious, sitting up there in the prow alone.

The night lasted for an eternity or two, then faded into a dull grey day. The sun never penetrated the clouds. The sea looked cold and sullen. And terribly, terribly vast.

Kesair came awake abruptly, surprised to find she had been asleep. Her muscles were stiff, her joints locked. When she tried to move she felt like a plant that had been frozen and would break rather than bend. She got to her feet slowly, holding on to the side of the boat.

When she stood and looked back at the others, she saw their faces turn toward her as flowers turn toward the sun. They sat waiting for her to tell them what to do next.

Seeing them waiting like that was a bit of a shock. I have to say something positive, she thought. They need it. *I* need it.

"We've passed safely through the night." She sounded pleased. "Perhaps we should offer a prayer now."

"A prayer?" They stared at her. Kesair had not been known as a fanatic before. Religion was unfashionable, an outmoded superstition. They believed Man was supreme in the cosmos, a belief Kesair had seemed to share. Before the catastrophe.

"I wouldn't care to pray to any deity who would let this happen to us!" the woman called Barra said angrily.

A murmur of agreement rose from the others. On their faces, Kesair read a threat to her newfound authority. If she tried to force the issue they might reject her.

She shrugged, and changed the topic to the distribution of food and assignment of tasks. After an uncertain pause, the group reverted to obedience. It was already becoming a comfortable habit. They were silently relieved that the embarrassing suggestion of prayer had been dropped.

Day wore on, became night, became day again. And again. They sailed this way and that, found no land, no people. Nothing. More and more, they simply drifted. It did not matter.

Social conventions were abandoned. Men and women openly relieved themselves over the side. Quarrels sprang up. The people were nervous, irritable, and apathetic by turns. Friendships were formed one day and broken the next.

Their food stores dwindled. The sea waited.

Byth droned on and on, listing an increasing catalog of physical complaints. The formerly brisk and bustling woman called Leel began sleeping the day away like a creature in hibernation.

Staring morosely at the sea, Ladra swore at the water bitterly, continually. He was inventive with profanity. Against her will, Kesair found herself listening to him. Once she laughed aloud.

He turned toward her, scowling darkly. "What are you laughing at?"

"Not at you. I was just enjoying your use of the language, that's all. You're very original."

He gazed at her for a long moment, then went back to cursing the sea. But after that he seemed more kindly disposed toward Kesair. That night when the food was distributed, he ate sitting beside her.

From his place opposite them, Fintan noticed the change in Ladra's attitude. He realized he was looking at Kesair differently himself. Before the catastrophe, he had paid her no attention. Women outnumbered men in the colony and he had always had his choice, which did not include Kesair. She was too tall, too fair, and he liked small dark women. More damning still, she was a loner. She did not seem to need a man. Fintan, who liked his women dependent, had ignored her. She was an exceptionally good weaver and did her share of the work, and beyond that he had no interest in her.

Before.

But now . . . he could hardly ignore the one person who had been able to take charge when he and the other surviving men were weary and defeated.

Surreptitiously, Fintan eyed the other female occupants of the boat. Old Nanno, two prepubescent daughters of a man who had been killed, an infant girl in her mother's arms. And forty-six women of childbearing age, including Kesair. Kesair, to whom the others deferred.

This gave Kesair an attractiveness Fintan had never noticed before.

Under his breath, he said to Byth, "Look at Ladra over there, trying to curry favor. Can't she see through him?"

"You sound jealous." Once Byth would not have commented on another man's emotions. But everything had been changed by the catastrophe. Byth stroked his chin, wondering when he had last shaved. None of the men shaved now.

"Jealous?" Fintan snorted. "Don't be ridiculous."

"Under the circumstances," Byth warned, "it wouldn't be a good idea to get too fond of any one woman. Think about it."

Fintan ignored him.

Byth shrugged. Arthritis bit deep into his shoulder and he rubbed the joint automatically, wondering how much damage the sea air was doing to him.

The color of the sea gradually changed. From slate-blue it became a warm, dark green. Kesair was the first to notice. She lifted her head and sniffed the wind.

"What is it?" Elisbut asked. Elisbut was a cheerful, chubby woman who made pottery and talked incessantly. "What do you smell?"

"Change in the wind," Kesair said succinctly. She did not want to encourage a flood of conversation.

Anything was enough to set Elisbut off, however. "I don't smell anything unusual, Kesair. Perhaps you're imagining things. I used to do that all the time. My mother—you would have liked her—my mother used to tell me I had too much imagination. Now I never thought a good imagination was such a liability in an artistic person like myself, but . . ."

Kesair was not listening. "We're going to change course," she shouted abruptly to her crew.

Within half a day they caught sight of a thin dark line on the horizon and knew they had found land.

Sailing in from the northwest, they made landfall on the rocky coast of what seemed to be a vast island. It was hard to be certain; most of the land was shrouded in mist. The boat ground ashore on a beach of white sand studded with black boulders. After dragging their vessel as far up the beach as they could, they secured it and set about exploring the immediate area.

"No sign of people," Ladra reported after scrambling up the nearest cliff and back down again. "But there is a sort of wiry grass up there, and I'd say we could find fresh water if we go in just a little way. We've been lucky. So far," he added darkly. "This could be a bad place. I wouldn't be surprised."

Kesair assigned armed scouting parties to explore the area more thoroughly. All brought back similar reports. Thin soil, unsuitable for farming, but a lushness of wild vegetation. A pervasive mist that rolled over the land, blew away, returned with a will of its own. Glimpses of distant grassland bordered by forest. Outlines of mountains beyond.

"If we have to start life over," Fintan said, "I would say we've found a good place for it."

They built a bonfire of driftwood that night on the headland above the beach. When Kesair found some of the women throwing the refuse from the boat into the sea, she ordered them to put it on the fire instead.

"What difference does it make?" they challenged. They did not want to carry armloads of rubbish up the slope to the fire. "One load of garbage in an empty ocean, what difference?"

But this time Kesair was adamant. Grumblingly, they obeyed. The tongues of the fire licked at the rubbish and a dark smoke rose from it, stinking of the old life.

Blue twilight settled over them. Down on the shore, the red boat gleamed dully in the last rays of the setting sun, then turned grey, like a beached whale dying at the edge of the sea.

As they ate their first meal on dry land, some people talked compulsively about their recent experience, retelling the boat-building and the battles and the flood, incidents which were already taking on a mythic quality in their minds. Others sat silently, simply trying to comprehend. Trying to realize that they were safe at last.

Kesair was not so certain of their safety. Any sort of danger might await them on dry land, on what seemed to be a very large and unknown island. They could die a more horrible death in the jaws of wild beasts than they would have suffered by drowning in the sea.

The next morning, Kesair organized work parties to build huts for the people and pens for the livestock. The men and women were to be housed separately, for the time being, and as leader she ordered a hut built for herself alone.

"Why don't we go farther inland?" Byth suggested.

"Not yet. We don't know what may be waiting for us. It's better we stay here for a while until we are established and used to the place."

The truth was, she was reluctant to leave the sea. But she did not say this.

They worked hard, bringing timber from the distant forest. They met no savage beasts, but twice they reported hearing a howling in the distance, as of wolves, and they were overjoyed to sight a herd of deer beyond the trees.

The group settled into a domestic routine not unlike the one they had known before the catastrophe. "We're lucky," she told Byth, who had become the closest thing she had to a confidant. "Among us we have most of the skills we shall need. We can make our own tools and clothing, we can build and repair."

She set up her big loom in the lee of her hut, where the morning sun supplied a clear yellow light.

Not everyone was ready to settle down. Some seemed devoted to grieving over what they had lost, hampering the work of the colony. Kesair learned she could rely on Elisbut, Fintan, Kerish, and the women called Ayn and Ramé to do what must be done, and enlisted them to help her encourage the others.

On a chill, damp afternoon when rain blew in from the sea in curtains of silver, Fintan came to Kesair's hut. He paused in the doorway, stooping, peering in, waiting for his eyes to adjust to the gloom. "Are you in here?" he asked uncertainly.

"I am," she said from a bed made of piled blankets. "I was just resting, listening to the rain."

Without waiting for an invitation, Fintan entered the hut. He gave off a smell of wind and water. "We need to talk."

"Sit there." The thought skittered across Kesair's mind that she should offer him food, or drink, but she was a solitary creature by nature and had never practiced the skills of hospitality. "Help yourself to whatever you want," she said lamely, making a vague gesture in the direction of her stores.

"Talk is what I want, some sort of plan. We can't just stay like this, Kesair. Winter is coming on, we probably need to go farther inland to avoid the worst of the weather. We don't even know how bad winter gets in this place."

"So how do we know it might be milder inland?"

"It stands to reason. And there's another thing . . ." His eyes were used to the dimness now. He could see her leaning on one elbow, watching him, her long legs stretched out beneath a blanket. Suddenly the hut seemed very small and intimate.

"What?" she said.

He swallowed. "We need to get on with our lives. We've been tiptoeing around this for weeks, but we must face the fact. As far as we know, we may be all that remains of the human race. If we don't reproduce ourselves, it could be the end of mankind.

"Of course, it could be too late already, I know that. But I feel an obligation to try . . ." He ground to a halt. She was looking at him intently, with an unreadable expression.

He picked up the threads of his thought. "People look up to you, Kesair. The other women follow you. If you were to urge them to, ah . . ."

"Mate," she said.

He had not expected her to put it so baldly. "Ah, yes. Mate. Have children, a lot more children . . ."

Kesair sat up, clasping her knees with her square, blunt-fingered hands. She locked his eyes with hers. "Fifty women alone on a large island with three men," she said in an expressionless voice. "Just imagine. Every man's fantasy."

He said huffily, "I'm not proposing an orgy, Kesair! You're an intelligent woman, you know exactly what I'm saying. You understand that—"

"—that you hope to use my mind to get at my body," she said flatly. "If you can. If I let you."

Stung by the truth in her accusation, Fintan retorted, "You don't have a very good opinion of men, do you?"

Kesair did not answer. He could have enjoyed an argument, but he had no coping skills for female silence.

Fintan tried to recall what he knew about her, seeking some sort of leverage. She was a latecomer to the crafts colony, having arrived with neither man nor child, only her loom and her skill, but she had proved to be an exceptionally creative weaver. Soon her work had been in great demand among the colony's customers, becoming a mainstay of their economy. No one had been willing to risk offending her by prying into her private life.

Very little was known about Kesair, Fintan realized. She was something of a mystery.

A most intriguing mystery.

He must get her to trust him. "I don't much care for the company of men myself," he told her confidingly. "I really prefer women, always have. I think women are the best of us." He favored her with his most winning smile, knowing his teeth were white and even and his eyes crinkled boyishly.

Kesair stared right through him, unimpressed.

Fintan choked back his annoyance. Did she not understand that men were now at a premium? That he could have his choice of any woman he wanted? He could walk out right now and it would be her loss, not his. He had forty-five others to choose from.

But he did not walk out. There were forty-five others, but Kesair was the leader. She was not beautiful, like Kerish, but she was special, she had an indefinable something extra. And he was Fintan, whose pride demanded he go for the best.

Wiping his smile from his face, he replaced it with a studiedly serious expression he thought she might like better. "What we need to do, Kesair, is to divide the women into three groups. Each man will take responsibility for one third of the women, do you see?" He paused. "Well, not Byth, perhaps. He may be a little old. But he can at least take a few and Ladra and I can handle the rest."

"Responsibility? What sort of responsibility? There is already a leader. Myself."

She is pretending to be stupid to irritate me, Fintan thought. She wants to be blunt; very well. I can be blunt. "Responsibility for them sexually. For getting them pregnant," he elaborated, trying to stare her down.

To his astonishment, she laughed. "Is that all? Fine. Pick out your—how many would you say, twenty each for you and Ladra, and ten for Byth?—pick out your twenty and get on with it. Just don't impregnate all the sturdiest ones at the same time, we need to keep an able work force. And wait for the younger girls to grow a few more years before you start with them."

Fintan's jaw sagged with dismay. What had happened to the titillating mating games a woman was supposed to play? He had imagined a very different sort of afternoon in Kesair's hut, listening to the rain on the roof, talking first impersonally and then very personally of sexual matters, advancing, holding back, weighing selected phrases with double meanings, gradually offering more intimate caresses. The mounting excitement, the thrill of the chase . . .

"Which women do you want?" Kesair drawled with supreme indifference. She twisted her upper body to put back a piece of chinking that had fallen from between the timbers of the hut wall beside her. The repair had her total attention.

Fintan got to his feet. "Not you, anyway!" he told her. He stomped furiously from the hut into slanting silver rain.

Kesair turned her head to watch him go. A light flickered in her eyes. He's proud, she thought. I like that in a man.

Fintan sought Ladra, whom he found at the edge of the cliff, throwing rocks down at the sea as if he were pelting an enemy. There was hatred and anger in every throw.

The sea had swallowed the world he knew. Ladra hated the sea. From time to time he yelled curses at it.

"Come with me to the men's hut," Fintan said to him. "We need to talk."

Ladra squinted at him from beneath dark, tangled eyebrows. Ladra was slightly taller than Fintan, with long arms but disproportionately short legs. He looked as if he had been made from the parts of several men. "Is it important?"

"I think so," Fintan replied.

Ladra hurled one last stone, then shrugged and followed Fintan. "I'm tired of being wet anyway," he said.

The men's hut was empty. Byth was elsewhere. Fintan and Ladra went in out of the rain. The hut was small and dark and smelled of mud and freshly cut logs.

"It's time we organized our social structure for the future," Fintan began earnestly. "I've been giving it a lot of thought and I've come up with a workable, sensible plan."

Ladra listened, frowning, as Fintan outlined his idea. Then Ladra said, "I don't much care for all this organizing. It smacks of a desire to control. And I think the desire to control has caused a lot of mankind's problems, Fintan."

"There will be more problems if we don't agree on a plan soon and start to follow it. You can't put this many people together in this sort of situation without trouble, sooner or later. I'm just making the most intelligent suggestion. People need to know what to expect."

"But Kesair wants us to use our energies for getting dug in here for the winter, making more tools and weapons, setting up some sort of defensive perimeter in case—"

"We can do all that too," Fintan interrupted impatiently.

"What does Kesair say to your plan? You did discuss it with her, didn't you? She and I should be—"

"You're making assumptions. You can't just appropriate a woman for yourself, Kesair or anybody else. We have to be sensible about our, ah, breeding arrangements. We have to use our heads."

"Our *heads?*" Ladra said with a grin. "That's not how I do it."

Fintan had the grace to laugh. "You know what I mean."

"I know what you mean all right." The other man sobered. "I suppose you expect the best women for yourself?"

"To avoid arguments I thought we might, well, draw lots for them."

Ladra shook his head. "I can imagine you trying to convince those women out there that it's all right for us to draw lots for them. Good luck. I don't want to be around when you try to sell the idea."

"You always criticize," Fintan complained, "but you never have a better suggestion."

Ladra said smugly, "As it happens, this time I do. The other women accept Kesair as leader. So have her make the assignments, just as she assigns work. If she's willing to accept this plan of yours at all, that is. I'm not sure she is, I'd like to hear what she thinks."

"She said we should get on with it," Fintan said with perfect honesty.

"Did she now? Ah. Well then." Ladra seemed satisfied.

He thinks Kesair will give herself to him, Fintan thought darkly.

When Byth returned to the hut and was told of Fintan's plan another problem arose. Byth was insulted at the suggestion that he take fewer women than the other men.

"But you're always complaining about your age and your infirmities," Ladra reminded him. "You even call yourself Grandfather!"

"And so I am, which is just my point. Before my wife died I sired seven children on the dear woman, all of whom grew up to have more children. They went out on their own long ago, but let me assure you I am patriarch of a large brood of extremely healthy . . ." A shadow crossed his face. "At least, they were healthy. Strong, intelligent. Exactly the sort of people we need. I can give the colony many more like them. Divide the women equally and I can take care of mine, never fear."

Later, Fintan said privately to Ladra, "How many women are going to want to go with an old man?"

"That will be Kesair's problem, won't it?"

Kesair. As he lay wrapped in his blankets that night, listening to Byth snore like pebbles rattled in a bucket, and Ladra toss restlessly in his own bed, Fintan thought of Kesair and brooded on the choices she might make.

The perpetually moist air of the land they had found lay lightly on his skin; permeated his lungs; surrounded and contained him. A damp, penetrating cold seeped into his bones.

Fintan pulled his blankets more tightly around his shoulders. He was uneasy.

He did not sleep well.

3

When he emerged from the hut in

the morning, the rain had passed and a radiant

autumn sunshine was gilding Kesair's face as she

came toward him. She was returning from a dawn

visit to the

seashore, a strange habit she had adopted. Beckoning her aside, Fintan told her of his discussion with the other men, and Ladra's suggestion.

"So Ladra thought of that, did he?" She smiled, which irritated Fintan. "Good for him. Of course I'll divide the women among you. They will see the necessity for it; I'll talk to them and explain. Some of them may not like it, however. It's a pity we don't have a better choice of men."

Fintan bristled. "What do you mean by that?"

"I mean, I assume I shall have to select one of the three of you for myself, and it's not a particularly appealing thought."

There! she thought. See how you like that!

Fintan bit back an angry response. The thought briefly crossed his mind that Kesair might prefer women, but he discarded the idea. There was something in the back of her eyes that told him otherwise, he was sure of it.

Perhaps she just was not interested in sex. But he did not believe that either.

When Kesair talked to the other women, she got mixed responses. Some were plainly horrified. "It sounds like dividing a herd of cows among three bulls," Leel complained.

"I don't see what else there is to do," Kesair said flatly. "There aren't enough men to go around, and we have to think of the future. If this island has enough resources to allow us to survive, we must start planning for the next generation here."

"I refuse to be a breeding animal!"

"That's your prerogative, no one's going to force you. You'll simply be left out." Kesair folded her arms, waiting.

Left out. Leel hesitated, considering the ramifications. Kesair had chosen the phrase deliberately, and it carried weight. In a more subdued tone, Leel said, "Can't we at least choose our men?"

"If we tried, there would surely be quarrels and resentment. And the distribution would probably be uneven. No, I think it's better we make an unemotional assignment and abide by it. We can do that, I know we can," she added with a confidence she did not feel.

Some of them accepted. Others refused for a while. But in the end they agreed. Kesair had been thinking about the matter for longer than they had, and had her arguments skillfully prepared.

The night before Kesair was to announce her decisions, she walked alone by the sea. Without even bothering to eat an evening meal, she had gone to the beach, drawn by the hissing of the foam. The white sand glimmered in the moonlight. A cold wind blew off the ocean. Kesair shivered, then wrapped her woolen cloak more tightly around her shoulders.

After tomorrow, she thought, our lives will be changed in ways we cannot yet imagine.

She had counseled a pragmatic, unemotional approach to the situation, but she was too wise to believe it possible. By its very nature sex involved passion, and when human passions were aroused anything might happen.

Like someone exploring a sore tooth with just the tip of the tongue, Kesair let her thoughts skim the surface of her personal history. She thought for one brief moment of the man who had hurt her more than she would have believed possible. She had thought her emotions were cauterized by the experience.

Now she knew they were not. She could feel. She could be hurt again. She did not want to be hurt again.

In sharply delineated footprints the soft sand recorded every step she took at the ocean's edge. A blurred area showed where she finally halted and stood gazing outward, lost in thought, then started forward as if to enter the water, hesitated, scuttled backward, stopped again, stood at last immobile. Caught. Held.

She breathed shallowly. She did not want the sound of her own breath to interfere with the voice of the sea. She listened, and that voice built, became a great rolling thunder resonating through her bones, a massive muffled booming as if some mighty heart were beating there, out beyond the breakers. A long sigh . . .

"What?" Kesair asked eagerly. "What?"

The new day dawned cold and crisp. As the people assembled in the open space around which they had built the huts and pens, Kesair studied their faces. The men looked more anxious than the women. In their faces was a tension, a wary watchfulness of one another.

By contrast the women stood quietly, looking from one male face to the other with a glance both dispassionate and measuring.

"The sooner we get this over the better," Kesair announced. "There is no way to divide fifty evenly, so I've decided that two men will take seventeen women each, and the other man will have sixteen. Fintan and Byth have seventeen." She saw the look of surprised anger on Ladra's face but went on smoothly, "Byth's group will include Nanno and the girl children, because I am sure Nanno would prefer being with a man of her generation and the children already consider Byth as a grandfather."

Ladra's expression eased slightly. "Fintan still has more women than I do," he pointed out. "Shouldn't I get the best ones, to make up for that?"

"'Best' women?" Leel challenged. "Do you think it's your place to grade us on merit? Are you asking for the prettiest as if the others were inferior?" Her eyes were blazing. Leel was thin and dark and very intense, with a temper like the crack of a whip.

Kesair smiled to herself. She meant Leel for Ladra; let the two of them blunt their bad tempers on one another.

"Silence, both of you," she commanded.

Smoothly, without pausing for comment or reaction, she called out the names as she had mentally arranged them the day before. Ramé, who was calm and steady, was assigned to Ladra. The reliable Ayn, who had nursing skills, was paired with Byth. Kesair wanted to have at least one woman whose common sense she trusted in each group. Elisbut she assigned to Fintan. Velabro for Ladra. Barra for Byth. Salmé for Fintan. Murra for Ladra.

When she paired Kerish with Byth an astonished light leaped in the old man's eyes.

"Kerish will warm your blood," Kesair told him, smiling.

So the beauty of the colony went to a grandfather. To their credit, neither Ladra nor Fintan voiced an objection. Each grudgingly admitted to himself the wisdom of the choice, and was thankful that at least his rival would not have Kerish. She was ideal for stimulating an old man's virility.

As the number of unassigned women dwindled, Ladra kept trying to catch Kesair's eye. Fintan did not look at her. He accepted the assignments impassively, with a brief nod to each woman who was named for him. He might have been accepting a portion of food, or clothing, for all the emotion he showed.

He does not want to be hurt, so he pretends not to care, Kesair thought.

The day before, she had decided to assign herself to Byth's group. Byth in the role of father figure was appealing to her. Her own father had been loved, but was long dead. Besides, Byth would probably not make much in the way of sexual demands on her, not when he had Kerish.

The naming went on.

Kesair had given so much thought to her choices that she could recite them automatically, allowing her tongue to follow the grooves she had worn in her mind. she hardly had to think, merely to say, "Ashti to Ladra, Datseba to Byth, Kesair to Fintan . . ."

The words flashed through the air before she realized what she had said. Her tongue had betrayed her. She drew in a startled breath, as if she could unsay the words by inhaling them.

Fintan was looking at her now.

She dare not contradict herself and say she meant Byth instead. She would look like a fool.

She made herself go on. "Leel to Ladra . . ." But her heart was pounding as it had pounded the night before, when, all her choices made, she had gone for a walk by the sea.

Fintan's grey eyes were gazing at her fixedly. Ladra was flushed with anger.

She swallowed hard, trying to steady herself. Listening to her own words, she realized she had almost completed the list of names. The mother with the baby she must now give to Byth, to make the numbers come out right.

When the woman smiled with relief Kesair felt a stab of jealousy.

Once the divisions were made, people were curiously uncomfortable with each other. No one seemed to know what to do next until Byth said, "Come to me, all my chicks. This occasion deserves to be celebrated."

After a momentary hesitation, his women joined him. The littlest girl, Datseba, stood close beside him and slipped her small hand into his.

Byth grinned. Ignoring the arthritic twinge in his shoulder, he made an all-encompassing gesture with his free arm. "Follow me, please."

He led them to the men's hut, where he kept his small hoard of personal effects. Each female was given something. Datseba received a tiny carved figurine he had once meant for his own granddaughter, but not sent to her before the flood separated them forever. Old Nanno beamed toothlessly when Byth wrapped his favorite woolen scarf around her neck. Kerish was awarded the only gold ornament Byth possessed. He presented it with a gallant speech. "This dims by comparison with your beauty," he said.

The others watched from a distance as Byth won the hearts of each of his women in turn.

"An old man can get away with that," Ladra muttered. He began calling the names of his own assigned women. They stepped forward, some willingly, several reluctantly. When they were gathered around him he turned toward Kesair. "Am I expected to build individual homes for them or what? How are we going to do this?"

Kesair gave him a blank look, suddenly embarrassed to realize her careful planning had not foreseen the next step.

Fintan spoke up, and she was silently grateful. "We should stay as we are through the winter, until we know what winters are like on this island. In the spring we can go out and let each group find a different location for itself, some place with good soil for farming.

"This winter will give us time to get used to the new, ah, arrangements, and to plan for the future. Plus we will have the security of being together through the hard season."

Ladra cleared his throat. "What are we going to do about beds? As it is, the women sleep in several huts, the men sleep in another, it's awkward, considering."

In spite of himself, Fintan glanced at Kesair. She met his eyes unflinchingly but said nothing.

He scratched his jaw reflectively, wondering why she was leaving it to him to answer. "I don't think we should rush things," he said at last. "This isn't the way relationships were . . . before. We're all going to have to get used to the idea. Allow some time, and I suspect it will sort itself out. We might build a few, ah, private huts, where couples can be alone together. When they want to. But it's up to you, of course."

Fintan's words relieved some of the tension. As if saved from some disaster, the people threw themselves into their day's tasks with excessive enthusiasm, talking about everything but the change in the social order. Yet Kesair noticed the way Velabro kept glancing at Ladra. The way Elisbut winked at Fintan.

Kesair said nothing to Fintan beyond the requirements of their tasks. She was more formal with him than she had ever been. He showed the same attitude toward her. There was a new brittleness in their voices when they spoke to each other.

If she is so indifferent to me, Fintan was thinking, why did she burden me with herself?

Is he angry? Kesair wondered. He said he didn't want me, but I didn't think he meant it. What if he did?

They had other things to worry about. Winter was rushing in upon them. Every day seemed perceptibly shorter than the one before, and an awareness of night and dark and cold permeated everyone's thought. Almost daily, Kesair examined their supplies, watching with alarm as they dwindled. She organized hunting parties. The men went after the red deer with limited success; they were unused to hunting for the sake of survival. The deer, who were accustomed to avoiding predators, usually escaped them. Two does and a half-grown buck were all the men could bring down in a fortnight of hard effort. Then the deer took to the mountains and were seen no more, hiding successfully in enshrouding mist.

"You've led us to this place to starve," Ladra accused Kesair.

She read the same accusation in other eyes. They were already cold, and growing increasingly fearful of hunger. They had found a good harvest of autumn nuts and berries, but these would not see them through the winter.

In an effort to cheer them, Kesair ordered a huge fire built in the center of the compound and kept burning night and day, so its warmth was constantly available and its light could challenge the increasingly gloomy atmosphere. There were numerous cloud-muffled days when the sun never broke through the heavy overcast and the people were trapped in a perpetual twilight.

Kesair fought their depression with the fire. They huddled around it gratefully.

In its light, however, she could see their faces growing thinner. She cut back rations again and yet again, ruthlessly, in an effort to make them last. But last until what?

Instinct drove her to the sea at last. Buffeted by a gale, she walked along the wind-whipped shore, watching great crested white dragons rise out of the surf and fall back, snarling. The ocean wore a savage face. Yet she stayed beside it, numb with cold. She remained until the icy wisdom of the sea seeped into the marrow of her bones.

With chattering teeth she returned to the compound.

The fire was a warm orange god, shedding beneficent heat and light on its worshipers.

But there were other gods.

"Extinguish that blaze," Kesair ordered.

Shocked faces turned to stare at her. "What are you saying?" Byth cried.

"We are spending all our strength gathering wood for the fire. Then we crouch beside it until it's time to go get more wood. We are doing nothing else, and we're wasting wood. If we moved around more briskly we wouldn't be as cold. Bring buckets of water, dig earth and throw it over, to extinguish the fire. Then let's start seriously finding food for ourselves. We can't afford to pamper ourselves any longer."

It was the least popular order she had issued. People whined, protested, argued bitterly. Byth the kindly, the avuncular, called her a fool to her face. Salmé accused her of being callous. Datseba began to cry. Byth put a protective arm around the girl and glared over her head at Kesair. He looked like an eagle defending its nestling.

Unexpectedly, Ladra got to his feet with a grunt and began kicking dirt on the fire. "She's right," he said. "Everyone has to be right sometime. Let's go hunting."

Fintan raised his eyebrows in surprise. Ladra had been the first to be disheartened by their lack of success as hunters and abandon the effort. "The deer are long gone," he pointed out.

"We weren't good at catching deer anyway," Ladra replied. "But we've seen lots of birds, and there are any number of small animals in the woods. I've heard them even if I haven't seen them."

No one had any experience of building traps or setting snares. They had never required such primitive skills. But the weapons they had tried to use on the deer were not suitable for birds and small game, so they had to discover new techniques.

Working together, Murra and Ladra invented a clumsy trap that was nevertheless capable of catching hares and stoats, and minuscule voles. Stoat and vole were only edible if one were starving, but Kesair ordered that they be cooked anyway, and the people try to acquire a taste for them. Hare, roasted or boiled with root vegetables, became a staple of their diet.

As a weaver, Kesair was the one to construct snares to hide in woodland undergrowth. These produced a constant supply of small birds to augment the diet, even in the worst weather. Particularly in the worst weather, when birds took shelter in cover.

They would not have to eat their few livestock. The land was supporting them. Cow and goat and sheep would live to see the spring and reproduce themselves, guaranteeing herds and flocks.

When they were sure they could make it through the winter, people's attention began to turn to other matters. Kesair had rewarded their diligence by allowing a fire in the compound at night, but smaller than before, not so lavishly wasteful of timber. Sitting around the campfire, eating their evening meal, men and women glanced at one another meaningfully.

Ladra and Murra were the first to go off together and make use of the private huts built on the far side of the compound. The others pretended not to notice. Since they shared quarters on the crowded boat, they had learned to erect invisible screens of privacy for the most personal functions.

The night Ladra took the first of his women to a private hut, Byth could not eat his meal. He sat staring at the food. Then he looked at Kerish, sitting cross-legged several paces from him, glowing from the heat of the fire, tearing meat from bones with her strong young teeth.

"Ah . . . Kerish," he said softly.

She glanced up.

"It's going to be cold tonight. I think I smell ice on the wind."

"Do you?" Kerish did not seem particularly interested. She was warm by the fire, as a cat is warm, languorous and easy in her body. She took another bite of meat.

Byth tried again. "I don't sleep well when it's very cold."

Ah, thought Kerish. Yes. She looked at him in the firelight. An old man, a ruin of a man. But the ruin of a man who had once been handsome. A woman with a little imagination could, in a dim light, see him as still handsome. And he was kind.

Ah, thought Kerish again. I might as well get it over with. It won't be so bad, not if I set myself to enjoying.

She rose and went to sit beside Byth. Close beside him. "There are three private huts," she said in a low voice. "One is occupied, but . . . perhaps you might sleep better in one of the others? If you had company?"

Watching them, Kesair felt the sea singing in her blood. Answering the tug of the tides. She glanced covertly at Fintan.

If he felt her eyes on him he gave no sign. He was talking to Elisbut. The potter was responding vivaciously, with smiles and expansive gestures and occasional laughter, obviously enjoying herself.

I don't care, Kesair thought. I'm only with him because I meant one name but said another.

I wish I were with Byth.

She rose and walked restlessly to the edge of the compound. They had established themselves on the headland. Below, no distance away, was the sea.

Out of the corner of his eye, Fintan watched her. He smiled and nodded to Elisbut, paying superficial attention, which was all she needed to encourage her flow of words. But his true focus was Kesair. He knew where she stood, how she stood—straight-backed, almost leaning forward, her arms folded across her chest for warmth.

He knew everything but what she thought and felt. Did she care about anything?

Below her was the sea. Kesair could see the luster of the water, far out. Its power was so immense, its presence so demanding, that her awareness of Fintan fell from her. The sea absorbed her thoughts as it had absorbed the existence of millions.

All those lives destroyed, she thought. Or were they? Do they still exist in some way, as part of the sea? Can life be destroyed? Or merely transmuted?

She had never thought such thoughts before. Where did they come from?

4

Once the mating dance had begun,

it continued throughout the winter. Mindful of the

injunction not to get all the strong women pregnant

at the same time, each man concentrated on only a

portion of his

group. Fintan spent time in the private hut with Elisbut and with dark-haired Surcha. But never with Kesair.

The little girls were very curious. Covering giggling mouths with their hands, they crept as close to the private huts as they dared and tried to hear what was happening inside. They made wild guesses. "I think the men and women go in there to fight!" little Datseba said. "They grunt and squeal, don't they?"

As the group waited for spring, there was a subtle shift in its dynamic. Kesair was the acknowledged leader, but as one woman and then another conceived, the pregnant women became the focal point of the community and their men strutted proudly.

Elisbut and Murra announced their pregnancies within days of one another. But it was Kerish who caused the most excitement. When she told Byth he had sired a child, his joy overflowed.

"What do you think of this old man now, eh?" he kept asking people. "This old man? Eh?" He could not stop grinning. He treated Kerish as if she were made of spun glass, and found tiny presents to give her. He wrapped her in his warmest blanket and quoted everything she said, no matter how banal.

The little girls laughed and giggled and watched with wide eyes.

More and more, Kesair spent her time alone on the beach. The susurration of the sea was her companion's voice. The incoming tide laid gifts at her feet. She found pieces of flint, bits of colored glass, twisted fragments of forged metal. Once a human thigh bone, sand-scoured to ivory.

What the sea had taken it gave back transformed.

She tried to get others to share and appreciate her growing awareness, but she could not adequately articulate her discoveries, and the others were too busy or preoccupied to listen.

"You're in danger of becoming a fanatic," Ladra warned her, "and nobody likes a fanatic. We've been through a lot, but you mustn't give in to these wild notions of yours, Kesair. You'll lose everyone's respect if you do. What has the sea done for us but flooded the land and killed people? I'll tell you what I think about the sea. I piss in it!"

Ayn put it more delicately. "I would like to stop and listen to what you're trying to tell me, Kesair, honestly I would. But you know yourself there is work to be done. You assigned it. You can't expect us to abandon our chores now, when we need every pair of hands, to come and listen to you talk about, well, about something no one understands. I'm sure you mean well, but it's really just superstition, isn't it? Worshiping the invisible, so to speak?

"We don't have time for that sort of nonsense anymore, Kesair. As a race we've long since grown beyond it. Come now, come away from the sea, back to the huts and the fire. And your loom, that's where you're needed. We need your talents and your strength and your energy more than you need to be staring out at the sea all the time."

Kesair began to feel a sort of pity for them. They were blinded by daily routines. They were deaf to the voices she heard.

Alone, she began collecting shells and stones, secreting them in a tiny cove sheltered by dark boulders. Almost every day she went there. Only the most bitter weather could keep her away. Answering some deep need beyond the design of rational thought, she began assembling her stones and shells into a tower, a conical symbol rising from the sand. On the rare days of pale winter sun and deceptive warmth she could spend a whole morning there, frowning at her handiwork, perhaps moving just one shell a fraction to the left.

At night she dreamed of the cove and the tower.

The days were growing longer, misty and mild.

The people began to talk of leaving the compound and seeking land to farm. As their infants grew inside them, Elisbut and Kerish and Murra and Surcha turned their thoughts inward, but their companions began looking outward.

Ladra became the spokesman for those who were anxious to find their own place and build new lives. Approaching Kesair, he said, "We've waited long enough. I want our share of the livestock and those sacks of seed we brought. My women and I are going farther inland, where there is land that will grow grain."

"What do you know of growing grain?" Kesair asked him.

He bristled. "Leel comes from a farming family, she knows. And we'll learn."

"You didn't used to be such an optimist."

"That was before. This is now. This is a new world, we can do as we like here and that makes everything different."

"Are your women able to travel?"

"The pregnant ones? Murra can, she's not too big yet. And Velabro. She doesn't expect to give birth until early summer, so we should leave as soon as we can in order to be settled in new homes by then. The winter's over, Kesair. Or hadn't you noticed? This is a good land with a mild climate. We're going to enjoy ourselves here."

"Is that what it's about?"

Ladra frowned at her. "You're aren't going to try to keep us all here, are you?"

"Why would I do that?"

"You enjoy being in charge. You're like Fintan, you want to tell other people what to do. I don't mind it, coming from you, but I have to go my own way."

"I never said otherwise," Kesair reminded him. "I agreed that the groups should split up, remember. When the time is right. But . . ."

"But what?" he asked with sudden suspicion.

"But don't you think you should make an effort to . . . to placate . . . to ask for . . . before you go, shouldn't you . . ." The words dried on her tongue.

"Are you trying to get us to pray again, Kesair? Forget it. You're getting tiresome, you know."

Preparations began for the departure of Ladra's group. Kesair supervised the meticulous division of provisions into three equal parts, counted almost to the last seed. She knew how Ladra would complain if he thought he was being cheated.

Then she went for her usual walk by the sea—and returned with a new suggestion.

"We're all going to need to find land we can raise crops on," she said. "and we can't predict what dangers may lie inland. I say the three groups should leave together now, and stay together until we have some idea what to expect in the interior of the island. When we're certain it's safe to divide our numbers, we can split up and each group can choose its own land."

Fintan said, "I'm surprised at you. I thought you would want us, at least, to stay here by the sea you're so fond of."

"I can leave the sea," she told him, adding cryptically, "as long as I stay near water."

The others approved of her suggestion. "Kesair makes good sense, as usual," Surcha remarked to Murra.

"She's strange, that one. Nothing like the rest of us. But you have to admire her," Murra replied. "Where would we be if not for her?"

Excitedly, the entire colony prepared for departure. Even old Nanno had spots of color on her seamed cheeks. The young girls were giddy, and Byth, bemused by approaching fatherhood, spoke dreamily of "the warm valley I'll find for me and my chicks."

Kesair paid one last visit to the sea. The water was deep green, streaked with foam. Their abandoned boat was a forlorn splash of fading ruby against the emerald water.

Slowly, thoughtfully, Kesair dismantled her tower. She put the stones and shells back where she had originally found them, except for one particular shell that she held to her ear, then tucked for safekeeping in the bosom of her gown.

Returning to her people, she assigned herders for the livestock and supervised the final departure arrangements. The soon-to-be-deserted compound presented a forlorn sight. "We can't leave it like this," Kesair said. "We must clear away the midden heaps, burn our garbage and those broken timbers, and . . ."

"Forget it," Ladra said. "Let them rot where they are. No one wants to waste time building up another fire."

The others echoed his words. Their future was tugging at them, they were impatient to go. If Kesair held them back a moment longer they might turn on her.

Reluctantly, she gave the order to leave. But the mess they left behind remained like a dark stain at the back of her mind. She could not stop feeling guilty about it.

Traveling inland, they used the watercourses to make their way through a chain of low mountains carpeted with heather and bracken. Because their pace was adjusted to that of the slowest among them, they had ample time to appreciate the beauty of the land they were crossing. Green, lush, misty.

It took Fintan's breath away. He frequently stopped to stare.

Once, captivated by a spectacular view of a series of lakes nestled among hauntingly lovely hills, he lingered to admire until the others were long out of sight. He did not realize Kesair had come back, worried, to look for him. But when he started forward again he caught a glimpse of her looking toward him from atop an outcropping of rock. Her figure was a dark column silhouetted against the sky, holding up the dome of heaven.

Fintan's breath was suddenly harsh in his throat.

Daily, the air grew warmer. A scent of green, as thick as moss, hung in the air. Soft, moist air. The pregnant women ripened. Their flesh took on the luster of pearls.

A sort of madness infected Ladra. Losing all restraint, he insisted on sleeping with every one of his women as often as he could. Soon he would not even wait until nightfall, but would pull the nearest woman behind a tree or a boulder and take her without ceremony, like a rutting goat.

Byth was appalled. "What's wrong with you?"

"Nothing's wrong with me, and my women aren't complaining."

"They are. To my women."

"They're boasting, because they know you aren't satisfying your women," Ladra said spitefully.

The old man's eyes blazed. "I'm not mauling them every chance I get, if that's what you mean. You act like a man demented, Ladra, and it's making the rest of us uncomfortable."

"You're just jealous!"

Hornetlike, anger hummed in the air between the two men. Kesair became aware of it. She stepped between them. "We can't afford to quarrel," she said. "Walk on now, you're holding us up."

At her urging they resumed the march. But like Byth, Kesair was worried by Ladra's behavior.

He could not control his passions. The very air he breathed was saturated with the impulse to life. The cells of his body responded. They combusted independently of his reasoning mind, burning him with lust. He could concentrate on nothing but the sweet heavy pressure in his groin, driving him, demanding, insatiable.

"I think Ladra's sick," Kesair remarked to Fintan. They were following a thread of water leading eastward from the mountains.

"What makes you think so?"

"Look at his eyes. They're glassy, wild, and he's sweating heavily. It isn't that warm yet. His face is ashen, too, as if the color's being leached out of it."

Fintan grinned. "I'd say everything's leached out of him by now."

"I'm serious. I'm worried about him."

"What am I supposed to do about it? I don't know anything about illness. If he is ill, and I'm not so sure."

But Kesair was sure.

Feeling her concerned gaze upon him, Ladra intepreted it as something else. He began watching for his chance.

Kesair did not always walk with Fintan and his other women. She preferred to find a path of her own, a little distance from anyone else. She would stroll along lost in her own thoughts, aware of the location of the others but not with them.

Ladra made it his business to know where she was. Even when with another woman, he knew where Kesair was; how near to him, how close to some place where he could cut her off from the others and take her the way she wanted. The way they all wanted. They all wanted him, wanted Ladra. Wanted, wanted, needed, had to . . .

His eyes glittered in his pasty face like broken glass.

On a morning of soft rain, they were late in leaving the camp they had made for themselves in a glade in an oak forest. Moving inland, they had found vast expanses of forest land, huge primordial oaks, elm, trees whose leaf and bark they could not identify mingling with more familiar species, all surging upward in search of the sun.

There was no sun this morning. The air was saturated with the mist that oozed from every pore of the land, bearing the scent of earth and water. The day had a curious languor. Kesair, lying in her blankets, reluctant to get up, had a fanciful half-dream of floating in her mother's womb. When she did arise her eyes were still brimming with the dream. Her lips curved in a private smile.

Watching her covertly, Ladra noticed.

Today, he thought.

They set off once more. Water oozed into the footprints they left behind in the mossy soil.

As they walked together, Byth confided to Kerish, "If there is a good valley beyond this forest we're going to stop there. I see no need to go farther, nor have we met any real dangers. Aside from game, this entire island is uninhabited. We could settle anywhere, don't you agree? So why keep on?"

Kerish, heavily pregnant, nodded. "We must stop soon." She smoothed her hands down the bulging moon of her belly. "We will have to stop," she added meaningfully.

The baby inside her shifted, made groping motions with its unseen hands, wriggled down toward the tunnel that led Out.

The forest was increasingly dense. They were following a

winding stream that offered the only open pathway, though its banks were slippery with moss and studded with frequent clumps of vegetation. Once Kerish slipped and cried out. Byth tried to catch her, but he was not quick enough. She saved herself by a desperate grab at a holly bush. The prickles tore her hands, making them bleed.

She caught her breath with a sob. "I have to stop soon," she said to Byth. "I can't go much farther."

He wondered if they should simply turn back. It would be a long journey to the last night's camping place. Better they go on. Or stop here, though the forest was damp and gloomy, an uninviting haven. It was hard to know what to do. He felt his responsibilities pressing down on him. My chicks. I must do what is right for my chicks.

Walking in the lead, Fintan suddenly called back over his shoulder, "I see a wedge of brightness up ahead. I think we'll be out of this forest in a little while."

Ladra grunted deep in his throat. He was walking a few paces behind Kesair, who as usual was eschewing the common path and treading her own way among the trees. She had taken off her cloak and stuffed it into the pack on her back, for it was warm in the forest. Warm and close.

Warm and wet. Ladra's eyes followed the clench-and-relax of her buttocks, clearly visible beneath the fabric of her gown.

Off to their left yawned the mouth of a small cave, almost hidden by moss and shrubbery as it backed into a hill. Ladra's darting eyes observed the cave; returned to Kesair.

"Kesair," he said. Very softly. "Kesair."

She heard him the second time and glanced back. "What is it?"

"Did you see that?"

"What?"

"Something just moved inside that cave. Something large. I think it's watching us."

"Are you sure?" Kesair stopped walking and turned to face the cave. "I don't see anything. Should we call Fintan?"

"I can do anything Fintan can do," Ladra said petulantly. "If there's any danger, you're safe enough with me. But I think we should take a look. Just because we haven't seen any large predators yet doesn't mean there are none. If one is in that cave, I want to know."

She nodded agreement and came back toward him. "Be ready," she warned. Her own long knife was already in her hand, taken in one smooth motion from the scabbard on her belt.

I am ready, Ladra assured her silently.

They advanced with cautious tread toward the cave. Its mouth was narrow, but it could be of any size within, burrowed into the tree-covered hill. Ladra held out one hand, signaling Kesair to move slowly.

The longer it took them to reach the cave, the farther away the others would get. If she should cry out, he did not want them to hear her.

When they had crept almost to the cave's mouth, he faked a stumble and dropped his own knife into the thickest undergrowth. "I've lost my knife," he hissed. "Quick, give me yours." He reached for it so suddenly and imperiously Kesair surrendered her weapon before thinking.

One slow step at a time, Ladra entered the cave. He had to duck his head under the low overhang, but once he was inside it was more spacious and he could stand. He was aware of Kesair behind him. "What do you see?" she whispered. "Be careful, don't go any farther!"

"I see . . . I see . . . it's all right, but come in here, look at this. Just look!" he said in a voice of feigned excitement, as if he had found some treasure.

Kesair entered behind him. She stood so close to him he could feel her breasts against the back of his upper arm. "What? I don't see anything." Her breathing was light and quick.

She wants it, Ladra assured himself. She knows why we're here.

Turning, he dropped his knife to the floor of the cave to free his hands. He caught her by the shoulders and pulled her against him.

"What are you doing?" She struggled to get her hands between their bodies and push him away, but Ladra held tight.

"Don't fight me, Kesair. This is what you're meant for." He bent his face to hers but she twisted aside, denying him her mouth.

"Let me go!"

"You're just saying that. Why don't you relax? We're all alone here, no one will bother us. It won't take long, I promise you, I never take long." He gave a wild laugh.

Kesair tried to get her knee up but he had her clamped so tightly against him that she could not. She had never thought Ladra was so strong. The fight between them became desperate; silent. She saved her breath for the struggle.

He pushed her toward the unseen back of the cave. She fought him every step, feeling a mounting panic beat like a pulse at the base of her throat. What difference does it make? a coolly rational part of her mind asked. Him or another. But the rest of her mind screamed silently, Not him! Not this one! It had nothing to do with rationality and everything to do with the integrity of her free will.

She redoubled her efforts and managed to break the hold of one of his hands. He grabbed for her again but she flung herself sideways, falling onto one knee on the cave floor, scrabbling with her free hand for purchase on the gritty stone.

Ladra did not give her a chance to get up but flung himself down onto her, knocking her flat beneath him. He gave a grunt of triumph and began tearing at her clothes.

His fingers closed on the shell tucked in the bosom of her gown. A small spiral shell, with a sharply fluted edge at its aperture.

The feeling of it was so unexpected Ladra snatched his hand back, thinking he had been grazed by unseen teeth. "Something bit me!" he cried in disbelief. "Something in your gown!" His fevered mind imagined a giant insect, some alien life form attacking him in the dark cave.

He half lifted his body off hers, trying to look at his hand in the dim light filtering in from outside. He thought he saw the ooze of blood.

Taking advantage of his distraction, Kesair gave a mighty heave and threw his body aside so she could roll out from under him. He reached for her again but she was too quick. She was on her feet as his hand closed on her gown. She strained; he held on. The fabric tore with an audible ripping sound and she was free. Kesair took the two paces to the mouth of the cave in one bound and was outside. With a great gasp, she drew the wet air of freedom into her lungs. She ran a few steps; slowed; looked back.

Ladra was not following her.

There was no sound from the cave.

He thinks I'll be curious and go back, she told herself. It's a trick.

Anger sizzled in her. She bent swiftly, pawed through the undergrowth until she found the knife he had dropped, and put it in her own scabbard. Then she hurried after the others.

She had almost caught up with them when her steps slowed of their own volition.

I am the leader, she thought grimly. I can't go off and leave him, even if I'd like to see him dead. And I would. I would!

She drew in a breath to call Fintan and ask him to go back with her, but never made the call. She did not want to give Ladra the satisfaction of thinking she was so afraid of him she had to ask Fintan for help.

I can handle Ladra myself, she thought. I'll control my fear and my anger too. I can do it. I *can*.

She gritted her teeth, biting down with all her strength on her seething emotions. Knife firmly in hand, she went back alone.

5

No sooner did Kerish see the light

ahead that meant the end of the forest, than the

vague disquiet that had troubled her belly all day

became something more defined. A spasm like a giant

cramp doubled her

over. She tried to call Byth's name but could not get her breath.

He was aware at once, however, and bent over her. "What is it? Are you all right?"

Old fool, she thought. You can see I'm not all right, do something! But she could not speak. The cramp was crushing her insides.

Byth straightened and looked around wildly for help. Some of his women were ahead of them, some behind. Fintan was still back among the trees somewhere. He did not see Kesair at all, though hers was the face he would have welcomed.

"Help!" he cried at random. He croaked like a frog, his voice breaking.

People hurried to them. The solicitous hands of other women touched Kerish, understood at once. A place was swiftly found for her and her bulky body eased down onto a mossy bed. The women crowded around her. There were hasty consultations. The young ones were frightened. The older women, particularly those who had given birth themselves, were calmer, insisting that everything was normal, there was no need to worry. They would care for her. With swift efficiency they divided themselves into groups to stay with Kerish and comfort her, and other groups to bring fresh water, gather clean moss, search through the packs for items that might be needed.

Ayn thoughtfully assigned herself to Byth and led him some distance away. "She'll be fine, they'll tend to her. You come with me now. You'd only be in the way and make her anxious. That's it, come along. We'll find a nice place where you can wait."

Had he been a younger man, Ayn might have encouraged him to stay with the woman. But Byth was paler than Kerish, and she was worried about him. With difficulty, she got him seated on a fallen tree near the stream, and tried to make distracting conversation with him.

When Kerish screamed the first time, though, he jumped to his feet and hurried back to her in spite of all Ayn could do.

By then Fintan had arrived, assessed the situation, understood he was less than useless, and gone looking for something to hunt while he waited. Most of the women, aside from those looking after

Kerish, were taking advantage of the halt to bathe themselves in the stream, or gather the shiny brown nuts that strewed the earth beneath some of the trees.

Fintan had not noticed that Kesair was not with the other women. Her absence did not cry out for his attention. She was inclined to go her own way. He assumed she was nearby, without giving it any specific thought.

A small furry animal sprang up almost under his feet and ran toward the light at the rim of the forest. Fintan ran after it.

When Kerish screamed a second time one of the women gave her a piece of cloth to hold between her teeth, and another gave her a piece of rope tied to a tree to pull on. They kneaded her belly to locate the infant. It had entered the birth canal.

There would not be long to wait.

Barra and Salmé supported Kerish in a squatting position. Old Nanno had put herself in charge. Her cracked voice guided their efforts. When Byth hovered too close she snapped, "Take him away, somebody!"

Hands tugged Byth a few paces from the scene of action. He protested every step of the way. "You're hurting her! Be careful! Can't you see she wants me?"

No one paid any attention to him.

Leel said in an awed whisper, "This will be the first child of the new world."

A sense of occasion overtook them. The women exchanged glances. Their eyes gleamed. Kerish, sweating, torn in half, struggled to bring forth life.

Her two screams had coincided with the struggle in the cave, so Kesair did not know. She only knew that she could not in good conscience go off and leave Ladra. He was sick; sick in his mind, of that she was convinced. His body had given off a sour, unhealthy smell that still clung to her clothing.

She fumbled at the bosom of her gown. The shell was missing. It must still be in the cave then.

For that reason alone she had to go back.

The dark cave mouth waited for her. She approached slowly. "Ladra?"

There was no answer. Nothing appeared to stir inside the cave.

"Ladra? You'll be left so far behind you can't find us if you don't come now." Kesair waited tensely, ready to run if he made any threatening moves toward her. But only silence greeted her words.

She stepped almost to the mouth of the cave and cupped her hands around her eyes, peering into the darkness. "Ladra?"

Then she saw him. He was lying on the floor, far back in the cave, with his knees drawn up against his chest. His face was turned toward her, a pale blur in the dimness. His mouth worked but no sound came out.

It's a trick, Kesair warned herself. "Come now," she said sternly.

He made no move to get up. Instead there was a whimper like an animal in pain, and his body thrashed weakly on the floor.

Kesair held out the knife so he could see she had it. Step by cautious step she advanced, ducking under the low overhang. She did not get within grabbing distance of him, but went close enough to see his face more clearly.

Ladra's face was bloated, twisted. "Annnhh," he moaned. "Aaaannnnhhhh." His eyes pleaded with her.

"What happened?" she asked in a shocked whisper. Suddenly she knew it was no trick.

"I'm . . ." His mouth struggled to frame words. "I'm . . . poi . . . soned. Poisoned. You poisoned me."

Kesair almost dropped the knife. "I did what!"

"That thing. Hidden. In your breasts. I . . ." His voice failed, but still his eyes pleaded for help.

"No poison could act that fast," Kesair protested. "I wasn't carrying any poison. Just a shell from the sea."

"Poisoned teeth," Ladra insisted. "Bit me. You . . . tried to kill me . . . why?" The last question was a piteous sob.

Kesair thrust the knife into her scabbard and bent down to try to help the man to his feet. But Ladra had no strength. Even with her aid, he could not stand. He was in undeniable pain.

Beside him on the floor she saw the pale gleam of the seashell.

Kesair picked it up. She turned it over, wonderingly, in her hand, then put it back into the bosom of her gown.

Ladra's eyes widened. "It will kill you!"

He is out of his head, Kesair thought. Aloud she said, "I'll go get help. But you're not poisoned, you couldn't be. It's a seizure of some sort. Don't worry, I'll get help." She was backing away from him as she spoke. She could not wait to leave the cave, to be in open air that did not choke her with the sour smell of him.

Once outside, she ran.

She came upon the others soon enough, although she had expected they would be far ahead by now. Instead she found them gathered beside the stream shortly before it emerged from the forest. In the center of the group was a figure that held their attention; they did not even notice her come running up to them.

"Ladra's ill," she called out. "I need someone to help with him. He can't walk."

Faces turned toward her. "Kerish is having her baby," Murra said.

"Oh!" Kesair hesitated. "Is she all right?"

"Seems to be."

"Then . . . can't we spare some people to come help me with Ladra? Where's Fintan? And what about Byth? Surely he's no use to Kerish right now."

Murra chuckled. "I don't think you could drag Byth away with a team of horses. But Fintan's around here somewhere, I think." She looked around, searching. Then she cupped her hands around her mouth and called, "Fintan? Where are you?"

"Be quiet," someone hissed. "You're disturbing Kerish."

The admonition was unnecessary, actually. Kerish was not disturbed. She was lost in the throes of birth, all her attention centered on the cataclysm within herself.

"I don't know just where Fintan is," Murra admitted to Kesair. "How ill is Ladra? Is it urgent? And where is he?"

"Back there." Kesair waved a hand vaguely. "I don't know if it's urgent, but I'm worried. He thinks he's been poisoned."

Murra's brow furrowed. "Did he eat some berries? What did they look like?"

"Not berries, and I don't really think he's poisoned. It's something else, but I need help. Stay there, I'll go find Fintan myself. I suspect he's gone on ahead to see what's there." She started toward the light beyond the forest.

She met Fintan coming back with a limp furry body in his hand. "Ho, Kesair," he called, brandishing his kill, "look at this!"

She averted her eyes. She was uncomfortable with death while life was beginning so close behind her. "Can you come help me get Ladra?"

Fintan's eyes dimmed with disappointment. He had expected praise; he had killed the creature with his first effort, a lovely clean kill. "What's wrong with Ladra?"

"He . . . ah . . ." Kesair pawed among the available words in her mind. She did not want to tell Fintan everything. "He caught hold of a seashell I was keeping and he thinks it's poisoned him. It couldn't have, but something has made him very sick. He's in a cave back along the trail, and he can't walk."

"What about the baby, is it born yet?"

"Not yet. But Ladra needs help now."

Fintan fell in step beside her. They made their way past the cluster of women around Kerish and on down the stream, deeper into the forest, until Kesair was able to point out the cave. "He's in there."

Fintan followed her to the cave mouth. She stepped aside and let him go in first.

Ladra lay as she had left him, knees drawn up against his belly. He was breathing shallowly but he was conscious. He said something unintelligible to Fintan.

"He's sick all right," Fintan affirmed. "But if we can get him on his feet with an arm around our necks, between us we can get him out of here."

Kesair did not really want to touch Ladra, but she forced herself. Between them, she and Fintan got him unsteadily to his feet and walked him out of the cave. He smelled worse than ever, a nauseating stench like something going rotten.

But his face was not as bloated Kesair noticed once they had him out in the leaf-filtered light of the forest. The illness, whatever it was, was abating. He stumbled but he could walk, and when he spoke again his voice sounded minimally stronger. "Thought I was going to die in there," he told them.

He did not mention his attack on Kesair. Nor did she.

Moving slowly, they rejoined the group. Ladra kept his eyes closed and let them guide him while he hung between them almost as limply as the furry creature had dangled from Fintan's hand.

They reached the others just as Kerish let out a great cry and a wet, bloody mass slid from her into old Nanno's waiting arms.

Within moments a boy baby was filling the forest with lusty cries.

In the excitement, no one paid much attention to Ladra.

Kesair and Fintan let him sit down, propped against a tree, and went to congratulate Kerish. It was Byth who was garnering the congratulations, however, his face shining like the risen sun. Kerish lay exhausted, watching the baby on her breast.

"Doesn't anyone care if I live or die?" Ladra's peevish voice asked at last.

When she was satisfied that Kerish and her baby were well, Ayn went to Ladra. She had the most experience among them in dealing with illness, but she could not explain his fading symptoms. "I don't think it's poison," she told Kesair, "but I couldn't be certain. It might be a kind I've never seen. Whatever it is, it's passing off anyway. I'd say he'll be all right. He'll have a day to rest. We won't expect Kerish and the new baby to move until tomorrow."

Instead of being reassured, Ladra took exception to Ayn's words. "She doesn't know what she's talking about. I almost died. I could still die. It's obviously something rare and dangerous, and no one knows what to do about it."

Kesair, making sure no one else was listening, said to him, "It was just a seashell I've carried in my gown all this way, with no harm to me. It couldn't hurt you. Your own guilt is making you sick, Ladra."

"Guilt? Guilt for what?"

"You know," she said in a low voice.

"I didn't do anything wrong. I didn't do anything you didn't want me to do."

"Did I act as if I wanted you to do it?"

"The fighting, you mean? That's just your way, I'd say. Some women like to pretend to resist."

"I wasn't pretending. And if you ever try that again, I'll fight harder. I'll kill you if I have to."

He gave her a shocked look. "You wouldn't! Consider! There are only three men now!"

"I'd rather there were no men, than to have to put up with you," she told him coldly.

Camp was set up around Kerish and her baby. The day of relative leisure was welcome. Fintan went back to his hunting, taking with him some of the women who had shown skills at catching small game. Nanno and Ayn looked after the new mother, a task that primarily consisted of keeping Byth from pestering them too much. He wanted to hold the baby, he wanted to ask Kerish how she felt, he wanted to do something for them. Anything.

He drove the others mad.

At last Nanno snapped, "If you want to help, gather more moss for diapering!"

Byth scurried away importantly. He spent the better part of the afternoon selecting, grading, and discarding bits of moss as if life or death might depend on them.

Ladra sat propped against his tree for a long time. The color slowly returned to his cheeks and the light to his eyes. Kesair was aware that those eyes followed her as she moved around the encampment. She began planning her paths so that trees interposed between herself and Ladra, blocking his vision.

Her warning had meant nothing to him. He did not take it seriously because it interfered with his fixed idea of reality.

She began to wonder if she would actually have to kill him eventually—kill him, or submit.

But it was not in her to submit.

That night they built a fire in a glade in the forest and roasted the game Fintan and his fellow hunters provided. Byth insisted the best parts, such as the liver, be given to Kerish. He forced more meat on her than she could possibly eat.

"Was he always like that, do you suppose?" Kerish asked Nanno.

The old woman's eyes were lost in wrinkles, but a smile lurked in their depths. "I knew him as a young man with his wife, and I assure you, he paid very little attention to his children then. Nor to the wife either. He had a wife and children because it was expected of him, and once he had them settled in his house he got on with his life. Oh, I'm sure he was fond of them in an absentminded way. But he took them for granted.

"Now he is no longer young, Kerish, and he has realized how fragile existence is. He is a different man."

"We are all of us different people," Kerish said. "I never imagined I would give birth in a forest and diaper my baby with moss. Me, who used to spend hours buffing my fingernails!"

"That was in another world," Nanno reminded her.

"Do you miss it? Do you wish we could go back?"

"Of course I do. But that's like wishing you could be young

again. We only travel in one direction, Kerish. Forward. Remember that, and waste no time regretting."

The baby at Kerish's breast whimpered and began seeking the teat again. His mother gazed down at him, then bent her neck to kiss the downy crown of his head.

Sitting opposite them, Kesair looked at mother and infant in the firelight. The picture they made was creating maternal stirrings in many of the women. She could not help noticing how they drew closer to their men, so that the three groups became more clearly delineated than usual. Even Ladra's women gathered around him, though of late they had been avoiding him whenever they could.

But it was Kesair his eyes sought.

She edged closer to Fintan. Salmé, sitting on his right, glared at her and refused to give ground. If Fintan was aware of the silent duel between the two women he gave no sign; he went on eating his food, his face impassive. With no word spoken, Kesair realized he would sleep with Salmé that night.

But she must talk to him. "Fintan," she said in a low, urgent voice, "there is something I must discuss with you. Tonight. It's a serious problem. I need you."

Salmé's lips tightened over her teeth and she moved still closer to Fintan.

Kesair reached past her, putting a hand on the man's arm. Immediately Salmé put her own hand on the arm, pinning it down. Her eyes were hot with challenge.

Kesair tried to make Fintan look at her but he would not. Nor did he respond to her touch. He sat immobilized, letting the women fight it out. Enjoying it, no doubt.

In that moment Kesair hated him.

She drew her dignity around her like an invisible cloak and relinquished her hold on his arm. "Very well. I shall handle the problem myself." Her voice was cold. She stood up and left them, walking with a straight back and high head into the sheltering darkness of the trees.

She knew that Ladra was following her with his eyes. But he did not come after her.

He was still feeling weakened, so he remained where he was, biding his time. There would be other chances. Tomorrow. Or the day after.

He had a score to settle.

The next morning Kerish insisted she could get up and walk if they did not walk too fast or too far without resting. So they pitched camp and set out. A doting Byth carried the baby, refusing to surrender it to any of the women. He only gave it back to Kerish for feeding.

"What if he drops my baby?" she complained to Ramé.

"He won't. Just look at him. He would rather die than let anything happen to that child."

They were soon out of the forest. Beyond lay a rolling meadowland that stretched to the horizon. "I'd say it's a central plain, if this really is an island as we think it is," Fintan remarked.

Leel paused, squatted on her heels, dug in the earth with her fingers. It was loamy and dark. "Rich soil," she said.

The plain was crisscrossed with watercourses, to which Kesair was inevitably drawn. They could not lose their way if they followed the water.

They were on open grassland under an open sky. Making sure there were others close by, she fell into step with Ladra. "This is good farmland, I'd say," she told him. "Fertile. And since we've met no serious danger, you might want to claim this region for yourself while the rest of us look farther."

"I'm in no hurry to leave you," Ladra drawled, enjoying the discomfiture in her eyes. "I'll stay with you a while longer. You can never tell what we may discover up ahead. Better land, perhaps. Or something . . . wonderful," he added meaningfully. He ran his eyes over her body like impertinent hands.

Kesair edged away from him, repelled.

But Ladra made no move to pursue her. He seemed content to watch her and make her uncomfortable.

He had never toyed with a woman in that way before, and he found he enjoyed it. It gave him a sense of power. It also was a form of revenge, and revenge was power too.

Ladra speculated as to whether Kesair might have told Fintan about the attack. Probably not, or Fintan would have done something. Or perhaps he was just waiting for Ladra to try it again, and catch him in the act. Then there would be a fight between them.

I am bigger, Ladra told himself. I would win.

He imagined bludgeoning the other man to the earth. The idea gave him an almost sensual pleasure. He strolled along with a tiny smile playing around the corners of his mouth, dreaming with his eyes open.

But Kesair had not told Fintan. After the scene with Salmé, she spoke to him no more than she must. His use of the other woman's body did not upset her, that was inevitable. But she could not forget how meekly he had submitted to Salmé and rejected Kesair when she needed him.

Crossing the central plain, they came to a valley of abundance at the confluence of three rivers. When they pitched camp for the night Kesair spoke to Ladra again. "This would be a fine place for you and your women."

"There is something I have to settle before we separate from the rest of you, Kesair," he replied. "I think we'll just stay with you a while longer. Until."

That night, wrapped in her blankets, Kesair fingered the knife she had taken to bed with her and wondered what it would be like to kill a man. Could she make herself do it? And what would the others do to her if she diminished the adult male population by a third?

I should discuss this with someone, she thought. But ever since she first joined the crafts colony, she had kept a certain distance between herself and the other women. Their talk seemed superficial to her, their interests were rarely her interests. And men had represented an area of life she had chosen to ignore.

Old Byth, fond as she was of him, would be little help to her in the present situation. And Fintan had rejected her.

Lying alone on the yielding earth, Kesair fingered the knife and thought of past and future. She was suspended between them.

We thought we were so highly developed, she mused. We believed humankind masters of the universe.

Now we are fifty-three people on an island. And I am contemplating murder.

Why can you not give in to Ladra? her rational mind demanded to know. Any one of the three would do as well as any other for the purpose of procreation. Surely it is not worth destroying what little civilization we have left, just to deny yourself to him.

But she could not submit to Ladra. Rationality had no power over elemental emotion. She had once been terribly hurt by a man, and she had been hurt again by Fintan's recent rejection. Some quality in him had begun the slow process of thawing her frozen passions, but that was now reversed. All she had left was the integrity of her inmost self, and she would rather die than surrender it to any man on demand.

Dying, killing, repeated her rational mind. After all that has happened, still you think these thoughts. Are you not revolted by the unquenchable darkness of the human soul?

I am, she answered. Yet she ran her finger down the knife blade again, testing its sharpness. She felt balanced on a knife blade between the old world and the new.

The blade was killing-sharp.

Close to her head, something crackled.

Kesair stiffened. Someone was creeping toward her in the darkness.

Her fingers closed on the hilt of the knife, easing it out from under the blankets. Suddenly she felt more alive than she could remember feeling. Every cell in her body tingled.

Whoever it was came closer.

The night was very still. The air was damp and heavy, and brought her an ominous, sour scent.

Ladra was stealthily approaching her bed.

Kesair felt a shock of surprise that he would risk such a move in the open, where one cry would alert the others. She was ten paces from the nearest sleeper.

Now she regretted even that distance, though keeping space between herself and the others was a well-established habit. She wished she were lying pressed close against Elisbut or Sorcha or even Salmé.

Her straining eyes made out the dim outline of the approaching head and shoulders. Ladra was actually crawling toward her on his belly, she realized with revulsion. Her hand made a small, convulsive movement, eager to use the knife.

"Kesair." His whisper was so soft she would not have heard it if her senses had not become preternaturally sharp with tension. "Kesair."

"Get away from me," she said in a low voice. She was embarrassed; she did not want the others to know.

"I have to talk to you." He wriggled closer.

"Talk? Talk isn't what you want from me."

"Oh but it is. Just listen." Ladra lay down beside her. He made no effort to touch her. "You tried to kill me," he said in that same insidious whisper. "But I forgive you. I want you to know I forgive you."

His unctuous tone infuriated her. "You can't forgive me for something I didn't do. I never tried to kill you. But I promise you, if you try to lay a hand on me now, I will."

"You should be nicer to me, Kesair. I'm the only one who appreciates you."

"They follow me as their leader," she said proudly.

"It isn't the same thing. You are the leader because you're . . . different. I understand that, I'm different too, in my own way. I could show you. We could make something very special together." His voice was soft, insinuating.

"You're different because you're insane," she said bluntly.

To her surprise, he chuckled. "Is that what you think? I'm insane because I don't subscribe to the same behavior as the rest of you? I am the sanest person among us, Kesair. I'm the only one who realizes that everything is different now; none of the old laws and restrictions apply. We can do what we like here, don't you understand? Don't you know how wonderful that is? We are free. *Free.*" The word hissed between them.

"Take advantage of your freedom, Kesair. Don't limit yourself to that wretched Fintan. Come to me. Be with me. Together we can explore ourselves, each other, this island, the whole world. It's all ours to take and shape, don't you see?

"You're still tied to the past. You wanted to burn the rubbish, rather than simply walk away from it. You can walk away from everything now. No more responsibilities. Just pleasure. Pleasure . . ."

Now he reached for her. Now his fingertips brushed her cheek with a touch as light as cobwebs. A touch as light as the kiss of sea mist . . .

She drove the knife into him with all her strength.

6

The tensile strength of living flesh

surprised Kesair. For a moment she was not

sure the knife had gone in.

Then she heard him gasp.

Some reflex made

her snatch her hand back as if to undo the deed. Too late, too late. The tug she had to give to remove the knife told her how deeply it had penetrated. She felt it grate against bone as she withdrew it.

Appalled, she lay frozen.

Ladra coughed. "You . . ."

"I warned you!" she said through clenched teeth. She was alternately hot and cold. Her entire body was shaken by the pounding of her heart.

"I . . ." Ladra stirred, gathered himself, struggled to his hands and knees. His head swung slowly back and forth.

Warm blood spattered onto Kesair's hand.

Ladra began crawling backward, away from her. She lay immobilized by horror. What to say? What to do? She could not think. Her paralysis of mind was more frightening than the menace of Ladra.

He somehow made his way back to his own bed without awakening anyone else. The wound was deep, his probing fingers discovered, but not close to the heart. Nor did it seem to have penetrated a lung. If he did not bleed to death he might survive.

Fighting waves of dizzying pain, he gathered moss to stuff into the wound. There was a roaring in his ears like the sound of the sea. He lay on his back, clinging desperately to consciousness. He was afraid he would never wake up if he let himself fall asleep.

The night was endless. The slightest sound was an assault on Ladra's raw nerve endings. All around him people slept, blissfully unaware that he might be dying. He hated them for their indifferent comfort.

This is me! he wanted to shout. This is my precious life seeping away!

But he did not shout. He lay in silence, fearing. Hating.

In the morning he was still alive.

Ladra was surprised to discover he was actually seeing the first flush of dawn. I am not going to die after all, he thought. His survival seemed almost anticlimactic.

With a great effort, he dragged himself to his feet and went to the stream to splash his face with cold water. It revived him a little. A close examination of the moss showed that blood was no longer seeping from the wound. He was weak, but he was alive.

Every movement hurt, however.

One-handed, he struggled to wrap his cloak around his body and fasten it so no one would see the bloody mess at his shoulder. Only then did he allow himself to make enough noise to awaken the others.

Kesair was already awake. She did not think she had slept at all. She heard him get up and go to the stream. She heard him return. He did not come anywhere near her.

At least she had not killed him.

She wondered how she felt about that.

She got up cautiously, surprised to find the world much the same as it had been the night before. Familiar forms surrounded her. Familiar sounds: coughing, farting, a groan of awakening, a muttered, sleepy conversation. The new baby's cry and Kerish's tender answer.

As Kesair bent over to pick up her blankets, the seashell fell from the neck of her gown.

She caught it in midair, instinctively. Holding it to her ear, she listened for a moment to the voice of the sea. Then she tucked the shell back between her breasts.

Though she watched him warily, Ladra gave no indication of what had happened between them. He moved stiffly as he gathered himself for the day, but he was able to walk. No one commented on his obvious discomfort. His women assumed it was a residue of his previous illness. The only one who reacted to it at all was Ramé, who trimmed a branch and gave it to him for a walking stick that he could lean upon.

When they left camp and got under way, however, Ladra moved so slowly even Kerish could outpace him. Eventually Ramé spoke to Kesair. "Ladra is in considerable pain," she said, "but he won't admit it and he won't let Ayn look at him."

"That's his right," Kesair said through stiff lips.

Ramé went to walk with Velabro. "Kesair is an unfeeling woman," she complained.

Velabro considered. "Aloof, perhaps. I wouldn't say unfeeling. And she may have her reasons," she added charitably. Velabro had a deep, slow, husky voice. Ramé liked to talk to her for the sake of hearing the music in her voice.

"Ladra's hurting, Velabro. Kesair should be more solicitous of him. She's the leader, after all. Our welfare is her concern."

"You weren't so solicitous of Ladra," Velabro pointed out, "after the last time he flung himself on you."

"That's different, I just got tired of him acting like a rutting stag. But I hate to see him suffer."

"Perhaps you should suggest to him that we stop, then. He might be willing, if he really is in pain. Leel says this is fertile soil. We could settle here and let the others go on, and Ladra could rest and get well."

"You make it sound simple enough, but it isn't. Think, Velabro. What will it mean? A band of women alone in a strange place with just one man—and him ill? Aren't you afraid?"

Velabro shook her head. "I was afraid when the sea rose. When the others came and killed our men and tried to steal our boat, I was afraid. I was terribly afraid when we were alone on the ocean. But I wore out my capacity for fear, finally. Now I just want to stop walking and stay somewhere and get on with whatever happens next. I suspect the other women feel the same."

Ramé quietly canvassed Ladra's other women. She found that they all were willing, even eager, to stop and stay. The weather was mild, the sun was shining, there was fresh water and abundant grass. The women who were in charge of the livestock were the most ready to stop traveling. Getting the animals through the forest had been arduous enough, but on lush pasturage they almost had to be dragged to keep them moving forward, exhausting their herders. "Let's stay right here," Ramé was told. "Look at the animals, they know best."

The next time they stopped to rest and let Kerish nurse her baby, Ramé spoke to Ladra. "Your women want to stay here and go no farther," she told him. "Leel says we could farm this region successfully, our seed would grow here. And you could regain your strength and—"

"I . . . am . . . not . . . stopping . . . yet," Ladra said, forcing each word as if it cost him great effort. But even as he spoke he swayed and almost fell.

Ramé caught him in her arms. "This is as far as we go!" she called to Kesair. "Ladra's ill, he's fainting!"

"We'll stay with you," Fintan said.

Kesair cried sharply, "We won't! Ladra's women can take care of him."

Fintan rounded on her. "Do you mean to leave him when he's sick?"

"I'm not . . . sick," Ladra insisted, fighting to stand upright again, pushing away Ramé's arms.

"There, you hear him, he's not sick. They just want to stay here, Fintan. So we'll leave them and go on."

"I'm going . . . too . . ." Ladra tried to insist, but waves of weakness were breaking over him. He met Kesair's eyes. His ears began to ring, as if with the roar of the sea.

"You're not going anywhere," Ramé said gently, taking hold of him again. Velabro hurried to help her.

Leel remarked, "I don't think we could find any better place than this no matter where we go, so we might as well stay here."

"I think that's a good idea," agreed Kesair. "The rest of you, prepare yourselves and we'll move on now."

"We can't just go off and leave them like this!" Fintan protested.

But Kesair would not listen. She seemed almost indecently eager to put distance between herself and Ladra's group. Byth was anxious to move on as well, he kept talking about the valley he wanted to find.

Fintan gave in, realizing that Ladra had not endeared himself to the others and no one would be heartbroken about leaving him. Besides, that had been the plan.

Still . . . he sensed something of a mystery about Kesair's attitude. When they were under way again, and Ladra and his women were dots in the distance, setting up their camp and staking out their animals, Fintan fell into step beside Kesair.

"Was something wrong between you and Ladra?" he wanted to know.

"No."

"Then why were you so anxious to get rid of him?"

She spun around and glared at him. "You wouldn't know, would you?"

"That's why I'm asking you. If there is some sort of problem, you should share it with me."

"I tried. You weren't interested." Her voice shimmered with icicles. "Now I'm not interested in sharing anything with you. Just service your women and leave me alone."

Fintan was mystified. The incident with Salmé was trivial to him, already forgotten. He found Kesair's attitude inexplicable.

But then, he reasoned, who could ever understand women?

They traveled on until Byth found his valley. As always, Kesair was following a river. It led between two hills that rose in gentle curves from the plain. Within the sheltering arms of the hills, which blocked the wind and trapped the sun, the river spilled into a crystal lake. An ecstasy of birds was in full song, and the valley surrounding the lake was fragrant with flowers.

"Here we are!" Byth cried, flinging his arms wide and ignoring his arthritis. "I knew we would find this place. We're home, chicks."

Indeed, the valley was beautiful enough to bring a lump to Fintan's throat. Had Byth not already claimed it, Fintan would have wanted it for himself. But he could not deny the old man. "This is your land, then," he agreed, "and we shall go on and find someplace for ourselves."

"Stay with us until we get settled in," Ayn urged Kesair. "Byth is not as strong as he thinks he is, and we would be grateful for some help."

Kesair had no hesitation about staying to help this time.

It was fortunate, because that meant they were still there several days later, when Ladra's women caught up with them. Several were already thickening with pregnancy.

Ramé led the group. Her face was haggard, her eyelids swollen as if she had been crying. Ashti, the youngest of the party, was still sniffling and wiping her nose on her sleeve.

Kesair hurried forward to meet them. "What happened to you?"

"He died!" Ashti wailed. "He was just sitting there, propped against a stone, and then he gave a sort of gurgle and blood started coming out of his mouth and he . . . and he . . ."

"Died," Ramé finished. "There was nothing any of us could do."

"It was horrible!" Ashti was crying. "Horrible! He kept struggling, and his legs were running but he wasn't going anywhere, and . . ."

Kesair said to Velabro, "Take her over there, away from the others, and give her a drink, will you?

"Now, Ramé, tell me just what happened."

"That is what happened. At first we could hardly believe he was dead. You saw how he was, he wouldn't even admit to being ill. Then all at once he was gone."

Listening to the conversation, Ayn was obviously puzzled. "I don't understand this at all," she said. "He was sick, then he got better. Then he was weak again, then he bled at the mouth, convulsed, and died? What sort of illness is that?"

"And how did he get it?" Fintan questioned. "Something fatal like that . . . could we all be subject to it?"

Seeing the fear in their faces, Kesair wanted to tell them. But she could not. She dared not. "No one else feels sick," she pointed out, "so we must assume this is something that affected only Ladra. Maybe an illness he'd had for a long time that we didn't know about."

They wanted to believe her but they were obviously frightened. Even Velabro was frightened. She found herself trying to comfort Ashti with words she did not believe. "Everything will be all right, we're safe, it's all right."

There was no conviction in the words. Ashti continued to cry.

In their panic to rejoin the others, Ladra's women had left most of their supplies behind. The cattle and other livestock had been abandoned to graze and run wild. Ramé, knowing Kesair would cling to the river courses, had been able to guess which way to go and so had found them, but her practicality had not extended to taking time to pack up and bring everything. She had been too afraid of being left behind.

There was only one thing to be done. Kesair arbitrarily divided Ladra's women among the two surviving men. She was annoyed with Ramé for leaving the animals, but assigned her to Fintan.

The urgency had gone out of them. They spent most of the rest of the summer getting Byth and his flock comfortably settled in their valley. It was only when the first chill winds blew over the hills that Kesair recognized the approach of autumn, and decided Fintan's group must be on its way. The valley would not support all of them on a permanent basis, and they would need to find their own place before another winter set in.

Leavetaking was hard. Ladra's death had made them aware of possibilities they had not wanted to consider before. Some of the women clung to one another and cried. But at last the final goodbyes were acknowledged, and Fintan and his party left Byth's valley.

After its first chill herald, the autumn was mild, a long and golden season. Kesair's rivers eventually led her to a vast deep lake with a strange red cast to its waters on certain days, and mountains standing like sentinels on either side. The land beside the lake, though hilly, was composed of rich loam, and there were fertile valleys not far away.

It seemed a good place to end their wandering.

A river flowing from the north fed the lake at its upper end, and that same river emerged at the lower end of the lake, wider, stronger, flowing toward the distant sea.

Surely flowing toward the distant sea.

I could follow the river and find the sea again any time I wanted to, Kesair told herself.

"There is timber here," she said. "We can build permanent houses of wood and stone, and we shall always have fresh water. There is no life without water."

She often stood by the lake shore, as she had once stood by the seashore. The same sense of reverence enveloped her. Instead of white sand she gazed upon reedy shallows, yet she could feel the water's presence just as strongly. Fresh or salt, it did not matter. What mattered was the element itself. It might be endlessly transformed yet it was always the same.

Holy, Kesair thought. Holy.

She wished the others could feel what she felt. She tried to explain to them.

In time, some listened.

Some did not.

In late winter, the body of water Kesair named the Red Lake was bitterly cold. Fires were kept burning night and day in the snug, small houses of stone and timber on the western shore of the lake, where the nearby mountains cut the wind to some extent.

Even on the coldest day, however, Kesair left the warmth of her hearthfire to stand beside the lake. Her house was hers alone, unshared. The other women lived five or six to a small cabin; only Fintan also had a place to himself. He invited the woman of his choice to it each night.

Kesair invited no one to hers.

Sometimes, she saw Fintan look at her in a way which she interpreted to mean he was going to ask her to his bed. Her reaction was always the same. She said something cruel or cutting or cold, and he invited someone else instead.

One by one, his women ripened with child. Kesair remained barren, big-boned and tawny-colored and barren, with angry eyes.

Salmé was also barren, though Fintan slept with her repeatedly. On the mornings after Salmé had been with him, Kesair spent a very long time beside the lake, communing with the water. Scooping it up in her shell, pouring it back.

"What are you thinking?"

His voice startled her from her reverie, but she did not look around. She knew Fintan was standing behind her.

"Thoughts are private," she said.

He ignored the rebuff. "You looked lonely standing here by yourself."

"I'm never lonely."

"I don't believe you. Everyone is lonely sometimes."

"You aren't. You couldn't possibly be."

"Because there's usually some woman with me? Surely you understand why, Kesair."

"Oh yes, I understand." Her voice was flat.

He waited. She said nothing more. How did we become so distanced from each other? Fintan wondered. Of all the women, she is the most intriguing, the one I thought would be closest to me once we got settled. "Kesair, what have I done to turn you against me?" he asked bluntly.

"Nothing." She was annoyed at his lack of subtlety, and she let him hear the annoyance in her voice.

He would not give up. "To tell you the truth, I'm getting very tired," he said confidingly. "Of the demands made upon me, I mean. It takes a lot out of a man, being the only male for so many. Sometimes I wish I could just sit and talk with an intelligent woman. Like you."

"You and I have nothing to say to each other."

"I think we do. There's mystery about you, you know. Layers to you. You've had experiences you haven't shared with the rest of us, that have made you what you are. I think I could learn from you."

She turned toward him then. Her expression was guarded. "Do you?"

"Of course. I admire you more than you know. The others are pleasant enough, but . . ." He smiled his winning, boyish smile, and gave a slight shrug.

Be careful, Kesair warned herself. His is a very practiced charm.

He's trying it on you simply because he can't bear to think any woman could resist him. "The others aren't stupid, you could talk to any one of them," she said aloud.

"Not the way I could talk with you. I need more than a warm body and someone to agree with me, Kesair. I'm not just a breeding animal. I need . . ."

He left the thought hanging unfinished on the cold air, like a cloud of vapor. She saw it there, hanging.

On the cold air, permeated with silvery light reflected from the cold lake.

Beyond the lake the mountains rose, each peak an icy solitude against the vast and empty sky. Cold. Cold.

The frozen liquid core of Kesair longed for the spring thaw.

Looking at Fintan, she saw heat in his eyes.

Turning from him, she looked at the water. Red Lake. Usually it was a deep, dark blue, but today it had taken on the strange red hue that occasionally resulted from the invasion of some unidentified life form.

The lake could not always maintain its integrity. Life intervened.

Byth is old, Kesair thought, and we have heard nothing from him since we came here. He might be dead by now. Fintan might be the last man I shall ever see.

The last man.

How precious is anger?

Abruptly she said, "I was thinking of Byth."

"Has anyone come with news of him?"

"No. I doubt if they could spare a messenger, and if they did, I doubt if a messenger could find us. We've come a long way from Byth's valley."

"I hope they're all right."

"This is a benevolent land, Fintan. We haven't seen any predators large enough to be a danger to us, and there are plenty of natural resources. Everyone is subject to illness and injury and age, but we all have a chance. We all have a chance," she repeated. "We've been very fortunate."

The day was still and cold. When a bird called in the distance, its voice carrying across the lake, the sound was like a spear of beauty lancing through the silence.

For once even the customarily busy human settlement on the lake shore was quiet. No sounds of human activity came from the huts. The women inside were resting, sleeping, mending their garments, tending their fires.

An ineffable and timeless peace hung over the Red Lake. Kesair and Fintan might have been the only two people in the world.

"Are we the only survivors, do you think?" Fintan asked in a low voice.

"We who made it to this island?"

"Yes."

"No. There are others."

She spoke with such certainty he looked at her in astonishment. "How can you say that? How can you know?"

"I know."

"You mean, you want to believe. So do I, Kesair; I very much want to believe that other people reached dry land somewhere, and life goes on. But I don't know."

"The sea knows."

"What are you talking about?"

Gazing fixedly at the lake, she replied, "Did you ever enter a room that was totally dark, yet you were aware someone else was already in it?"

"I suppose so." He thought for a moment, remembering. "Yes, I have."

"Your senses told you of that other person through some faint disturbance in the air."

"Perhaps. But that was an enclosed room. You can't expect me to believe you somehow sense survivors on the other side of the ocean . . ."

"I don't. I told you. The sea does, the sea is aware of them and if you listen to it . . ."

He was beginning to lose patience. This was more of that wild mystical talk of hers that some of the others had complained of before. "We aren't anywhere near the sea, Kesair."

"We're near a lake. And all water is one water."

How tranquil her voice was; how at peace she sounded. Was she mad? Fintan wondered. If so, was she more comfortable in her madness than he in his sanity?

"Do you expect me to believe you talk to the *water?*"

She shook her tawny head. In the cold blue light of winter her face was pale, her eyes large and luminous.

"I don't talk *to* water. What could I possibly say of any

importance to a force so much greater than myself? I merely listen. I am quiet, and I listen."

Mad, Fintan decided. Yet there was an allure in her tranquillity, in the knowledge and conviction she contained deep within herself. He was inexorably drawn. "What does the water tell you?"

"Whatever it wishes to tell me. Tales of other times. Ideas from the stars." She paused meaningfully. "How to survive, if we but listen and learn.

"The water brought us this far, across the sea, along the rivers and streams. It has forgiven us the damage we have done and allowed us to start afresh. But we must not make the same mistakes again, Fintan. No god is endlessly forgiving."

"No god . . . are you saying you worship the water?"

For the first time, she took her gaze from the lake and fixed it on him. The radiance in her eyes took his breath away. "We have not worshiped anything, Fintan, except ourselves and our own puny achievements. And see what has happened to us. We are reduced to abject helplessness. We are forced to admit our total dependence on that which is beyond our control. Earth and air, fire and water. The fine trappings and comforts we prided ourselves on having are stripped from us. The way of life we knew is gone forever.

"But some things remain because they are immortal. And is not the immortal, holy?

"In the future, if we are to continue to survive, we must revere the holy, the essential, the powers above our own. We must not put our faith in temporary things. We must listen to the immortal voices of sea and lake, river and stream. They have great powers, Fintan. We must listen and obey."

"Create new gods, you mean? We put that behind us long ago. We've outgrown superstition."

"By 'we' you mean humankind? And where is humankind now?" Kesair made a show of looking first in one direction, then another. "Gone, most of them," she concluded. "But the water remains."

He could not find a way to refute her. He was aware that a few of the women had begun to listen to her, during the long winter nights when there was little to do but sit around the fires. A few of them now joined her each dawn beside the lake, to dip up water in a jug and pour it over their hands into a basin, then empty the basin back into the lake. He had thought the ritual harmless, women's foolishness.

Perhaps it was.

Perhaps it was homage to a power that should be placated by people in a situation of tenuous survival.

Kesair believed this, and her belief carried its own power. Standing face to face with her in the silvery loneliness, he could feel the power.

What had she said? Water sustains life?

It does, Fintan thought. I cannot deny it.

She was looking at him intently.

"The water remains," he echoed.

The tension in her face eased. "That is the beginning of understanding. We are starting over, Fintan." She reached into the neck of her gown.

To his disappointment, she withdrew a simple seashell. She held it up. "Look, Fintan."

He looked, puzzled as to what she wanted.

The shell was white with the faintest rosy tinge that darkened to a deeper color within its fluted lip. Round at one end, it spiraled to a pointed tip at the other. When he looked more closely he realized how beautiful it was.

We share a love of beauty, he thought. I could make something of that . . .

"Listen, Fintan."

Kesair held the shell to his ear, pressing the fluted edge against the curled ear flap that was so like the curve of a shell.

Obediently, Fintan listened, keeping his eyes on hers.

She waited.

At first he heard nothing but a sound that might be the muffled beating of his own heart.

Then, faintly, he became aware of something else. He began to listen with his whole being.

The sound grew in intensity. Became a roar. A roar of ancient power, the roar of a billion voices held within the shell, muted to softness, but immortal.

Fintan's eyes widened with delight.

"I hear the sea," he said.

Fire. Fire! Firefirefirefirefirefire.
Let there be fire.
Hot hotter hottest singeing singing soaring burning blazing conflagration inferno holocaust.
Let there be light.
Sparking flashing flaring flaming illuminating glowing gleaming glaring dazzling radiant.
Let there be life.
Vigor ardor intensity vehemence fervor passion fury magic inspiration genius brilliance.
Thoughtless explosion of power giving birth to all thought, all awareness. Vast outgoing surge of creative passion studding the universe with stars, smoldering in the souls of planets.
Simmering scorching scalding sizzling bubbling boiling molten inflaming energizing consuming.
Firefirefirefirefirefire.
Fire is. Fire was. Fire will be.
Mindless.
Allmind.
Fire.
Fire.
Fire!

7

Meriones awoke with a sense of

guarded expectation. It felt like a day when

something good just might happen.

He opened his eyes to the light of the

Mediterranean reflecting from

the plastered walls of the second-story sleeping chamber. Beyond the window, the dawn glowed rose and gold. The music of the waking city was a harmony of voices and bustle, carts creaking, neighbors calling out to one another, shutters being thrown back.

Meriones stretched lazily beneath the linen sheet. The other half of the bed was empty. Tulipa had been up since before dawn, pouring a bowl of milk for the house snake that guarded their spirits when they slept, building a fire in the bake oven in the courtyard, setting up the small folding table beneath their one olive tree for their morning meal. As usual, she talked to herself as she worked, pitching her voice so it was certain to carry through the open window to Meriones.

Tulipa had lost interest in spending the early morning in bed with her husband. When he tried to lure her back she was quick to point out it was his fault she must leave him. "Who will milk the goat if I do not?" she would ask. "Who will cook our food or sweep our share of the street? There are no slaves here such as are to be found in the houses of more famous musicians. The wife of The Minos' favorite says she doesn't even know how to use a broom, can you imagine? But I do. I'm just Meriones' wife. I know how to do all manner of tiresome tasks. I have to get up right now and empty our night jar, so the whole house doesn't stink of it. I have no time to loll in bed with you."

As soon as she began, Meriones would shrug and smile his shy smile, offering little tokens of peace between the flying arrows of her words. "I am sorry . . . of course, you're quite right . . . you do work very hard, I know . . . yes, yes . . ."

But she had to run on to the end, always. And loudly, so others heard. In the city the houses huddled close together.

"She will be different when the children start to come," Meriones had once said apologetically to Phrixus, who lived next door.

"I doubt it," commented Phrixus, who was older. "Sometimes the marriage rites bring forward the worst in a woman. Your Tulipa told my Dendria that she had married beneath herself and regretted it."

Meriones had hung his head at these words. "Tulipa's uncle was Keeper of the Bulls. I'm just one of the countless musicians at the palace, with no royal blood to give me status."

"How did you come to play the lyre?"

Meriones had hesitated before answering. When he spoke his voice was low with embarrassment. "My grandmother was brought here as a slave from the Islands of the Mist. Are you surprised? Not many know; Tulipa would rather die than tell anyone. My grandmother taught me to play a small stringed instrument that had belonged to her father. It was the only possession she had been allowed to bring with her."

"You don't have to be ashamed, Meriones," Phrixus had said. "Almost everyone on Crete has ancestors who came from somewhere else, and a lot of them were slaves. After all, the commerce of the world goes through our harbor. Slaves are treated well here and their descendants can prosper, you are proof of that yourself. So be proud—and start siring some descendants of your own. They will keep Tulipa too busy to scold you."

But although Meriones and his wife prayed daily to the Good Goddess and observed her rituals, and Tulipa made several pilgrimages to the cave of the deity of childbirth, her belly remained flat while her tongue grew sharper.

Now as Meriones emerged, blinking and yawning, from the windowless ground floor of his house into the brilliant sunlight of the courtyard, she began on him at once. "That thief at the oil merchant's shop sold me a whole pithos of rancid oil, husband. It was delivered yesterday. I just unstoppered it and the vile smell turned my stomach over. What will I boil tonight's meat in? Why does everyone think they can take advantage of us? It's your fault, Meriones. Because you are unimportant we are sold rancid oil and we live on a crowded back street with no view of the harbor."

"We have a nice house," Meriones replied. "You seemed to like it well enough when we married, and you said nothing about the view then." Trying to hold on to the good mood he had awakened with, he looked admiringly at his little house of stone and plaster. Its exterior walls were painted the cheerful yellow of field flowers. As was the custom in Knōsos, the ground floor was windowless to insure privacy, but the upper story was windowed front and back to catch the light and draw the salty breezes from the harbor.

A man's status in the community could be judged from the view he commanded, and in the ninety cities of Crete there was intense competition for a panorama of the mountains or the dark glittering sea. The day room and sleeping chambers were at the top of the house, so their occupants could enjoy the scenery and be removed from domestic activities taking place at ground level in the megaron, or hearth room.

Meriones' house boasted no view more lofty than that of the paved street in front and its own tiny courtyard behind, but the building itself was bright and comfortable. Privately, Meriones thought it a fine achievement for the grandson of a slave. Yet many of his class lived as well or better, for the wealth of the sea kings lapped like a tidal wave over the inhabitants of the island of Crete.

Tulipa was not really dissatisfied with the house. It was her life and her husband that displeased her. She sat tapping her foot while Meriones ate, then sent him on his way with a negligible pat on the cheek, her mind already casting about for some way to avoid the chores waiting for her. She felt they were making her old before her time. Perhaps she could put off airing the bed until tomorrow— "Meriones will never notice anyway" she muttered to herself—and spend the morning with her friends Lydda and Dendria, gossiping over bowls of spiced fruit juice and comparing the faults of their husbands.

"Men are all alike," one of them would say with a sigh, and the other two would readily agree.

Meriones swung around the corner and set off up the main street of Knōsos, heading south, inland. He blended immediately into the crowd, one more slender, almond-eyed young man in a throng of chattering townspeople. He walked with his chest thrust out and his back arched, swinging his arms freely and flexing the arches of his feet to produce the exaggerated, jaunty gait that identified a Minoan of Crete anywhere in the known world. It was a walk that had taken him years to perfect. A strain of rogue blood in his veins resisted the effort, but had at last been overcome.

Now anyone seeing him would have thought him pure Minoan. The dazzling sunshine of Crete had tanned his skin to copper. His black hair was folded and knotted at the nape, with oiled curls hanging over his ears in the latest fashion. Around his waist he wore a linen apron embroidered in gold thread, emblem of one who had access to the palace of The Minos, the greatest sea king of all, Lord of Knōsos, god-king of the Minoan empire.

Meriones' waist was tightly girdled to accent its abnormal smallness, the result of wearing the heavy copper girdle that was fastened on children of both sexes almost from birth. "The tinier the waist, the more elegant the person," was a Minoan axiom.

Meriones was considered elegant indeed.

A stray hound trotted out of a narrow alleyway and came to a halt at Meriones' feet, looking up at him hopefully. He stopped and returned the dog's gaze. "I'd be glad of a companion as far as the Sun Gate," he told the white hound, "but they won't let you come into the palace." When he began walking again the dog trotted at his heels, its feathery white tail waving like a plume.

They threaded their way through a polyglot of lean dark Egyptians and ebony-skinned Nubians, Syrian traders and Cycladic purchasing agents, Libyans and Amorites and Hittites, porters and sailors and laborers who jostled one another and laughed or swore as the occasion dictated. Nobles in sedan chairs claimed right of way. Small donkeys, overburdened and uncomplaining, picked their way over the paving stones and ignored the impatient hands jerking their headcollars.

As Meriones moved inland toward the great sprawling palace known as the House of the Double Axes, the shops and small businesses that lined the main street began to give way to public areas furnished with fountains and flowers. Curving walkways led to luxurious villas set well back from the road. The tang of the sea was replaced by the heady aroma of flowering trees. Behind walls painted in blue and yellow and coral, caged birds could be heard singing, their music mingling with the laughter of children.

The land lifted, the houses climbing with it in a series of steps, bright blocks of color forming a random mosaic across the hills. Had he looked back, Meriones would have seen the cobalt sea and the mass of lateen-rigged ships crowding the harbor. Instead he gazed steadfastly ahead, contemplating immortality. Beyond Knōsos great Zeus himself lay sleeping, pretending to be a mountain.

Meriones and the dog passed a small stone shrine by the side of the road, heaped with floral offerings and containing a glazed jar of seawater with a realistically painted octopus curling its tentacles around the vessel.

Meriones paused. The hound flopped down in the dusty road beside him and scratched behind one ear with an audible sigh of relief.

A vendor carrying a wickerwork tray stepped out from behind the shrine. "An offering for the god of the shaking earth?" he suggested.

Meriones considered. The sun was warm. The ground felt stable beneath his feet. The flower-bedecked shrine to Poseidon gave no hint of the unstable temper of the god. Still . . .

"It never hurts to be cautious," the vendor urged. "Only last year, at Phaistos . . ."

"Yes, yes, I remember." Meriones quickly selected a sprig of mint from the man's tray and added his offering to the heap, though he was embarrassed to see how small one sprig looked amid the piles of gaudy, more expensive flowers. The vendor was looking at him with contempt, like Tulipa. He pressed a coin into the man's hand, whistled to the dog, and hurried away.

The sunbaked road broadened into the Royal Avenue as it led into the valley that sheltered the palace of The Minos from the greedy gaze of sea pirates. Not that there was any real danger of invasion, not anymore. For several centuries Crete had ruled secure and unchallenged at the heart of the world's seaways.

And sometimes the god who ruled those seas reminded man of his ultimate power by shaking the earth.

With the white hound at his heels, Meriones crossed the stone bridge that spanned the stream east of the palace. The House of the Double Axes, called Labrys in the court language, spread out before him as if a bag of jewels had been spilled from a giant's hand, tumbling down the valley in gay profusion.

No huge perimeter wall protected Labrys. Its guardian was the power of the sea's mightiest fleet, defending not only Knōsos but the other cities of the Cretan sea kings. Instead of a fortress, the palace of The Minos consisted of a number of elegant villas surrounding a central core of chambers and halls. Some of these villas, which served as homes for the vast array of officials and functionaries required by The Minos, rivaled the king's own quarters in splendor. But none could compete with the royal residence in terms of sheer size.

"There it is," Meriones said to the dog. "I spend every day of my life there—except feast days, of course. The palace is a city in itself, you know. There's a maze of passages and storerooms and private chambers inside. It took me years to learn my way, but I did," he added with shy pride.

The dog wagged its tail and grinned up at Meriones.

Labrys had been built from the heart outward, as a tree grows, until it sprawled in giant tiers like a child's blocks. The heart itself was the Great Central Court through and around which all life flowed. Four main gates led into the complex. The westernmost, called the Bull Gate, was the ceremonial entryway, with a pillared portico fronting on a broad paved courtyard. The south gate was the Zeus Gate, facing the mountains. To the north was the Sea Gate. Meriones approached by the eastern Sun Gate, following a walkway through flowered gardens. He wove his way among increasing crowds of gaily dressed men and women in animated conversation, hands fluttering, voices trilling. In addition to the customary courtiers there was the usual scattering of long-haired folk from Boeotia and Attica and Euboea, travelers from Pylos and Lerna, even a few flint-eyed warriors from Mycenae and Tiryns.

Everyone came to the House of the Double Axes.

Meriones, like most citizens of Knōsos, was fluent in several languages. He smiled from time to time at some overheard witticism, and translated for the dog's benefit.

As he climbed the broad stone steps that led to the Sun Gate itself, the giant Nubian warrior at the top of the stairs looked down at him. His usually impassive face cracked into a smile.

"Not another dog, musician?"

Meriones glanced ruefully at his companion. "I'm afraid so. They follow me and I can't help encouraging them. I would like to have a dog of my own but my wife says they make her sneeze." He gave the white hound a last fond pat, then handed it over to the Nubian, who held it by the scruff of the neck until Meriones disappeared inside the palace, and then gave it a shove, not unkindly, and sent it on its way.

Meriones made his way through the corridors and service rooms that lay between the Sun Gate and the residential quarter. Like all public areas of Labrys, the royal apartments featured spacious open rooms, often divided by the same dark red columns that were used to support the exterior porticoes. The columns tapered downward in the distinctive Cretan style, and were as integral a part of palace design as the painted frescoes glowing on every wall. The famous Grand Staircase was renowned throughout the Mediterranean world for its scenes of cavorting sea creatures, blooming lilies, and elegant court life. Numerous light wells provided adequate illumination for the appreciation of such beauty, even in the inner recesses of Labrys.

But Meriones did not reach the Grand Staircase. His progress was interrupted by Santhos, Master of Musicians. "You have a new assignment," the round-faced Santhos announced. "You won't be playing in the royal apartments for a while. The queen is very dissatisfied with the quality of work being done by the goldsmiths these days, and wants a musician sent to play in their workrooms and inspire them."

Meriones' erect posture slumped. The workrooms of the royal craftsmen were in the northeast quarter of the palace, a comparatively dreary place where a musician himself might despair of inspiration. But there was no point in arguing.

Meriones forced a smile, straightened his spine and saluted Santhos. He strode off jauntily, springing upward from the balls of his feet, looking as if the prospect of days spent in gloomy workrooms was the thing he most desired.

Watching him go, Santhos said to himself, "Thank Zeus for men like Meriones. Musicians are so temperamental. Most would have refused."

The craftsmens' workrooms were on the ground floor beneath the Great Eastern Hall. In separate cubicles, men fashioned furniture, fabrics, tableware, jewelry, the myriad items required by the huge community above them. The chamber of the goldsmiths was in a favored position, with a light well and freshly painted walls, but Meriones' heart sank when he entered. It was hot and cramped and utilitarian rather than elegant. Tulipa would be angry if she learned of this.

Half a dozen men were working at benches and tables. They all looked up as he entered.

"I am a musician of The Minos," he began formally. His words dropped like stones into a sudden silence. "I have been sent to make music for you while you work. Is there, ah, a bench, a stool . . . ?"

They stared at him unresponsively. Meriones felt his ears reddening. Why couldn't someone else have been sent? Why did these things always happen to him?

Then one of the goldsmiths, a ruddy, thickset man with bloodshot eyes and an uncut mane of sandy hair, stepped forward and guided Meriones to a stool. "Here, musician, perch on this. And play quietly, don't distract us."

The man's voice was harsh with the accents of distant Thrace, but Meriones felt a sudden warmth toward him and smiled gratefully. "I'm called Meriones," he offered.

"Hmmm." The other turned back to his table. Then he said "Hokar" over his shoulder as an afterthought before forgetting Meriones entirely and returning to his work.

Meriones sat on the edge of the stool, trying simultaneously to be inspiring and inconspicuous. He was a success at one of the two, for the goldsmiths paid no further attention to him.

In mid-afternoon two slaves arrived, bringing watered wine and a tray of bread and cheese. Hokar put down the gold plate he was working on and stood up, stretching. "I need to walk," he said casually to Meriones. "Do you know your way around this place?"

"Yes, absolutely."

"Come, then." Hokar headed for the door, massaging the muscles of his shoulder with one hand. Glad of the break, Meriones followed him.

"Working with gold is like working with the sun, isn't it?" he said, to make conversation. "I mean, molten gold looks like liquid sunlight, doesn't it? I envy you, really. It must be wonderful to be able to make beautiful things . . ." His voice trailed off. Hokar did not appear to be listening.

They sauntered along hallways that wound a baffling route toward the Great Central Court. Once, when Hokar was about to make a turn that would take him into a warren of storerooms, Meriones corrected him with a gentle hand on his arm. Nothing more was said until they reached the colonnaded walkway overlooking the Court. There they stood shoulder to shoulder, watching the constant crowd swirling across the mosaic tiles.

"I've never known a day so hot," Hokar remarked. Sweat was pouring down his face.

"It is hot," Meriones agreed, "hotter than usual. And so still." That seemed to exhaust the fund of conversation. The two men were quiet for a time.

Then Meriones volunteered, "The women of Knōsos are the most beautiful in the world, don't you think?"

"You haven't seen the women of Thrace," Hokar replied. But his eyes were following a Cretan priestess of the Snake as she minced past. Like all women in the House of the Double Axes she was fashionably pale, her powdered complexion a marked contrast to the glossy black of her hair. Kohl rimmed her dark eyes, accentuating their almond shape. Her slender body was clad in a flounced skirt of multicolored layers that swung beguilingly above her bare feet and dainty rouged toes. A gem-studded belt defined the impossible smallness of her waist. Above it her breasts bloomed, pushed upward by a tight saffron-colored bodice that clung to her shoulders and upper arms but left her bosom bare. Her erect nipples were sprinkled with gold dust.

Meriones saluted the priestess and made flattering gestures with his hands, to which she responded with a few softly lisped syllables.

"You understand her?" Hokar queried.

"Of course. That is the court language, the Old Tongue still favored by the nobility and the priestly class. One could not be long in Labrys without learning at least a few words of it."

"I'll be the exception. If I have to learn to sound like a dove cooing I prefer to be speechless."

Meriones chuckled. "It's a difficult language," he agreed. "You never hear it now, outside of the palace. Crete speaks the New Tongue, the language of the markets. You're quite good at that, I notice, which proves you have a gift for language as well as for creating beautiful objects. I also have a gift for language. I speak several, even one I learned from my grandmother, who spoke the tongue of the Islands of Mist."

"You talk a lot," Hokar observed. "all Cretans talk a lot, don't they?"

"We enjoy the arts, including that of conversation."

"There is a lot to enjoy here," Hokar remarked. His eyes were now following a graceful woman dressed in a vivid shade of orange, her fingers and toes weighted with jewels, her nipples painted a brilliant blue. She returned his frank stare with an amused smile.

"You'd never see anything like that on the mainland," Hokar said. "My cousin Tereus would consider it an invitation to rape."

Meriones was shocked. "She is merely sharing her beauty! To ignore her would be rude, but it would be ruder still to abuse her as a result of her generosity."

"Hmmm." Hokar dug his unpolished fingernails into his beard, scratching. "I suppose it's this Cretan worship of beauty that creates such a good climate for artisans, so I shouldn't joke about it. We're given opportunities here we would receive nowhere else. I devoted years of my life to obtaining an invitation to come to Crete just as an apprentice goldsmith, whereas in Thrace I was already considered a master."

"What is Thrace like?"

"Rugged country. Breeds rugged people. We have no patience with effeminate manners in Thrace."

"We are not effeminate," Meriones protested, stung at last by the other's patronizing tone. "We are an *elegant* people. You mainlanders don't understand elegance."

Hokar grinned. "Not in our heads, perhaps. But watch me at work and then tell me my hands don't understand elegance."

That night over their meal Meriones spoke to his wife about Hokar. "He's a gruff sort of fellow, devoted to his work. He keeps to himself, mostly. But I know he has a kind heart, and he's a brilliant artisan. It's a treat to watch him, it truly is. I wish you could see him take those big paws of his and move them this way and that—and then something delicate and exquisite emerges. I could watch him for hours."

Sundown had marked the beginning of a feast day, and Tulipa had purchased a small kid in the marketplace. The remnants of the meal, still redolent of spice and honey, lay on their plates. She picked idly among the bones. "You are always trying to make friends with the most unlikely people, Meriones. If you must attach yourself to someone, why not to someone important who can do you some good?"

"But I like Hokar. He was nice to me, in his way, and I take it as an honor. Did I tell you he used to make sword hilts for the warrior princes on the mainland?"

Tulipa sniffed and wiped her greasy fingers on her forearm, working the grease into the skin to keep it soft. It was a habit of the lower classes, one no court lady would have allowed herself. But Meriones made no judgment. After all, as she so often reminded him, her uncle had been a person of importance.

"You fasten yourself onto someone who doesn't care if you're alive or dead," she continued in an aggrieved voice, "while I sit home alone, fading away for lack of entertainment. If you made some really important friends perhaps you could get me invited to the palace."

"If we had children you wouldn't be bored," he ventured. "Shall we . . . go upstairs now?"

"No. I don't want to. Listening to you rave on and on about some common Thracian has given me a headache. You are so thoughtless, Meriones."

"I'm so sorry! I didn't realize." Meriones jumped to his feet. "I'll go dip a cloth in cool water and vinegar to put on your head," he promised, hurrying away.

As the days passed, Meriones continued to play in the chamber of the goldsmiths. Hokar gradually accepted his patiently proffered friendship. They began taking a daily stroll together in the gardens, though as long as the heat wave continued even Meriones, who dearly loved sunshine, had to make a conscious effort to keep his step fashionably brisk.

"No one can remember it being so hot for so long," he once commented. "I used to think it could never be too sunny, but now I wonder. Is it hot in Thrace, Hokar?"

"In the summers it is. But we pay no attention."

Hokar enjoyed talking about his homeland, so Meriones constantly plied him for details. The Thracian spoke glowingly of the mountains of his boyhood, and of things he had seen in his travels as an apprentice goldsmith. He alluded to the growing power of the citadels of Mycenae, and described chariot races so vividly Meriones could almost see them. Inflamed by his own words, Hokar embossed a scene of chariots and charioteers into the rim of a platter he was making for The Minos' table.

At last the heat broke. The brief Cretan winter arrived, bringing raw damp air that bit into a man's bones. It was the Season of the Dying God. In the House of the Double Axes the chambers were divided into smaller, more heatable rooms by means of sliding wooden panels. These rooms were heated by bronze braziers. Fires were built in the central hearths of the megaron. Meriones enjoyed staring at the bright tongues of flame, children of the sun. His grandmother, who remembered the Islands of Mist as being always cold, had taught him an appreciation of fire.

Meriones personally tended the fire in the brazier in the goldsmiths' chamber.

He never tired of watching his friend at work. Once Hokar had begun on a piece he tolerated no distractions and would lash out at anyone foolish enough to disturb his concentration. Meriones learned to time his music to the rhythm of the Thracian's work pattern.

Melding with the music, Hokar so lost himself in his art that it seemed no man was involved, just a pair of skilled hands taming the molten gold, the melted sun, turning it into exquisite jewelry and tableware and ornaments for the palace.

To Meriones, Hokar's gift seemed like magic.

"The queen is very pleased with the work coming from the goldsmiths now," Santhos reported to Meriones. "You may become a permanent fixture here."

In the Season of the Borning God Meriones invited Hokar to come to his house for dinner, to celebrate the arrival of spring.

"Will I be able to get home afterward before dark?" the Thracian inquired.

"Where do you live?"

"In a little house at Arkhanes, in the shadow of the Hill of Tombs."

Meriones whistled. "It depends on what time you leave my house, then. That's a goodly distance. We can loan you a lamp. Or you can spend the night with us. My wife will make up a pallet."

As they talked, the two men were standing side by side in one of the gardens, eating their bread and cheese and watching a pretty girl play with a chained monkey. "Do you have a nice place?" Hokar asked.

Meriones beamed. "I think so. It was a great piece of luck, getting it. For some reason the old Minos—the one before this, that is—took a fancy to my music toward the end of his reign. He had grown quiet, and I think he liked me for playing softly. He chose me alone to play for him on Last Day, so for a brief time I was very important at Labrys. My reward was enough to buy my house, and Tulipa married me."

"Tell me about Last Day, Meriones. What was that like? We have no such custom in Thrace."

"It's the sight of a lifetime! The final day of the Nine Years' King must be more spectacular than any that has gone before, to show our gratitude to him for a prosperous reign. The Bull Dances are better than ever. Outstanding teams of Bull Leapers compete with each other for the honor of performing on Last Day, and the bull who proves to be bravest and most agile in the Bull Dance is sacrificed to Poseidon at the end of the day."

"You always offer a bull to Poseidon?"

"We make many offerings to the sea god, but it is the gift of the mightiest creature on earth that pleases him most and keeps him from shaking the land."

Hokar nodded. "I've heard that Poseidon Ennosigaion ripples Crete from time to time, though I've yet to experience a bad earthquake here."

"Ah well, they do happen," Meriones admitted. "But we build to allow for them, and we do those things that keep us in good favor with the gods. And with a joyous spirit!" he added quickly. "That is the Cretan way—with a joyous spirit!"

"Tell me about the sacrifice. Would it make a good scene to depict on a gold bowl?"

Meriones hesitated. "I don't like to talk about sacrifices, really. I never enjoy seeing blood spilled. But if you want the details . . . the priest of the Double Ax, the two-faced ax that faces both toward this world and the netherworld, sacrificed a huge pied bull in the Central Court, and its head was brought to this very chamber, to have the horns gilded."

"Was the old Minos sacrificed too?"

Merioned recoiled. "Of course not! What a ghastly idea!"

"I just wondered. It is the custom in some lands, sacrificing the king at the end of his reign. It's supposed to restore fertility to the soil."

Meriones was quite pale. "How grim." He swallowed, hard. "No, we don't practice human sacrifice on Crete. It is unbearable to imagine."

"Yet the sign of the Double Ax is everywhere in this place," Hokar pointed out. "It must have some significance beyond the killing of bulls."

"Ah, well, er . . . I suppose it is a symbol from the olden times. Long ago . . . but surely not now . . ."

"This is a huge place. There could be rites carried out in Labrys that you would know nothing about, Meriones."

"Oh, I hardly think so, not the way people love to talk. You are very bloodthirsty, Hokar."

"I'm not, I'm realistic. We Thracians are earthy people, that's all. But if this bothers you, tell me instead about what happened to the old Minos."

"Ah, yes." Meriones looked relieved. "I stayed with him until the end, playing the music he liked. Then the priestesses took him to the Chamber of Robes and removed all his finery, sending him out naked to his women. How they sobbed, his queen and concubines! But that was just part of the ritual, there was nothing to be sad about, really. They wrapped him in a simple robe and led him away. I stopped playing just as the priest brought forward the new Minos, a young man at the peak of his strength, naked, freshly bathed, and took him into the Chamber of Robes. There he was dressed in the royal clothes, still warm from his predecessor. That's important, the warm part," he added.

"And the former king?"

"I saw them bringing a covered sedan chair from the Zeus Gate to take him away. I believe he was taken to a distant palace such as Phaistos to live out his life in luxury, for he had been a good king and we prospered during his reign."

"But do you know for certain if he's still alive? Has he ever been seen since?"

"Oh no. At the end of his nine years a Minos must disappear from the sight of his people forever."

"I see." Hokar nodded. His eyes were on the omnipresent sign of the Double Axes, depicted over the nearest doorway.

On a languid blue evening when

the rusty voices of the gulls had ceased and bronze

lamps of welcome burned in residential windows,

Hokar dined with Meriones. At the

conclusion of

the meal he wiped the crumbs from his beard and belched appreciatively.

Tulipa sniffed. The man was crude. His hairy face offended her. Men should be clean-shaven and polish their nails. But at least he had brought her a present. For the sake of the silver bracelet he had given her, she would try to overlook his rough edges.

Now the two men lolled at their ease beside the table in the courtyard, watching idly as Tulipa cleared away and brought a fresh pitcher of wine.

"Your wife is a good cook," Hokar remarked when she had gone back into the house. "I never had birds stuffed with barley before, or those little shellfish."

"And raisins soaked in fruit juice," Meriones said. "They were especially good. Did you like them?"

"Mmmmm. Does she always cook like this?"

"Always," Meriones was proud to say. There was no faulting Tulipa's cooking, even if she hated domestic duties otherwise. "Have you never married, Hokar?"

"Never. Though at a time like this, I can see some of its advantages. But I've always been devoted to my work. That takes my energy, I have no time left over for women. My art is my life. My only passion."

"Ah now. Ah now." Meriones smiled a sly smile and waggled a forefinger in front of Hokar's eyes. "That isn't true. I've seen how you look at the girls in the palace, particularly those young ones, the new Bull Leapers."

"Any man would look at them, but looking is all I want to do. Can you imagine trying to catch hold of one? They are all muscle, those girls. And they have hardly any breasts. They look like the boys."

"They have to be slim and strong. It's a very hard thing to do, the Bull Dance, and demands the greatest athleticism. Bull Leapers are recruited from every land, you know. It is a high honor to appear in the Bull Court."

"Recruited? Kidnapped, you mean. In Thrace we heard of young people who were seized and taken aboard Cretan ships and never heard of again. Rumor was, they disappeared into the bowels of Labrys."

"You make it sound as if something awful happened to them,"

Meriones protested. "But they were taught a high art instead. Dancing with the bulls, leaping over their horns, somersaulting in teams through the air while a bull charges beneath you . . . it is not only beautiful to watch but it tests the courage of both human and bull. The best Bull Leapers become famous."

"If they live long enough," Hokar commented. "What about the ones who are killed learning this 'art'?"

"Killed?" Meriones raised his eyebrows. "I've heard of no one being killed."

"I suppose you wouldn't," said Hokar. "I suspect it's kept very quiet. Like the old Minos."

A shiver ran down Meriones' spine. "You're just saying that."

Hokar relented. "I enjoy teasing you," he said. "I mean no harm by it, forget I said anything."

The rest of the evening went well. At one stage, Meriones went next door to bring Phrixus over to meet the goldsmith. "He's very important at Labrys, you know," the musician said under his breath to his neighbor.

"I hear you had an important visitor from the palace yesterday," Dendria said with barely concealed envy when she met Tulipa at the well the next morning.

Tulipa affected nonchalance. She yawned, she patted her hair, she studied her nails. "Oh, yes? My Meriones knows everyone who matters." Balancing her filled water jug on her head, she walked away, swaying her hips.

Several days later, Hokar mentioned that his cousin Tereus, who was captain of a sizable trading vessel, should be arriving in the Cretan harbor soon. "You would enjoy meeting him, I think. He's very full of life, is Tereus; he's been everywhere and seen everything and he tells great stories."

"We'll invite him to my house for dinner," Meriones decided, flushed with his recent social success.

Tulipa was not hard to convince. She was wearing Hokar's silver bracelet, which she had shown several times to Dendria and Lydda. This Tereus might bring her something even better.

On the appointed evening, Hokar came straight from the palace with Meriones, and the two settled in the courtyard to await Tereus. They did not wait for long. A brawny man with a jutting jaw pounded on the outer door. When Tulipa opened to him, he scarcely noticed her. Looking past her into the interior of the house, he bellowed, "Hokar! Where are you?" At an answering shout from the courtyard, he pushed past Tulipa and found his own way to the rear of the house.

She trotted after him, wide-eyed with indignation.

Hokar got to his feet as Tereus appeared in the doorway. "Meriones, this is my cousin Tereus, captain of the *Qatil* out of Byblos," he said.

Tereus filled the doorframe with his broad shoulders. Vitality radiated from him like heat from a brazier. He made Meriones feel insignificant, and when his brilliant blue eyes swept over her household Tulipa received a distinct impression of contempt. This was a man who demanded much. Whatever life was lived in the house of Meriones, the musician was insufficient for his appetites.

He was polite enough in his unpolished way, however, and thanked Meriones—though not Tulipa—for receiving him. As the three men sat at the table Tereus had great tales to tell of ocean voyages and sea monsters and terrifying storms. His stories were so vivid Meriones often forgot to eat, sitting with his mouth agape and the food congealing on his plate.

When Tulipa finished serving the men she drew up a chair to the table for herself, so she could listen to Tereus. His accent was no thicker than Hokar's, and she understood most of what he said.

She understood very clearly when he remarked, "Only on Crete do women dare sit at the table with the men. Elsewhere they know their place and keep it."

Tulipa's cheeks burned. She looked to Meriones, expecting him to defend their customs, but he only stared at his plate and toyed with his uneaten food.

Snatching up her husband's plate, Tulipa strode furiously into the house.

"That's better," said Tereus. "Women get in the way of serious conversation. Meriones, my cousin tells me you have served in the house of The Minos for a long time."

"Since I was old enough to take off my waist-shaper."

"Then you have good knowledge of the place, of its staffing, the habits of its purchasing agents, and so forth?"

Meriones had been surprised, and secretly, guiltily pleased at

Tereus' handling of Tulipa. And he was flattered at the way the ship's captain made him feel important, privy to the inner workings of the House of the Double Axes. "Oh yes," he said, waving his hands. "I know all the stewards, the keepers of the stores, everyone."

"Hokar said he thought you might. You are the very man I need, then." Tereus leaned forward, folding his thick arms on the tabletop. His voice dropped to a more confidential tone. "I have a very special cargo from my last voyage and I would like to sell it here, to the household of The Minos. A sea king can afford the kind of price which would give me enough money to buy my own ship at last, and not have to bow my head to some Syrian owner who never sets foot on deck."

There was something about the emphasis Tereus put on his words that made Meriones nervous. "If you have a valuable cargo I suppose the quartermaster already suggested the best market when you cleared it through him? And the ship's owner—a Syrian, you said—will he not get the profit?"

Tereus and Hokar exchanged glances. The goldsmith gave a barely perceptible nod. "Meriones is all right," he said softly.

Tereus dropped his eyelids halfway over his eyes so their expression was veiled. "I have not discussed this particular cargo with the harbormaster, Meriones. Do you understand? Nor will it be reported at Byblos. There is a bit of profit in it for you, too, if you keep your mouth shut and put me in contact with the right buyer. Would you not like to have a bit of wealth to impress your wife?"

Meriones felt his mouth go dry. "What is your cargo?"

Tereus smiled lazily and leaned back, resting his broad shoulders against the plastered wall behind his chair. "My last voyage was through the Pillars of Herakles and then north, following the coast," he said. "A dangerous trip into unpredictable waters. Not many are willing to make it. Our final destination was to be the lands at the edge of winter, where people collect lumps of raw amber on the seashore after storms. To trade for amber, we took flint from the Islands of Mist."

"You have been to the Islands of Mist?" Meriones asked in an awed whisper.

"Of course. We started from Byblos with timber and jade, and pearls from Dilmun. These we traded along the way for obsidian, for copper, then for Nubian ivory, and that in turn went for textiles and bronze which we traded in the Islands of Mist for tin and flint and, on the westernmost island, gold."

Meriones' existence was circumscribed by the luxurious, enclosed atmosphere of palace life. But Crete was the land of the sea kings, so he had heard tales of the far places beyond the horizon, tales of Ugarit and Mitanni and Assyria, of wild Iberia and fabled Babylon. Now he was looking at a man who had personally sailed to the very kingdom of winter, where blond giants farmed steep fields and amber lay free for the taking on rocky beaches. Meriones strained to envision a land of deep fjords and long blue silences.

But he was more interested in the Islands of Mist. "My grandmother came from the Islands of Mist," he said.

Tereus lifted his eyebrows. "As a slave? Then you understand what sort of cargo I brought this time. I hope you won't be offended when I say the best slaves are from those rainy islands. Their skin is very white and they are highly prized throughout the Mediterranean. I try to pick up a few good ones each voyage, to sell privately."

Meriones suffered confused emotions. Slavery was very much a part of life, and central to Cretan economy, as it was everywhere in the Mediterranean. Thousands were traded each year at places like Kythera, where men dealt in nothing else. But, remembering his grandmother, he found it hard to think of people like her as if they were merely cargo, so many cattle to buy and sell. "Is that this special, valuable cargo, then?" he asked Tereus. "Captives taken from the Islands of Mist?"

"Yes. Five of them, three females and two males. The females are young, very pretty. They would be valuable anywhere. But the men . . . that is, one of them . . . ah, this one is something very special.

"If your grandmother came from those islands, what do you know about them?" Tereus asked Meriones.

"Only a little. How green they were, how mild the climate. How many lakes and rivers they had."

"It is the inhabitants who are interesting," Tereus said. "They are strong and brave and are ruled by warrior princes. In some ways they remind me of Thracians. But they live intimately with gods I do not know: water gods, weather gods, gods of the wild places. And they build stone ritual centers with as much engineering skill as the Egyptians, though in a very different style. I have seen nothing anywhere that raises my hackles like the great stone circles in the Islands of Mist.

"One of the slaves I brought back with me this time is some sort of priest. Not such a priest as you have here. I believe theirs is a fading race, though once it may have been very powerful. Their sorcerers can still do things to freeze a man's marrow. This old fellow should be worth a fortune as a worker of magic, or at least a royal diviner. For all I know the old man can predict the shaking of the earth, which would make him beyond price, eh? And even if he fails in that he can do a lot of other tricks."

Meriones was shocked. "You would take a priest and sell him as an *entertainer?*"

"I would sell the woman who bore me if she were still alive and the sale would enable me to buy my own ship and be answerable to no man."

"Your mother would cheerfully cut your throat if you tried such a thing," Hokar interjected.

"My mother was a proud woman and a warrior in her own right. She would have understood my desire to be my own master."

Meriones was frowning. "I just don't like the idea of selling priests as slaves. Angering the gods is dangerous."

Tereus said, "His gods aren't our gods, I told you that. Besides, if I can turn over a cargo twelve times in a voyage and avoid the pirates of Mycenae, I fear nothing."

"But—"

"Never mind, just do as I tell you and fortune will smile on us. The gods of whatever land support the successful, have you not noticed? Put me in contact with someone at the palace who is empowered to purchase slaves—expensive, unusual slaves, by private treaty—and I will present my treasures for his inspection. Here, at your house."

Meriones was startled. "Why at my house? Why not take them direct to Labrys?"

"They are, shall we say, unpredictable. Especially the old man. Hokar tells me you know a little of the language they speak, so I want you present throughout the negotiations to persuade them to be cooperative. It will all go more smoothly here, in a private house."

Watching Meriones closely, Tereus assessed his exact degree of resistance. He immediately poured another bowl of wine for Meriones, saying, "And of course I will pay you extra for the use of your house. Agreed? Good, good!"

When Tereus left them for a few moments to go and relieve himself behind the wall, Meriones said to Hokar, "I always seem to be letting people talk me into things. I can never say no when I should. I admire your cousin. I doubt if he has that problem."

"He has others," Hokar replied. "Is there any more wine?"

Meriones gazed solemnly into the pitcher Tulipa had left on the table. "It's empty," he reported with regret. "But I think we have some milk flavored with kinnamon."

"Milk!" Tereus guffawed as he returned to them. "Men don't drink milk, even flavored with spices! Once this deal is concluded, my wasp-waisted friend, you'll be able to afford amphorae of wine, one for every day of the week." He clapped Meriones heartily on the back.

Much later, in the privacy of their bed, Meriones made the mistake of telling Tulipa about Tereus' offer.

"You certainly are going to help that big Thracian sell his slaves!" she insisted, sitting bolt upright in the bed. "If you don't, I'll go back and live with my mother!"

For a moment—only for a moment—Meriones was tempted.

After several false starts when his courage deserted him, Meriones spoke to Carambis, Master of Slaves, and a meeting was arranged. Carambis had been party to such deals before and knew exactly how much padding could be concealed within the price he would ultimately collect from the palace treasurer. A nice little profit would be made all around, if the slaves lived up to their description. The new Minos was known to have a taste for exotics.

Tereus' men were to bring the slaves from the ship to Meriones' house before dawn on the appointed day, and hold them there until Carambis arrived for the inspection. Tulipa disliked having so many strangers under her roof, but the promised commission placated her.

Meriones had less easily dismissed reservations.

When he heard the muffled knocking at the street door in the predawn darkness, he thought for the tenth time, I wish I had not agreed to this. Tulipa burrowed more deeply into the bed and pretended not to hear, so it was Meriones who padded downstairs on bare feet and opened the door.

Four husky seamen pushed past him into the small passage opening onto the megaron. The area was filled with the stench of their unwashed bodies. Meriones was aware of huddled forms being dragged and shoved with them, and the thump of a fist on someone's back. He lifted his bronze night-lantern in an effort to make out faces, but only succeeded in casting distorted menacing shadows on the walls, figures that gesticulated like dark frescoes come to life.

Tulipa joined them in the megaron. She shrank against the wall and rolled her eyes at Meriones.

"It's all right," he assured her with a total lack of conviction. "These men are from Tereus, with the, ah, guests, we talked about."

One of the seamen grinned, a flash of broken yellow teeth in a swarthy face. "Guests, is it?" he mimicked. "Look at this one." He thrust one of the bound, cloaked figures into the lantern light and uncovered its head. "You have strange tastes if you invite people like this to be your guests."

A thin old man stood blinking before them. He was taller than either Meriones or Tulipa, as tall as any of Tereus' men. His gaunt face looked like wrinkled parchment stretched tight over a skull. A fringe of white beard edged his jawbone, then slanted upward to meet the tangle of his uncut hair. His eyes were set deep in cavernous sockets. When they accepted the light and were able to focus he turned their full glare on Meriones. Strange eyes, colorless, burning with a life more intense than any other in the room.

Meriones involuntarily took a step backward.

The old man murmured something and struggled to free his hands. Instantly his captor pulled the cloak over his face and spun him around to face the wall. "Here, that's enough of that," he warned. To Meriones he said, "You don't want to let him look at you too long, or make those signs with his hands."

Tulipa asked in a harsh whisper, "Why not?"

"It's just better if you don't," the man replied. "I am Jaha Fe, third officer on the *Qatil*. My men and I will stay here and guard these guests of yours. Is there anything to eat while we wait?"

Without complaints for once, Tulipa hurried away to prepare food. When she was gone, Jaha Fe winked at Meriones. "Now these women, they could be guests in my pallet any time. Want to see?"

Meriones nodded, though his eyes kept straying to the cloaked figure of the old man. Jaha Fe unwrapped the nearest woman and pushed her toward the light.

She was beautiful, even by Cretan standards. Her skin was as luminous as seafoam.

"I think she's the daughter of the old man," Jaha Fe said. "Or granddaughter, could be."

Her frightened glance skittered about the room until she met Meriones' eyes. He offered a shy smile. She said something in reply.

Meriones struggled with the scattered fragments of childhood memories, put together a few words, discarded them and tried again. A sound emerged that might have been the sighing of wind in the cypresses of Knōsos, a confusion of sibilants and aspirants that startled him as much as anyone else. But the girl flashed a grin of acknowledgment and replied in the same tongue.

"What's she saying?" Jaha Fe demanded to know. "Get her to tell you her name."

Sweating, for the heat had returned to Crete, Meriones struggled with the forgotten language of his grandmother. His words came haltingly, but his understanding of the language improved as he listened to the girl. "She is called Ebisha," he translated at last, pleased with himself. "It means something like . . . Green Eyes."

"And she does have them!" Jaha Fe exclaimed. A roll of laughter relieved the tension in the room.

Meriones did not go to the palace that day. Even if he had not been instructed to wait for Carambis to come and inspect the slaves, he would have been unwilling to leave his wife alone in the house with the Thracian seamen.

He spent his time in conversation with Ebisha, who was pitifully eager to talk now that she had someone who could understand. She spoke with longing of her lost land, a land of many tribes, ruled by warrior chieftains who were very much under the influence of the priests. According to Ebisha, the inhabitants of the Islands of Mist were obsessed with the supernatural. They envisioned a community of spirits freely mingling with the living, interacting with them as if both seen and unseen were members of one ongoing community. This concept was inexplicable to the Cretan mind, whose vision of the netherworld was a simplistic paradise.

Ebisha told Meriones of priests who manipulated the power in the standing stones that dotted the islands, drawing down that power in some extraordinary fashion to make crops grow and heal the sick and control the weather to their advantage. This was not magic, she insisted, when Meriones tried to apply that term to the priests' actions.

"Not magic," Ebisha said. "Priests use . . . what is. Earth, fire, water, stone. They know how to use. They . . . shape. Make happen by shaping. My grandsire"—she nodded toward the old man—"he makes happen."

Meriones looked toward the tall, gaunt figure that was still standing immobile, facing the wall. He shuddered. It was as if something alien, cold beyond cold, had come into his warm little house.

Tereus arrived before Carambis. There was no mistaking the way Ebisha's face lit up when she saw him, though the other slaves turned their faces away from him. "He is like a chieftain of my own people," she told Meriones. "As soon as I saw him I wanted him to put his hands on me. I knew he wanted it too."

"Did he . . . on the ship?" Meriones asked, surprised to find the thought angered him.

"No. But he will, he will." She looked past Meriones to Tereus and smiled.

Tereus was paying no attention to her. Instead he had the old priest brought before him and asked Meriones his opinion of the man's saleability. The priest stood silently, glaring out of his skull-like face, eyes blazing with a light that might have been madness or even the manifestation of a god. Once, perhaps, they had been as green as Ebisha's, but all color had long since been burnt out of them by the heat of the spirit within.

"Tell him he will go to the king of Knōsos," Tereus instructed Meriones. "Tell him that if he pleases the king, he will have a good life and be treated well."

Meriones repeated the message. The old man's only response was a contemptuous flicker of his eyelids. "I don't know if he will cooperate," Meriones said doubtfully.

"He must," Tereus grated. "I didn't haul this ugly old weed all the way here just to have him turn obstinate when the time came to prove his value. He's worth more than the rest of them put together, and I mean to make a lot of money with him."

"Shall I ask him to do a feat of sorcery that would impress Carambis?"

"He had better; a damned impressive one."

"What can your grandfather do?" Meriones asked Ebisha.

The girl cast a wary glance at the old man. "He is a servant of the sun. He can ask the sun to hide his face and darken the land. He can summon the wind."

Meriones said he was vastly impressed, but he doubted those acts would be suitable for performing in a small house. Besides, thinking about them made him nervous. "Can he cause a lump of glass to change color?" he asked Ebisha. "Or charm a snake? Those are the sort of tricks The Minos enjoys."

Ebisha's eyes were cold. "You mock him."

"No! I did not mean—" His apologies were interrupted by Tulipa's entry with a tray of food. Meriones was too tense to eat, but Ebisha showed an appetite that outstripped even that of Tereus and his crewmen. She and the other captives—with the exception of the old man, who ate nothing—stuffed food into their mouths as if they had been starving for days.

"Didn't you ever feed them?" Meriones asked Tereus.

"I offered them what I feed my crew. They didn't seem to think it was food."

One of the crewmen laughed.

The old man behaved with a dignity that never deserted him. His hands had been untied to allow him to eat, though the guards watched him closely every moment. He lifted the bowl Tulipa offered him and carefully examined its contents without touching them. Then he placed his bunched fingers against the bottom of the bowl in its exact center and chanted something under his breath. The ritual completed, he put the bowl down, the food uneaten, and sat back, withdrawing into some private place beyond their reach.

Carambis arrived in a painted sedan chair befitting his station.

He was a bulky man, obese by Cretan standards, with a jowly face and a voice that gurgled upward from deep in his belly. The glitter of his eyes betokened a lustful nature, and Tereus shrewdly presented Ebisha to him first.

"Ah, this is a gem," Carambis agreed. "She looks like something from a lapidary's workbench. Silver skin, jade eyes."

Tereus said, "I understand the wife of The Minos collects exotic handmaidens? Think how she would prize this one!"

Carambis circled Ebisha, then signaled for her to be stripped. She stood with her head up, watching not Carambis, but Tereus. Aside from faded briar scratches on her legs and rope burns on her wrists, her body was unflawed.

But Tereus did not see her beauty. He saw instead a proud wooden galley, fresh from the boatbuilders, and felt the deck beneath his feet. One of those new ribbed coasters, with space for thirty oarmen and a square sail for long-distance voyaging.

The bargaining for Ebisha was so intense it made Meriones uncomfortable. He left the room, joining Tulipa in the courtyard. "What will our share be?" she asked him at once.

"I don't know. It depends on how much Tereus makes, I suppose."

"Didn't you agree to a sum in advance?"

"How could I?"

Tulipa's lips formed a thin line. "You are an idiot."

But Meriones was not thinking of profit. He was feeling guilty, as if he had somehow betrayed the girl with green eyes and the others. The blood in their veins flowed, to a small extent, in his. He heard its voice crying out.

In time the negotiations for Ebisha were concluded, and one by one the others were examined, argued over, sold. The day grew stiflingly hot. When Tereus noticed how heavily Carambis was sweating, he insisted they conclude their business in the courtyard and ordered Tulipa to bring them cool drinks.

"I'm not his slave," Tulipa muttered. But she brought the drinks.

By this time there was only one captive left to sell. Tereus had saved his prize until last.

"Look at this creature!" he enthused. "Is there not a divine madness in his eyes? This man is a high priest among his own kind, a sorcerer without equal."

Carambis looked skeptically at the old man. "What is this? Do you think we have any use at the House of the Double Axes for skinny old sticks like this one? It is you who are mad, Tereus."

"You don't understand, Carambis. I have with my own eyes seen the priests of the Islands of Mist exhibit abilities beyond the range of mortal men. The female pharoah in Egypt would pay any price I asked for this creature, but I . . . ah, have no authority to take the *Qatil* to Egypt."

Carambis smiled an oily smile. "I understand your situation perfectly. But I never buy fruit without taking a bite of it first." He folded his arms across his ample chest. "If he is as good as you say he is, have him do something right now. Prove your claim."

The scene that ensued was painful to all concerned. Tereus gave orders, Meriones translated them to the best of his ability, and the seamen struck the old priest when he stood immobile, indifferent, turned to stone.

"I think you're trying to sell me a deaf-mute by pretending he's something else," Carambis accused Tereus. "This deal begins to stink in my nostrils. Do not try to swindle me, or you will find no safe harbor in Knōsos."

"But this priest is worth a fortune!" Tereus protested, feeling the decks of his own ship fading away beneath his feet. "Meriones here says he can make the sun stop shining just by casting some sort of spell."

Carambis curled his lip. "If that's true he's too dangerous to have at the palace, and if you lie he's not worth a sack of meal. Either way, I want nothing to do with him. He's your problem; you brought him, you dispose of him. But not to the House of the Double Axes. As for the rest of this lot, I'll send men to collect them before dark and you'll be paid for them once they're in our custody."

Tereus simmered with anger. He bit back the words he wanted to say, however. It would be foolish to make an enemy of Carambis if he ever hoped to sell slaves to the palace again.

When the Master of Slaves had departed in his sedan chair, Tereus rounded on Meriones. "Why did you fail me? Why didn't you make that wretched old fool perform!"

Meriones held his hands palm upward in a placating gesture. "I did my best."

"Your best is no good, then. And I've lost a lot of money. That old man is of no value except as a diviner or sorcerer for a king's household. I might be able to sell him to one of the princes of Mallia—though I doubt it. I can't waste time trying, I'm due at Byblos."

"What will become of him, then?"

Tereus shrugged. "We'll throw him overboard," he said casually. "As soon as we're at sea again."

"No! You mustn't! I mean . . . I did my best . . . he is an intractable old man . . . but you mustn't kill him because I failed . . ." His words somersaulted over each other. Then he stopped. He drew in a sharp breath, his eyes lighting with inspiration. "There is a Cretan colony on the island of Thera."

"What of it? It's not even on my usual route," Tereus said. "My owner avoids them, they have a nasty reputation."

"But they're very wealthy," Meriones argued, "and their number includes scholars and wizards and all sorts of strange people who are reputed to do remarkable things. Why not take the old priest to Thera and try to sell him to them? It is the one place that might value him. I'm almost certain of it."

"What do you know about anything?" the Thracian sneered. "You're a bumbling fool, Meriones, and I'd be another to take any advice from you."

Meriones replied, miserably, "I never wanted to be involved in this anyway. I was only doing a favor for a friend."

"Then you can't expect much recompense in return," the Thracian said abruptly. "I'm willing to pay you for the food and the use of your house, but that's all."

Meriones felt his heart sink. What would Tulipa say?

Tereus gave Jaha Fe and his men orders to stay with the captives until they were collected, then bring the payment to the ship. This done, he stalked out of the house, dragging the old priest with him like a goat to the slaughter.

Meriones watched with a pained expression. At the last moment, Tereus relented enough to call back, "Oh, all right, if I get something for this old fool on the island of Thera, I'll see that you receive a share. But I don't expect to make a fortune for him in Atlantis."

9

Meriones went to the palace next

day without his usual jaunty gait. The white hound

ran out to meet him, recognized his depression, and

sat down in the road, whining.

"I'm sorry, Meriones,"

Hokar said when he had heard the entire story. "I thought it would be a good opportunity, I didn't know it would turn out badly."

"My wife isn't speaking to me. and that old man will be killed unless the Atlanteans buy him."

"They will," Hokar said confidently. "Those Cretans on Thera will buy anything that's truly unusual."

"They won't know he's unusual unless he shows them."

"Ah, they'll make him show them. They have ways, in Atlantis," Hokar added mysteriously.

"What ways?"

"I don't actually know. I've just heard whispers."

Meriones nodded. "We've all heard whispers. But no one knows very much about what they do over there."

"I for one don't want to know," Hokar told him. "I'm more interested in that girl you mentioned. Tell me about her."

Meriones tried to describe Ebisha, but his words could not bring her to life. "I'll play her for you instead," he told Hokar, taking up his lyre.

He stroked a delicate melody with a recurring throb like a beating heart. The music was as lovely as any he had ever played, with the exception of the songs he had composed for Tulipa in their first days together.

Craftsmen wandered in from other chambers and stood in rapt silence, listening.

When Meriones finished playing, Hokar said, "If that is Ebisha, I want to see her."

But no one saw Ebisha for a while. She had vanished into a perfumed opulence where even slaves lived lives of comparative luxury, and would not reappear until she had been refined and polished into a work of art worthy of the queen's service.

Knowing her destiny, Meriones did not worry about her. But sometimes at night as he lay sleepless, with Tulipa's rigid back like a wall turned to him, he thought of the old man. He did not know the old man's name, even. Ebisha had refused to tell it, saying, "Names of holy men belong to the tribe. Not for use by strangers."

An old man stolen from his home, his dignity assaulted, his scrawny body lashed by some slavemaster's whip . . .

Then Meriones remembered the priest's eyes, and he shivered and pulled the bedclothes over his head, though the night was hot.

Meanwhile word of his newly lyrical music reached the ears of Santhos, and he found himself reassigned to the royal apartments. He hated leaving Hokar. They promised to meet from time to time in the mazes of Labrys.

One scorching morning when the perfumed air lay heavy in the halls and even the liveliest courtiers were lethargic, Meriones was sent to the queen's megaron, the pillared "public room" in the center of her suite.

There he saw Ebisha again.

She knelt beside the queen, holding open an olivewood casket inlaid with ivory, from which the wife of The Minos was selecting jewelry. The queen pointed to a rope of pearls spaced with carnelian and lapis lazuli. The pearls were the perfect accompaniment to the bodice the wife of The Minos wore, an exquisite garment dyed in royal Tyrian purple. To obtain that dye a thousand tiny sea creatures had been crushed in their shells. The bodice might be worn only once; the queen rarely repeated her costumes.

But Meriones was not looking at the queen. He was staring in admiration at Ebisha, who was very changed.

The briar scratches and rope burns were healed. Her nails were smoothed, shaped, painted carmine. Her oiled hair was twisted and curled into a fanciful sculpture, revealing the elegance of her skull shape. She was dressed in the height of Cretan fashion. An ankle-length skirt of pleated tiers in contrasting colors fell from a tight belt, while her upper body was naked except for a short-sleeved, tight-fitting bodice that encircled her bare breasts like a frame.

Feeling Meriones' eyes on her she turned toward him, recognized him, smiled.

The queen signaled to Meriones to play. When he responded with his latest composition she clapped her hands with pleasure. "What a lovely song! I have not heard it before, it is like water tinkling." She rippled her fingers descriptively through the air. "Is it your own creation?" she asked Meriones.

"Yes, lady. I call it 'Green-Eyed Girl.'" Glancing at Ebisha, Meriones saw her smile again, pleased.

The queen followed his glance. "Well done," she commented. "Green is my favorite color, as that scoundrel Carambis knows. He found this green-eyed girl for me and paid a pretty price, I suspect.

But we are well pleased with her. Play us some more of your music now."

During the long, hot day, Meriones found several opportunities for snatches of conversation with Ebisha. He was surprised to discover she had already acquired a rudimentary understanding of the New Tongue. She insisted on using it with him, trying to improve herself. It was hard not to laugh at her grammar, but her eagerness impressed him.

Once she said, "I hear from my grandsire."

Meriones stiffened. "How?"

"He has ways. He gets word to me."

"Where is he?"

"On an island called Thera."

Meriones was relieved. "That's good, he's safe, then."

The girl frowned. "Not safe. They hurt him when he does not give them his gift. But he cannot give it to them. It is his, you see? It is not theirs. His, for his people."

Meriones did not see. But he hated the thought of men on Thera abusing the old man. "What about you?" he asked Ebisha the next time they could talk together. "Are you happy here?"

"Happy?" She puzzled over the word. "I am not free. So I am not happy. But I am not cold, or wet, or hungry. So is good. Some good. Is wonderful place, here. Is magic here."

"Magic?" Meriones thought she misunderstood the meaning of the word.

"Oh yes. The queen walks through that doorway to her water closet, she calls it. She sits on stone there. Her droppings are carried away by water poured through drains. Is magic, yes?" Ebisha smiled her radiant smile at Meriones.

"Yes," he echoed, chuckling.

When he was with Ebisha, Meriones' normally buoyant spirits returned.

Although he missed Hokar and the goldsmiths' chambers, he could not deny that he was infinitely more comfortable in the royal apartments. The queen's megaron was exquisitely furnished with gilded benches, tiled floors, mosaics on every wall. The ceiling was decorated with spirals of plaster as perfectly formed as seashells. Ebisha commented many times on their beauty.

By prior arrangement, Meriones and Hokar met in the palace gardens one twilit evening as both were on their way home. The goldsmith related what little gossip he knew; Meriones told him of life in the queen's megaron, and of Ebisha.

"I'd still like to see her," Hokar confided. "That music you used to describe her has haunted me ever since."

His opportunity came soon enough. An ambassador presented the queen with a delicate gold pectoral, a gift from one royal family to another. Somehow it was dropped and the shape of the soft gold was distorted on the hard floor. The queen ordered a goldsmith sent quickly to her apartments, to repair the pectoral before the ambassador should see it.

The task fell to Hokar. He entered the megaron in the company of the Master of Craftsmen, rehearsing the words of thanks he would say to the queen if the opportunity arose.

Then he saw Ebisha, and all words went out of his head.

There was discussion about the pectoral. ". . . A tap with the hammer, here, and perhaps the slightest twist just there . . ." and Hokar nodded his head and set his hands to their task, but they worked without a conscious thought to guide them. Hokar's true attention was concentrated on the girl.

When the pectoral was repaired to the queen's satisfaction, he forgot to thank her humbly for the honor. He left the megaron with his eyes filled with Ebisha.

Hokar sought out Meriones every chance he got, always to talk about Ebisha. "How is she? Did she notice me, do you think? What is she like?"

Meriones ransacked his memory for tidbits about the girl. When he mentioned her admiration for the plaster spirals on the ceiling of the megaron, Hokar was excited. "I shall make a piece of jewelry for her! And you will give it to her, Meriones. And tell her it comes from me."

Another favor. Meriones wriggled uncomfortably. "It isn't really appropriate, Hokar. To give gifts to slaves, I mean. Nor for me to be the carrier either. You see—"

"Nonsense, it's just a small token, who could object? In a way you're responsible for her being here, Meriones. You should want her to be happy. And a gift will make her happy. How can you refuse?"

How indeed? Meriones asked himself gloomily as he walked home later, through a stifling heat so intense it threatened to press the air from his lungs.

It was worse than the heat wave last year. It was worse than any weather he could ever remember.

When he reached his house he entered eagerly, longing for its cool darkness. But the air inside was stuffy and still, hardly less unpleasant than outside. Passing through to the courtyard, he found Tulipa lying on a pallet under the olive tree with a cloth dipped in cool water pressed to her forehead.

"The heat gives me a headache," she greeted him. "Be quiet."

"I wasn't going to say anything. Is there something I can do for you?"

"Make the heat stop," she replied petulantly.

But no one could make the heat stop. Day by day it mounted, fraying nerves, spoiling food. Tulipa's headache had become so constant he no longer questioned its reality. It was not a device she used to make him feel guilty. She was in real pain. Dark circles appeared under her eyes and she could not eat. She did not even have the energy to scold him.

He grew increasingly worried about her. She was losing all her pretty roundness; her bones showed through the skin of her face, strangely reminding Meriones of the skull-like visage of the old priest from the Islands of Mist.

The more ill Tulipa became, the more Meriones recalled how dear she had been to him in their early days together, when he had been as enchanted by her as Hokar was by Ebisha.

He went to every physician in Knōsos, and every herbalist, seeking help for his wife. But nothing stopped her headaches.

When he played his lyre in the queen's megaron he was distracted and it showed in his performance.

"What is wrong with you?" Ebisha whispered to him. "The queen frowns when you play. Does not sound the same now."

"My wife is sick and I'm worried about her."

"She has a pain?"

"In her head."

"Ah." Ebisha nodded. "My grandsire could heal."

"Much good that does me!" Meriones burst out before he could stop himself. The heat was getting to everyone.

Next day, Hokar met him at the Sun Gate and pressed an object wrapped in linen into his hands. "Give this to Ebisha, and tell her it's from me."

He had to wait for his chance. At last came a time when the megaron was briefly all but deserted, its usual throng of chattering, chirping courtiers gone to bathe in the pools or lie panting on their beds. Ebisha remained, and Meriones beckoned her to join him behind one of the pillars. "I have a gift for you from Hokar the goldsmith."

"Who?" But she took the parcel and unwrapped it.

Then she gasped. "Look!" She held up a necklace as fine as spiderweb, made of tiny gold links. Spaced along the chain at regular intervals were six miniature gold nautilus shells, repeating the spiral design in the ceiling of the queen's megaron.

The gold flashed in Ebisha's fingers. "It is the metal of the sun!" she cried.

"This is too elaborate and costly for a slave," Meriones tried to tell her. "You won't be allowed to keep it. Give it back and I'll return it to Hokar and explain."

Ebisha's eyes brimmed with tears. "I cannot keep?" But she handed the necklace back to Meriones without protest.

Tulipa would have held on to it and argued vehemently, he thought. Aloud he said, "It would make trouble. Hokar should have known this." He turned away, unable to bear the look of disappointment on her face.

When he could, he returned the necklace to Hokar in the goldsmiths' chamber. Hokar looked as disappointed as Ebisha had been. "But it's not anything lavish," he protested, "just a trial piece I made that didn't work out. I thought no one would mind."

Meriones turned the glittering trinket over in his fingers, studying it. "Are you saying it's not perfect?"

"Yes."

"Then you lie," Meriones replied softly. "It's the best thing I've ever seen you do. This is no trial piece at all, and if the queen had caught Ebisha wearing it I don't know what would have happened. The queen herself has nothing finer. More elaborate, but not finer."

Hokar was crestfallen. "But I want her to have something to

remind her of me. I wish I were a painter. I'd reproduce her face and form on every wall in Labrys."

Meriones was beginning to lose patience with his friend. "If you care for this girl you have to be quiet about it, Hokar. The courtiers and servants of the palace aren't encouraged to . . . well, you know . . ."

"I know. And I don't need any encouragement. Just one look from those green eyes would do it. Meriones, you have to arrange for me to see her again."

"Aren't you listening? She's a slave. We are not supposed to have anything to do with slaves."

"Then I'll buy her!"

"How could you? Carambis paid a high price for her, more than you make in a season, I'd guess."

"I'll think of something," Hokar said. His mouth became a grim, determined line.

When he left the palace that evening, Meriones did not stride out with his usual arched-back, arm-swinging ebullience. He trudged with his head down, his thoughts alternating between Tulipa at home and Hokar and Ebisha in the palace. A presentiment lay like a cloud on his spirit.

He walked through heat so thick as to be palpable, even though the sun was setting. The omnipresent sea, nibbling at the northern coastline, had lost its luster and turned dull and sullen.

The music of Meriones had also lost its brightness. Santhos spoke sharply to him the next day. "What's wrong with you? Your music sounds more like a dirge, and that is not the sort of music we like in the palace. The queen is displeased."

"I have worries."

"Everyone has worries! But our personal concerns must not dim the color of the royal apartments. Now Orene is playing your songs, and he sounds better than you do. Correct yourself or you will be playing for the cooks in the kitchens!"

Meriones struggled to throw off his melancholy. He could not bear to think of reporting another demotion to Tulipa.

Day after day she lay in the sleeping chamber, or under the olive tree. The olive tree was better, she said, because it was not quite as hot in the courtyard as it was in the upper rooms of the house. But there was no escaping the heat anywhere.

She had grown very thin. On her behalf Meriones offered gifts of food and wine and faience beads at the shrine of every god who might have any connection with good health and healing. But the sacrifices were wasted. Almost every day, Tulipa suffered a savage headache.

"Sometimes I wish you would plunge a knife into my skull and let my brains spill out," she told Meriones. "That would ease the pressure."

Her pain tortured him. His early tenderness came flooding back and he sat on the edge of the bed, stroking her hand, fighting back tears.

He spoke privately to Ebisha in the queen's megaron. "You said your grandsire could heal?"

"He can."

"You said you have ways of getting word to him?"

She gave Meriones a guarded look. "Why?"

"I need . . . I mean, my wife needs, really . . . she is very ill, you see, and nothing anyone does seems to help. I have grown desperate, Ebisha. I thought perhaps . . . your grandsire . . ." He ran out of words. His dark eyes pleaded.

"Meriones, I—" Ebisha clamped her mouth shut suddenly. Looking up, Meriones saw the queen watching them.

"We'll talk later," he said under his breath.

But that same day Santhos came to escort Meriones to the palace kitchens.

"This is your last chance," Santhos said. "Do well here, and you will stay in the House of the Double Axes. Fail here, and you will go."

But how can I play when my heart is a lump of lead in my breast? Meriones wanted to ask.

He sat on a bench; he strummed his lyre. No one listened. The kitchens bustled like a hive of bees from before dawn until long after dark. Everyone was hot, bothered, in a hurry. They brushed past Meriones, cursed at him if he was in the way, shouted at one another over the constant clatter of cooking utensils.

Worst of all, he was not allowed to leave until all work was done in the kitchens for the day, which meant very late at night. He had to make his way home in the dark when most of Knōsos was long since asleep. He could not meet Hokar anymore; the goldsmith was also snoring in his bed by the time Meriones made his weary way through the Sun Gate and headed for home.

He barely had time to prepare a sketchy meal which Tulipa usually could not eat, fall on his bed for a troubled, brief sleep, and arise still in the dark to go to the well for the day's water. Then he must be on his way back to the palace, leaving his suffering wife behind him physically but carrying her every step of the way on his conscience.

He arranged with Phrixus and Dendria to look in on her and do what they could for her, but it was not enough. Nothing was enough.

Meriones began to fear his wife might die.

A different man might, perhaps, have welcomed freedom from a scold. But Meriones had a gentle heart. Long ago, he had given that heart to Tulipa. It would go into the grave with her. A girl like Ebisha might stir lust in him, or even tenderness, but he had given his wife a part of himself he could not take back, and thus would never have to give again to any woman.

The music would die with Tulipa, Meriones thought.

He was desperate to find help for her. When he could slip away from the kitchens he haunted the passageways leading to the royal apartments, hoping to see Ebisha. At last his patience was rewarded. He managed to signal her with his eyes as she walked past at the end of a procession of slaves, carrying bales of fabric to the queen's seamstresses.

From the citadels of Mycenae and Tiryns a huge tribute was sent each year to The Minos of Knōsos—cattle and oil and wine and every manner of merchandise. Goods were stored in the vast warehouses beneath the palace, but only briefly, for most were used as soon as they arrived. The royal family indulged in an orgy of consumption meant to impress the Mediterranean world with the unrivaled wealth and power of Crete.

Within the last few days a shipload of rare and costly fabrics had arrived in the harbor. The goods were immediately transported to Labrys, where the royal family would make their selections from the best of the best. When their choices were made, complete new wardrobes would be sewn not only for The Minos and his family, but also for every member of their court.

The minions of The Minos would bloom like fresh flowers.

The Minos had recently decreed that each season's clothing was to be burned at the end of the season, a ceremonial destruction of the old and celebration of the new. This unprecedentedly lavish gesture could not fail to impress the other sea kings.

Ebisha could barely see over the folds of shimmering cloth she carried, but she nodded to Meriones as best she could. When the procession of slaves passed an open doorway she slipped inside and Meriones quickly joined her.

They found themselves in one of the many bathing chambers scattered throughout the palace. Its walls were lined with alabaster decorated with frescoes, and the terra cotta bathing tub stood in a recess ornamented by columns. A brazier burned continually, casting flickering shadows.

As she talked with him, Ebisha rested her burden on a marble shelf meant to hold sponges and bath oils. Meriones was saying, "My wife is very ill and no one can heal her."

"I am no healer."

"But your grandsire is a magician. Tereus said so. And you are in touch with him. Is there some sort of magic he might do, perhaps? I could find a way to send payment to him, I would gladly . . ."

Her eyes filled with pity. "Meriones, I tried to explain before. I can't talk to him, not the way you think. We exchange our . . ."—she struggled with words—"our feelings. I know his emotions. No more than that."

"You couldn't ask him to help Tulipa?"

"No. I am sorry. Nor do I think he would," Ebisha added honestly. "He is very angry. They treat him badly in this place where he is; they hurt him. He is . . ."—she sought for the right word again—"he is *simmering* with anger. He would not want to help. He wants to strike out." Her eyes were very large. "His feelings frighten me, Meriones."

"I'm sorry about all this, Ebisha."

"Is not your fault."

"I was involved."

"If not you, Tereus would have used another person. You at least were kind to us. You tried to help, you argued for my grandsire's life.

"Perhaps it would have been better if he died," she added in a low voice.

Meriones put a hand on her arm, trying to comfort her in spite of his own pain. Then he saw the slender gold arm ring she wore, half concealed by the sleeve of her tight-fitting bodice.

The arm ring was gold.

"Where did you get that?"

Ebisha's lashes lowered over her green eyes. "A gift from a friend."

"Hokar the goldsmith? You've been seeing him?"

"We meet sometimes," she admitted.

"And you're taking presents from him? Don't you know how dangerous it is?"

"He wants me to have them."

"But what about Tereus?"

"I will not see Tereus again," Ebisha said with female practicality. "I know that. Hokar I see every day. He is good to me. He says he will buy me out of the palace and give me my freedom."

Hokar was obviously telling the girl a pleasant little lie. "He can't buy you," Meriones said. He did not want her to be deceived, even by his friend. "Hokar is well rewarded for his work, but a master craftsman does not make enough to buy a favorite of the queen."

Ebisha lifted her head. In the flickering light her green eyes blazed. "I was born free," she said.

"I know, but look at you now. You have beautiful clothes and all you can eat. And I know the queen doesn't beat you. What more could you want? You are fortunate, really."

When she spoke, Ebisha's voice rang in the alabaster chamber in a way that curiously reminded Meriones of his long-dead grandmother's voice. "I come from a race of free people," she said. "I was born free, and even if Hokar has to steal to get me out of here, I shall die free!"

Her words made a chill run up Meriones' spine.

10

Several days passed, days of unrelenting heat. The House of the Double Axes lay languid beneath a blazing white sun. People longed in vain for the first cool breeze off the sea that would hint at the Season of the Dying God.

Tulipa was dying. But she did not die. It was as if she held death at arms' length, somehow, which made it even more painful for Meriones. It was agonizing to leave her in the mornings, yet equally painful to return at night, not knowing what he might find.

When he found her alive, he knew the agony would continue.

"There is a growth in her head," a physician finally told him. "It is the only explanation."

"Can't you do something?"

"The Egyptians have a technique for opening the skull and operating on the brain, but the only Egyptian physician on Crete is in the court of The Minos. He would not treat your wife."

Meriones knew that already. Early in Tulipa's illness he had tried to gain access to The Minos' private physician and been forcefully turned away.

I am no one. Just a minor musician. As Tulipa said, I am nobody.

Pain lapped in him like a rising tide.

Santhos caught him by the arm in a passageway of the palace. "There you are! I've been looking everywhere for you. Why aren't you in the kitchens, where you belong?"

"They never miss me," Meriones said truthfully.

"That's immaterial. You are supposed to be there. If you disobey, I shall be blamed. And I promise you I will pass on to you any punishment I receive!"

Santhos had caught him just as Meriones was about to attempt another visit to the royal apartments. In desperation, he was going to try to find and appeal to the royal physician himself. But Santhos took hold of his arm in a painful grip and dragged him back to the kitchens, where he proceeded to place a scullery boy on guard over Meriones with orders to report to Santhos immediately if the musician left his post even for a moment.

When the final meal of the day was cooked and Meriones was at last allowed to leave, he stepped from the perpetually lit halls of the palace into a Stygian darkness. The night was starless and oppressive. Leaving by the Sun Gate, he had to make his way down the stair very carefully to avoid losing his balance and falling. It would have been easy in the dark to step by mistake into one of the gutters that ran down beside the stair, part of the elaborate system of drains and baffles that slowed the flow of rain runoff and prevented the flooding of palace floors on the lower levels.

But there had been no rain in a long time. Meriones found himself longing for a storm to lighten the air.

When he reached Knōsos, and his own street, a dark shape rose before him. By the light of a lantern burning in a nearby window, Meriones recognized Hokar. The goldsmith's face was haggard and his eyes were sunk in dark hollows.

But it was not the heat that was affecting him.

"I'm in terrible trouble, Meriones. I need your help as my friend," Hokar said urgently, whispering as if afraid they would be overheard.

"You'd better come into my house and tell me about it." The musician longed to take off his sweaty clothing and sponge himself from the water barrel in the courtyard, but that would have to wait. Leaving Hokar in the megaron, he took time only to tiptoe upstairs and check on Tulipa.

She was awake. "I think I feel a little better, Meriones," she said to his vast relief. "Just a little. The headache is not as bad as it has been."

His heart pounded with hope. "Are you sure? Are you getting well?"

"I don't know about that, but I do feel somewhat stronger. Perhaps I could eat a little broth . . . ?"

Meriones plunged back down the stairs. Ignoring his guest, he busied himself with cooking pots until he had put together a concoction of leftovers that would, he prayed, do his wife some good. He carried a bowl up to her and watched with held breath while she sipped it. When she yawned and fell asleep again he returned to his guest.

Hokar was waiting patiently. "I have nothing else to do," he said.

"What's this trouble you're in?"

Hokar was reluctant to say outright. He came at the subject with uncharacteristic obliqueness. "There was a wrestling exhibition in the Great Central Court today, you know. Everyone who could went to see it."

"I know. The cooks made up countless platters of food to pass among the spectators. Fish, mostly. My clothes still reek of it. But what has the wrestling to do with your trouble?"

"The craftsmen were given permission to attend, and everyone in our chambers went. Except me. I stayed behind, crouched down behind my workbench so no one would notice."

Meriones felt a cold hand squeeze his heart. "Why?"

Hokar would not meet his eyes. "Ebisha." His shoulders slumped. Then he burst out, "I can think of nothing else, Meriones! She fills my mind the way my work used to!

"She said she would be my woman if she was free, but I know it would be very costly to buy her from the palace. So I stole what should be enough gold from our supplies. I buried it in the terraced gardens. They were deserted for once; everyone was at the wrestling. I did not dare keep it on me in case the loss was discovered and we were searched. Then I joined the others at the Great Central Court. No one noticed I had not been there all along.

"The theft was discovered almost as soon as we returned to our chambers. They thought someone might have come in from outside and taken the gold, but they couldn't be sure. They searched us, and I suspect they sent men to our homes to search us again when we arrived at the end of the day.

"That's why I didn't go home tonight. I couldn't face another search. My hands have begun shaking."

"I'm not surprised! I don't know how you managed to do it in the first place."

"It wasn't that difficult. The gold wasn't locked away."

I suppose not, Meriones thought. Theft had never been a problem in the palace. It was well known that anyone caught stealing simply vanished, and there were whispered rumors of some horrible fate that awaited them deep in the bowels of Labrys, lost forever amid its labyrinthine twistings and turnings. The fear of the unknown kept most people at the palace honest.

Unfortunately, the Thracian's desire for a woman had outweighed his fear—for a while. The fear appeared to be catching up with him now. He had gone very white around the eyes and his hands were, indeed, shaking.

"I don't know how I can help you," Meriones told the unfortunate man.

"Would you if you could?"

Without thinking, the musician nodded assent.

"You can," Hokar said eagerly, "because no one would have any reason to suspect you, you haven't been near our chambers for a while. I'll tell you just where I hid the gold. You watch for your chance and retrieve it for me and hide it in a safer place. The gardens were just a temporary solution. The gardeners might dig there any time and find it."

"But you can't take raw gold to Carambis and offer to buy Ebisha with it! Everyone will know exactly how you came by it!"

"I'm not going to approach Carambis at all. I've thought it out. We'll take the gold to Tereus the next time he puts in at Knōsos. I'll allow him a large cut of it, and he will use the rest to buy Ebisha himself. Once she's out of Labrys she and I will leave Crete on board the *Qatil* and make a new home for ourselves far away somewhere. An artisan can always find work."

"This is madness, Hokar," Meriones said flatly. "You have no right to ask me to get involved."

"I thought you were my friend," the other chided him. "In Thrace, friendship is sacred to the death. Is it not that way on Crete? Is it not that way with you?" Hokar knew when a metal lacked the tensile strength to hold firm under the hammer. Meriones would give in if pressed hard enough. "Think what I will lose if I am caught, Meriones! Would you have my death on your conscience?"

Meriones squirmed. "Don't put it that way."

"Then say you'll help me."

Meriones had a vision of the great bull being led in for sacrifice, its piebald hide washed and gleaming, flowers wreathing its neck. He remembered the way the bull had lifted its head and looked with sad eyes at the inevitability of the ax.

"I'll help you," he said at last. "But you'd better go home now. It's better if we're not seen as being too friendly from now on."

"I'm afraid to go home. If any of The Minos' men are there I might give myself away, coming in so late. So nervous."

"Drink enough of my wine to slur your speech and relax you," Meriones instructed, thinking fast. "If there are guards tell them you've been at a party. Laugh a lot. Seem carefree. You can do it, if you drink enough beforehand."

Hokar's beard split in a grin. "I knew I could rely on you, Meriones. The gods put you in my path."

"I wish the gods would put someone in my path to help me,"

Meriones muttered to himself. Hokar, intent on his own problems, paid no attention.

The musician fed the goldsmith wine until the man's speech slurred convincingly, then sent him on his way. "Now remember to act much drunker than you are," he instructed. "And cheerful. Unworried. That's the important part. You must act as if you have nothing at all to feel guilty about. You've just been having a wonderful time at a party."

He pushed Hokar out the door and watched, worrying, as his friend weaved his way up the narrow street and out of sight. Hokar was clutching the last jug of Meriones' wine in his fist.

The musician's inspiration saved the goldsmith. There were guards from the palace waiting at his house to search him again. When he arrived, however, he was so drunk and seemed so jovial they could not believe he was guilty of anything more than overindulgence. He even insisted they share his jug of wine with him.

"We've had a long wait for nothing," one of the men said. "It's the least we deserve." They leaned against Hokar's wall and drank the last of the wine before returning to Labrys.

Meanwhile Tulipa lay on her bed and dreamed. The pain's easing had left her prey to a curious hallucination. She thought it was the season of the Festival of the Snake, the time sacred to females.

The wombs of donkeys would be swelling with foals. New kids would soon be suckling the milk goats. It was the season, in her fevered mind, of fertility. Pilgrimages would be made to the inland mountains to conduct the rites sacred to the Good Goddess. Men were excluded as long lines of women snaked up the slopes, carrying torches and singing.

Tulipa imagined herself among them, begging the boon of motherhood. She thought she felt a cosmic response shudder through her barren belly.

In the darkness of predawn she became aware of Meriones lying beside her. "We're going to have a child," she murmured.

He was instantly awake. "What did you say?"

But she had sunk back into her dreams. When he tried to question her she muttered crossly, not remembering.

Could it be possible? Meriones felt a jolt of joy. A child!

Suddenly the future became very precious to him.

He bitterly regretted promising to help Hokar. What if they were caught?

He went to Phrixus' house to ask Dendria to stay with Tulipa for the day. "She might be with child," he explained. "I don't want her to be alone."

Dendria raised her plucked eyebrows. "Tulipa, with child? I shouldn't think so."

"I'm not certain. But she might be. And I'm very worried about her."

"If you're that worried you should stay with her yourself," retorted Dendria, who had better things to do.

But Meriones dared not stay home. He did not fear the wrath of Santhos as much as he feared doing something unusual that might cause suspicion.

To his relief, Dendria reluctantly agreed to keep an eye on Tulipa. Only a little late, Meriones hurried off toward the palace, forcing himself to his usual jaunty gait, even whistling a little, as if he had not a care in the world.

He had not gone very far before he encountered the white hound. The dog stood with its head cocked on one side, not completely fooled.

"Come on," Meriones coaxed. "Walk with me." He snapped his fingers and made cajoling noises.

The dog cocked its head on the other side, but then it came. The two walked on together. The dog was panting already, its red tongue lolling.

As they climbed up from the city toward the palace, Meriones glanced back as he often did to enjoy the view. Almost the entire Cretan fleet, largest in the Mediterranean, was in. The ships' captains were waiting for a freshening wind to blow along the northern coast.

But the air was leaden and still. There was a sullen haze to the north. The fleet which was Crete's pride and power would stay where it was until Poseidon showed a more amiable face.

Somewhere on the sea Tereus is heading for Crete, Meriones thought to himself. I'll need to retrieve the gold and have it ready for him when he arrives.

"My cousin's current trading voyage is just to the major ports of call in the Mediterranean and Aegean," Hokar had said. "He will return to Knōsos before long."

So they did not have much time.

"This is going to be dangerous," Meriones said under his breath to the dog.

The hound wagged his tail. With a last glance at the ships and the sea, Meriones set off again, springing upward from the soles of his feet as if he had not a care in the world.

No one could see the thoughts roiling in his head.

According to Hokar, the gold had been hastily buried in a shallow hole beneath a red-flowering bush that smelled of honey. The bush was to the left of the steps leading down to the largest of the many pools in the terraced gardens.

The gardens were popular with courtiers and visitors to the palace alike. As long as daylight lasted, there were usually a number of people wandering through them.

But as Hokar had pointed out, "Now that you are assigned to the cooks you arrive very early and leave very late. If you know a way to reach the kitchens by going through the gardens, you could actually be there when it's dark and no one else is around. I could never do that. We arrive later and leave earlier. And besides, they will be watching us. No one will be watching you. Get the gold for me, Meriones, and hide it in a safer place until Tereus gets here."

Meriones did indeed know how to reach the kitchens by way of the terraced gardens, but it was a highly circuitous route. One he might have to explain if he was questioned.

As he walked along, he had a flash of inspiration.

"I'll say I'm picking flowers to garnish the royal platters!" he told the dog.

By the time he reached the palace a sultry heat was already building up. With a casual salute to the guard, and a farewell pat to the white hound, Meriones entered the Sun Gate. But he did not follow his usual route. Instead he trotted briskly down endless passageways, up stairs, around corners, across courtyards, until at last he reached the garden.

To his disappointment, other people were already there. The time he had spent arranging for Dendria to stay with Tulipa had cost him; the sun had risen before he ever left Knōsos. He had no chance of getting the gold this morning. But he plucked flowers just the same and took them to the cooks, to establish his story.

The cooks were delighted. Garnishing food with flowers at once became the fashion in the House of the Double Axes.

That night Meriones left by the same route, but once again he found people still loitering in the gardens, trying to find a breath of air in the darkness.

To his dismay, when he reached home Tulipa was alone. "I sent Dendria away," she said in a petulant tone. "Her voice cuts into my head like a knife into a melon. I wish we could go away, Meriones. Really go away, I mean. To someplace cool. To the mountains . . ." She sighed.

"The heat will break soon, everyone says so. It can't go on much longer like this. The Minos has offered sacrifices to be made to Poseidon in exchange for cool winds from the sea."

"I think the gods are angry with us, Meriones," Tulipa replied. "It will take more than sacrifices to placate them. Look at me. You must have done something to make the gods angry and I am being punished." Weak tears of self-pity crept down Tulipa's sunken cheeks.

Meriones was frantic. He had done everything he could think of to help his wife; he was doing all he could to help his friend; neither situation was getting better. He felt caught, trapped, helpless.

He was exhausted, but he could not sleep. At last he left his wife alone in their sweat-soaked bed and went down to lie on the cool paving stones of the courtyard for a few hours, until the light of the false dawn summoned him back to the palace.

The stones were hard and unyielding, but they had already given up their heat. They soaked up his body heat instead, giving him a measure of relief.

Lying pressed against the ground in his courtyard. Meriones was one of the first to feel the rumbling deep in the earth that signaled the awakening of the gods.

11

En route to Knōsos again in hopes

of exchanging a cargo of oil and spices for Cretan

pottery, Tereus was still dreaming of his own ship.

He had come to hate every plank of the Qatil

because it belonged to someone else.

He considered his prospects. The men in the Cretan colony that called itself Atlantis had been willing to buy the old priest, so Tereus had left the man on the island of Thera with them. But they had not paid much for him. They said he was an unknown quantity whose worth would have to be proved.

By now, Tereus told himself, they should have found ways to force that old savage to reveal his talents.

And if he's as good as I think he is, they might now be willing to buy more like him. We could discuss their commissioning me to go back to the Islands of Mist and capture other sorcerers. It could be enormously profitable.

Yes indeed.

If the old man has proved himself.

Tereus made a decision.

"We're going to call in to Thera again before we go to Crete," he informed his helmsman. "I have some enquiries to make."

The helmsman did not like the sulfurous look of the sky toward Thera, but he knew better than to argue with Tereus. He changed course at once.

At first the blue sea hissed as always, running past the prow. Then it grew sluggish, almost oily. They were making slow headway in spite of their best efforts. But even when the air became gritty and his crew started coughing, Tereus insisted they hold to their course. If a man protested, he felt the lash of Jaha Fe's whip across his shoulders.

They began meeting other vessels coming out from Thera. Luxurious pleasure galleys as well as ordinary fishing boats, everyone of them packed with white-faced, staring people whose household goods were piled around them. It appeared to be a migration, as if the population of Thera had in some common madness decided to take to the sea.

Leaning on the rail of the *Qatil,* Tereus stared down at them. No one waved to him. No one called a greeting. Some of the women, he observed, were crying.

A larger vessel, a trader like the *Qatil,* approached. Its captain was an old acquaintance with whom Tereus had shared wenches and wine in many ports. He hailed the other ship and it drew alongside.

The *Qatil* put down a boat so Tereus could go over to the other ship.

Its captain wasted no time with pleasantries. "Everyone who can lay hands on a boat is leaving Thera," he told Tereus. "They would rather be at sea than wait on the island to face the wrath of the god."

"What god?"

"Ennosigaion. Earth-Shaker! For days he has been growling underground, and Zeus supports him with a rain of ashes from the sky. The air stinks like rotten eggs. Thera is unsafe, Tereus. I implore you, turn your ship about and come away with us before it gets any worse."

Tereus looked toward the island barely visible through the murky air. Its solitary peak thrust upward from the sea like a warning finger. For the first time he recognized a certain malevolence to the shape. Near the southern tip of Thera was the commercial town of Akrotiri, mercantile hub for the sprawling Atlantean colony that had expanded up the slopes to command sweeping views toward their native Crete.

Akrotiri; abandoned. Atlantis . . . a cold worm stirred in Tereus' belly.

"The gods cannot threaten me," he said to the other captain with too hearty a laugh. But as soon as he was on board the *Qatil* again Tereus gave the order to put about and make for Crete. The helmsman responded gladly.

There was not a breath of wind to stir the sail. Oars were their only power now. The sweating oarsmen labored, grunting, impelled by a nameless fear. Jaha Fe no longer needed to use the lash on them. In the sullen, lowering light, they were doing their best to leave Thera behind them.

On Crete, Meriones was also doing his best that morning. After several frustrating days when he had found someone in the gardens every time he passed through, today he found the gardens deserted. People were being kept under roofs by the persistent grit that fell like rain from the sky.

Meriones hurried to the bush Hokar had described. Crouching down, he dug with feverish fingers into the soft earth at the bush's roots. It was volcanic soil, friable and loose, and offered little resistance. He scrabbled hurriedly. In a moment more he had the package in his hands.

He glanced nervously around to see if anyone was watching. The gardens were still deserted.

Meriones stood up. The package was both bulky and heavy. But when he sucked in his belly as hard as he could, he was just able to thrust it down between his belt and his flesh, where it would be somewhat hidden by his embroidered apron.

If anyone looked closely his shape would have seemed very suspicious. But no one was paying any attention to Meriones that morning.

For several days the people of Crete had been living in a state of accelerating apprehension. Poseidon was flexing his muscles and rippling the earth from one end of the island to the other. Meriones had felt the first tremors as he tried to sleep in his courtyard. Since then, subterranean movement had become almost constant. From long experience, Cretans knew how to build to withstand the milder attacks of the Shaker's temper, but the continual rumblings were wearing everyone's nerves. Dogs howled. Goats went dry. Children awakened crying.

Tulipa's headache had returned, increasing to alarming proportions.

Householders along the northern coast were complaining of a greasy ash that settled on everything, ruining food and fabric. Men began wandering down to the harbor to talk to experienced seamen, then stand and stare at the ugly light in the north. On their way home they visited the various sacred shrines and left lavish offerings to Poseidon Earth-Shaker.

People invented excuses to visit the inland mountains, or relatives in the south. Then they gave up making excuses and began fleeing openly, running from the unnatural evil that hovered on the northern horizon.

First singly, then in families, they had descended on the palace to demand protection from their god-king. But as they pressed in upon him, The Minos had panicked. He gave orders that the guards were to admit no more outsiders.

The court concluded that expendables such as craftsmen and entertainers would be next. It looked as if only the royal family and the most influential officials would be granted sanctuary within Labrys.

Meriones had come this morning, against his better judgment, to make one final attempt to retrieve the gold for Hokar before access to the palace was denied him. He would have preferred to stay with

Tulipa. No one, he felt sure, would have noticed or cared. People were too preoccupied.

But his promise to his friend compelled him.

Now that he actually had the gold, his first thought was to turn around and go home. But that would look more suspicious than if he had not come at all. No, he decided, better to wait until after dark, then leave as usual.

Finding a hiding place in the meantime should not be too hard, really; not for a man who knew Labrys so well.

Entering the palace, Meriones made his way to the upper levels. There an antechamber had been set aside for the exclusive use of the musicians, who visited it when they needed to repair their instruments. Aside from that, the room was never visited.

Meriones slipped into the chamber and pulled the door closed after him. The room was empty. With a sigh of relief, he dug the bulky package out from his clothing.

He could not resist opening it for just one look.

When he folded back the last flap of cloth, Meriones drew in a sharp breath. Gold gleamed like fire, like chunks of stolen sunlight. Pure, raw, massy gold, in nuggets worth a fortune.

So much gold! No wonder it was heavy. He realized at once that he could not leave it here, no matter how well hidden. He had planned to secrete it at the back of a small cupboard crammed with bits of wood and wire and pots of fish-glue. But that would never do, not for such a treasure. It would surely be found. Questions would be asked, musicians come under suspicion . . .

He would have to take it with him. No one would pay any attention to him now, he reasoned, not with Labrys rocking on its foundations. There would be no better time to get the gold out of the palace.

He wedged it back between his apron and his loincloth, wincing as the bulky nuggets dug into his belly. He wasted valuable moments readjusting his leather girdle to hold the package in place. His waist was no longer elegantly slim, he noted ruefully.

Then he brushed his hands and stepped out into the corridor trying to look nonchalant.

The atmosphere was changing rapidly. People's expressions were tense, their movements frenetic. Officials scuttled up and down the passageways, exhorting others to remain at their posts. Until the last, the minions of The Minos would strive to keep order.

But it was rapidly becoming a lost cause.

The bellowing of a bull reverberated through the stone-walled chambers of Labrys. Meriones realized sacrifices were being offered in an attempt to placate Poseidon Ennosigaion. The Great Central Court would run red with blood.

Priestesses howled eerily. Incense thickened the air.

Men and women started running; directionless, panicky.

"I don't suppose anyone will be expecting me in the kitchens today," Meriones remarked to no one in particular. Then, hitching his apron to make certain the gold was secure, he set off in search of the nearest safe exit.

He was almost knocked down by a man who came bolting out of an antechamber. "Watch where you're going!" the fellow snarled, sweeping Meriones aside with a wave of his arm.

"I'm sorry, I didn't mean . . ." The musician waved his fingers apologetically. But the other had already run off.

The floors were shuddering violently, Meriones realized with a thrill of horror. Not only walls, but the foundations themselves might collapse under such an onslaught!

A bull broke free from the sacrificial pens and ran headlong through the palace, his frantic bellowing adding to the mounting hysteria. A madness seized the palace animals. Pet monkeys bit and clawed. A hound savaged a royal child.

Cracks appeared in the smiling faces on the frescoes. Tiles fell with a clatter in the bathing chambers. Something grated; something crashed. Cries of distress were coming from the royal apartments. Plaster crumbling added its dust to the already polluted air. An enormous spiral shell made of stucco fell from the ceiling of the queen's megaron and crashed at Ebisha's feet. With a shriek of terror, she ran from the room. No one tried to stop her.

Hokar also was running through the dust-choked hallways of Labrys. A rumor that the gates had already been closed and barred had reached the workrooms, stampeding the craftsmen. Each was determined to find some way out for himself.

Upset and disoriented, Hokar lost his way. He found himself at the head of the Grand Staircase just as Ebisha came running up it.

People swarmed over the stairs. Someone bumped into her and she fell to her knees. With an oath, Hokar plunged down the steps to help her. The face she lifted to him was blank with fear.

He caught hold of her arm. "We must get out of here. Can you stand?"

Ebisha jerked free of his grasp and shrank back.

"I'm Hokar," he said, "don't you know me?"

She shuddered like the trembling earth. "Hokar?" The syllables sounded meaningless on her lips.

"Yes, Hokar the goldsmith, remember? Stand up now, that's it. Here, this way . . . do you know how to get out of here?"

"Out of here?" She was mimicking his words without understanding.

The air was darkening perceptibly. Even the light wells failed to dispel the gloom. A cloud seemed to have blotted out the sun.

Hokar guided the dazed Ebisha back to the top of the Grand Staircase, where he tried to figure which way to go next. Broad corridors lay in either direction but gave no clue of their destinations. "Which way does that go?" he asked Ebisha, pointing along one.

She stared at him with wide green eyes.

He swore under his breath and started in the direction he had pointed, drawing her with him by putting one strong arm around her trembling shoulders. "I think this is the way toward the Zeus Gate," Hokar said to no one in particular. "It's the gate nearest Arkhanes."

The mention of Arkhanes made him think of his little house there with a sudden, fierce longing. Everything in that house was Thracian in style. Familiar. His own.

He would take Ebisha there.

Someone wearing the stiff formal headdress of an offical stumbled past. "Which way to the Zeus Gate?" Hokar shouted at him. But there was no answer. The goldsmith's voice was lost in the wordless scream that was becoming the voice of Labrys.

People were running everywhere. The press of bodies shoved Hokar and Ebisha until passing through a doorway, they found themselves on the colonnaded porch that overlooked the Great Central Court. Below them people scampered across the mosaic tiles like a nest of disturbed ants. "The Minos has deserted us!"

someone cried. "He has evacuated his family and left us here to die!"

The last restraint dissolved. Whether the rumor was true or not, it was enough to instill blind panic.

People began clubbing each other with their fists, fighting for space, for air, for access to an exit, or just to relieve their unbearable emotions. Meanwhile the floor beneath their feet heaved and buckled like a living thing.

Ebisha screamed and clung to Hokar. He could hear her gasping names—the names of gods, he supposed—but they were not names he recognized.

Everyone seemed to be crying some name aloud. Some called on their mothers, others cursed or prayed to The Minos. Or Poseidon. Or Zeus. Or any of a hundred other deities, large and small, the particular image of a particular belief to which one might cling when the world was collapsing.

Nothing stopped the collapse, however.

The crowd was a mob, a mindless sea that moved like a tide first in one direction, then another, sweeping Hokar and Ebisha along with them.

Ebisha had one frightening glimpse of a great dark hulk lying on the floor of the court below. It was the corpse of the last bull to have been sacrificed to Poseidon. Forgotten now. The sacrifice refused.

"Hokar!"

The goldsmith heard his name, but in the melee he could not tell who was calling him.

"Hokar! Over here!"

He craned his neck. Then he saw a slim arm waving frantically.

"Hokar! It's me, Meriones!"

The musician hurried toward them, twisting and weaving through the crowd. When he reached Hokar he managed a harried grin of relief. "What are you doing here?" he asked his friend.

"Trying to find a way out. I got lost. What are you doing here?"

"Trying to find a way out. I was in this part of the palace looking for a place to hide your, ah . . ."

"My gold? You have it?"

"I do. But we don't have time to worry about it now. After we get . . . Look out!" Meriones cried suddenly. He grabbed Ebisha and pulled her aside just in time to keep her from being trampled by a clot of running men.

"What are you doing with this woman?" Meriones asked Hokar while Ebisha stood, panting, flattened against a wall.

"Trying to get her out too. I want to take her with me to Arkhanes. But there's a rumor that the gates have all been barred."

"Possibly," Meriones conceded. "But even if they are, there are many ways out of a palace as big as Labrys. Not everyone goes in and out through a public gate, Hokar. I haven't been here all these years without discovering that. I was just trying to decide which exit to use myself. I don't think anyone will question us under the circumstances."

"You talk too much!" Hokar snapped. "Just get us out of here if you know a way!"

Meriones nodded. "Come on, then. And bring her," he added, nodding at Ebisha. "Let's leave before the ceiling falls on us."

Taking a deep breath, Meriones plunged into the swirl of the crowd like a bather diving into a cold sea. Hokar glanced up at the ceiling, turned pale, hooked Ebisha with his arm and ran after Meriones.

For a measureless eternity they struggled through packed passageways and crowded corridors. Meriones, who was shorter than Hokar, kept disappearing. Finally Hokar caught hold of the fold of hair at the nape of his friend's neck and held on with all his might, though the pull brought tears to Meriones' eyes. Hokar dared not let go. If they lost Meriones he and Ebisha would be truly lost.

They ran up some steps and down others, scuttled across audience chambers, dodged through counting rooms, sidled along narrow passages meant only for slaves, and eventually emerged from a steep stairwell to find themselves on the lowest level of the palace. The walls of unplastered stone smelled of niter. A pervasive gloom was relieved only occasionally by a few plain bronze lamps burning in small niches set into the walls.

They had left the maddened crowd behind, but its roar could still be heard, echoing through the labyrinthine corridors of the palace.

Meriones paused, looking around. "There is an entrance down here somewhere that gives porters coming up from the sea direct access to the main storerooms. If we can find—"

He was interrupted by a thundering crash almost directly above their heads. The walls around them vibrated, the huge blocks of stone ringing like gongs.

"It's going to fall on us!" Ebisha cried. "We'll be crushed!"

The goldsmith folded the woman in his arms and bowed his head over hers protectively, as if he meant to take the weight of the palace on his shoulders rather than let it touch Ebisha.

In that moment, Meriones envied his friend. "It won't fall on us if we can get outside," he said urgently. "Come on!" He began running again.

They followed him through unlit areas floored with bare earth and rubble; stumbling, their breath burning their throat, the world they knew disintegrating around them.

"Here we are!" Meriones whooped suddenly, plunging toward a common planked door standing ajar in the thick wall.

The trio emerged into a daylight they scarcely recognized as daylight. The sky was as dark as mid-winter dusk, but with an evil yellowish cast.

The porters' entrance was let into a north-facing wall in the foundations of the palace, and had been abandoned at the first tremor of the earth. A flagged pathway led away from the doorway, but Meriones did not follow the paving. Instead he hurried away from the palace at an acute angle, making for the open ground beyond. Here the land began to slope upward, out of the royal valley.

The trio climbed the slope in silence, trying not to hear the screams and crashes coming from Labrys behind them. Other people ran past them from time to time, their faces distorted with terror.

Meriones led the way to the rim of the valley. There he paused. "You said you wanted to take Ebisha to Arkhanes," he reminded Hokar. "You'll want to go that way." He pointed.

Hokar's jaw dropped. "Aren't you going with us?"

"I can't, I must go home to my wife. I should never have left her this morning. I wouldn't have, if I'd thought things were going to get so bad."

"And they may well get worse," Hokar warned. "If we're separated now, we might never see each other again. Stay with us, Meriones, let's all help each other. Don't try to go back to Knōsos now, you might not make it. Stay with us," he repeated, putting all the strength of his personality into his urging. "Please!"

Just for a moment, Hokar thought he could hold Meriones. Then the earth shuddered as if Poseidon Ennosigaion was stalking across the land on giant feet, rumbling destruction with every stride.

Ebisha flinched and gasped.

"I have to go home to Tulipa!" Meriones cried frantically.

Hokar unleashed his temper. "Go, then! Desert your friend. Be a coward, who cares? Who needs a wasp-waisted lyre player? I can take care of Ebisha without you!"

Meriones blinked. Then he gave a thin-lipped nod, turned on his heel, and hurried off in the direction of Knōsos.

Hokar stared after him with rising dismay. When the musician was almost out of earshot, he relented and called out, "Meriones? My friend? Be . . . careful!"

Meriones heard. He paused and turned around long enough to give Hokar a Cretan salute. Arching his back like a bow, he made a fist and pressed his knuckles to the Palace of the Brain. "My friend," he echoed. "Try to be . . . cheerful."

Then he spun around and ran for home.

He had run for some distance before he became aware that his movements were being hampered by a bulky object thrust between his loincloth and apron.

He had forgotten to give Hokar the stolen gold.

12

A *dead calm lay on the sea.*

On board the Qatil, *Tereus felt his hackles rise.*

"Pull!" *he yelled at his oarsmen.* "PULL!!!"

But it was too late. A growling roar, far away at

first, swiftly came

closer, increasing in volume until the ship's timbers vibrated and men clapped their hands over their ears. It sounded as if the ocean floor was being wrenched apart.

The roaring grew to unbearable intensity then doubled; trebled. A tremendous thunderclap reverberated throughout the Aegean Sea, slammed across the Ionian Sea, rang the waters of the Mediterranean like a giant bell.

While the world still shook with its force, a second thunderclap boomed with enough power to dwarf the first. Then, impossibly, there was a third, mightier and more terrifying than anything that had gone before. It was a sound to freeze the blood and stop the heart. It was a sound to announce the end of the world.

Geysers of steam shot upward, hot fountains jetting from the sea bed into the sky. Pumice and ash rained down to meet them. The air stank of strange gases released from the bowels of the earth. When horror had exceeded all limits, with one final gigantic blast the world exploded.

A volcanic eruption mightier than any within the memory of mankind tore the entire side out of the island of Thera and hurled it into the sky. A monstrous flower of incandescent light blossomed, burning white, hot beyond heat, setting the air ablaze and drawing all breath, all life into itself. An enormous pillar of boiling smoke, shot through with orange sparks like evil eyes and lit from within by a lurid glow, rose from the disemboweled island. The cloud mushroomed upward, billowing into a burning sky.

The first shock wave rapidly radiated outward. It hit the *Qatil* like a battering ram. Tereus fell face forward on the deck, clawing long splinters out of the wood with bloody fingers. He screamed and did not know he screamed.

Outraged, the sea rose on its hind legs to bellow fury at the heavens.

Meanwhile, Meriones was pounding down the familiar road that led to Knōsos, his house, his wife. He hardly noticed when the white hound darted out from somewhere to join him. The animal was whimpering with terror. Man and dog ran together, fear making them lightfooted.

They had gotten as far as the long hill commanding a view of the harbor when the voice of Poseidon thundered across the sea and knocked Meriones flat on the earth.

He lay dazed, then pulled himself to his hands and knees, spitting earth and pebbles. The god again cried aloud, with a great booming voice. Meriones wet himself in his terror and drew up into a ball, waiting to die.

The god roared with the greatest anger that had ever been unleashed in the world. Meriones knew he was dead. He thought his heart stopped.

But he did not die. He lay helpless while the tremendous explosions echoed and reechoed throughout Crete. Eventually, the musician realized that he was still alive. Probably. He got to his knees again, very shakily, and tried to find the courage to stand.

The ultimate blast slammed across the sea, threw him on his face once more as the whole world rocked on its foundations. The northern sky caught fire, became a sea of molten flame.

Meriones did not try again to stand. What was the use? He lay with a calmer mind than he expected, his head turned sideways, cheek pressed against the road. "This is the end," he heard himself say. No one contradicted him. But somewhere close by, a dog whined piteously.

Meriones shifted enough to be able to see the white hound lying in a heap beside him. He reached out and drew the dog against his body. It did not seem any more injured than he was. Merely scared to death.

Scared to death. The term had new meaning. It meant being so scared that fear itself was slain and one waited placidly, like a bull awaiting sacrifice. Looking at the ax.

Listening for the voice of the god.

Then the god fell silent. Seventy miles to the north, the sea was rushing in to form a seven-mile-wide lake of boiling water and steam embraced by the ruined crescent of lava cliffs that was all that remained of the island of Thera.

From the shock of that monstrous reforming a great wave spread out and moved across the sea. In deep water it was like a ripple traveling across a pond when a stone is dropped in. But as the giant ripple neared the land and the sea bed was shallower, the wave swelled upward, building into a mighty wall with a crest towering hundreds of feet into the shocked sky.

With the speed of the gods, the wall of water rushed toward Crete.

Meriones felt a certain disappointment that he was not dead. Instinct told him the dead might be the lucky ones. But he was unquestionably alive. Slowly, expecting to be knocked down again at any moment, he got to his feet and examined his bruises. They were numerous but not serious. Then he turned the same attention on the dog. It had no broken bones but whined continually, a thin, high-pitched moan that did not sound like a dog at all.

He picked it up and cradled it against his body. The feel of another warm and living being comforted them both.

Meriones' gaze moved along the road toward Knōsos, noting how the paving slabs had heaved. For the first time he realized there were a few other people on the road. He saw them as dark lumps illuminated by the hideous light of the flaming sky. Some of the lumps were stirring, groaning.

Others lay unmoving and silent.

Meriones thought suddenly of Hokar and Ebisha. What had happened to them? Should he go back? He looked over his shoulder, indecisive, then thought of Tulipa and whirled around again, gazing toward the city and the harbor . . .

. . . and stood transfixed.

The cloud that had been Thera was clearly visible on the horizon, glowing like a firebed. In the foreground of this horror were the residents of Knōsos, staggering away from a city reduced to rubble. They resembled the survivors of a destroyed army. Some wept, some cursed, some moaned in pain. Some whimpered like the white hound.

The foremost reached Meriones and passed him, unaware of him. They had no thought but horror and escape. They went on, leaving Meriones staring.

He saw the wave come up out of the sea. But it could not be a wave. It could not be anything known and familiar. It was a giant, malevolent entity from an underworld that spawned monsters. Irresistible, it sped toward the harbor where the masts of the fleet still rose like a forest of sticks.

The tidal wave slammed against Knōsos, smashing the glory of the world's largest fleet into splinters. In the blink of an eye the forest of ships was devoured by the ravenous sea. Its appetite unassuaged, the monster swallowed the shoreline and gobbled up the ruined city beyond, crushing everything beneath a mammoth wall of water.

Staring, unbelieving, Meriones waited, fully expecting the tidal wave to continue inland and cover Labrys in the valley, then rage up the slopes of the mountains themselves, putting an end to one insignificant musician and the brilliant world of Crete.

It came very close.

But the land had a strength of its own. As the tidal wave swept across it the earth robbed the waters of their energy. At last they fell back, exhausted by their own fury. The water drained off toward the sea with a ghastly sucking noise, leaving a spoor of dirty foam and piled mountains of unidentifiable debris.

Still Meriones stood, and stared.

He did not know how much time passed. It seemed eons. Surely he had been watching there since the birth of the world, witness to the contest between land and sea for supremacy.

Where a rich seaport had been was now nothing. The little yellow house was gone. Tulipa's goat was gone. The olive tree was gone.

Tulipa was gone; gone with Knōsos.

Its streets had disappeared beneath the mud and slime that frescoed the site. The stench of the sea bottom floated up to Meriones and he bent to one side to vomit, spewing out his horror without ever turning loose of the dog clasped tightly in his arms.

Knōsos was gone.

Tulipa was gone.

As if from a great distance, Meriones heard the shrieks and wails of the survivors.

But Tulipa was gone.

Knōsos was gone.

"I would be gone too, but for Hokar's gold," he heard himself say to the dog.

The sound of his voice stilled the hound's whining. It twisted in his arms and tried to lick his face with its wet tongue.

"How strange," Meriones said wonderingly. "I could be out under the sea with Tulipa. Isn't that strange?"

His voice sounded calm, unemotional. He might have been commenting on a minor event in an ordinary day.

He did not notice the tears running down his cheeks.

He stared at the sea and the burning sky, and the empty place where the city had been.

"Hokar's gold," he said after a while in the same uninflected voice.

His body turned itself around and began to walk in the direction of Arkhanes.

13

Shortly after Meriones left them,

Ebisha's strength deserted her. Her legs felt like

water. She sat down abruptly on the unstable earth

and stared helplessly up at Hokar. "No more,"

she said.

He gave a worried glance at the peculiar sky, then reluctantly sat down beside her. "Just for a little while," he said. "We can rest for a little while, then we have to go on."

"Where?"

"To my house, in the hills beyond this valley. It might be safer there."

"Can we breathe there, in the hills?" Ebisha coughed, shook her head, coughed again. "The air is so bad here. So thick."

"It will be better at Arkhanes," he assured her with a confidence he did not feel. He sat with her for a little while then tried to get her on her feet again. When he tugged at her arm she sat like a lump of soft clay, unwilling to move. "Come to my house now," he pleaded. "I have something for you there, something I've been keeping for you. It is the gold . . ." Suddenly he remembered. His stolen gold. Meriones said he had it, but Meriones was gone.

Gone off with my gold, Hokar thought. His mouth narrowed into a bitter line.

"What do you have for me?" Ebisha asked, pulling his attention back.

The words were ashes in his mouth. "The gold necklace I made for you, the seashells." It's all I have left, he was about to add, feeling the anger flame in him.

But at that moment the first blast struck.

Ebisha screamed and cowered against the earth. Hokar stood swaying, his ears ringing. Then the second great thunder drowned out all other sound and hurled him to the ground.

As the final explosion ignited the sky, he twisted violently to shield Ebisha's body with his. Wrapping his arms around her head, Hokar pressed his face down beside her and waited for death.

Waited in a ringing silence.

Slowly, astonished to find himself alive, Hokar began trying to disentangle from the woman. A white-hot pain lanced through his hip.

Ebisha was crying in soft little hiccups.

When Hokar tried to stand, his wrenched muscles screamed. He tugged at Ebisha. "You must help me," he told her through gritted teeth. "I'm hurt. I don't think I can get up alone."

With an effort, she controlled her sobbing and peered at him through a curtain of disheveled hair. "Hurt?"

"My hip." Waves of pain lapped at him. "But we cannot stay here. Help me."

Ebisha got to her feet. Then she bent and helped Hokar drape an arm across her shoulders. She wrapped both her arms around his chest.

Very slowly and very carefully, between them they got him upright, standing.

Hokar was briefly nauseated, but it passed.

"That's better," he breathed. He straightened his spine and lifted his head, moving out of her embrace to stand independently. "I'm all right now," he said with conviction.

But when he tried to walk he knew he was not all right. The injured hip could not be trusted, and every movement of his leg was a painful effort.

Ebisha, watching him through narrowed eyes, moved close again without being asked and draped his arm back across her shoulder. She could not afford weakness when he needed her strength.

They set off once more in the direction of Arkhanes.

People were streaming past them. A small child, bloody and naked, appeared in their path, shrieked unintelligibly, and fled like a mindless animal. Moments later they came to the collapsed house where the child's family lay crushed. One clenched fist protruded from the rubble.

There was nothing to be done. Hokar and Ebisha went on.

Once the goldsmith glanced back toward the north, but the sight of a monstrous tower of flame invading the heavens so appalled him that thereafter he kept his eyes fixed on the ground in front of him. The ground was cracked, broken, the familiar way to Arkhanes already altered beyond recognition. But better than fire in the sky.

Shielded by the contours of the hills, Hokar and Ebisha were spared the sight Meriones would never forget, the massive wall of water rushing down on the defenseless coast. The concussion of the tidal wave was, to them, indistinguishable from the other tremors running continually through the earth.

The tidal wave did not reach the House of the Double Axes. The valley rim that had shielded Labrys from the rapacious view of sea pirates in former times now sheltered the palace from the most savage pirate of all. Poseidon did not carry away the treasures of The Minos.

But Hokar and Ebisha heard a change in the quality of the distant screaming. An added wail of terror was carried to them on the wind from the northern coast.

Hokar forced himself to a shambling run, a sort of hobbling hop half supported by Ebisha trotting beside him. Surprisingly, the effort eased his pain as if he were forcing some misaligned portion of himself back into place.

The hot wind, the long overdue wind, was blowing more strongly every moment, bringing a cloud of pumice and ash. In time it would begin delivering the fragmented flesh of Thera.

Hokar and Ebisha journeyed through nightmare. For a while he stopped thinking of her as a woman. Getting-Ebisha-to-Arkhanes became a task he had set himself, like fashioning fine gold wire. His mind fixed on that as the only reality, rejecting the unreal surrounding them and the surreal horror of the situation.

Struggling, stumbling, cursing, he guided her—he the cripple and she the crutch—through an endless filthy darkness in which a thousand raging fires were springing up as blazing cinders began to rain from the sky.

Hardly a structure they saw was still intact. Homes and farmsteads, their stones scattered, littered the land with rubble. Dazed people wandered about as aimlessly as dazed livestock.

Some survivors, less dazed than others, had already begun looting.

As Hokar and Ebisha approached Arkhanes, several times they encountered small groups of men going from one ruined homestead to another, taking anything of value they could find. Snatching, grabbing, grinning, running.

"They are like the men who capture free people to make them slaves," Ebisha said with repugnance.

But the looters did not bother them. They were so ash-covered and begrimed they looked as if neither ever had anything worth stealing.

Arkhanes had been a small but important town. It was on one of the main roads leading from the south, and was also the site of the royal tombs of minor members of the ruling families of Knōsos. Generations of sisters and nephews and mothers-in-law slept there peacefully with their grave goods piled high around them, fearing no grave robbers, for graves were sacred in the land of the sea kings.

At least, they always had been. Before.

"My house is just up ahead," Hokar told Ebisha with obvious relief. "If it's still standing."

The goldsmith's house was at the end of a road leading to the Hill of Tombs. An ugly glow behind the hill might have been sunset—or sunrise—who could tell?

Hokar directed Ebisha to the familiar pathway. Now he was looking ahead. He could hardly believe his stinging eyes.

His house stood relatively unharmed, with just a slight cant to one side.

They hurried gratefully inside.

The door could not be closed behind them. The doorframe was out of alignment. Putting his shoulder behind it, Hokar forced the door as far as it would go, which was no more than halfway, then sat down, panting, on the nearest couch.

The pain in his hip had become only a memory of fire. But suddenly he was desperately tired. He just wanted to sit. Not think, not feel. Just sit. He hung his head and closed his eyes.

Ebisha stood indecisively for a moment, then began exploring the goldsmith's house.

It was nothing like the House of the Double Axes. Simple to the point of being stark, it was a utilitarian residence for a man usually occupied elsewhere. A few couches, one of which served as a bed; some low wooden tables; a couple of chests carved in designs she did not recognize. Coarse woolen rugs hung haphazardly on the walls—though with a sense of color, bright dyes enlivening the plain white stucco. On one of the tables was a pitcher with dying flowers.

Ebisha smiled to herself when she saw the flowers, and nodded, as if they carried a particular message.

"Is there any water?" she heard Hokar say behind her.

She took the flowers from the water and carried the pitcher to him. He drank gratefully. The water was flat and stale but it cleared the dust from his mouth.

When he ran his tongue over his teeth afterward, he could taste the dead flowers.

Gingerly, he stood up. His hip ached, but it was bearable. Crossing the room to an assortment of householders' tools leaning in one corner, he selected a heavy metal bar. With the bar he pried up a flagstone from the floor.

There was a hollow beneath the flagstone, and a small parcel wrapped in linen in the hollow.

Wordlessly, he handed the parcel to Ebisha.

When she unwrapped it her eyes widened. "The necklace!" She turned the thin links over in her hands, her eyes following the spiral design of the tiny nautilus shells.

Hokar said diffidently, "It's . . . ah . . . the best thing I've ever done. Not very heavy though. If I had more gold . . ." He broke off, scowling. The memory of the stolen gold burned in him.

"You have a very great gift," Ebisha said reverently. "I think the gold speaks to you."

Hokar was embarrassed. "That's not possible. I'm just, ah, good with my hands."

"You don't think gold can speak to a craftsman? I do. Everything has a voice. Not as powerful a voice, perhaps, as one of the immortals, but . . ."

"What do you mean by 'the immortals'? Are you talking about the gods?"

Ebisha's forehead pleated with the effort to explain. "Not like the gods you have here, Hokar. Not giant men and women or magical animals or some blend of the two. The immortals my people know and understand are alive, but in a different way. They are the very forces of life. They provide what we need for our existence as long as we treat them with respect, but they . . . they are not . . ." She broke off, coughing.

When the seizure passed she resumed, "Water is one of the immortals. Among my people are some to whom the water speaks. They can find it hidden far beneath the earth. They hear the voice of unknown springs and show others where to dig their wells. The water calls to them, and they listen.

"My grandsire has a different gift. He knows the soul of fire. Fire is another of the immortals. Something in the fire speaks to my grandsire and he listens. They . . . communicate. He can make sparks leap from his fingertips or set a tree afire with a glance. Do you understand?"

Baffled, Hokar shook his head. "It's magic. I know nothing of magic."

The lurid light of the flaming sky shone through the window, painting the interior of Hokar's house the color of blood.

A face peered around the half-open door. "Hokar?" someone inquired. "Is this your house? Are you in there?"

Hokar stiffened.

Ebisha gave a squeal of joy. "Musician!"

Meriones entered the house warily, as if expecting it might collapse at any time. Hokar wanted to hurry forward and welcome him, but something held him back. "Why are you here?" was all he could say. His tone was surly.

Meriones peered at him. "I had to bring your gold to you," he said. It was the only answer he could think of.

Hokar exhaled a great sigh of relief. "You brought it back."

"Of course I brought it back, did you think I—you did! You thought I'd stolen it for myself!"

"Of course not," Hokar said, too heartily. "It never entered my mind!"

"It never entered my mind either," Meriones told him in a soft, sad voice.

Abashed, Hokar hurried tardily forward and clasped Meriones by both hands. "What about your wife? Did you reach Knōsos?"

"Knōsos is gone. Tulipa is gone."

"Gone? What do you mean, gone?"

"Gone. The sea took them." Meriones' tone was flat and dead.

Hokar and Ebisha exchanged shocked glances.

Something whined at the door. A very lean, very dirty white hound crouched there, wagging its tail to placate its god for the sin of having followed him.

The faintest spark of life crept back into Meriones' voice as he said, "It's all right, this is my friend's house." He did not think Hokar was the sort of person who would object to a dog in the house. He snapped his fingers and the hound ran to him.

"What's happening out there?" Hokar wanted to know.

"It's very bad. The air is thicker than water and cinders and other things are falling out of it. Fires are springing up everywhere. And looters," he added, relieved that Hokar had asked no more about Knōsos and Tulipa. "You should bar your door, Hokar."

"I can't, it won't close. The frame is twisted. But we'll be all right here."

Meriones was not so sure. The atmosphere in the house was only slightly less foul than outside. The wind blowing across Crete from destroyed Thera was bringing not only volcanic ash and debris but poisonous gases.

Ebisha coughed again, and again, more harshly each time.

The three sat on Hokar's couch, the woman in the middle and the dog crouching at their feet. They sat and waited. There was nothing else to do.

Sounds drifted in from outside. Crashes, shouts. Then long sullen silences broken only by the howl of the wind. Then different crashes, other voices shouting.

It might have been day or night.

"My throat is so dry," Ebisha gasped, reaching for the water pitcher on the table beside the couch. But the pitcher was empty. She clawed at her throat beneath the gold necklace she had slipped over her head.

"Where's your well?" Meriones asked Hokar. "I can go for more water."

"It's a good trot down the road, in a little square half hidden by shrubbery. Not easy to find unless you know just where it is."

Ebisha coughed again, violently. Her eyes pleaded.

"You go then, Hokar," said Meriones.

Suddenly Ebisha said, "Both of you go!"

"But I want to be with you," Hokar protested.

"I shall be all right for the time it takes you to fetch water," she insisted. "Just go now. The dog will watch over me."

She had grown accustomed to palace habits. At Labrys, men and women insisted on privacy when they relieved themselves. Bodily functions were circumscribed with rituals. It had been a long time since she last emptied her bladder and it was aching dreadfully, but she was reluctant to say this aloud. If the two men would just leave her alone for a little time she could take care of herself in private.

The more Hokar argued to stay with her, the more she urged him to go. And each time she spoke made her cough.

At last he gave in. "But we'll be back very soon," he assured her as he walked, somewhat stiffly, toward the door.

It would be good to do something other than sitting passively, he suddenly realized.

Meriones had a last word for the dog. "Guard her well!" he ordered the hound.

The white dog, which had started to follow him, sank back on its haunches with a disappointed whine, but stayed with Ebisha.

Outside the house the unnatural twilight closed in upon them at once.

There were other people at the well. A nervous scuffle had broken out. Everyone was in a hurry to fill the various water vessels they had brought. Once people waited politely at the well, each taking their turn. Not now. The eerie light, the quivering earth, the stinking air combined to strip away the patina of civilization and reveal frightened animals snarling at one another over water rights.

One man shoved another hard. The second man staggered back against an elderly woman. She dropped the vessel she carried. It crashed on the paving stones. Glancing down, Meriones saw that it had been a finely made piece of pottery formed to resembled a leather bag with a lip, with pottery handles simulating twisted rope. Rose in color, it was decorated with a repetitive double ax motif common to Cretan ware.

Smashed.

As Cretan pottery was ceremoniously smashed every year in an ostentatious display of wealth intended to give employment to more potters and enhance the economy still more.

Holding his own water pitcher against his chest, Hokar managed to edge closer to the well. Then a fight broke out in earnest. One burly man hit another in the face with his fist. In seconds, the area boiled with fury. People relieved their pent-up emotions by hitting out at whoever was nearest, for no reason at all.

Meriones had never liked fighting. He tried to stay out of the melee, but when he saw Hokar being pummeled by a pair of men he swallowed hard and plunged forward to try to help his friend. "You leave him alone!" he yelled.

The crowd swallowed him.

Meriones was, however, tougher than he looked. His was a wiry and agile strength and his reflexes were quick. He gave as good as he got and found, to his surprise, that it felt good to be hitting something.

Yelling wildly, he began to hit harder.

The crowd at the well was so intent on their impromptu war that they did not hear other voices crying out in the town, warning of the arrival of the looters.

Someone hit Hokar a thundering blow to the side of the head and the red world turned black. He slid down and away, into a ringing silence.

But consciousness did not totally desert him. He could still feel the pain in his hip, and he somehow knew he was in a sitting position with his back against the cold stone of the well-curb. Confusion swirled around him like spirits swirling through the netherworld.

His mind wandered off in a dream of its own. He envisioned the long, satisfying afternoons in the goldsmiths' chamber at Labrys. He fancied he heard the sound of the lyre, and he smiled to himself. Sitting dazed on the shaken earth of Crete, his ears temporarily deaf to the funeral laments of a shattered civilization, he lived again at his workbench. His fists uncurled and reshaped themselves as if holding his tools. He reveled in the rich satiety of designs running through his mind, waiting for his art to give them substance.

He thought he was watching his hands shape the gold necklace for Ebisha. He saw the shells . . .

"Ebisha," he groaned, clawing his way back to the here and now.

Meriones was bending over him. "Hokar? Are you all right?"

"No. Not. No."

"Can you get up?"

"I don't want to," Hokar said with conviction even as he reached for the hand Meriones was extending.

The pain in his hip woke afresh, but somehow he got to his feet. "What happened?"

"The fight's over. I think we all won. Everyone got their water and went home. I've been trying to get you to open your eyes for ever so long."

"Ebisha!"

"We'd better get back to her," Meriones said. "I don't want to worry you, but I heard someone say there's been looting not far from here."

"Why didn't you leave me and go to her right away, then?"

Meriones looked shocked. "You're my friend. How could I leave you here with men fighting all around you? And I couldn't carry you, you're too big."

"Ebisha," Hokar said again. This time it came out as a groan.

He leaned on Meriones' shoulder and reverted to the hobbling hop that was the nearest he could come to a run. The two men hurried up the road toward Hokar's house, neither speaking. They sped through a smoky, permanent dusk. Beneath the cloud of volcanic debris no daylight could survive.

Other survivors were still picking their way through the streets, not only of Arkhanes, but of the other cities and towns of Crete that had suffered the volcanic fury and its aftermath. They were digging at the collapsed walls, seeking friends and family, trying to identify landmarks, talking to one another—or at one another—in fragmented, disjointed snatches. Words drifted to Hokar and Meriones: ". . . the entire fleet . . . six generations to rebuild . . . collapsed on top of them, and no one . . . have you seen her? A little girl, only this high . . . burning, still burning . . ."

As they neared the house with the gaping door, Hokar and Meriones slowed by mutual unspoken accord. Nothing looked any different than when they had left it.

And yet.

"Don't go in there," Meriones said suddenly. "Let me look first." He pushed Hokar's arm from his shoulder and advanced toward the house alone. Hokar made no move to follow him.

Meriones was not afraid. As far as he was concerned, the worst possible thing had already happened. Nothing he might find in Hokar's house could be as bad as seeing the tidal wave that took Tulipa.

But Hokar was afraid. He stood frozen with anticipatory anguish.

Meriones edged his body around the door and peered into the gloom. At first he could not see anything. Then his eyes began to make out details.

An overturned table.

A couch hurled halfway across the room.

Meriones flinched in spite of himself. "Ebisha?" he whispered hesitantly.

A voice answered him. Not a human voice. The faint whimper came from beneath an overturned table.

Meriones flung himself down beside it. The hound lay there, thin ribs heaving, a bloody slash along them showing where the dog had been attacked with a knife. The hound tried to lick Meriones' hand.

"Did you fight for her?" he asked it. "Did you try to save her?" The dog whimpered again. Meriones' heart sank.

He knew what had happened as surely as if he had been there. Looters had stumbled across Hokar's house and seen the gleaming necklace Ebisha wore. He glanced to one side. The flagstone with the hollow beneath it was still in place. Meriones and Hokar had hidden the gold nuggets there before they went for water, and it appeared undisturbed.

But even in the gloom, looters would have seen Ebisha's necklace.

Gold. Deadly gold. Meriones stood up. "Ebisha?"

"Is she there? Is she all right?" Hokar called anxiously from the doorway.

Meriones knew he was not thinking clearly. He was too tired, and his brain was numbed by grief. Yet he must try to shield his friend, if he could, from an awful discovery.

"You stay there, Hokar!" he ordered sharply. "I'll find her, just a moment now . . ."

He fumbled about the room, stumbling over furniture. The dog tried to crawl after him, then sank back and lay panting.

Meriones came to the couch lying on the floor like a slain animal, feet upward.

Not lying flat.

There was something beneath it.

Meriones took hold of two of the legs and eased the couch onto its side.

Ebisha, a lifeless heap, had been underneath the couch.

Meriones held his breath for one agonized moment before calling out to Hokar. Let Hokar think, for that moment longer, that she might be alive. It was a small gift to give.

Meriones touched the dead girl's shoulder with gentle, regretful fingers . . . and felt her stir beneath his touch.

"Hokar!" he cried. "She's here, she's alive, come quick!"

Hokar flung himself into the room as if he had never been injured.

Between them they righted the couch and lifted Ebisha onto it. Some random part of Meriones' mind noted that she was heavier than Tulipa. Bigger-boned, from a bigger race.

Tulipa. Don't think about her.

Ebisha coughed and opened her eyes. "Aaannh?" she asked uncertainly.

Meriones told her, "You're alive, we're here. It's all right."

"Aaannh." Her eyes closed again, satisfied.

A hasty examination showed her to be stunned, but uninjured. Only the dog was injured. It whined pitifully, begging for Meriones' attention.

They had brought no water after all. Meriones had to run back to the well to fetch some. Every step of the way he expected to be attacked, but he was unchallenged.

He filled the pitcher and ran back to Hokar's house. Some water sloshed from the pitcher as he ran, but he arrived with most of it.

Ebisha was awake. She lay cradled in the goldsmith's arms. With one hand Hokar kept stroking her hair as if to assure himself she was real.

She was coughing when Meriones entered the house. She reached eagerly for the pitcher and gulped down half its contents. She choked, spluttered, drank the rest.

The coughing eased. She managed a wan smile. "The dog saved me. Strangers came. They saw the necklace and tried to take it from me, but the dog attacked them and fought them. They had knives, though. They would have killed us both. But then the necklace broke and they took it and ran because the dog was growling so savagely. They hurt him, but he never stopped growling!"

Meriones went to the dog and knelt down beside it. He stroked the animal's head tenderly. "You're going to be all right," he said. "We'll take care of you. You're safe now." The dog thumped its tail weakly against the flagstones.

"You're my dog now," Meriones added.

The feathery tail wagged harder. He could have sworn the hound understood.

He made another trip to the well, and got enough water to drink and to bathe the dog's wound. He was as gentle with the hound as he had been with Tulipa, pouring all his care and concern into his task, venting his amputated love.

They stayed in the house, waiting, but they did not know what they were waiting for. No one else bothered them. Hokar retrieved the gold nuggets from their hiding place, then seemed to lose interest in them. He sat with the package held loosely in his hands as he stared off into space.

Meriones eyed it. A thought occurred to him. "Hokar?"

"Mmmm?"

"Where did you get the gold for Ebisha's necklace?"

There was no answer. Meriones persisted. "Did you get it the same way you got those chunks of raw gold?"

Hokar looked down.

"Ah." Intuition moved through Meriones, forming a mosaic in his mind. "You stole it. And because you had stolen, you thought I would steal too."

Hokar said nothing.

Meriones carried his thoughts a step further. "Tereus stole Ebisha and the others from the Islands of Mist. They were free people, but he made them slaves. There has been too much stealing. We've made the gods angry, that's why this disaster has befallen us."

Ebisha looked intently at Meriones. "Do you think your gods did this? Do you think they are powerful enough to do this?"

Meriones ran his hands through his hair. "They must be, how else could it happen? So we must find a way to placate them. We have to give back what was stolen."

"Not my gold," Hokar said abruptly. His fingers clamped on the package in his lap. "I need this to buy Ebisha's freedom."

Ebisha said in a wondering voice, "I think I'm free already. Who at the palace cares now what has become of me?"

"She's right," Meriones agreed. "The pair of you could vanish completely and no one would ever ask questions. So many have vanished . . ." He paused, swallowed hard, went on. "If there are any ships left—and there must be—in time you could even make your way to the Islands of Mist. Take Ebisha home, return something that was stolen."

At the word "home" a great light dawned in Ebisha's green eyes.

Hokar responded to its blaze. "I suppose we could go down to the coast and ask about Tereus and the *Qatil;* they were due in. If we can't find them, there will surely be other ships taking refugees out. Everyone will want to leave Crete after this."

"Not everyone, but many," Meriones agreed. "I would like to leave myself. There's nothing left for me here," he added in a low voice.

Ebisha clapped her hands. "Then come with us to the Islands of Mist!"

Meriones looked at Hokar, who had believed him capable of theft. "I don't know . . ."

Hokar rightfully interpreted the musician's dubious expression. "You must come with us," he said. "You're my friend. My friend forever, beyond any doubt."

Meriones slanted his gaze sideways, to the injured hound lying nearby. "And my dog?"

Hokar laughed. "Bring him. We owe a debt to that dog."

"Hear that?" Meriones asked the hound. "We're going to the Islands of Mist!"

The dog lifted its head, wagged its tail, and grinned.

They gathered what food they could find and a waterskin, then made a bundle of these using one of Hokar's blankets. In the bottom of the bundle were the gold nuggets. Ebisha was assigned to carry the bundle, while Hokar leaned on her shoulder.

Meriones carried his injured dog.

Their waiting over, and firm in their resolve for a new beginning, the trio set out for the coast.

They traveled through an alien landscape. In places the hot ash was knee-deep and getting deeper. Great cracks had opened in the earth. Some of these revealed fire raging in their depths, devouring debris. Scorched, singed, and shaken, the Minoan empire was in ruins.

"The Mycenaean warlords have been waiting for an opportunity like this," Meriones remarked, unable to walk long in silence. "When they realize what's happened here, they'll probably attack Crete and take over the Mediterranean."

Hokar was not listening. He was not interested in politics or military adventurism. His eye was drawn to a burned tree standing alone against the sky. Its twiggy, blackened branches formed an elegant pattern, like freehand filigree by a master craftsman.

I could copy that, Hokar was thinking.

He was so intent he did not notice the fissure in front of him until he lost his balance and swayed precariously on its brink.

With a shriek, Ebisha grabbed for him.

At the bottom of the fissure a roaring fire waited.

Hokar tumbled forward.

Ebisha caught him at the last possible moment. But she had to drop her bundle to do it.

The bundle fell into the heart of the flames.

"My gold!" Hokar cried in dismay, reaching toward it.

Simultaneously, Meriones felt a stirring inside himself, like intuition. Like inspiration. His voice boomed above the roar of the fire. "Let it go!" he commanded.

As if in response, a red-gold belch of flame soared upward, driving Hokar and Ebisha back. Meriones stood alone on the edge of the fissure. Alone with the fire.

As it scorched his skin, awe bubbled through his blood. An ancient heritage came alive in him. His grandmother's voice sang to him in the hiss of the flames.

"Yes," Meriones whispered. "Yes."

Suddenly he *knew*, beyond thought, beyond question, what elemental power had been unleashed when Thera exploded. In the flames he saw, for one heart-stopping instant, the face of the old priest who was Ebisha's grandsire.

"Yes," Meriones said a third and final time. He arched his back and pressed his knuckles to the Palace of the Brain in salute. Then he stepped back to safety.

"The gold is gone," he told his companions. "We have given it to the fire."

The stone sat on its hillside and thought. Its thoughts were not cerebral. It had no cerebral cortex. Nor were they visceral. Stones do not need viscera. The thoughts of stone are the thoughts of earth, compacted, weighed down by the eons, thrust upward by cataclysm, encased in ice. Immobile for millennia. Then pushed, shoved, dragged, dropped.

The stone sat where the glacier had abandoned it. The surrounding landscape slowly changed. Vegetation appeared, softly mantling the ice-scraped soil. Trees grew. Great lizards came. And disappeared. Mammals rubbed their itching sides on the stone to rid themselves of parasites.

Rain poured over the stone; rain from its cousins the mountains, who helped shape the weather, controlling wind currents and influencing the amount of precipitation.

Sun shone.

Change followed change.

Two-legged mammals arrived. They recognized the stone as fearsome and holy and bowed in worship before it. In what served as its consciousness, the stone thought this behavior just and proper. It was part of the sacred earth.

Then different, paler, bifurcated beings arrived, and began slaughtering the worshipers of the stone.

14

Annie Murphy sat in the twilight of

her fine frame house with the book on her lap. It had

grown too dark to read unless she lit a lamp, and

Annie did not like to waste oil. There would be

God's daylight tomorrow

and she could read more. Meanwhile, her thin fingers stroked the leather cover of the book. The smell of new leather drifted up to her. Her fingers caressed the gold stamping on the cover. It read: NEW HAMPSHIRE AS IT IS. A GAZETTEER. And the date, brand-new, gleaming gold: 1855.

Annie Murphy sighed a contented sigh. She was a wealthy woman, by her reckoning. She had a fine new book to read that would last her through the hard New England winter to come and well into spring.

"No bigger than a bar of laundry soap after a hard day's wash," was the way she described herself. Tiny, meticulous, she ruled the Murphy household with an iron hand. There was only one way—her way, and nothing less than perfection would suffice. But her eyes twinkled as easily as they snapped, and her fine-boned face and slim little body radiated good humor.

She had peculiar eyes for a descendant of Irish immigrants, almost almond in shape, dark, exotic.

"My Annie's family had someone born on the wrong side of the blanket sometime," her husband said to his cronies down at the feed store. He, Liam Murphy, was as Irish as they came, there could be no doubting his pedigree. His blazing red hair and freckles were indisputable proof. "I come from the Murphys of Wexford," he loved to boast. "The Boys of Ninety-eight."

But the heroes of the most recent doomed Irish rising against English oppression meant nothing to hard-bitten New Hampshire farmers gathered around a potbellied stove in the feed store at Conway. What mattered was the oppression of the oncoming winter and the anticipated depth and duration of the snow it would bring, which would shape all their lives for the next six months.

"You reckon it's gonna be next May again, afore mud season?" Benjamin Osgood was asking Daniel Foster.

"Don't know yet," the other replied. "Ask me next week."

Daniel Foster was the local weather prognosticator. He had an uncanny record for accuracy, as well as owning Conway Feed and Grain. The two combined to make him an important personage indeed.

Ben Osgood sighed and tugged at his lower lip. A balding farmer, he had courted Annie McDonnell, as she was then, before Liam

Murphy married her. Annie's forebears had emigrated from the glens of Antrim in the north of Ireland back in 1719, seeking religious freedom. As good Presbyterians they had been welcomed into strongly Protestant New Hampshire.

But Annie had a blot on her escutcheon. One afternoon she had entertained her new beau by reading to him from her family Bible and Ben had discovered, to his dismay, that her mother came from a long line of Donegal Catholics.

The religious tolerance of the Osgood family did not extend to Papists. Ben married someone else, and Annie eventually married Liam Murphy, who adored her and was clearly happier with her than Ben Osgood ever was with his wife, a repressed and judgmental Freewill Baptist.

When Ben was in Liam Murphy's company, he was inclined to suppress an envious sigh from time to time.

Liam was saying, "My wife Annie'd sure like to know how you predict the weather, Dan'l. She 'lows as how it'd be a right valuable skill for me to have for my ownself. Lord knows it's hard enough to make a livin' when the weather's with you. When it's agin you, a man can starve to death."

Daniel Foster smiled thinly. "Weather prediction is a valuable skill," he agreed, "and I make too much money sellin' my predictions to farmers like you, to start givin' away the secret. But that's just like Miz Murphy; alluz thinkin', ain't she?"

Liam glowed with pride. "She's got a good head on her. Reckon it comes from all those books she reads. I fetched her home a new one when I was down to Moultonborough. Thing called a Gazetteer. Tells about soils and crops and towns and history. Annie's interested in all that."

"Cain't think why," Ben Osgood interjected. "Woman oughta be interested in her house and her children."

"Annie is interested in 'em," Liam told him. "She plans to teach our children outta them books. But she says this here Gazetteer has a lotta information in it that'd be useful to a farmer. She'll read those parts out to me in th' evenin's. She'll read every word in that there book. She loves to read anything about New Hampshire and the mountains. She purely loves this part of the country."

Ben Osgood snorted. "Don't set much store by bookish women, myself," he said contemptuously. "My wife now, she's a good

Christian woman and she puts up good preserves. That's what a man needs." He tilted his cane-seated chair back and laced his fingers over his belly as if he were the final authority on women.

To himself, however, he was thinking, I wonder what it would be like to be married to Annie McDonnell? That busy little way of walkin' she has. And the quick smile on her. She's alluz thinkin' of somethin' to help Liam. Liam Murphy's not much of a farmer. Never been much of a farmer. He couldn't grow rocks in a field if Annie didn't keep a fire lit under him.

Bet she lights a fire under him in bed too.

His mind far away, Ben tilted his chair back farther, crucially misjudging the weight-to-angle ratio. The back of the chair grated against the wall, then the legs shot forward and deposited Ben Osgood, chair and all, on the sawdust-covered planks of the feed-store floor.

The other two men guffawed.

Ben, red-faced, scrambled to his feet. "There's a devil in that thing!" he said of the chair.

"Ain't no devil," Foster retorted. "You lean back too far, you fall. It's a natural law, and cain't no one go agin natural law."

With a sullen scowl, Osgood shrugged into his coat and stomped from the store.

"Man ain't got no sense of humor," Daniel Foster remarked.

Liam Murphy gave a lazy grin. "You ain't exackly famous for your sense o' humor either," he told Foster. "My Annie says you're as mean as a ruptured goose."

Lean and irascible, Foster was not inclined to take an insult from any man. But he was not offended by Annie Murphy's statement. Everyone knew she had a twist to her tongue. She also had exotic dark eyes that tilted up at the corners, and a ready laugh. Foster was perversely pleased to think she had spoken of him at all.

"Mean as a ruptured goose," he repeated, mouthing the words to get their full flavor. "Happens I am, I reckon. To them as gits crosswise of me." He sounded proud.

Unconcerned, Liam Murphy yawned and ran his thumbs under his suspenders, easing the pressure they were bringing to bear on his flannel shirt. Liam was easily the tallest, strongest man for twenty miles in any direction, and another man's temper didn't worry him much.

Nothing worried him much, as long as he had Annie. She did the thinking and the worrying for both of them.

"Reckon I better get on home myself," he remarked. "Days're closin' in. I like to be with the wife when the light's gone."

Such open acknowledgment of fondness for one's spouse was rare among Conway people. Privately, Foster thought Murphy was tied to his wife's apron strings. But just as no one wanted to make an enemy of the man who owned the feed store and predicted the weather, so no one would make fun of big Liam Murphy.

"Give the missus my regards," Foster said.

Liam got to his feet, stretched, scratched himself in both armpits, retrieved his heavy coat from its peg, then vocalized the all-purpose New England "A-yuh" and left the store.

Murphy had been the last man in the feed store that evening, aside from the proprietor himself. When he had been gone a suitable time, Foster ambled over to the front door. He looked up and down the dirt road that was called, rather grandly, Main Street.

No one was approaching from either direction. Lamplight glowed from the windows of the false-fronted hotel across from the store. Off in the hills, a hound bayed at the cloud-shrouded moon.

The darkness crouched among the mountains, waiting.

Foster shivered, crossed his forearms over his chest, and rubbed his upper arms to warm them. Then he stepped off the porch and walked around the store, fastening the heavy wooden shutters, known as Indian shutters, tightly over the windows. He went back into the store, shut and bolted the door, and barred the Indian shutters from the inside. A second set of interior shutters was then also closed and barred.

He took his rifle down from the rack behind the stove and lovingly cleaned it, squinting down the barrel, wiping the highly polished stock with a soft cloth, working the mechanism to be certain it was in firing order. Overhead he heard the creak of the floor that told him his wife was moving about in their apartment over the store. She would be putting his supper on the table. It was time to go.

He made a final round of the store, checking both shutters and door again.

Then he shouldered his rifle and climbed the stairs.

Meanwhile, Liam Murphy reached home. Home was a cabin that

had been built by his neighbors, according to custom, the week after Annie agreed to marry him. Not a town house, it was constructed of pine logs, well chinked, with two rooms and a sleeping loft. The house was connected to the much larger barn by an enclosed dogtrot. The barn had been raised first, of course, being the more important structure.

Liam lifted the latch, pushed the door open, and called a cheerful, "Annie! Where's my girl?"

"Ssshhh, you great ox, you'll wake the children."

"They abed already?"

"Of course they are. I put the baby to bed before the sun goes down. She's fretful without lots of sleep."

"I thought Johnny might still be up," Liam said hopefully. Seven-year-old Johnny was his father's pride and joy.

Annie bent to the fireplace, lowering the cast-iron pot on its chain to heat up stew for Liam's meal. "I couldn't keep that boy up forever, waiting for you." Her voice was brittle.

"Aw now, Annie, I was just down to the feed store, talkin'. No harm in it."

"No harm? Sometimes menfolk stay talking at Foster's till all hours."

"Not me," he assured her. He tried to put his arms around her. She pretended to avoid him, then yielded, letting him pull her tight against his chest. The bottom of his red beard brushed the top of her head, where the glossy dark hair was sleeked back into a bun.

With her nose pressed against Liam's body, Annie inhaled the familiar, beloved smell of him, the smell of male sweat and wool flannel and, on a deeper level, the fragrance of the stony soil he worked, permanently absorbed into his flesh.

Her voice muffled against his chest, she asked, "What way did you come home?" and immediately bit her lip.

"Same as I alluz do," he replied with the infinite patience of one who has been asked a question too many times. "Up the orchard road to Mason's top field, then 'cross Dalrymple's meadow."

"You didn't see any Indians? You didn't go near the rock?"

Liam laughed, a comforting earthquake of a laugh that rumbled out of his chest and into Annie's bones. "'Course not. I told you afore, I ain't scared of Injuns but I know better than to go near their sacred rock."

"That's good," Annie murmured.

But she knew her man. She knew Liam Murphy would not let anything dissuade him if he ever took it into his had to come home by way of Pine Hill. And he might just do it sometime, to prove he was not afraid.

As he sopped up the last of the stew with the last of Annie's buttermilk biscuits, Liam remarked, "Mason got a mighty fine lot o' hay outta his top field this year. He had a good barley crop too. Got the rain just right, and a dry spell for harvest. That man has all the luck. Wish I was him this year," he added wistfully.

Annie shook her head. "If everyone had to hang their troubles on a clothesline for the world to see, and you were told to pick one, you'd pick your own."

"Meanin' what?" Liam asked, amused as ever by his wife's sayings.

"Meaning Susan Mason told me in town last market day that her husband has a tumor in his belly Dr. Smith can't fix," Annie said. "She sat right there in her nice shiny new cut-under buggy, with me sitting waiting for you in our old spring wagon, and told me with tears in her eyes. So don't ever wish to change places with anyone else, Liam. You don't know what you might get."

When they lay in bed later, Liam's healthy snores shook the rope supports that held the ticking mattress. Annie lay open-eyed beside him, but it was not his snoring that kept her awake.

She was reproaching herself for mentioning the stone. If she kept on reminding him of it, sooner or later he would be perversely tempted.

"Keep your mouth shut, Annie Murphy," she whispered angrily to herself, drawing the patchwork quilt up under her chin. "You just keep your mouth shut."

But she was afraid she could not, any more than Liam could stop snoring.

15

In the morning, Liam went off to

help the Burbanks mend a section of their fence.

Johnny dutifully recited his letters for her, then

Annie set him to work sorting strips of rag to be

woven into rag

rugs. Each pile of strips was a different color, and he had to study the colors and match pale blue with dark blue, bright red with dull red. She gave Mary a sugar-tit and settled the little girl at a safe distance from the fire to play. Then she opened her book again.

Annie sat close to the window, letting the dull light of a grey autumn day fall across the page as she read: "During the long and distressing war with the Indians it required all the energy of the people of New Hampshire to save themselves from utter destruction. But the glad return of peace brought with it a desire to develop the resources of the infant state."

"Return of peace," Annie muttered to herself, glancing out the window to a stand of pitch pine beyond the house. Pitch pine was a valuable commodity; tar and turpentine were manufactured from such trees. But Conway people did not cut pitch pines. According to local legend they were protected by the Indians, who would be angry. The Indians supposedly made some sort of medicine from them.

Annie stared at the trees and thought of the income they could bring, an income that would enable her to enroll Johnny in one of the new academies springing up farther south. "Learning is power," had been one of Annie's father's axioms.

His words came back to her. She returned to the book. Perhaps within its pages she might find some sort of power to use against the persistent menace that—in spite of boasts to the contrary—continued to influence life in parts of New England.

She had intended to read the book straight through, as was her custom. Books were scarce and expensive and each one a joy to be savored and prolonged. But now she found herself skimming through the pages, looking for something . . . something . . .

Her eye was caught by an entry on page 172 and she stopped to read: "CONWAY, Carroll County." Annie's eyes danced. "That's us," she murmured to herself. "Right here in this book." She read on, learning that Conway was 72 miles from Concord, and the Saco River in this region was about 12 rods wide and an average of two feet deep, though it had been known to rise 27 feet, and in a few instances 30 feet, in 24 hours. The largest collections of water were Walker's Pond and Pequawkett Pond, the latter being 360 rods in circumference. Pine, Rattlesnake, and Green Hills were the most considerable elevations in the town, situated on the northeastern side of the river.

Then Annie tensed. She put her finger to the exact line and read more slowly, her lips shaping the words. "On the southern side of Pine Hill is a detached block of granite, or bowlder, which is probably the largest in the state—an immense fragment, but which doubtless owes its present position to some violent action of Nature."

There it is, she thought to herself. There's the rock.

But the Gazetteer gave no further information, none of the strange and bloodstained history of the stone.

Annie's shoulders slumped in disappointment. But she read on. "Considerable quantities of magnesia and fuller's earth have been found in various localities. The soil is interval, plain, and upland. The plain land, when well cultivated, produces crops of corn and rye. The upland is rocky and uneven, and to cultivate it with success requires long and patient labor."

Annie nodded. Indeed it does. A mn must be out from dawn till dusk, breaking his back with a mule and a plow and a sledge for the stones. And even then you can't be certain anything will grow. What if the spring is too cold or the summer too hot or the rains don't come? What if your crops survive, only to be destroyed before you can harvest them by an early frost or an early snow?

How did the Indians manage to do so well here? Annie wondered. They prospered effortlessly, compared to our endless labors. And they begrudge us the land still. This would be a good place if the soil was more fertile and the fields weren't full of stones and the forests didn't conceal lurking Indians.

"There are in this town 5 hotels, 10 stores, 1 lathe manufactory, and 1 paper mill," she read on. "The Congregational church was established here in 1778. The Baptist church was formed in 1796. There is also a society of Freewill Baptists.

"On the 1st of October, 1765, Daniel Foster obtained a grant of this township on condition that each grantee should pay a rent of one ear of Indian corn annually."

Annie shook her head. Daniel Foster's ancestor and namesake had been as tight with a penny as the current feed-store owner himself. One ear of Indian corn. Fine rent for a whole township.

"Number of legal voters in 1854, 458," the Gazetteer further informed her. "Value of lands, improved and unimproved, $171,597. Number of sheep, 1017. Domestic stock, 1660. Domestic horses, 267."

There ended the description of Conway. Annie gave a sarcastic snort. Five hotels, ten stores, and a paper mill sounded more impressive than it was. "It's easier to acquire a grand name than it is to keep freckles off it later," Annie said to herself. "People who read this book and come to Conway expecting to find a city are in for a shock."

She gazed out the window again, recalling how splendid the town had sounded when Liam described it to her during their courting days. But the hotel where they spent their honeymoon, which he had made sound like a palace, was cold and drafty and had one two-seated backhouse to accommodate all its patrons.

She had promised herself then that life would get better. She had dreams for herself and plans for the children she hoped to bear. "You'll have to push that young man of yours," her father had warned her. "Liam has a good heart, but he's too slow to catch snails."

Annie had pushed. She was still pushing. She urged Liam to consider new crops and new ways of planting them, she did her full share of farmwork and still found time to keep an immaculate house and braid bright rag rugs for the floors. She had persuaded her bemused husband to build an imposing pine bookcase for her growing collection of books.

She was not a woman to be intimidated by stony fields or lurking Indians. Or heathen idols disguised as boulders. No.

All at once, Annie was tired of worrying. She closed the book abruptly, stood up, and went to take her cloak from the peg.

"You, Johnny, mind your sister while I'm out. Keep her away from the hearth, and if she gets hungry give her a bit of buttered bread and some of that buttermilk."

Annie slung the cloak around her shoulders and gave a last look around her house, making sure everything was in order as she always did before going out the door.

"Where you goin', Ma?" the boy asked.

"I'm going to look a problem in the face, so I'll know it's not sneaking up behind my back. Now, you busy yourself counting the dried apples in those baskets while I'm gone. When I come home I expect you to tell me how many tens of apples we have."

The freckled lad nodded eagerly. He thought he was helping. Annie knew he was learning.

As she walked away from the cabin, she noticed the day was

relatively warm in spite of its overcast skies. "Almost like Indian summer," she remarked to herself. But the phrase brought a chill. It referred to a season of terror, the warm dry days that often followed harvest; days when hostile Indians swooped down to slaughter hapless farmers and steal their provisions.

"Such things wouldn't happen," Annie's father had firmly believed, "if the white men had tried to establish amicable relations with the Indians from the first. We treated them badly, though, so how could we expect them to respond except with savagery and hatred? Hatred is too often the result of knowing only one side of another person, Annie. Remember that, and be tolerant."

The only daughter of Jackson's only doctor, Annie had adored her father and taken his word as gospel. Then one spring day, two young men from the distant town of Conway arrived in the area to attend a wedding—and Annie met Liam Murphy and Ben Osgood. Within a year, she had left her father and Jackson behind.

How strange that such a trip, no more than a day's buggy ride, could make such a difference in one's life!

"Bad Injuns still come outta the forests to visit a big rock on Pine Hill," Foster's frowzy wife Tabitha had confided to Annie at her first Conway quilting bee. "They bow down to it like a heathen idol. Don't you never go near it, and when your children start to come, don't let them near it neither." She had dropped her voice to a whisper. *"That there rock eats babies."*

Annie had responded with a burst of disbelieving laughter, making an enemy of Tabitha Foster.

In the years since, however, Annie had realized just how thoroughly locals avoided the boulder on Pine Hill. In time an amorphous fear had begun to infect her, as if transmitted subliminally; fear of the rock she never saw, fear of the close-crowding forests, fear of the wind howling with an inhuman voice from atop distant, brooding Mount Washington.

In a way no one could express, Conway seemed haunted by some malign montane presence as the village of Jackson had never been, though Jackson was a remote community high in the mountains and Conway was a bustling farming town in the Saco River valley.

Annie had grown accustomed to the local paranoia, yet some part of her mind never ceased to question and resent it. Annie McDonnell Murphy had not been raised to be a fearful person.

On this grey autumn day she was at last marching resolutely to face what she perceived to be the source of the fear, and put it to rest. Her spine was ramrod straight with determination. She crossed two stubbled fields, climbed over a stile, then made her way along a meandering livestock trail winding through dense stands of brittle, dying sumac.

Pine Hill lay between the Murphy farmstead and Conway town. Deliberately avoiding the vicinity of the stone made the journey to and from town longer.

With the loving attention of one who is delighted by scenery, Annie had explored most of the area beyond the farm before her babies had started coming. But she had never visited Pine Hill. Still, she knew where it was: a short distance above the Portland road.

The path she was following disappeared in a trampled mire of dried mud and cow dung. She paused and cocked her head, relying on an inborn sense of direction that was her pride. "This way," she decided, and set off again, briskly, whistling to herself.

Right where she expected it, Pine Hill rose above her, its slope crested with a mane of dark pines. She climbed the north side, picking her way through briars, and looked down from the top.

The boulder waited below. Its identity was unmistakable.

Annie stared down at it, impressed in spite of herself. The solitary stone had a presence. It appeared to be as tall as two men and as big around as a very large haystack. She started down toward it. She had stopped whistling.

The closer she got, the bigger it looked.

The boulder was as dull as the sky. Its weathered surface was grey and harsh, though as Annie picked her way toward it through clumps of sumac, she thought she glimpsed a lightning streak of quartz or mica, glittering.

"Nothing to be afraid of," Annie said aloud in a no-nonsense voice. "Just a granite boulder, like the book says. New Hampshire's full of granite. What makes you special?"

But the question had been asked for the sake of hearing a human voice speak. Anyone, looking at that particular boulder, would think it was special.

The boulder stood in solitary splendor. No granite outcropping supported it. The earth at its base was beaten flat, devoid of rocks or even pebbles.

What had the Gazetteer said? ". . . doubtless owes its present position to some violent action of Nature."

Not God, no. Nature. "Heathen idol," Annie said scathingly. "God had nothing to do with you. Sitting there like Mount Washington itself, glowering at me. Ignorant savages might think you're special, but I know you're just a rock, and a rock can't do anything *but* sit."

Emboldened by her own words she ventured closer, until she was standing beside the stone. The nearer she got, the larger it seemed to be. The surface of the boulder was abraded and pitted like an incredibly ancient face, but it was clearly inanimate. Harmless. Just, as Annie said, a rock.

Her lips quirked at the corners. "If that isn't like Conway people," she remarked, as her father would have done. "Scared silly of a rock." She could almost feel Dr. McDonnell standing beside her, though he'd been dead for five years. She could almost hear his practical, no-nonsense scoffing at pagan superstition.

Her mother, however—her mother with her Donegal-blue eyes and her fey sensitivity, her mother who secretly put a bowl of milk outside the door on All Hallows' Eve, for the "good people"—her mother would not have scoffed at the stone. Her mother would have signed the Cross the moment she saw the thing, something older than Protestantism rising in her. She would have known the stone for what it was: angry, aware. Malign . . .

Annie gave herself a furious shake. "Foolish woman! Anyone would think I didn't have the sense the good Lord gave me. I'm as bad as the Conway people, believing wild stories." She glared at the boulder. "You're nothing but a rock. A great big ugly dead-forever rock. Now that I see you, I can stop worrying about you. Be shut of you. I can tell Liam to come home this way any time he pleases, he'll just be under our roof that much sooner." She fixed the stone with a determined look. "Indians indeed. For good measure, we might just cut that stand of pitch pine and make some money out of it!"

To emphasize her words she gave the stone a defiant slap.

When her palm touched the rock, a jolt went through her body from her head to her heels.

Annie reeled backward.

Dazed, she struggled to keep her balance. She threw up her

hands, palm outward, toward the rock, as if to ward off . . . A wave of force hit her like an invisible wind, and she found herself hurled through the air to fall heavily into a clump of sumac some yards from the boulder.

She lay facedown in the sumac, smelling its drying, dying dustiness. Lights were flashing behind her eyes.

I've been struck by lightning, was her first thought. But there was no storm. The day was characterized by a soft grey overcast like mountain mist sinking into the valleys.

Annie swallowed hard. If not lightning, what . . .

Then she heard, or felt through the earth, approaching footsteps. Someone was coming toward the rock from its southern side, climbing the gentle slope of Pine Hill, pushing his way through the undergrowth.

The clump of sumac and the boulder itself concealed Annie from whoever was approaching. She could hear him, though. She heard the masculine grunt with which he deposited some burden at the base of the stone.

"Selah," she heard Daniel Foster's voice say, enunciating the Indian word clearly. It was a word Annie knew. It was both a greeting and a term of respect.

There was a pause, then Foster's footsteps moved away again, back down the hill, toward Conway.

She had been shocked, perhaps injured. Surely any woman in such a circumstance would have called out for help to a man she knew. But Annie Murphy did not call out. She lay as still as she could, hardly daring to breathe for fear he might discover her. She could not have said why. But she waited until he was long gone before she cautiously gathered herself and got to her feet.

Emerging from the sumac, she felt herself for bruises or broken bones, but there were none. She had been stunned but not hurt.

Stunned by what?

She advanced a few wary feet toward the stone. Nothing happened. It was as inert as it had first appeared to be.

She did not want to go any closer, but she walked around it in a wide, wary circle, watching it every step of the way.

On the downhill side she found the burden Foster had put down there. A bulky bundle wrapped in burlap lay at the foot of the stone.

She started to reach toward it. Then she drew back. Her curiosity was not strong enough to make her go close to the stone again, not now, not with her body still bruised and tingling from whatever it had done to her.

It had done.

The stone did it, she thought, not wanting to believe.

Believing.

She stared at its weathered face. "But I meant you no harm," she heard herself say in an aggrieved voice like a little girl's.

The stone watched her.

She knew, now, that it was watching her.

Her feet began backing away.

When they had carried her beyond a certain point, she whirled around and ran for home.

She did not stop running until she had almost reached the porch of the cabin. Then she slowed, stopped, stood half bent over with her hands on her knees and her heart hammering against her ribs, trying to catch her breath.

I can't believe I ran away from a rock, she thought.

I can't believe that rock flung me through the air either.

But it did.

It did.

Annie straightened slowly and squared her shoulders. Let whoever . . . whatever . . . was watching, see that she was in control of herself again.

With steady tread, she mounted the porch and went into the cabin.

Johnny lay curled up on a rag rug in front of the fire, sound asleep.

But there was no sign of baby Mary.

Annie saw again the burlap-wrapped bundle at the foot of the boulder.

That there rock eats babies.

16

Tabitha Foster looked up eagerly

when her husband entered the feed store.

"Anything?" she asked.

"Nothing." He shook his head.

She came out

from behind the counter, wiping her hands on a none-too-clean apron. "Did you see anybody?"

"I told you. Nobody."

"But people keep askin'!"

"Don't you think I know that?" he snarled at her. "I'm doing all I can. If you think you can do better, you try it."

"Ah, no." She shrank back. "No, Dan'l, don't say that."

"Then shet your mouth and don't criticize me." He shrugged out of his heavy jacket and went to take Tabitha's place behind the counter. "Anyone come while I was out?" he asked her.

She stood timidly in the middle of the room, looking as if she would dodge behind the nearest barrel at any moment. "Only Zeb Bigelow."

"What'd he want?"

"Same as the rest of 'em. He wants to know how bad the winter's gonna be, should he be orderin' . . ."

"What'd you tell him?" Foster interrupted.

"To wait till you got back and ask you."

"You tell him where I'd gone?"

"'Course not!"

Foster sighed tiredly. "Long trip for nothing." He adjusted the suspenders that held up his heavy woolen trousers, then looked down, frowning. He stooped to brush bits of dead stem and leaf from his lower legs. "I'm tired, Tabby. Fetch me a cup of coffee."

She scampered away, relieved to be out of his immediate presence.

Foster sat staring into the dark shadows in the corner of the feed store. His thoughts were far away. He did not even notice when Tabitha came back and set a cup of steaming coffee down beside him.

"Here, Dan'l," she said, waiting for him to become aware of her and dismiss her. She did not like to be around him when he came back from the boulder. Trouble sat on him then like a blackbird on a fence.

Tabitha knew her husband feared and hated the Pine Hill boulder. All local people did. It was not merely a focus of superstition. A real and bloody history was attached to it.

When Daniel's and Tabitha's parents were small children,

growing up in the Foster and Gray households a mile from one another, local men had fought off a band of marauding Indians. They had chased the savages to Pine Hill and the great boulder. There the white men had killed the Indians, every one. And scalped them for good measure, some claimed.

It was common knowledge that ever since, vengeful descendants of those Indians lurked in the wilderness beyond the town, never forgetting, never forgiving. A danger even when most other Indians in New Hampshire were long since pacified. Sometimes, it was rumored, they even returned to their sacred stone on Pine Hill to conduct blasphemous heathen rites.

People did not talk about it very much, not openly, anyway. Only Daniel Foster had the courage to drive his chestnut mare and his buggy out to Pine Hill on a regular basis.

Conway, as everyone knew, was the Fosters' town. Always had been. Even the massacre that had taken place on Pine Hill was not sufficient to make a Foster give up what was his, something his father and grandfather had claimed before him: the right to visit the stone and have prophetic visions of the weather.

So Tabitha's husband made his trips to the boulder, and from time to time returned with valuable knowledge. But it cost him. It cost him dear.

Tabitha gazed sorrowfully at his withdrawn, haggard face, then went back upstairs, unable to bear his presence any longer. When he had been to Pine Hill it seemed as if he came back poisoned, she thought to herself.

Foster continued to stare into the shadows. The cup of coffee cooled unnoticed beside him.

Meanwhile, at the Murphy cabin Annie's shriek of horror had awakened her son abruptly. He sat up on the rag rug, knuckling his eyes. "Mama?" he said fuzzily.

"Where's the baby!"

"Baby?" The boy gazed vacantly around the room. Then awareness returned. "The baby. Oh! I got sleepy, so I took her cradle up into the loft where it's warm and put her in it up there. Even if she got outta the cradle I knew she wouldn't try to come down those steps and get too close to the fire. She cried a while, then she went to sleep. I guess I did too."

But Annie did not wait for the end of his explanation. She was already scrambling up the steep steps to the loft.

As Johnny had said, the loft was the warmest part of the house due to the nature of heat rising. And there was baby Mary, sleeping peacefully in her pine cradle.

Annie stood looking down at her, waiting for her heart to stop pounding. Now why, she asked herself, did I think . . . ?

That bundle. That bundle Daniel Foster left at the rock. It was the right size to hold a baby.

A cold finger of fear traced up her spine.

For the rest of the day, she could not make herself settle to any task. She could not even read. She paced the floor, picked up her sewing and put it down again, half swept the floor and then propped the broom in the corner. Every sound from outside brought her to the door, looking out anxiously.

When at last Liam returned she hugged him even harder than usual.

"I don't smell dinner cookin'," he complained.

Annie made an impatient gesture. "I'll start it in a minute but I have to talk to you first." She glanced around to make sure Johnny wasn't listening. "Liam, you've lived here all your life; do you know of any children, any babies, who've disappeared in Conway?"

"What are you talkin' about?"

"Babies. Have any just . . . disappeared?"

Liam scratched his head. He suspected Annie was going to have to scrub his scalp again with yellow soap. Nits were in his hair, he could feel them. "Ever' now an' then some child wanders off an' ain't never found," he said slowly, remembering. "They fall in the river. Or perhaps the Injuns gits 'em. It happens. Why?"

"What about babies? Babies like our Mary?"

"Mary's old enough to toddle. I reckon she could wander off iff'n you didn't watch after her so good. But you never leave her alone, so I'd say she's safe, Annie."

I don't dare tell him I left Mary alone today, Annie thought. And I'll never do it again!

But what about those other children? God help us, what about the other little ones who have disappeared over the years?

Every rural community, as Annie knew, had its share of disappearances. Liam was correct when he said children wandered off and were never found. It had happened in Jackson too. And perhaps Indians occasionally did steal an unwatched baby.

But . . . but . . .

Annie's mother had loved to tell stories. In her soft, low Irish voice, she had recounted the tales her grandmother told her: Donegal stories, filled with rebel princes and magical women who could assume the shapes of seals. And one tale that had never failed to give Annie a delicious tingle of fear.

Crom Cruach, the terrible pagan stone of Ireland to whom infants had been sacrificed before the coming of Christianity.

Were there such stones everywhere in the world? Annie wondered. Were they thrust up by some violent action of Nature to serve as its avatars? Nature. Pagan, pantheist, Nature.

The same Nature New England farmers struggled with every day of their lives, trying to wrest a living from the grudging land.

"What're you askin' about this fer now?" Liam was inquiring. "You seem all het up."

With a mighty effort, Annie laughed. "Just my never-ending curiosity," she replied. "Seems like I heard Charity Allen say something at the last quilting bee about some baby that had disappeared, and I got to wondering."

"I don't recall no baby disappearin'. 'Course, one coulda got lost way out in the country and we might never hear about it. Lotsa folks live in the hills and don't come inta town from one summer till the next. It's even a right smart journey for us," he added.

Annie had expected to be able to tell him he could cut distance off that journey. But she said nothing.

Tardily she busied herself preparing a meal. If Liam was surprised to find his wife uncharacteristically unprepared, he did not say so. He settled happily into his chair and watched her hips as she bent over her pots and saucepans at the hearth.

Might be she's gettin' fretful, he thought. Women are mysterious. They take all sorts of vapors. Might be a good idea for Annie to have another baby, give her something more to think about.

Liam smiled to himself, watching his wife's hips.

For several days, Annie never got beyond shouting distance of the cabin. She even moved the hen boxes from the barn to the dogtrot, so she could gather her eggs without being away from the baby more than a couple of minutes.

But the fear rankled her. At night, when Liam took her in his arms and pressed his mouth on hers, she tried to respond. But her thoughts kept skittering off. Even when he sucked her breast like a hungry baby, his crisp beard brushing her flesh in a way that had always heightened her pleasure, she could not totally surrender to him and forget everything else. Some part of her mind insisted on picturing the boulder on Pine Hill.

"What's wrong with you?" Liam finally asked one night. He had returned to earth from his usual thundering, cataclysmic climax, only to find Annie lying wide-eyed beneath him, not sharing. She who had always shared, whose sensuality was his greatest joy.

"Nothing's wrong with me," she said quickly.

But he knew there was.

It can't go on like this, Annie decided. She felt as if the stone had moved into their house and was lying between them like a rock in the bed. Its shadow seemed to fall over everything she did.

Then the first snowflakes fell. A scattering like freckles in buttermilk, but a precursor of the blizzards to come.

"Reckon I better get on inta town and talk to Dan'l," Liam announced the morning of that first snow. "Find out how deep it's gonna be and how long it's gonna last. Might want to lay up more vittles in the root cellar. Ain't too late to buy more apples an' turnips if we need 'em."

"Don't go to Foster!" Annie exclaimed without thinking.

"What?" Her husband stared at her. "Not go to Dan'l? What're you talkin' about?"

But she could not tell him. The complicated layers of imaginings in her mind could not be peeled apart and exposed like the layers of an onion. And without a satisfactory explanation to give, she refused to hang on to Liam irrationally like a whining woman. She had too much pride.

After he had gone, she berated herself. Surely there were ways she could have described what had happened to her, and how she felt about it, without sounding like a fool.

I have to go back to the rock, she thought. I have to know if I imagined all that. Perhaps I did. I'll know, when I see the rock again.

But she desperately wanted not to go.

"Character is the sum of the choices we make in life," had been one of her father's favorite axioms.

She would go, she knew it. She would make the choice and go, rather than cowering at home.

This time, however, she did not leave Mary in Johnny's care. She dressed both children warmly and took them in the opposite direction from the rock, across fields to the Baldwin farm which lay northwest of the Murphy property. She asked May Baldwin to keep the pair for the day.

"You goin' inta town, Annie? If you are, I'd 'preciate if you'd get me a quarter bolt a' calico."

"I'm not going into town."

"You ain't?" May's slack jaw showed her surprise. For what other reason would a woman leave her children in someone else's care? "You goin' visitin' downcountry, then?"

Annie nodded. "That's it, I'm going visiting downcountry. I'll be back afore dark and fetch the children. Obliged to you, May."

"Say nuthin'," the other woman responded automatically. She stood in her open doorway, listening to the crescendo of noise rising behind her in her cabin as the Murphy children joined into the daylong riot of the Baldwin seven. Her eyes followed Annie back down the path toward the Murphy farm.

"Somethin' not right about her today," May said to herself. "Seems like she's poorly, somehow."

But Annie was as strong as three cups of hastily drunk strong black coffee could make her. She had been tempted to take a swig from Liam's jug of hard cider, but decided against it. She might need all her wits about her.

The sky was white with unshed snow. It would start falling again soon, she knew, and not stop. Not stop until the drifts reached the eaves of the house and yard-long icicles hung from the porch roof. Not stop until people huddled inside their houses like a race besieged, listening to the wind howl from distant Mount Washington.

How long? How deep? How cold?

Daniel Foster knew.

How?

Did the stone do things to him, as it had to Annie?

She had to make herself keep going toward it. At every bend, she was tempted to turn and run back. When she climbed the stile between two fields she teetered at the top, a breath away from going back down the steps she had just come up.

But she was Henry McDonnell's daughter and she kept going.

At last she saw the grim grey stone on the slope of Pine Hill, waiting for her.

But this time the stone was not alone.

Daniel Foster glanced up guiltily when Annie Murphy materialized on the crest of the hill above him. "What're you doin' here?" he called out, knowing she could see him.

She hesitated before answering. She must be very careful. She could not simply turn and run away; that would make him very suspicious. But she was dismayed to discover him there, and more dismayed by the fact that he carried yet another burlap bundle.

Foster was equally astonished. No local had surprised him here in all the years he had visited the place.

Of course, Annie Murphy was not really a local. Perhaps that was why she had not been sufficiently intimidated by the legends that kept others away and allowed Foster sole use of the stone.

She angled down the slope toward him. "I have as much right to be here as you. This isn't your land."

"Ain't yours neither," he pointed out. "And folks don't usually come here nohow."

Annie assumed a wide-eyed innocence. "Oh? Why not?"

"You know. You've heard the stories."

"You mean the local superstitions? My father raised me to pay no mind to superstition." She did not add that her mother had been a most superstitious woman.

"Ain't superstition," Foster insisted. "S'truth. There's a lotta death happened at this rock. Band o' dirty savages was killed here when my pa was a boy. That's why the Injuns in these parts are still hostile. Conway men killed a pack of 'em here, same as some men down in Albany once killed an Injun chief called Chocurua. Chased ole Chocurua to the top of his tribe's sacred mountain and killed him dead," Foster added with relish.

"I know that story," Annie interjected. "Chocurua was a gentle man who'd done the white settlers no harm, but a band of hunters killed him for the sport of it. As he was dying he pronounced a curse on his killers and their descendants. That was long ago, but my father still used to go all the way to Albany to treat people down there. They suffered from a strange complaint of the abdomen that eventually killed them. He used to make a long journey down there in his buggy, once or twice a year. The malady intrigued him. But he refused to credit it to the curse of Chocorua."

"Then your pa wasn't as smart as he shoulda been."

Annie bristled. "He was the smartest man I ever knew! He would have been smart enough to wonder why you're here, Daniel Foster. And just what sort of offering you bring to this pagan stone!" she burst out, too incensed to guard her tongue.

Foster hugged the burlap bundle against his chest. "None o' your business," he said sharply.

There was a recklessness in Annie Murphy. Side by side with her studied sensibility was a wild recklessness that had once made her thrust her hand into Liam Murphy's trousers as they sat courting in her father's parlor. In all his life, Liam had never imagined a woman would do such a thing. Not a nice woman. He had caught fire from Annie's fingers.

Now the fire was in Annie. As always, it surfaced when she least expected it. This time it made her grab for the burlap bundle.

Shocked, Foster tried to fight her off. But her small body concealed a wiry strength he did not expect, and an agility abetted by desperation. She wrenched the burlap out of his grasp and dropped to her knees with the bundle cradled in her arms, almost at the foot of the boulder.

Before Foster could stop her, she unwrapped the package.

Then she sat back on her heels and stared.

17

"Maize?"

"Corn. Injun corn," Foster verified,

bending to rewrap the bundle.

"But . . . I don't understand . . ."

"'Course not. Ain't

none of your business." As Annie stared up at him, Foster tucked the end flaps of the burlap neatly under the lengthwise fold until the package was secure again. Then he carried it a step or two, and set it down against the base of the stone.

"Selah," he said.

Annie was still sitting on her heels, watching him in bewilderment. "You give corn? To a rock?"

"A bowl of milk to the good people, the fairies, to keep them from doing us harm," her mother had once explained. Her mind made the leap from milk to maize.

"I think I understand," she said slowly.

"No you don't. And like I told you, 'tain't none of your business."

"But it is. I mean, I thought . . ."

Foster's eyes narrowed. "What did you think?"

"I thought . . . your wife said the stone eats babies."

To her embarrassment, Daniel Foster laughed. "'Course she did! I tell her to say that, same as my ma said it, and her ma afore her. Keeps people away. But you thought . . ." He glanced at the burlap. It was Daniel Foster's turn to be shocked. "Lordy, you thought I was bringin' *babies* to this thing . . . ?"

Confounded, Annie dropped her eyes.

"Well, I never," the man muttered. "Is that all you think of me, Annie Murphy? And I've alluz had admiration for you, with your book learnin' and your hard work and all. Now I come to find out you think I steal babies and give them to the Injun rock."

"I'm sorry," Annie said in a strangled voice. "I don't know what got into me, thinking something like that. I don't know how to apologize." She had made a dreadful mistake, she knew. Daniel Foster was the most important man in Conway. Directly or indirectly, almost everyone depended on him in some way, including her Liam.

Conway Feed & Grain was the only such store within twenty miles. If he refused service to anyone, they were effectively ruined. And if Annie Murphy was any judge of character, Foster was mean enough to refuse service to someone who insulted him as badly as she had just done.

How am I going to explain this to Liam? she wondered, sitting there with her head down and mortification burning through her body.

Daniel Foster was equally uncomfortable. He had spoken the truth; he had always admired Annie Murphy. Every man in Conway admired Annie Murphy. She was a breath of fresh air, a bright and laughing spirit. A sharp tongue, but a light foot and a twinkling eye that a man could not help responding to. Foster was horrified to think she believed him capable of so monstrous a crime.

"Ain't necessary to apologize," he muttered. "I can see how you thought what you thought, I suppose."

"But if it isn't true . . . I mean, why the corn?"

"You've found out my secret," Foster admitted. "The weather. You alluz wanted to know, didn't you? Well, now you do."

"The weather?" Annie was baffled.

Leaving the burlap bundle where it was, Foster came back and sat down beside Annie on the cold ground. He did not feel the cold. It was a warming experience, sitting close to little Annie Murphy. From this distance he could see the way her dark hair pulled loose of its bun and clung in tiny tendrils to the pink shell-shape of her ear. For the pleasure of sitting beside her—alone in the country, far away from prying eyes and wagging tongues—he would trade his secret. For that pleasure and more, perhaps.

"It started with my grandfather's grandfather. He was granted the township in return for—"

"One ear of Indian corn annually!" Annie interrupted. "I read it in my Gazetteer."

"A-yuh, that's it. But it was a funny sort of rental. The corn was to be paid here, at the Injun rock. Brought here and left."

Annie raised her eyebrows. She was aware of Daniel Foster's intense gaze on her, but his words were more interesting. "Paid to the Indians, is that what you're saying? But I thought the rental was paid to the local authorities, or—"

"Paid to the true owners of the land," Foster said. "We took their land, y'see, and we give 'em their own back for it. It was somethin' worked out in Conway long ago, and as long as my family abided by it, the Injuns never attacked us the way they did other places. But then there come a day when we forgot or the man who was supposed to deliver the corn to the rock got waylaid, or somethin'. Nobody knows what. Anyway, the rental wasn't paid. And the Injuns come outta the forest and attacked the town.

"The men got muskets and drove 'em off, finally. Chased 'em all the way back to this rock. And killed 'em here. Legend has it that the redskins' blood splashed on this stone.

"After that there were no more Injun attacks, but people didn't forget about the corn rental again either. In fact, my grandfather started bringin' more than just one ear, to be sure. And one day, after he delivered the rental, he came back sayin' he knew what the weather was goin' to do. He warned of a great storm fixin' to blow in on us. He begged people to get all their stock into their barns and prepare themselves, though there wasn't a cloud in the sky at the time.

"And he was right, Annie. A terrible wind blew up. Took roofs off cabins, blew down the front of the hotel, did all kinds of damage. But no one was killed, 'cause he'd warned people to hide in their root cellars and the storm blew over 'em.

"After that, people started comin' to him reg'lar to learn what the weather was likely to do. They were willing to pay money for it, and he was willing to take their money. But afore he could give a prediction he alluz had to visit this rock, and he alluz had to bring a gift of Indian corn."

Annie's eyes were fixed on his face. They were as bright as two stars. "Well, I never," she breathed. "And you still do it. You come here and leave the corn, and then . . . then what? How do you learn about the weather? Do the Indians meet you here and tell you?"

"Mebbe I ain't willin' to say," he replied. "Man should keep some of his business to himself, if he's anyway smart."

But she had to know. How could she bear it if she didn't know?

"I won't tell anyone," she promised.

"What'll you give me for it?" he countered with heavyhanded playfulness.

There was no mistaking his intention. Annie stiffened. "My thanks," she said coolly. "And the gratitude of my husband, who, as you surely remember, is a very large and powerful man."

Foster understood well enough. Her sudden icy dignity, combined with the implied threat, meant he had got all he was going to get from her unless he forced her.

Had she been a different woman in a different setting, he might. But the proximity of the rock restrained him. Its presence, glowering over them, drained his audacity. The thing always had scared him, he thought resentfully. And not because of the wild stories Foster womenfolk circulated about it either.

The situation called for caution. Liam Murphy would beat any man to a pulp for molesting his wife. Foster did not want Annie carrying a tale back to her husband. He bargained with what he had. "If it'll make you happy," he said ruefully, "I'll tell you about the weather. But remember you promised not to let it go any further."

Annie nodded agreement. But she stood up and put a bit of distance between herself and him, just in case.

Foster observed without comment. "The Injuns held this rock sacred because they said it talked to them," he related. "It was part of the earth, which in their way of believing things was also part of the sky and the weather, everything all mixed together. I don't understand it, heathen gibberish. But they believed it for centuries. They came here to touch that rock and have visions. In those visions, they saw what the weather was going to be like, and they arranged their lives accordingly. Bad winter comin', they went south. Mild winter, they stayed put. That sorta thing.

"My grandfather discovered by accident that when he touched the stone he had visions too. Sometimes, not all the time. He was afraid to tell anybody, afraid he'd be accused o' witchcraft. So he passed the secret down only to his eldest son, my pa, and he passed it on to me."

Annie asked, "Is it witchcraft?"

Daniel Foster shook his head. "I'm no witch, Annie. I can't do no magic. All I can do—sometimes, like I said—is see a vision. Kinda cloudy and far away, hard to see, but when it comes to me it shows me . . . it's hard to explain. It just shows me. In return for the corn."

"The Indians don't tell you about the weather?" she asked, unsure what he was saying.

"Not the Injuns. It's the rock, their sacred rock. My pa figgered bein' able to see visions from the rock was something passed on in the blood. Like inheritin' a good singin' voice. He figgered mebbe it came easier to Injuns than to whites, but us Fosters had a little bit of it. The visions ain't clear, but we can see 'em. Sometimes."

"Did you see a vision the last time you came to the rock?"

Annie's question surprised him. "Ah . . . no. I laid my hand on the rock but I couldn't feel nothin'. Like it was empty, somehow."

"Empty? What did you expect to feel?"

"What there alluz is afore a vision comes. A sort o' hum. You can feel it more'n hear it."

"Can you feel it now?" Annie wanted to know.

"I ain't touched the rock yet. I was just fixin' to when you come over the hill."

Annie gave the man a penetrating look. She would have dismissed his tale as foolishness, had she not received a mighty jolt from that same boulder. "I don't believe a word of it," she said emphatically, knowing how he would respond. "You're storyin' me, Dan'l Foster."

"I am not!"

"Then show me. Show me now."

"I cain't do it with you here," he muttered.

"Why not? Are you afraid it won't work? Are you afraid I'll know it's a lie?" she taunted.

Beads of sweat formed on his forehead. "It ain't meant for any but the Foster men, it's our secret."

Your profitable secret, Annie thought to herself. Maybe it is witchcraft. A lie is a poor substitute for the truth, but it's the only one anybody's found so far. If it is witchcraft, of course you'd lie about it to save your skin.

Memories of witchcraft lingered in New England, even in enlightened 1855. Annie was not certain she believed in witches—there was too much of her father in her for that—but she was not certain she disbelieved either.

Her mother would have believed.

And there was *something*. That boulder had thrown Annie through the air as if she were a piece of chaff.

Annie had to know.

"You've told me so much already," she said to Foster, "you might as well show me the rest. I promised you I wouldn't tell, and I won't. My word is as good as my husband's. What is it you do, Dan'l? Do you put your hand on the stone like this . . ."

She reached out as if to touch the boulder, encouraging him. She had no intention of making actual contact, however. The memory of the last time she touched that rock was sharp within her.

But Foster did not know she was only pretending. The stone was his, his secret, his family heritage though dark and filled with mystery. He would not share. With an inarticulate cry, he grabbed for her hand to stop her from touching the boulder.

Foster's sudden move startled Annie, causing her to dodge to one side. She slightly lost her balance, and inadvertently put out a hand to save herself.

Her hand touched the stone.

Later, thinking back, she would be able to recall the very peculiar sensation she had felt in that fraction of a second before her skin made contact with the boulder's surface. This time there was no jolt, no shock. Instead, she had felt her hand being irresistibly drawn as if by a powerful magnetic force.

Then the world as she knew it disappeared.

18

She was in a high cold place.

Mountains rolled away from her. Peaks seemed

to be below her. She had a sense of vast distances,

as if she could gaze south to Massachusetts, east to

Maine, west to

Vermont . . . yet she could not gaze. She had no eyes.

She did not need eyes.

Her entire being was a sensory organ.

She was aware of weight, mass, heat, fragility, temperature, color—an incredible spectrum of unimaginable colors!—texture, movement, upheaval, solidity, somnolence, energy.

Her awareness was total and generally unresponsive. She observed. She partook.

But she could respond; she knew that.

If there was a threat, she could respond.

She observed the vast mountain chain sprawled around her. It was rather like lying on a bed, looking down along one's own body. But she knew it was not Annie Murphy's body. It was not even female. Gender had become an irrelevant abstraction.

Many things had become irrelevant. Others had acquired all-consuming importance.

She partook of the passage of time as if it were the workings of heart and lungs and intestines within the body; building, repairing, altering, tearing down, redesigning, replacing, removing, a constant process of change that was necessary because existence itself was a constant process of change. But change could be a positive, or negative, force.

With an effort beyond comprehension, the tiny, stubborn seed of Annie Murphy's individual consciousness resisted absorption and struggled to assert itself; struggled to question and know.

What is this?

What am I?

I am in a high cold place.

No.

I *am* a high cold place.

Yes.

Partly.

She redoubled her efforts. With senses that were not mortal senses, she reached out and explored. She could not see, hear, touch, taste, smell. Yet she saw wind. She heard ice. She touched light. She tasted energy. She smelled time.

She was the massive patriarch settlers had named Mount Washington, and simultaneously she was the granite boulder, the glacial erratic Indians had worshiped on Pine Hill. She was Mount

Katahdin and chunks of amethyst in the hills above Kearsarge and grains of sand in the bed of the Saco River.

She was earth, she was stone.

Positive and negative forces coursed through her being, forming a circuit between earth and sky, connecting with clouds, streaking the air with lightning, striking into the silt of eons like the finger of God touching Adam's clay and bringing forth life.

She saw the solar wind and felt its song.

The seasons were hers. She knew, intimately, snow and sun, wind and rain. The least flake of snow was important to her because in its minute way the snowflake, frozen child of Water, would have an incalculably small but irreversible impact.

Every drop of moisture brought change, adding its impetus to the rivers that carved and recarved the face of the planet, swelling the seas that gave birth to the glaciers and gnawed away the land.

Every wind that blew drifted sand, eroded rock, resculptured the surface. Made a difference. Was felt. Must be endured.

The entity in which Annie Murphy's consciousness was suspended was like a flayed giant. It had no layer of toughened skin to protect its raw nerve endings. Those nerve endings were bared afresh by every breeze and raindrop. Earth felt everything done to its body. The shifting of a single particle of soil was measured on the same scale as the shifting of the continental plates. Both affected the being of Earth.

Earth was aware and vulnerable. Every cell of its being was aware of its vulnerability to the forces that acted upon it.

Annie, linked with it, was aware.

The planet knew what winds would blow and what precipitation would fall. In its own self-interest, the massive totality of Earth was continually observing every weather pattern, assessing with the experience of eons what each change would mean for itself. Every change mattered. Every change altered the fabric of its existence.

Earth contained an instinct for survival proportionate to its mass.

That which was still Annie Murphy felt a thrill of terror. She realized she was somehow partaking of the consciousness of something infinitely larger than herself. At the same time, she also seemed to be trapped within various separate aspects of that entity. She was a mountain; she was a grain of sand.

Her terror mounted. In a few moments her identity must surely be stripped from her by sheer force. What had been Annie would be irretrievably fragmented, dispersed among a trillion particles of soil and stone. She would be lost in the ponderous indifference of a planet.

She knew the fear the dead might feel if their brains continued to function while their bodies disintegrated. The fear of being absorbed into the earth, made one with the darkness. Spinning away into infinity. Lost. Lost to life as she knew it. Lost forever.

She grew as cold as all the glaciers that had ever glittered beneath a polar sky. She was frozen with a fear no human could imagine, yet her consciousness had expanded enough to imagine it.

I am a cold high place, she thought with resounding horror. And I shall be here forever.

Then, bubbling up through her fear like a spring of bright water, came an unexpected wash of sympathy. She felt a huge and tender pity for the flayed giant that was so beautiful, and so vulnerable. The massive peak rearing its head through ice and thunder. The grain of sand, enduring.

This is my land, she thought.

My land.

Oh, my lovely land!

The nerve endings of her spirit intuitively recognized kinship. Her flesh had been nourished by this soil, ingested with the crops she had eaten. She was not separate from Earth. She was one with Earth.

Yes.

As she should be.

Yes.

And it was both terrible and good.

The boulder on Pine Hill had recognized in her the innate devotion to and sympathy for the land that characterized both the Irish and the Indian. The love of place in Annie Murphy had spoken to the stone, and the stone had answered.

Invisible lightning had flashed and a circuit had closed.

When she touched the boulder a second time it had welcomed her in.

Now she was Mount Washington, brooding above the clouds, whipped by gales no human could withstand. Glorying in its strength, grim in its endurance.

Now she was the boulder on Pine Hill, fearsome and holy . . .

19

"*Gawdamighty! Annie? Can you*

hear me? Gawdamighty! Miz Murphy? Miz Mur-

phy! Talk to me! Gawdamighty!"

Daniel Foster feverishly chafed Annie Murphy's

hands. She was

aware of him as from a great distance. He was a puny being, less than an ant, a thing of no importance, and he labored frantically over another thing of no importance.

Annie observed.

The boulder observed.

The woman's body lay prone on the beaten earth in front of the stone, with Daniel Foster crouching over her. His face was pale, his eyes were wild. He kept repeating "Gawdamighty!" like a prayer as he struggled to restore her to consciousness.

Annie/boulder observed with a vast indifference. Why would any being wish to spend a few flickers of eternity in a parcel of flesh, isolated from similar fleshly beings by a total lack of communal consciousness, doomed to pain and disease and a swift extinction?

Boulder/Annie watched and pondered these things.

Once Foster shot a glance at the stone. Fear frosted his face.

His efforts were pathetic, but the human impulse behind them touched that which had been Annie Murphy. He had meant her no harm. He was a greedy, penurious man who forced his wife to live above the store when he could have built her a fine frame house with a dozen rooms, if she wanted—but he was not an evil man. Just flawed. As all humans were flawed in their various ways.

As stone was flawed. Boulder knew about fissures and cracks that would break open under pressure. Boulder knew about fire and heat and crushing weight, bearing down, solidifying.

Annie's thoughts were merged with boulder's thoughts.

Foster felt her hands growing colder in spite of his rubbing. He sat her unresisting body up, head propped against his shoulder, and began gently slapping her face with is free hand. "Annie! Miz Murphy! Gawdamighty, your husband will skin me alive . . . Annie!"

The mention of Liam reached Annie in some far place. With an effort, she reached out. But it was very hard to break free of boulder. Boulder wanted to keep her, incorporate her heat and light into its cold self. Boulder remembered glaciers, and bitter, grinding cold. Boulder remembered being dragged over the earth by the ice until it formed a great gouge in the soil, like the trail left by a huge animal . . .

No!

Annie made a terrible effort and wrenched herself free. It felt as if every cell of her body was being torn from every other cell.

She screamed with pain and opened her eyes. "Liam!" she gasped.

Daniel Foster's pale face hovered over hers. "Thank Gawd," he breathed. "Are you all right? Talk to me, Miz Murphy."

She swallowed, then moistened her lips with her tongue. She tried to remember how to shape lips and tongue. But the only shape they would take was to make the name of Liam.

"We better get you home, Miz Murphy," Foster said anxiously. "Gawdamighty, I never meant this to happen. I told you not to touch that rock. Didn't I say that? You tell your husband I said that. You tell him I never meant you no harm. But you wouldn't lissen to me. You wouldn't lissen."

Annie fought with her vocal cords and finally managed to say, brokenly, "Not your . . . fault."

"Thank Gawd you admit that! Well, come on now, let's see if we can get you on your feet and to home. Can you stand up?"

"I . . . think so." She was beginning to feel a little more at home in her body. But it was a strange sensation. Her body was so small. And so liquid!

It had the gift of movement, however. Movement was wonderful, miraculous! Just to be able to lift one part of oneself from the earth by the action of bone and muscle . . .

Annie gave a delighted laugh. The laugh shocked Foster almost more than anything else. It seemed so out of place.

Maybe her mind was hurt! Who knows what might have happened to her? One minute she seemed perfectly all right, then the next minute she was lying flat on the ground, not even seeming to breathe, her body as rigid as stone.

He watched, baffled, as she experimented with walking, taking her first steps with all the uncertainty and joyful discovery of a baby.

One foot and then the next foot, Annie thought to herself. Lift them, move them! Move forward!

Her face was split with a grin.

Foster hovered at her shoulder. When she was sure of her balance she reached out one hand and pushed him away. "I can manage by myself."

"Are you sure? That was awful, Miz Murphy." Thinking fast he added. "Like you had some kinda fit or somethin'. Are you given to fits?"

With every beat of her heart, her thoughts were growing clearer. "No, Dan'l," she said firmly. "I don't have fits. Not ever. No one in my family has ever had fits. This was something else. You know that."

He cringed visibly. "I don't know what you're talkin' about."

"Yes you do." She frowned at him. "Now you stand aside, Dan'l. I can get home under my own power, thank you very much." She bit off her words precisely and forcibly.

"Are you sure? I mean, what're you gonna say to your husband?"

"Why should I say anything to him?" Annie replied coolly. She almost laughed again at the relief on his face.

But she knew she could not tell Liam about this. She could not tell anyone. It was impossible to describe. Besides, she could well be accused of witchcraft, the accusation Daniel Foster feared. What other explanation could there be?

But for the first time in her life, she was not curious. She no longer sought answers. Answers seemed . . . irrelevant.

Turning her back on Daniel Foster, she began climbing the hill toward home.

The boulder watched her go.

Daniel Foster watched her go.

Then he shook his head, slowly.

His most recent offering of Indian corn still lay by the stone. He slouched over to it and stared down. Then, warily, he reached out and touched the stone himself.

Nothing.

A cold rough surface.

No hum.

No pictures, however cloudy, in his head.

Nothing.

He was a skinny, angry man, standing on the side of a bleak November hill with his hand on a huge boulder.

He stood there a long time. Then with a grunt, he put his hand down by his side again and turned away, heading back toward Conway. He left the corn, however. Just in case.

He always left the corn.

And when he came back the next time, it was always gone.

Meanwhile, Annie made her way toward home. As she walked, her head kept filling with unbidden images. They swarmed around her like a cloud of blackflies. Sometimes she even raised a hand and brushed at her face as if to brush them away. But they returned, or some variant of them returned.

She saw clouds above . . . and below her. Heard wind change its course. Sensed ice pellets high above, ready to fall. At the same time she felt heat, cold, compression, erosion. Was aware of warm blood trickling over a stony surface. Sounds of screaming.

She shook her head again and brushed at her face. When she moved her hand away, she saw her dear, familiar cabin, just across the next field, and broke into a run.

When Liam Murphy returned home for his dinner he found his wife making biscuits. There was nothing unusual about what she was doing. As she did every day, she kneaded the soft dough, cut it into circles with a round tin cutter, dredged the circles in a little melted lard, arranged them two deep on the metal biscuit tray, and set them close to the fire.

"Someday," she had always said, "we'll have one of those big cast-iron stoves with ovens in it, like my mother's."

Liam paused in the door as he sometimes did, watching her work while she was still unaware of him. In a moment the draft from the open door would make the fire leap up and she would turn around, and smile, and come into his arms.

The fire leaped up but Annie did not turn around. She went on working as if her thoughts were a million miles away.

Johnny and little Mary hurried to their father, however. The boy clung to Liam's arm with unusual tenacity; the baby lifted her own chubby little arms in a plea to be picked up.

"I'm home, Annie," Liam announced, surprised she had not already come to him as well.

She glanced around with a start. For one heartbeat her face was blank, as if she did not know him.

Then the moment passed and she was in his arms too, the four of them joined in one big hug.

Yet throughout the meal, Liam could not help noticing the nervous way the children, particularly Johnny, kept glancing at their mother.

While Annie was busy with the washing-up, the boy approached his father. "Somepin's wrong with Mama," he said in a confidential tone. "Ever since she went visitin' this mornin'."

Liam called across the room to his wife. "Annie, you go visitin' this mornin'?"

"Not that I recall," she said, her voice muffled because her back was turned toward him.

"Tarnation, sugar, you can't go visitin' an' not recall! It's a right smart walk from here to anywhere."

Annie's shoulders shrugged dismissively.

Baffled, Liam turned back to his son. "What's wrong with your mama, Johnny?"

The boy shuffled his feet. "I dunno," was all he could say.

For the rest of the evening Liam kept a watchful eye on his wife. Most of the time she was herself, merry and bustling. But occasionally she seemed to stop, almost in mid-motion, as if she saw something. Or heard something. Then her eyes held a faraway look, and if he spoke to her, he had to repeat himself more loudly before she would answer.

"Are you feelin' poorly?" he asked several times. But Annie always insisted she felt fine. And she had not gone visiting. "I just took the children over to May Baldwin's for the day to give myself a little rest," she said.

The mere idea of Annie saying she needed a little rest was so foreign to her nature it worried Liam more than anything else.

That night in bed, when he reached for her, she felt as rigid as stone. "Annie?" he said anxiously.

She softened at once beneath his touch and snuggled against him in the old familiar way. Yet nagging doubts continued to gnaw at the back of his mind.

Something was wrong. Johnny knew it, even if he couldn't identify the problem. Even the baby knew. She would not stay on Annie's lap anymore, but insisted on getting down almost as soon as her mother picked her up.

Liam Murphy was not a particularly sensitive man, but his family was his world. The subtle disruption in the atmosphere troubled him.

He would have been more troubled had he known that, sometime before dawn, Annie had awakened beside him sweating with fear.

The dream that was not a dream had intruded upon her sleep and dragged her into another time and place. A cold high place. A peak—not Mount Washington, she realized instinctively—whose slopes were fragrant with dark pines. At the foot of the mountain was a crystalline lake that reflected the trees as if they were warriors gathered around its shores.

There were warriors.

No.

A warrior.

No.

A chief. A strong, noble man in his middle years, dressed in deerskins, with soft moccasins on his feet. Feet that knew every step of the way up the mountain. Running feet.

Pursued.

The Indian's breath rasped in his throat.

He paused once and looked back. The sun, low in the sky, cast bloody reflections on the still water of the lake. Between himself and the lake, hurrying up the slope after him, was a band of men carrying long rifles and shouting encouragingly to one another. "There he goes!" "Up there!" "Lookit him run, the old fool! After him now, git 'em afore he goes to ground!"

Chocorua's moccasined feet ran lightly up the slope toward the summit, hardly disturbing a grain of soil. The air was thin and sweet, like pure water. Nestled amid stony outcroppings were beds of emerald moss, soft as down, upon which a weary man could sleep. But he dared not stop. He ran on.

He left the moss and rocks behind and began the steeper climb to the utmost peak of the mountain. The earth knew his feet; they had made this trip many times before. Since his young manhood Chocurua had climbed the sacred mountain to sing his tribe's greeting to the rising sun.

Now the sun was dying in the west.

A gunshot rang out from down below, echoing and reechoing among the mountains. Then another, sharper, closer. Lead spang and spattered against stone a man's length from the running Indian.

They were playing with him. He was a sharp silhouette against the skyline above them, and the best shot among the hunters could easily have picked him off. But it was more fun to chase him and shoot close to him, keeping him moving, adding to his fear.

He heard their laughter below him.

Chocurua knew some of those men. He had sold them otter skins and beaver pelts, and made them welcome among his people as was the custom of his tribe. In hard winters, he had taken some of his own provisions to the white settlers, who seemed to have little gift for providing for themselves from the natural bounty around them.

On this day he had encountered the party of hunters by the lake, as he was stalking a deer. Although the chief of his tribe and a man with grandchildren, he was proud that he could still bring down a deer quicker than any man of his age.

But the deer he had chosen for his arrow had a fine set of antlers. The white hunters had seen it, too, and were in hot pursuit. They fired their guns but did not hit the deer and it bounded safely out of range. Then, seeing Chocurua, in their frustration they accused him of driving their quarry off on purpose.

When he protested his innocence they turned on him and attacked him in place of the deer.

They would kill him. He had no doubt. He had seen it in their eyes, hot with baffled bloodlust.

Knowing they would kill him, he had fled up the sacred mountain. Perhaps he might have eluded them if he had set off in a different direction, but he did not think so. They were young, some of them mere boys, and they had stamina and speed. So he had chosen to come to the summit to die; to give his life's blood to the mountain his people recognized as holy. It would be Chocurua's last and greatest gift to the spirits.

He could go no farther. The hunters were coming up behind him, shouting their triumph. At bay, he turned to face them. He lifted his head and began to sing.

The first shot slammed into his body. He staggered with the impact. He kept on singing. His voice rose through the clear air, chanting the song of the mountain.

The second shot hit him. It took all his strength to stay on his feet. He swayed, then felt the reassuring solidity of stone at his back. Gratefully, he let himself lean against the stone.

The song continued.

The hunters gathered around him in a circle, jeering. "Crazy old fool, stop that godawful racket!" one shouted at him.

The guns spoke.

His right foot was shattered. At the same moment a sheet of white-hot pain enveloped his left leg.

The hunters laughed. They meant to kill him by inches.

Chocurua had reached the end of the chant for the stone. According to custom, he should have begun again, singing through a precise number of repetitions. Instead he drew a deep breath and turned his head slowly, from one side to the other, so he could look each man in the eyes.

In a voice that did not quaver—with the stone at his back supporting him—Chocurua pronounced his curse. Upon his killers, their posterity, their habitations, and even their possessions.

Then he closed his eyes and, with a calm face, resumed the song of the mountain.

The shot that killed Chocurua blew his belly open.

Annie Murphy, in the dream that was not a dream, felt the impact of the shot that had passed through him as it thundered into the stone.

She felt his hot blood splashed across her face.

She screamed.

"Wha'? Wha'?" Liam sat up in bed, befuddled by sleep but already fumbling for the rifle he, like all farmers, kept within reach at night. There was always a chance of some predator attacking the stock.

Annie grabbed Liam and clung to him. She was shaking.

"What is it?" he asked more clearly. "Annie?"

"A nightmare," she mumbled. "Just a nightmare."

Liam was surprised. His wife was not given to having nightmares. In fact, if one asked him, he would have said she was the least fearful of women.

"What kinda nightmare, sugar?"

She shook her head and would not answer. What can I say? she thought. Can I tell him I became a rock and an Indian was shot against me?

Can I tell him how I became that rock?

Annie was an intelligent woman. She knew, in the year 1855, there were only two explanations. Madness, or witchcraft.

Neither was acceptable.

"It's fading already," she lied. "I don't remember. I s'pose I was just too tired, Liam. Lie back now, let's sleep. I'm all right, truly."

He lay down beside her again, but he was still troubled. There was something wrong with his wife, no doubt about it.

But what?

For the rest of the night, Annie fought off sleep. She was terrified of finding herself in another of the dreams that were not dreams. The memories of stone.

The morning came at last. She got up, red-eyed, the inside of her head feeling scraped out by weariness, and took the bellows from the hearth to blow life into the banked embers and build up the day's fire.

Liam was unusually reluctant to leave the house that morning. He kept finding small chores to do that enabled him to keep a watchful eye on Annie. Aware of this, she went out of her way to make everything appear normal. She kept her emotions under iron control and showed him a cheerful surface.

At last he had no option but to go out and tend the stock, fetch the water, chop the firewood.

Annie stood listening to the reassuring sound of his ax as he split logs in the barnyard.

She was surrounded with familiarity. The fire crackled merrily. The smell of good cooking permeated the cabin. Her children's playful chatter was peaceful music.

Everything was normal. She was Annie Murphy, flesh and blood and bone.

And stone.

It came upon her so suddenly she had no time to prepare. One moment she was reaching for the broom to sweep the floor, the next moment she was a slab of rock on the floor of a riverbed scoured by the sand the rushing water drove across her surface. She lay in cold and darkness as she had lain for centuries; as she might lie for centuries more. Or forever. Cold. Still.

She was back in the warm bright cabin, paralyzed with horror.

Johnny was tugging at her arm. "I ast can we have some buttermilk?" he said in a tone that told her he had already asked the question several times, to no avail.

With a guilty start, Annie recovered herself enough to pour out buttermilk for the children.

She was appalled to realize this could happen to her at any time, with no warning and no protection.

Was it a curse put on her by the stone?

If so, why?

What had she done?

She tried to think of her possible crimes, but could find none that would merit such a punishment.

Perhaps it wasn't meant to be a punishment.

Perhaps it was something that just . . . happened. Like the Fosters being able to touch the stone and predict the weather. Perhaps she, too, had a gift for communicating with the stone. With stones.

Just a thing that happened.

Suddenly she recalled a madman who had lived in the tiny village of Bartlett when she was a child. Her father had occasionally driven over to Bartlett to care for him when he injured himself. Annie remembered Dr. McDonnell saying at the dinner table the night after one of those visits, "It's like he lives in another world. Some of the time he's with us, some of the time he's simply somewhere else."

Was that man mad? Annie wondered now.

Or did he, like herself, truly have a terrible and unwanted access to a world beyond ordinary human senses?

She gazed in horror at her children. Foster had claimed the gift of dealing with the stone was passed down through his family. If so, would Annie's children inherit the curse that had befallen her?

Suddenly she grabbed up the baby, who had been happily playing at her feet, and pressed little Mary to her breast with such hungry urgency that the child began to cry.

"Mama, you're hurtin' Mary!" Johnny protested.

Annie quickly set the child down. "I was just hugging her," she said. She could not meet her son's worried eyes.

For the rest of the day, nothing untoward happened, to her vast relief. There were no more of the flashes of altered consciousness she dreaded. She could—almost—convince herself they might have been dreams.

Almost.

For the evening meal she decided to open one of the jars of preserves she had put up the preceding year. Preserves were stored in a cupboard in the dogtrot, where they would stay cool but were protected enough to keep from freezing. Annie loved opening the cupboard doors and looking at row upon row of glass-encased fruit, ruby and purple and amber, gleaming like the jewels of summer.

She chose a jar of sweet mountain blueberries, Liam's favorite, and took it back into the cabin. When she had pried up the disc of paraffin wax that sealed the jar, she held the preserves under her nose and took a deep sniff. Her senses flooded with memories of hot summer days shrill with cicadas, and long dark shadows sleeping under leafy trees.

"Mama!" Johnny, who had watched her alertly throughout the day, was scandalized. "You told us never to smell our food!"

Embarrassed, Annie put down the jar. She had felt an irresistible desire to enjoy a human memory. Stones could not appreciate the fragrance of blueberries; could not reminisce about sunny after-noons spent berrying with a small, freckled boy who put more fruit into his mouth than he ever put into his basket.

That was an Annie Murphy memory.

While she was preparing the boiled mutton and potatoes that would be their meal, Liam appeared in the doorway, clapping his mittenless hands together. "It's jus' startin' to get cold," he reported. "Been mild for a mighty long time now. Reckon we might not see snow till after Thanksgiving, for a change. Might be able to order a little less feed, make up for it with grazin'."

Annie turned toward him. Her eyes did not seem to see him, however. "No," she said in a strangely hollow voice. "Order the feed. Order extra."

"What're you sayin'?"

"The snow will start by the end of the week and not stop. Blizzard after blizzard."

"Where'd you hear that?"

She did not answer.

The next morning, Liam left his chores undone and went into Conway. His first stop was the feed store. Money was tight; he did not want to order extra feed if he did not need to, but he would spend the required fee to get advice from Daniel Foster.

Foster, however, refused him. "Cain't tell you, Liam," he said succinctly.

"Tarnation, Dan'l, cain't you give me some idea?"

"Nope." Foster's face was as closed as a spring trap.

"Why not?"

"Don't know," was the unhappy reply.

Daniel Foster had been giving that same reply to other farmers for days. By this time of year, he was usually able to make a surprisingly accurate prediction of the winter to come. But since Annie Murphy's first visit to the boulder on Pine Hill he had had no prophetic visions.

"Waal . . ." Liam Murphy drawled, rocking back on his heels, "reckon I better listen to Annie, then. She says we're gonna have one helluva blizzard afore the week's out. Then another and another, right on up to April with no letup at all, hardly. She says I oughta get all our feed and supplies in now, and I should order extra corn, bran for mash, blackstrap molasses . . ."

He went on, ticking off the list on his fingers while Foster listened with growing alarm. The feed-store owner was glad of the order, but dismayed to hear that Annie Murphy was now predicting the weather.

He had a dark suspicion as to how she was doing it.

Three days later a monster blizzard hit, well in advance of its usual season. By that time Liam had his stock in the barn, his loft crammed with feed, his firewood cut, additional flour and salt and thread purchased, carrots and turnips and potatoes snugly bedded in fresh hay in the root cellar, and was just doing a final check of the shingles on his roof when the first flurry began.

By the time he had come down off the roof and put his ladder away in the barn, the howling wind was so full of snow it was impossible to see more than a few feet. He returned to the cabin through the dogtrot and settled down in front of the fire with a sigh of satisfaction.

"Just made it, Annie. Thanks to you," he said. If she had been acting strange lately, it was forgiven and forgotten in the relief of the moment.

Other farmers were not so fortunate.

20

The exceptionally early blizzard

caught most people unprepared. Livestock was

trapped in the open and frozen. Great drifts blocked

roads. Supplies ran low. People huddled together in

snowy siege, measuring

the level of oil in their lamps and food in their larders and worrying.

At last the snow abated, but only briefly. During that period men hurried into Conway from outlying districts, telling harrowing tales of blizzard losses and clamoring for supplies.

An angry band descended upon the Conway Feed Store. "Why didn't you warn us, Dan'l?" they demanded to know. "Any time afore this, when there was a major storm a-comin', you've let us know."

"I didn't know myself, this time," Foster protested. But they were in no mood to be lenient.

"You've cost me!" Nathan Nesbitt accused. "You've cost me a heap o' money in dead livestock, Foster, and I won't forget it! Any other man wants to set up a feed store in this area, he'll get my business afore you!"

There was a mutter of agreement.

Grudgingly, the men placed feed orders with Foster against the winter to come. But he could feel the resentment in them. Three generations of Fosters had prophesied local weather with uncanny accuracy. Until now.

They would not trust Daniel Foster again. That source of income had suddenly dried up.

Yet Annie Murphy had known about the blizzard.

"Annie Murphy robbed me," Foster growled to his wife.

"How'd she do that?" Tabitha wondered. "She ain't even been in town since harvest."

"She robbed me," he repeated stubbornly. "And I ain't one to forget."

Yet how could he prove it? he asked himself. How, without revealing his own involvement, could he accuse Annie Murphy of knowing the weather through ungodly means? Any mention of witchcraft on her part would bring the same accusation down on himself.

Besides, he was not certain it was witchcraft. His father had told him, "It's a curse, boy. A curse on the Fosters for what my pa helped do to them Injuns. That there stone calls us out to it from time to time to remind us o' what we done, and at the same time it makes us see things we got no business seein'.

"But when a man is faced with two evils, he'd be a pure fool not to try to make a profit outta at least one of 'em," the elder Foster had concluded.

Throughout his manhood Daniel Foster had made a good profit, indeed, from the visions the stone caused. Now that profit looked like it was being taken from him by a woman from another place entirely, a woman with no claim to it at all that he could see!

He raged silently, wondering how to get his own back. His wife, noticing that his mouth had become a thin, hard line, avoided him. She knew her man. As Annie Murphy had said, Daniel Foster could be mean.

He had a whole long, hard winter to brood on his loss. The weather was too unrelentingly savage, the roads too badly drifted to allow him to go out to the boulder on Pine Hill. But once mud season set in with the melting of the snow, he would. He vowed to return to the stone every chance he got, until he caught Annie Murphy there, stealing from him. Stealing his visions. Then he would . . . he would . . .

He was not sure what he would do. He had the whole long winter to brood about it, though. And if he forgot for a moment someone was bound to come into the store and remind him. "You sure messed up this time, Dan'l," some man would say with the ill-concealed pleasure people take in pointing out the failings of others. "Lookit that snow out there. Heaviest since '45. And the earliest. How come you didn't know, Dan'l? Eh? How come you didn't know?"

Then his questioner would laugh a sly laugh at his obvious discomfort. And Foster would promise himself anew to be revenged somehow on Annie Murphy, when the snow finally melted and he could catch her sneaking out to the stone.

But Annie had no intention of ever returning to the boulder on Pine Hill. There was no need. From day to day, she knew what the weather was going to do before she opened her eyes in the morning. Her bones knew. The message was carried through them by the same energy that hummed through the granite of New Hampshire.

With the knowledge, came the visions.

Days might pass without one. Then, horrifically, just when she had begun to relax a little, she would find herself bonded with stone. With a mountain or a pebble or, occasionally, with the entire chain of the White Mountains themselves. In and of and with the mountains, her soul unwilling witness to geologic history.

"Annie's got very strange," a worried Liam at last confessed to his nearest neighbor, Ezekial Baldwin.

"How so?"

"She goes off, like. Into some sorta daze. Don't seem to hear me when I speak to her, don't seem to know what's goin' on for the longest time. Then all at once she's back."

"She's broody," Baldwin declared with the authority of a man who had sired seven children.

But though Liam watched Annie's waist hopefully, it showed no sign of thickening.

The long winter passed, punctuated by Christmas and New Year and the first eager references to sugaring-off. "When the sap rises," Daniel told Johnny, "we'll sugar-off."

The prospect was almost more exciting than Christmas. The boy remembered from former years the sound of metal tubes being banged into the sugar maples, the clank of buckets as they were carried around and suspended from the protruding metal, the slow drip of the running sap into the buckets, the incredibly sweet fragrance of the boiling sap. And best of all, the thrill of dropping a ladle full of hot sap onto unmelted snow and then eating the confection thus formed.

"When, Papa?" the child asked almost every day. "When is sugarin'-off gonna be?"

"Not yet, boy, not yet. Not till the thaw starts and the trees begin warmin' up."

"When will that be?"

"It's in God's hands," Liam said.

But Annie knew. She knew almost to the exact moment. Liam returned to the cabin from the barn one morning to have her meet him at the door, with one word on her lips.

"Thaw," she said.

"Not yet, Annie. It's fixin' to blow up another blizzard out there!"

She shook her head. "Thaw," she repeated.

The blizzard the sky had threatened never developed. A wind blew up the spine of the mountains, driving the clouds before it like strayed sheep. In the wake of the wind's passage the sun shone, the earth warmed.

Water dripped steadily from the melting icicles along the eaves.

It was the earliest thaw in a decade.

Liam looked at his wife with wonder in his eyes.

"Go into town as soon as the road's passable," Annie told him.

"Order your seed, you'll be able to plant. Mud season's not going to last long this year."

She could feel it; could feel the heat in the stone underlying New Hampshire, knew the snow would melt and run off and the earth would dry early, ready for the seed.

When Liam entered the Conway Feed Store a surprised Foster greeted him with, "Didn't 'spect to see you for a while yet, Murphy."

"Wanna order seed now," Liam replied. "Brought the wagon. Gonna be plantin' soon."

The men gathered around the potbellied stove laughed. "You're soft in the head," one told him. "It's way too soon, we'll be wadin' in mud a while yet."

"Nope. Annie says get ready to plant."

Foster did not laugh. He sold Liam the seed. There was something cold and angry behind his eyes, however.

The viscous New Hampshire mud firmed, and in that brief but glorious season between the mud and the coming of the black flies and mosquitoes, Liam Murphy planted his crops before anyone else. His harvest would be the first to market, commanding the best prices.

No one would laugh at him anymore.

"I reckon I'm gonna be able to build a reg'lar second story on this house, 'stead of just a sleepin' loft," Liam told Annie proudly. "Have us a coupla bedrooms up there. Mebbe even put a pump inside so you can have runnin' water indoors for your cookin'."

She smiled wanly. "That'll be nice."

"Nice! It's what I alluz meant to do, give you as good a house as your pa had in Jackson. Better, even. Give you the finest house in the Saco Valley, you'll see."

"That's nice," she said again.

She was not the same Annie. The change was deeply troubling to Liam. Yet the change included an uncanny ability to predict the weather, an ability that was worth more than gold to any farmer.

The Lord giveth and the Lord taketh away, Liam concluded.

He never suspected his wife of witchcraft. She was Annie.

It was high summer before she visited the boulder on Pine Hill again. She did not want to; would have given almost anything not to go. But Liam's crops were in the ground and the rains had not come. With the passing of months, her tormenting vision had faded. Sometime around midsummer she had ceased to be certain of the weather.

Liam stood on the porch of the cabin and gazed out at the sky. Hot, blue, shimmering. Cloudless.

"You reckon we're gonna have rain soon, Annie?" he called over his shoulder to his wife. It was a question he was asking with increasing urgency. The dirt was powder dry. Crops were visibly wilting.

Annie stood behind him in the doorway. "I don't know."

"You've known all year, why don't you know now?" He turned to look back at her. For the first time, he noticed streaks of silver in her dark hair.

"I just don't." Annie went back into the cabin.

Liam took Johnny to the fields with him that day. As soon as he was out of sight, Annie bundled up the baby and carried her to the Baldwins' farm. "I need her tended for a while," she told May Baldwin, who responded with a lifted eyebrow but a willing nod. Folks did for one another. Raising barns or tending babies, folks did for one another.

Annie set out for Pine Hill with a pounding heart. I can't let Liam down, she thought.

Perhaps the stone would speak to her again, and in the speaking renew its gift.

Or it might kill her. She accepted the possibility. Anything with so much power might kill her. The journey on which it sent her might be enough to stop her heart—or leave her trapped forever this time, inside stone.

Yet Annie went on.

The stone eats babies.

Daniel Foster had said that was a lie.

But the stone had claimed victims; Indian victims. As the mountain in Albany had claimed Chocurua.

Maybe the stone will want my blood this time, Annie thought.

She tried to make her feet stop walking. But they were on the path now. They walked on in spite of her.

Up the hill that sang with summer. Toward the crest, then down. Toward the stone.

It waited for her.

It had no choice. No particle of earth, whether loose sand or compacted rock, could move by itself. An outside agency was required.

So the Pine Hill boulder must wait as the earth itself waited, for the action of wind and fire and water, for lightning and glacier and earthquake.

For Annie.

Annie Murphy was a better conductor for its petrified thought than Foster men had ever been. The aura of her energy was strong and clear, easily used to forge a connection with other cells of the earth. Mountains, rocks, pebbles, sand. Annie's energy could link the whole.

The stone, solitary, waited.

Annie stopped a few yards short of its weathered face. "I'm here," she said aloud as if to announce her presence to a sentient being. A sovereign being, with the power of life and death.

The stone waited. It could do nothing else.

Step by reluctant step, Annie moved closer. "Help me," she said.

The stone had no comparable concept for "help." To help implied physical action.

The stone could only wait.

"I should have brought you something, shouldn't I?" Annie said, tardily realizing. "Corn, maybe. But we don't have any crops yet. Be a while. Maybe not at all, if we don't get the rain. I need to know about the rain."

She took a last step forward, until she was close enough to touch the stone if she merely reached out her hand.

"I need to know about the rain!" she pleaded.

"I knew you were doin' this!" cried a triumphant voice.

Daniel Foster came running toward her. His face was as black as thunder.

"Stealin'!" he shouted. "that's what it is, Annie Murphy. You're stealin' money outta my pocket! The stone don't talk to me no more. It talks to you. You gotta make it stop, you gotta make it talk to me again. You don't need them visions!"

He skidded to a stop beside her—careful not to touch the stone.

She tried to give him a blank look, but Annie was not good at dissembling. "My husband needs to know the weather same as any farmer," she said.

"Give my gift back to me and I'll do his predictin' for free," Foster offered.

She looked at him sadly. "I don't know how to give it back."

"But you sure knew how to steal it, didn't you?" he accused.

"Not on purpose. Swear to God, I didn't do it on purpose. It just came to me. I touched the rock, and it came to me."

"'Twarn't meant for you. It's mine!" Blood suffused Foster's face. The cords in his neck stood out strongly above the open collar of his blue shirt. Annie was afraid he meant to hit her. She took a step back, away from him, away from the boulder.

He followed like a cat stalking a bird. "You give back what you stole from me."

"How?" At that moment Annie would have gladly given him the gift—the curse. To be rid of it forever!

A slow smile curled Foster's lips, though it never reached his eyes. His eyes were like two chips of flint.

"You don't never come to this stone empty-handed, that's what my pa taught me," he said. "Alluz bring an offering for the stone. If you want somethin', you gotta give somethin'."

Annie glanced around. She saw no burlap bundle. "What did you bring this time?"

His smile widened. "I didn't bring anything. You did."

"I didn't . . ."

"Yes you did. You brought yourself."

A shudder ran through Annie's body. I knew this all along, she thought with horror. I knew the stone would want my blood.

Abruptly, Foster dodged to his left, trapping her between himself and the boulder. "Come to me, pretty Annie," he said softly. He held out his hand. "Come to me. You owe me a debt. You're gonna pay it. We alluz pay our debts in Conway."

He's mad! she thought with horror.

Foster reached for her. She shrank back against the boulder, expecting a lightning flash, a monstrous jolt, a moment of unbelievable pain . . .

Nothing happened.

Annie Murphy stood with her back pressed against the rough surface of the granite and stared at Daniel Foster.

He hesitated, vaguely surprised. The length of the woman's torso was pressed against the stone, yet she showed no reaction.

"Don't you feel anything?" he asked.

"No."

"No hum?"

"No."

"Don't you . . . see somethin'? Anything? Kinda murky, like? Like clouds gatherin', and a sense of the weather about to change . . . ?"

"No," Annie told him a third time.

His face tightened with anger. "The stone's gone dead to you too, has it? You've damaged it somehow, that's what you've done. Fool woman, interferin' where you didn't belong. Outsider. I shoulda known, I shoulda . . ."

What he should have done, Daniel Foster never said. As he spoke, he reached for Annie's shoulder, and the moment his fingers closed on her the words froze in his mouth. He stood like a pillar of stone, mouth gaping, eyes bugging from his head.

Annie felt something run through her like a mighty river. Her body was covered with instant gooseflesh as her hair stirred and lifted. Vision dimmed. Foster's face was replaced by a silvery shimmer that flickered like the outer limits of consciousness. A vast nausea swept through her, followed by a sensation of cold as hot as fire; of heat as cold as ice. A diamond-lit memory of hurtling through the space between the stars . . .

She came back to herself.

She stood beside the Pine Hill boulder. The smell of sun-baked stone was in her nostrils. She could hear wind soughing in the pines on the crest of the hill. Somewhere a bird sang three crisp, sweet notes, paused, then followed them with an elaborate trill.

Daniel Foster stood unmoving. His face was the color of ashes.

Annie's mouth opened. But when she spoke, the voice was not hers. She felt incorporeal fingers fumbling through her mind, selecting words that then were spoken by her lips with a ghastly hollow resonance, as if emerging from some deep cavern.

"We," said the voice. "We."

Annie and Foster both stood rooted, unable to do anything but listen.

"We are . . . earth," the voice went on, gathering strength and certainty. "We are earth. You are only . . . the eyes and ears of the earth. But . . . you are think . . . ing, thinking, the earth's thoughts."

The voice fell silent. The silence swelled, occupying all space, holding Annie and Foster at its center like prisoners in a bubble.

"You . . ."—more fumbling with concepts in Annie's mind— "you presume. You must not presume."

The voice ceased. Annie had a sense of vast dark spaces and intense compaction; flickering fires; unbearable compression, unborn explosion. Whatever had spoken seemed to be moving away from her. Before it was gone, its mystery unexplained, she tried to probe its intellect as it had probed hers, seeking some common experience or emotion. She felt resistance. She pressed harder. The fire of her mind burned through the resistance. Something opened to her.

You are thinking the earth's thoughts.

There was no love, no hate. The entity was incapable of either, as neither was required for its survival. Likewise, it had no understanding of birth and death as humans understood those things.

But it did have a sense of justice. In the vast planetary scale all things must be kept in balance.

The entity was aware of construction and destruction. Of exhaustion and replenishment.

Of give and take.

It took. It gave accordingly, in kind, as it perceived with its nonhuman intellect.

What it gave might be accepted by humans as a gift or a curse, a bounty or a famine. But on the earth's scale, it was always a matter of maintaining the balance.

The earth did not care how humans were affected. They were specks on its surface, apparently unable to make a lasting impression.

Or could they?

Annie was dimly aware of some ancient memory, old even by the standards of the entity. Creatures, specks, long ago, striving, achieving, changing things . . . erecting crystalline forms that were . . . cities? Then catastrophe.

No. The idea was too far back, she could not grasp it. The

thoughts of the entity were slipping away from her altogether. She made a final effort to hold on. But all her focused curiosity could not prevail against the vast shifting of thought that was like a slipping of giant plates beneath the earth's unstable crust. The slightest echo of that shifting was enough to throw Annie to her knees, the link broken.

For a few moments her mind would not work at all. She was a body and nothing more. The heart beat, the lungs worked, but there was no conscious process to direct anything else.

She came to very slowly. Her eyeballs were painfully dry. She had not blinked for a long time. She was on her hands and knees, her vision fixed on the ground some eighteen inches from her eyes. The earth was beaten flat by generations of feet, but seen so close up it had a variety of textures. Annie was looking at individual grains of soil, minute threads of plant life, a tiny scurrying of black ants emerging from one hole and disappearing into another, a few crushed twigs, a pearly sliver of fossilized shell from some remotely distant past.

She blinked.

Her eyes watered profusely.

She swallowed, forcing saliva down her parched throat. With an effort, she lifted her head and looked around.

Daniel Foster was still standing in front of her, his own expression slowly clearing.

"Are you all right?" she said with a rusty voice that was at least her own.

The feed-store owner looked down at her in astonishment. "What you doin' here, Miz Murphy?"

"Don't you remember?"

He shook his head. "I don't remember nothin' since I got up this mornin'. Nothin'!" he repeated wonderingly.

He stared at the woman. She didn't look the same, somehow. He tried to remember how she should look, but his thoughts were cobwebbed.

Annie stood up. She was as stiff and sore as if she had been on hands and knees for hours. When she glanced at the sky and saw how far the sun had traveled, she gave a gasp of disbelief.

"I have to get home!" she cried. "I have to collect the baby and start dinner!"

Being able to say those words brought a peculiar relief to her, as if she were painting an image of normalcy over a window that opened onto an appalling vista.

Foster nodded, beginning to shift his weight from one foot to the other, trying to loosen locked joints. "A-yuh. You do that, Miz Murphy. I gotta get back to town myself. Cain't figger out what I'm doin' way out here anyway. Was I s'posed to go to Portland today? Where'd I leave my horse and buggy?" He turned and looked vaguely toward the road.

Annie glimpsed Foster's chestnut mare tied to a tree in the distance, waiting patiently in the shafts.

But there would be no buggy ride for her. She must walk across fields, and she would have to hurry if she was to be home before Liam and Johnny returned from the day's work, their bellies growling.

Wearing a baffled expression, Foster bade Annie goodbye and started toward the road. The blank in his mind was worrisome. But the more he tried to remember, the more solid his mental fog became. His brain was like a child's slate, wiped clean with one swipe of the cloth.

Everything pertaining to the boulder on Pine Hill was gone.

Annie could feel her own memories fading. She was aware that she had made a giant leap of understanding, but it was going from her as swiftly as the details of a dream fade with the coming of morning.

If I could tell it to Liam right now, maybe I could remember, she thought.

But Liam was not there. And Daniel Foster was hurrying away as if the hounds of hell were after him.

Annie circled around the boulder and began climbing the gentle slope of Pine Hill. Halfway to the top, she turned and looked back at the stone.

I wonder if it's lonely, she thought with a strange stir of sympathy.

No. Stones can't feel things like that.

Stones can't feel.

But they think. They are aware.

With an uncontrollable shudder she hurried on up the hill and through the pines, then began running for home.

I have to get home before it rains, she thought.

She ran under a blazing blue sky.

But by the time she was breathlessly mounting the Baldwins' porch to collect baby Mary, the first fat raindrops were splattering on the dry earth.

The creak of the porch floorboards brought May Baldwin to the door with Mary in her arms. Her jaw gaped open when she saw Annie.

"Lordy," she breathed.

Annie thought she was astonished by the rain.

"Much obliged," Annie said, taking the baby from the other woman's arms and turning quickly. "Gotta run or we'll get drenched," she called over her shoulder. "Much obliged, May!"

She sprang from the porch and pelted off toward the Murphy homestead.

May Baldwin stared after her in stunned disbelief.

Mary screamed and writhed in her mother's arms, making it hard to run. "Hush up now," Annie panted. "I know I scared you, grabbin' you like that, but we gotta hurry."

The baby kept on screaming.

When she reached the cabin, Annie let out a sigh of relief. As soon as she was inside she closed the door against the rising wind, and looked anxiously toward the banked fire. There was still a glow of coals; it would blaze up quickly once she got the bellows after it.

She set Mary down and the child, still screaming, scuttled away from her.

"Hush up, now!" Annie repeated. "A person would think you don't know your own mama!"

She busied herself with the fire, keeping one eye on the obviously distraught child. Raindrops were setting up a steady barrage on the roof. "Going to be a good soaking rain," Annie announced with satisfaction to the room at large. "Last all day and all night, most of tomorrow."

She could not say how she knew. It was in her bones, like her sense of direction.

The baby cried herself into a violent case of hiccups. Only then did she allow her mother to pick her up. Annie paced up and down the cabin floor, holding the child and crooning to her.

From time to time the child turned wondering eyes on her mother's face.

At last Annie put her down in the almost-outgrown cradle. For once Mary did not complain. She snuggled down gratefully as if returning to the security of the womb.

Annie busied herself preparing a meal. She went into the barn and used Liam's grindstone to put a fresh edge on her household ax. Then she went out into the yard and caught a hen that had grown too old to lay. She swiftly beheaded the bird, plucked and cleaned it, and had it in the pot in a matter of minutes. She was soon floured to the elbows as she made dumplings to go with the chicken.

"Sweet corn would be good with this," she decided. "And some green tomatoes, sliced thin and fried the way Liam likes them."

She whistled softly to herself as she worked. From the depths of the cradle Mary could not see her mother, but she heard the familiar, comforting sound, and relaxed. By the time her father and brother came home she was fast asleep.

Annie was putting the final touches on the meal. When she heard the thud of familiar footsteps on the porch, she called out, "There's dry towels there by the door. You men dry yourselves off before you come in my house, hear?"

The door creaked on its hinges. Annie turned around with a smile to welcome her menfolk.

There was a gasp of total horror.

Liam Murphy dropped the armload of firewood he was carrying in from the porch. The split logs fell to the floor with a clatter. At once Mary screamed from her cradle.

"What's wrong with you?" Annie demanded of Liam. "Listen to that, you've woken the baby when I just got her to sleep a while ago!"

Then she realized that both her husband and son were staring at her as if they had never seen her before. Johnny shrank back, putting his father's bulk between himself and his mother.

"What's wrong with you?" Annie asked again.

In a strangled voice, Liam replied, "What's wrong with *you?*"

"What do you mean?"

"Come over to the mirror, Annie." He took hold of her arm and led her across the room to her mother's oval mahogany-framed mirror, hanging in a place of honor between the two front windows.

"Look," Liam said.

Annie looked.

The rainy light coming through the windows fell softly on her face. But even its gentleness could not soften the image reflected in the mirror.

Bright, merry Annie Murphy was gone. In her place was a woman with the seamed and fissured face of a person twice her age. The eyes were ageless, and haunted.

Instead of sleek dark hair, the face peered from beneath hair as snowy as the peaks for which the White Mountains were named.

Annie's mind struggled to reconcile what she had expected to see with what she was actually seeing.

She raised a trembling hand to her head.

The figure in the glass did the same.

"My hair's gone white," Annie said in a disbelieving whisper. She turned toward Liam, seeking some sort of reassurance. "What happened?"

He could only stare at her. "I don't know! Don't you know? Good God almighty, woman, don't you know?"

Annie swung her incredulous gaze back to the mirror.

Her eyes locked with the haunted eyes in the glass.

In one dizzying moment she was sucked out of herself and plunged into a whirling vortex that spun her among a kaleidoscope of images. Incredible heat, the universe exploding, incredible cold, a sense of vast space, spinning, slowing, cooling, an infinity of time passing. A wrenching upheaval. Destruction, reformation. Great sheets of ice, grinding inexorably. Warming, melting. A swarm of motion on the surface. Crystalline shapes rising in clusters to sparkle in the sun.

Then cataclysm. Change.

Ice melting, seas rising. More motion, other construction. Volcanoes erupting like giant pustules. Lava flowing, seas boiling. Cataclysm. Change.

Faces! Faces that seemed to surface from somewhere deep inside Annie herself and imprint themselves over the images spinning past.

She saw, for one clear moment, a large tawny woman holding a seashell against a misty green background. Then she was gone. Countless other faces sped past, blurring. Hundreds, thousands.

Then another figure etched itself sharply on Annie's awareness. She saw a slim bronzed man with an abnormally small waist and almond-shaped, tilted eyes. He stood on the brink of a flaming abyss.

She wanted to shout a warning to him, but before she could he turned away, only to reappear against the misty green backdrop that had framed the tawny woman. Then he faded and was gone, to be replaced by another succession of figures rushing by in a measureless stream. Men, women. Faces. Faces with features Annie began to recognize. One had a familiar width of browbone. Another had a certain set to the shoulders. A third had, like herself, tilted eyes.

Family features, developing over the centuries.

Intuitively Annie understood. She was seeing connections. The people she was glimpsing as they were swept along by the river of time were her people. She was as much a part of them as sand and pebbles and boulders were part of the mountains.

The mountains! Suddenly they rose triumphant in her vision, brushing all else aside. Mount Washington, Mount Katahdin, Chocurua's mountain; vast and massive ranges whose names she did not know. The mighty mountains, enduring. Witnesses to the antediluvian past and the unimaginable future. Time viewed from the mountaintops. Eternity in stone.

"Some people worship mountains," Annie heard herself murmur in a faraway voice. "Some people see no difference between mountains and God."

Then she fainted in Liam's arms.

It was the first and only time in her life that Annie Murphy fainted.

Eight months later, when the Murphys' second son was born, people attributed the startling change in her to her pregnancy.

"Takes some women like that," Nellie Smith confided at the church's box supper. Nellie's husband was the local doctor. "My Zebediah says being in the family way changes a woman's whole system."

May Baldwin disagreed. "Not like that, it don't. It don't turn a woman's hair pure white between sunup and sundown."

"I don't think this is a proper conversation for a church social," Felicity Osgood said primly, pretending she was not listening avidly.

Ignoring her, Nellie went on, "Miz Murphy's doing fine now, my husband says. She's back on her feet and taking up her chores. Her hair's still white, but when he was out there the other day he said her wrinkles were softening. Nursing a baby softens a woman, you know. It was just such a big strong baby that having it was a shock to her body."

"I should think so!" Agatha Dalrymple exclaimed. "Having a sixteen-pound baby would be a shock to any woman!"

The Widow Mason giggled. "I alluz knew that Liam Murphy was a strappin' big man."

The others, except for Felicity Osgood, laughed outright.

Tabitha Foster commented, "The Murphys are gonna need a lot o' strong sons, the way things are goin' out to their place. That farm used to be piss poor, you know. Then last autumn Liam Murphy brought in the biggest harvest in these parts, and he's doubled his order for spring seed. Seems like he cain't put a foot wrong."

May Baldwin agreed. "That's true. He's alluz ahead o' the weather these days. How you reckon' he does that, Tabitha, when your husband ain't sellin' weather predictions no more?"

The question was asked with gleeful malice, as all present understood. Tabitha Foster kept her burning face lowered to her sewing as she replied in a low voice, "Don't know. Just lucky, I guess."

The others resumed their gossip. According to Elizabeth Wheeler, whose husband Matt owned the hardware store, "Liam Murphy's ordered a special new indoor pump all the way from Concord, to put by Annie's sink. Reckon there's gonna be more celebratin' when that comes."

"Take more than a new pump or a new baby to make a woman get over havin' her hair go white," Susan Mason said.

May Baldwin gathered spittle in her mouth and licked the ends of the thread she was trying to push through the eye of her needle. "I'd be right happy to see Annie perk up a mite," she told the others, when the thread was safely through. "She alluz used to be whistlin' or singin'. Sometimes when the wind was right we could even hear her over to our place. But ever since last summer—long afore she got big with that baby—she's gone quiet. Turned in on herself, like."

The other women continued sewing without comment.

Tabitha Foster did not think to remark that her husband's demeanor had changed at about the same time, as if some burden had been lifted from his shoulders.

The two had no connection in her mind.

Everything that is, is alive.

Life did not come into this world. The life forms of the earth are a natural product of the earth, as the living planet is a natural product of the living universe.

Life in any form is part of life in every form. One, indivisible. The terrestrial spark is connected to the most distant star, just as the collective consciousness of the earth is one cell in the infinitely greater creative intelligence of the universe.

It is said, no one can know the mind of God.

Yet we are the mind of God.

And so we dance for joy.

We dance to the music of life, which ripples and shimmers across the universe. Even in the coldest depths of space, something is dancing the dance. Something is part of the music.

Every molecule of air on earth has its part to play in the whole. Myriad life forms dance in what appears, to human eyes, to be empty air.

Air is not empty.

Air is alive.

The angels of the air sing the songs of the spheres.

21

A hot wind was blowing the White

People away. In the gathering silence, the Real

People met to dance the Ghost Dance and their dead

came alive again. Their land was repeopled

by ghosts.

One of the ghosts was George Clement Burningfeather, who went to the reservation because he had no better place to go.

Throughout his life George had been suspended between two worlds. His name was indicative of his dilemma. His mother liked to claim that her paternal ancestors came over on the Mayflower, which was a lie. The Clements had been in New England for generations, however, as had her maternal ancestors, the Murphys. George's mother didn't talk about the Murphys very much. They were hard-working Irish farm folk and not suitably patrician from her point of view.

George's father was also a New Englander, but of considerably older stock. He was a relict of the all-but-extinguished tribe of Pennacook Indians, and when he had had too much to drink he claimed to be a prince of the tribe.

When she had had too much to drink at a cocktail party in Boston, Samantha Clement met him and believed him.

She thought he was exotic, and was soon showing him off to her friends in Manchester and Concord, expounding on the romance and hinting at the virility of the noble savage.

In point of fact, Harry Burningfeather was neither noble nor savage, and once his virility was blunted by familiarity, he tired of the white woman who had seduced him into marriage. He skipped out for parts unknown, leaving her pregnant with George.

Although the birth certificate said Burningfeather, Samantha raised her son to be George Clement. Period. She reverted to her maiden name and stripped the house of anything that could possibly remind her of her Indian interlude.

Except George.

Who had a questioning mind.

One look in a mirror was enough to assure the boy that his Amerindian features came from somewhere other than Mayflower stock. When he started going to school, other children who had listened to their parents' gossip were happy to tell him about his origins.

He came home crying, dirt-smeared, with a bloody nose and a black eye, and vehemently informed his mother, "I'm George Burningfeather and you shoulda told me!"

Samantha tried to spank it out of him. But there was a stubborn streak in the boy. The more she spanked, the more Indian he became. When her back was turned he sneaked into her room and used her lipstick to streak his face with warpaint.

From that point on, there was war between Samantha and her son. She provided him with a good education, smart clothes, a decent secondhand car when he entered college, and an icy reception whenever he was foolish enough to appear at home with his father's features stamped on his face.

Inevitably, he escaped as soon as he could.

George Clement Burningfeather attempted to escape to the stars.

Metaphorically speaking.

But by the time George graduated, the space program as such had run out of impulsion. With NASA as his goal, George had acquired a thorough grounding in the sciences, but no one was sending manned missions into space anymore. There were too many problems demanding attention on earth.

George had to settle for being an earthbound meteorologist, his only extraterrestrial explorations taking place among the wind currents and isobars in the atmosphere. His job was to try to figure out why the climate was going belly-up. Metaphorically speaking.

"We'll lick this thing, of course," his immediate superior assured him. George hated that term. It implied that he was T. Dosterschill's immediate inferior, which he was not. Except on payday.

"There's nothing science can't accomplish," Dosterschill frequently insisted with a bland arrogance that set George's teeth on edge. "Improved recycling techniques, improved substitutes for toxic chemicals. We'll get a handle on this. We have to. No one's willing to give up the way of life technology's made possible. Hell, I don't intend to start keeping my beer cold in a wooden icebox with a cake of ice either, know what I mean?"

George knew what he meant. What George did not know was how to make mankind's tardy efforts have any meaningful impact on a problem that was rapidly escalating. Recycling was not enough. Neither was cloud seeding nor improved methods of nuclear-waste disposal nor writing endless papers on the Greenhouse Effect.

Nothing science could do made an appreciable difference.

When the question was of academic interest only and there were very few academics left to ponder it, George went to the reservation.

It wasn't a Pennacook reservation. There weren't enough Pennacooks left to need one. It was simply the nearest Indian reservation George could discover through a cursory search in the deserted library, but it would do.

"Fuck you, Dosterschill," he said the day he hung up his identity badge for the last time in the echoing locker room. Dosterschill wasn't there to hear him. He had been one of the earliest casualties in their particular department.

The two black men, Hill and Webber, were still there, as was scrawny little Gerry Gomez, the one they called Whitesox. A couple of the women too—Mary Antonini and the blond with the long legs, the one the guys never believed was a natural blond. She was still at her desk when George walked for the last time toward the big glass double doors. "I won't be back," he called to her over his shoulder.

"Have a nice day," she said. The words sounded foolish but there was nothing else to say.

Given all the electronic information available, finding a reservation had been easy. Finding a bus that was still running in that direction was the hard part.

Finding any public transportation at all had become very hard indeed. But George didn't want to drive a car. He felt it would be curiously inappropriate to take a car with him in his flight to his chosen world.

All his life, George had had a strong sense of what was appropriate.

The bus rattled down an empty superhighway between expanses of parched earth. Heat waves shimmered on the pavement ahead. When George boarded the bus, there were two other passengers, but they soon got off. George moved up to sit behind the driver and stared over his shoulder at the mirages. If the driver saw them, he didn't say.

He didn't say much of anything, though George tried several times to start a conversation. At last the bus driver growled, "Look, fella, you got your troubles and I got mine, okay? I don't wanna hear yours, and I don't wanna talk about mine."

What happened to the friendly, courteous driver on the TV ads? George wondered.

For that matter, what happened to TV?

Not enough people around to produce television anymore. Not enough people to watch it, either, or buy the products it tried to cram down their throats, the glossy, elaborately packaged, outrageously trivial necessities that people had come to believe they could not live without.

Gone with the wind, George thought. The few of us who remain don't need the tube anymore.

The few who remain. Myself and the bus driver.

The great empty yawned beyond the smeared windows of the bus.

At last the vehicle shuddered to a halt. "Your stop," the driver said.

Shouldering his duffel bag, George got out. He hadn't brought much with him. A closetful of suits he would never need again had been left behind, along with the stereo and the CD and a superb collection of jazz. And an avalanche of polyethylene grocery sacks trapped between the refrigerator and the wall.

In George's duffel bag were two pair of clean jeans, T-shirts, socks, underwear, a Levi's jacket, a pair of cutoffs, a canteen, a compass from L. L. Bean, a Swiss army knife, matches, a dog-eared copy of *The Martian Chronicles* and another of *Tomorrow the Stars*, a small cache of emergency rations, a flashlight with spare batteries, a dop kit containing toiletries, and a string of rosary beads.

The rosary had been passed down through the generations of his mother's undiscussed Murphy ancestors, then buried at the bottom of Samantha Clement's cedar chest, out of sight and mind. When she died and George was going through her things, he found it and pocketed it on an obscure impulse.

He had briefly considering putting a packet of condoms in his duffel bag, then laughed ruefully.

How ironic, he thought. AIDS and contraception have both become irrelevant.

For a while he played a dark game with himself. Spot the Irrelevancies. Mink ranches. Renewal notices for magazine subscriptions. Sunlamps. Politicians' promises.

Insurance.

The broken line down the center of the highway.

When the game became too depressing, he stopped.

He stood on the heat-shimmered highway and watched the bus dwindle into nothingness. He doubted if the driver would bother to finish the run. For miles, the man had been driving with one hand and using the other to scratch furiously at the bleeding back of his neck.

George started walking. According to the directions, the reservation lay some two miles west of the highway. He squinted at the brassy sky. The glare was so pervasive he could not tell west from east. He paused long enough to take the compass out of his bag, consult it carefully, and clip it to his belt before starting off again.

He soon came to a road, of sorts; two deep ruts carved in the now hard-baked earth. The ruts were deep enough to break a man's ankle if he stepped wrong.

Sweat trickled down the back of George's neck.

He was thankful for his hat, a fine old silver-pearl Stetson from his college days, when he was a country-music fan. He had long since abandoned both hat and country music, but he had resurrected the hat again from the back of his closet. A Stetson kept a man's face and neck in the shade.

He shifted his duffel bag from one shoulder to the other, trying to remember if he'd put the Vaseline back in the bag. He'd smeared himself liberally with it before getting off the bus, covering all exposed skin . . . but had he left it on the seat when the driver called out his stop?

Feeling suddenly panicky, he threw down the duffel bag and began pawing through it. Must have done, must have done, must have put it back, wouldn't dare go out without it anymore . . . ah! There! He gave a great sigh of relief. The petroleum jelly was in his dop kit, with the white gunk for his lips and a bottle of aspirin in case he got too hot.

George put the white ointment on his lips and applied a second coat of Vaseline to his face and the backs of his hands. It wasn't as good as a real sun-block, but those had disappeared from drugstore shelves months ago.

When the reservation finally appeared on the horizon, it proved to be a disheartening straggle of ramshackle buildings with the dreary look of a place where dreams were born dead.

Well, what did you expect? George asked himself.

As he got closer he made out two rows of army-type wooden barracks sagging beneath unmended roofs. There was a store, of sorts, with rusted gas pumps in front, a porch, and a screen door permanently ajar, since the screen was too torn to be of any use anyway. Beside the store a few goats bleated in a barbed-wire pen, and some scrawny hens, half-denuded of feathers, scratched in the dust.

Beyond the barracks were some individual shacks with roofs of corrugated tin. The temperature under that tin must be enough to cook a roast, George thought. Surely no one tries to live in there, at least during the day.

So where is everybody?

His guts twisted. There might not be an "everybody." There might not be anybody.

He had just assumed this would be one place where . . .

George began to run forward in spite of the heat.

"Hallooo!" he shouted. He could hear the desperation in his voice.

There was a muffled response from inside the store. A tall, lean man came out onto the porch, shading his eyes with his hand. "What do you want?"

George squinted up at him. "My name's George Burning-feather."

"Burningfeather." The man came to the edge of the porch to get a better look. "Take off your hat."

George complied.

Instantly he was aware of the unshielded sun beating down on him like a weapon.

The man on the porch studied his features. "What tribe?"

"Pennacook. Well, half," George added, knowing dishonesty would be inappropriate at the end of the world.

"Half. Yeah. Well. I never heard of the Pennacooks."

"New England tribe. All gone now, or almost."

"'Cept you?"

"I'm the only one I know of."

"And you're just half."

"Yeah," George agreed, "but I'm alive. And I don't have any skin tumors."

The man said, "Then you better put your hat back on quick. At least until you get up here on the porch." He turned away and went back into the store.

George followed him with a profound sense of relief.

It took his eyes a few moments to adjust to the low interior light, after the fierce brightness of the day outside. Then he saw that the store was far from empty. A couple of dozen people sat, stood, leaned, lounged around its walls, occupying straight chairs, perching on boxes, propping their elbows against shelves. Men, women, children. A gawky teenaged boy. A little girl with huge black eyes and her thumb in her mouth.

The sight of the children gave George a jolt of joy.

The children had been the first to die. Out There.

Already he was thinking in terms of Out There and In Here.

"This here's George Burningfeather," the tall man told the others. "Says he's a Pennacook. New England tribe."

"How come he didn't go back north, then?" a man wanted to know.

"The database in our library didn't show any reservations in the part of New Hampshire I came from," George explained. "And since I was living down here, and this was the nearest one, I just sort of . . . gravitated here, I guess you'd say."

"Yeah," said the tall man. "We know. Getting pretty bad out there, is it?"

George shifted his duffel bag from one shoulder to the other, uncomfortably aware that no one had invited him to set it down. "Pretty bad," he confirmed grimly.

"Many left alive? We got a radio, but it's broke."

"Some. Not enough to keep the country running, though."

"How about the rest of the world?" another man asked. "White people dying everywhere?"

"*People* are dying everywhere," George corrected. "Caucasians are losing the highest numbers to malignant melanoma, but the various viral diseases are getting everybody."

"Africans and Orientals too?"

"Everybody," George said again. "There's more than enough death to go around, from a number of causes."

"What about survivors?" the tall man asked.

"The last reports I read said that aboriginal people like the

American Indians and the Maoris in New Zealand appeared to have the highest survival rate overall, but we don't know why. Could be genetic, could be pure accident. There aren't enough scientists left alive and working to find out."

"'We'?" said the tall man suspiciously. "You some kind of scientist too?"

"Not a biologist or a geneticist," George said quickly. "Just a meteorologist. I mean, I was. Out there."

"A specialist in the weather," one of the women said. "So you understand why it's gone so wrong."

"Nobody fully understands," George told her regretfully. "We only know some of the factors involved. Once the problems began multiplying exponentially, we—"

"Expo what?" someone interrupted. Indian eyes stared at George like polished stones.

"Faster and faster," he simplified, hoping he wasn't sounding condescending. "It all began going sour at once. Drastic changes in the climate, the expanding hole in the ozone layer, a decrease in breathable oxygen in the atmosphere—we think that might be partly the result of the huge number of trees cut down in the rain forests—it just piled up on us. Added to that there were so many pollution-related allergies. And the diseases. All those deadly new viruses, one after the other. People dying." George blinked as if to blink away a memory. "People dying," he repeated. "Most of the experts who might have come up with some answers died with the rest."

"Are you saying there's no one left alive who knows what to do about the heat?" a man asked, as if it was somehow George's fault.

"What to do about it? No. But we do believe it's an unnatural planetary warming caused by environmental damage."

"Caused by man," said the woman who knew what a meteorologist was.

"Yeah," George admitted. "It very much looks that way."

"But man doesn't know how to undo the damage." She was not asking, she was stating a fact.

"Yeah."

George looked at the woman with interest. Her speech indicated education. She was in her early thirties, perhaps, though he had no skill at assessing the age of an Indian face. Her features were unlike his, less rounded, more chiseled. A different tribe. One of the Plains Indians?

Sweeping his gaze around the room, he became aware of a variety of different types. This reservation was occupied not by one tribe, but by individuals from many.

As if reading his thoughts, the woman said, "We're all survivors, like you." Her face softened slightly, not enough to be a smile, but at least enough to mitigate the severity of her bone structure. "My name's Katherine," she said. "But people call me Kate. Kate-Who-Sings-Songs."

"And I'm Harry Delahunt," the tall man volunteered tardily. "That's Sandy Parkins over there, and Jerry Swimming Ducks and his wife Anne, and Will Westervelt—he's half Indian, like you and . . ." Harry continued around the room, introducing people. They variously nodded, raised one forefinger in token greeting, or just met George's eyes impassively. Their names were as diverse as their faces. Some used Indian names, others did not.

George rotated in the center of the room, acknowledging each person in turn. When the introductions were over he said, "Can I put this duffel bag down? I feel awkward standing here holding it as if I might have to leave again any minute."

Instead of replying, Harry Delahunt looked toward the far end of the store. Following his gaze, George saw someone he had not noticed before, sitting half hidden by shadows. It was an old, old man, with grey hair streaming over his shoulders like a waterfall, and a face fissured by age.

The face turned toward George.

He felt eyes looking him up and down.

The face nodded.

"Put 'er down," said Harry.

The duffel bag thudded onto the floor.

"You got any food in that thing?"

"Some candy bars. Beef jerky. Trail mix."

"Hunh!" Harry gave a contemptuous snort. "We don't eat that junk here. Kids might like the candy bars, though."

"Are you low on food?" George glanced at the well-filled grocery shelves.

"We got enough," Harry replied guardedly. "If we're careful."

Kate-Who-Sings-Songs said, "You're welcome to share what we

have." She looked toward the old man in the corner. He nodded. "If you're willing to eat what we eat," she added, smiling at George.

"That's kind of you," he said gratefully. He dug in the duffel bag and produced the candy bars. He offered them to the children. The gawky boy snatched his eagerly, but the little girl with the huge eyes stayed where she was, peering around her mother's skirts.

George went to her and hunkered down as low as he could get, holding out the candy bar. "It's real good," he said softly, slipping into the prevailing speech pattern. "But you don't have to eat it if you don't want to."

He continued to offer the candy bar. The little girl rolled her eyes up toward her mother, who gave a curt nod.

Slowly, shyly, one small brown hand was extended. Inch by inch, it reached toward George. He didn't move. He didn't even breathe.

The little fingers touched the shiny wrapper and stroked it. But she didn't take hold. Just stroked. Her eyes were huge.

"It's yours if you want it," George said.

All at once the fingers closed on the bar and snatched it away.

The people in the store laughed. Kind, fond laughter, the laughter of adults enjoying their children.

George felt a knot of tension loosen in his belly.

22

The ice was broken. A man called

Bert Brigham offered George a can of beer.

"Ain't cold, of course," he said.

"I'm not used to refrigerated drinks anymore,"

George told him.

He pulled off the tab and took a deep drink.

The others watched his throat muscles working.

When he had finished the beer, George put the tab back into the aluminum can and set it on the counter. "Thanks," he said. He could have drunk a second one, but he didn't ask. Nor did anyone offer. They had seen how he emptied the first can without stopping. They knew he was thirsty.

Everyone was thirsty.

The land was thirsty.

Parched.

George turned to Harry Delahunt. "You've told me everyone's name but his," he said, indicating the ancient figure in the corner.

Harry smiled enough to reveal tobacco-stained teeth. "He's Cloud-Being-Born. This is his reservation. Was. His family lived here. Most of 'em up and went off to the city to find jobs. Few came back, not many. His daughter, and then his granddaughter—that's her over there—stayed and took care of the old man. Reservation rotted around 'em. Then people began coming back. Not his tribe. Other people, like you, like me. He don't know where his tribe is. But this is his place, he was born here and he means to die here. So I guess he's the chief. And we're the Indians," Harry added with a humorless, eroded laugh.

"Cloud-Being-Born," George repeated. It was an evocative name. Poetic, he thought. He approached the old man respectfully.

The wrinkled face watched him.

He could not tell if the man was even breathing. He might have been carved from stone.

"How old is he?" George asked over his shoulder.

Cloud-Being-Born moved his lips almost imperceptibly. "A hundred and seven," said a voice like paper rustling.

George stared at him.

"A hundred and seven winters," the old man repeated. "You. Come close. Let me see you."

With a sense of awe, George moved closer, bending down so Cloud-Being-Born could see his face. Close up, he could also take a good look at the old man. He saw eyes sunken into deep sockets, a nose like an eagle's beak, rising proudly from between collapsed cheeks. A slash of a mouth, lipless. There was a smell of great age:

dusty, acidic yet not sour, not the sickly smell of the inmates of "convalescent homes" and "Golden Age nursing homes." Cloud-Being-Born's incredible antiquity was healthy.

"You," the old Indian said. "I see spirits in your eyes."

Harry Delahunt barked his strange laugh again. "Spirits is a right good idea," he said. "We got to welcome Burningfeather here properly!" Ducking behind the counter, he produced an assortment of smeared jelly glasses and a bottle with no label, containing what looked like water. A tiny portion was poured into the glasses, one for each woman. Then the bottle was passed among the men, starting with George.

He managed one cautious sniff at the bottle neck before he drank.

It smelled like nothing.

It smelled like rain, maybe. Or clouds.

He tilted the bottle back and took a swig.

His mouth filled with fire. Tears spurted from his eyes. Everyone laughed. Harry pounded him on the back. "Happens to everyone, the first time," he said. "That's the old man's firewater. It's some kinda powerful."

George felt as if his throat was being eaten by lye. But once the liquor hit bottom, a delicious glow began to spread through him, a sense of ease and well-being. He drew a gasping breath, coughed, wiped his eyes and looked around.

They smiled back at him.

These are my people, he thought.

"Dam' good stuff," he managed to say.

"Dam' right," Bert Brigham agreed. "Pass that bottle here."

The bottle was handed to each man in turn. No one took more than one swig before handing it on. Meanwhile, the women took tiny sips, glancing at one another with sparkling eyes. The little girl's mother hiccuped delicately.

The bottle reached Cloud-Being-Born. He accepted it with a grunt and took not one, but two swallows. Then he passed it back the way it had come.

Everyone, George included, took a second drink.

He was not quite as overwhelmed by the liquor the second time. "I'm glad I came," he said as he passed the bottle to Harry.

"Mmmm."

"I'm just not sure . . . why I did, though."

"Why you did what?"

"Came here. Why we all . . . came here," George elaborated.

No one replied.

The bottle was passed again. Then another bottle materialized and at an unspoken signal from Cloud-Being-Born the second bottle was emptied like the first. Heat faded; shadows lengthened. George was vaguely aware of the sun setting, and someone— Kate?—gave him some saltine crackers to eat with hunks of rat cheese, strong and crumbly.

Later, he did not know how much later, he found himself sitting on the porch in the dusk, dangling his legs in space. He was fuzzily aware of people moving around him, coming and going. It did not seem to have anything to do with him. From time to time a bottle filled his hand. He drank. The roseate glow spread through him.

He turned to the shadowy bulk of someone sitting beside him. "Why?" he asked with the intensity of the very drunk.

"Why what?"

George struggled to remember the question, and why he had asked it. "Why'd we come here?" he queried at last, peering owlishly at his companion.

A voice answered from the far end of the porch. "The Ghost Dance brought us."

That's important, George thought. That man is saying something important. He half turned and tried to focus his eyes on the person who had spoken, but he was having trouble with his eyes. They saw double. Sometimes quadruple. He shook his head to clear it but that set off a frightful clanging in his ears.

With a groan, George canted sideways until his cheek touched the splintery planking of the porch floor. At least that stopped his head from spinning. He stroked the planks with his fingertips. Splinters . . .

Splinters of light dissolving behind his eyes, giving way to velvety darkness. Darkness without stars.

Very much later, George awoke. He was totally disoriented. He did not know where he was or even why he was. He lay in darkness. He opened his eyes and it was still dark, but the thud of his eyelashes striking his eyelids when he batted his eyes made him flinch with pain.

He had the worst hangover of his life.

Something stirred nearby.

"I hope I'm dead," George muttered. "If I'm not, kill me, will you?"

"You'll be all right," said a voice. Female voice. George's bruised brain registered the fact without interest. Something hard touched his lips. "Drink this."

He sipped obediently, too weak to resist. The taste was like the way green grass smells.

George sank back into the starless night.

The next time he awoke, the dim grey light of dawn was streaming through a glassless window above his head. The air was almost cool. He was lying on a narrow cot, with a thin, worn cotton blanket pulled up under his chin.

His head did not hurt.

George sat up very slowly, waiting for the sledgehammer blow of pain that never came.

"Are you feeling better?"

Kate stood in the doorway, looking in at him. He realized he was in one of the shacks he had noticed the day before.

George turned his head gingerly, examining his surroundings. It was definitely one of the shacks; when he looked up, he saw the underside of a corrugated tin roof. Better get out of here before the sun hits that, he thought. Beside the cot on which he lay was a cane-bottomed chair. His Stetson hung from one of the chair posts. At the foot of the cot was a cheap pine dresser, decorated with a pitcher of freshly picked wildflowers.

Flowers?

Where did anyone find flowers still blooming?

"Where am I?" George asked, feeling like he was reading the lines from a corny old movie.

"Your house."

"*My* house?" George started to toss the blanket back and get up. Kate vanished from the doorway.

Air on his body warned him he was naked. Then he noticed his clothes folded neatly on the dresser beside the flowers. His duffel bag was on the floor at the foot of the cot.

"Hey, who undressed me?" he called out.

There was no answer.

Dressing thoughtfully, waiting for the hangover that never returned, George tried to recall the night before.

He remembered the bottle. Bottles. Oh yes, he remembered them all right. And somebody singing? Stories being told? Had he told some? About wanting to go to the stars, maybe.

He couldn't remember.

He found his wallet lying underneath his jeans. Citywise caution made him check its contents.

All there. Useless money, useless credit cards. Even the photographs. Someone had taken them out, probably to look at them, and put one back upside down. It was the snapshot of Stacey with her cloud of glorious red hair.

George blinked, trying not to remember the last time he'd seen Stacey. That was in the hospital ward, with her hair gone and her eyebrows and eyelashes gone and her face the color of old cheese. "Only family members," they'd said. But when he explained that he and Stacey had planned to marry as soon as she got her degree, a sympathetic nurse had relented and allowed him a few minutes. To say goodbye.

Hyden-Fischer Syndrome. One of the proliferating plague of viral diseases that had sprung up since the discovery of AIDS several decades back. When they first read about this newest one, Stacey had joked, "Looks like something's trying to exterminate the human race, George. AIDS, which we still haven't totally conquered, then NEEP, then AZ12, and now this Hyden-Fischer thing. What next, do you suppose?"

What next indeed.

He stared at the smiling face in his wallet, then folded the leather abruptly and jammed it into the hip pocket of his jeans.

He clapped the Stetson on his head and went outside.

Light and heat hit him simultaneously. Though the sun was barely clearing the horizon, it was already swimming in a sick yellow haze. The day promised to be another scorcher.

What next? George thought. I'll tell you, Stace, since you weren't here to see it. Lucky you. What next was a huge increase in skin cancer fatalities. The good old sun there did that, with the help of the hole in the ozone layer.

And if that isn't enough—if some few of us should manage to keep on living anyway—there's a joker in the deck.

We're running out of oxygen.

Bitterly, George surveyed the dreary landscape of the reservation before him. The earth was baked beige. The few straggling trees were dessicated. The only green remaining was in random clumps of weeds sheltered by the shade of fenceposts.

A lot of America looked like that, George knew.

A lot of the rest of the world was as bad or worse.

As his eyes accustomed themselves to the glare, however, he noticed a group of people on the far side of the barracks, moving around busily. Curious, he sauntered toward them. Then he stopped in astonishment.

They were tending a thriving vegetable plot. Hilled rows of well-worked soil alternated with narrow trenches. Men and women were hoeing weeds and staking up drooping plants. The children were bringing buckets of water to pour into the trenches.

Although he was no expert, George thought he recognized the feathery tops of carrots—he'd seen them in the supermarket—and heads of cabbage. Cauliflower, broccoli, pole beans.

Even a few flowers, like punctuation, at the end of each row.

Life was being coaxed from earth that was, elsewhere, refusing to nurture life.

George grinned. Trust the Indians, he thought. No machines, no fancy gadgets. Hand tools and sweat and kids to carry water.

He walked toward the nearest neat row. The woman called Kate, who was tying up bean runners, glanced up at him and smiled. "So you decided to come out for a constitutional."

"Yeah." He smiled back. "How the hell are you doing this?" He waved a hand to indicate the vegetables.

"The same way we've done it for thousands of years."

"No, I mean . . . seriously."

"I am being serious. We grow only what we need, and do as little damage to the earth as we can."

"That's all? You mean, like organic farming?"

"Even less sophisticated than that," she assured him. "This is purely subsistence level."

"You weren't born here," George said bluntly. "And you've had an education."

"Right on both counts. I'm Comanche, if you must know. Born in Oklahoma, educated in Chicago. Widowed in New Orleans," she added without inflection.

"I'm sorry."

"Why? You didn't know him."

"No, of course not, but . . . hell. I'm just sorry, that's all."

He felt his neck burning in spite of the Stetson. This woman made him uncomfortable. She was, he suspected, the one who had undressed him last night. The one who had left the flowers. And looked at his pictures.

"My fiancée died too," he said.

Kate nodded, her eyes on her work again. "White girl."

"Yes."

"Some white people are surviving."

"Not many."

"Not many people period," Kate said. She moved to the next bean pole, knelt beside it, her fingers working automatically, sure and deft. "You weren't telling us much we didn't already know, yesterday. Except when you said that aboriginal people seemed to be surviving better than anyone else. Is that true?"

"It's what I heard. Or read, rather. The report I saw named American Indians, Maoris, Inuit—"

"Alaska?"

"That's right. But I don't know how accurate it was, Kate. I read that report not long before I left, and we were hearing a lot of hysterical claims by then."

"Not long before you left," she repeated. "Do you think that's why you came here? Because you hoped you'd have a better chance for survival on an Indian reservation?"

"No," he told her honestly. Her dark eyes demanded honesty. "I've always thought of myself as an Indian, I suppose that's why I came. To be with my own at the end of the world, some romantic notion like that. Sounds silly, doesn't it?"

"No," she said shortly.

George went on, "Besides, if there is some gene-linked ability to survive our current disasters, it doesn't affect everyone. Indians and Maoris and Inuit are dying, we know that. Just not as large a percentage of them, perhaps. And I'm only half Indian anyway, so it might not do me any good at all."

Kate finished tying up the runners to the last bean pole and started to get to her feet. Without thinking, George reached out and took her hand. She gave him a swift, startled glance, then accepted, rising with a fluid grace.

He was concentrating on the way she moved when she said, "The diseases of civilization, like measles and chicken pox, killed vast numbers of aboriginal natives who had no immunities to them.

Wouldn't it be ironic now if the natives were the ones to survive the last, worst plagues of civilization?"

George forgot her grace and admired her mind. "Ironic indeed," he agreed. "Nice and neat and savage. But unfortunately, even they won't be able to survive the—" He bit off his word.

"The what?" Kate asked sharply. "They won't be able to survive the what? What didn't you tell us?"

"I told you. I said there was a decrease in breathable oxygen. I just didn't make a big point about it. There's no sense in scaring people when nothing can be done."

"Decreasing oxygen," Kate said slowly, her eyes widening as the message sunk home.

He nodded reluctantly. "Yes. We're running out of air we can breathe. Haven't you noticed that your lungs have to work harder than they used to? Don't you get tired easier, even over and above the heat? The people with weak lungs or emphysema or TB died quite a while ago, Kate. When the air is gone, we'll all go. End of story."

"When the air is gone," Kate said. He watched her draw a deep breath, tasting it with a sudden, desperate hunger. Her eyes met and locked with his.

"We won't die today," he told her. "Or even tomorrow. It'll just be a little harder to breathe tomorrow."

"But we will die. Everything that needs oxygen as we do will die." She searched his face for denial.

"Yes," he had to tell her. "Within the foreseeable future." The phrase had a new and awful meaning.

Kate stood still, breathing. Feeling the apparatus of her lungs work.

"Well then," she said at last. Turning from him, she walked down the row and picked up a hoe someone had dropped. "In that case, we don't have a lot of time, George. So we shouldn't be wasting what we do have. Here, take this and chop some weeds."

"After what I just told you, you still want to chop weeds?" he asked in disbelief.

"They won't chop themselves," she said briskly.

George shook his head and made an attempt at the weeds. But after a few efforts he admitted, "I'm afraid I can't tell a weed from a valuable plant."

Her lips twitched. "Some Indian you are. I'll bet you think milk comes out of cartons too. Here, give me that hoe before you do more harm than good. You might as well get a bucket and help the children carry water. Everyone who wants to eat has to work, and we need to finish tending the garden and doing the outside chores before the day gets any hotter."

So George Burningfeather found himself bustling between well and vegetable patch, carrying water. He watched Kate out of the corner of his eye. Stolidly pursuing an age-old task, she could have been any primitive female. Yet she had an air of confident self-possession that almost amounted to sophistication, as if her experience in the non-Indian world had altered her very genes, adding a new element. Yes, a new element. Kate was an amalgam. Earth and fire. And water—those liquid eyes.

Whoa, George, he told himself. Armageddon came and went and we lost, no contest. The world is ended, at least for the human race. There's no point in thinking the thoughts you're thinking. All that's left is to fall down and die, and that won't be very long.

Will it?

He looked at Kate again, calmly tending the vegetables.

And at the damned vegetables, green and growing. They did not have human lungs, they were a different life form.

Other life will inherit the planet we despoiled, George thought sadly. I wonder if they'll know, or care, how beautiful it was. Once.

His eyes stung. He blamed the pollution.

When the outdoor chores were completed, everyone gathered in the general store. It seemed to be a combination meeting place, day center, and dining room, with people willingly sharing a communal existence. Apparently other buildings were only used for sleeping.

I wonder where Kate sleeps? George asked himself.

Breakfast consisted of homemade bread, homemade jam, slabs of a peculiar substance Anne Swimming Ducks identified as goats'-milk butter, and instant coffee from a jar, the water boiled on a tiny camp stove.

"This is our second-last jar of coffee," Will Westervelt told George. "Don't suppose you brought some in that bag of yours?"

George said ruefully, "I didn't. I've been trying to give up caffeine."

Someone laughed.

"Why?" Harry asked. "Not good for your health?"

This time everyone laughed.

To keep the laughter going, George added, "I've given up smoking too."

They roared.

When the laughter died down, an ancient voice said, from the shadows at the end of the room, "No smoke. No pipe. How can you burn up your anger if you do not smoke it away?"

The people in the store met one another's eyes with brief, embarrassed glances, then looked away again.

"Cloud-Being-Born clings to the old traditions," Mary Ox-and-a-Burro, the mother of the little girl, explained to George. "The buffalo robe, the peace pipe, the Ghost Dance . . ."

Harry shot her a warning look. She fell silent.

"Ghost Dance," George said. "Someone mentioned that before. Last night?"

"Lotta things got mentioned last night," drawled a thickset man perversely known as Slim Sapling.

"And forgotten," added a man called Two Fingers.

But George persisted. "What is the Ghost Dance?"

Bert Brigham said, "Hell, I don't even like talkin' about this. Can't we just let it go?"

"We cannot forget the Ghost Dance," said the voice in the corner.

23

George felt Kate's light touch on his

arm. "Come out on the porch," she said in a low

voice, "and I'll try to explain it to you. There's no

point in upsetting people in here."

Feeling their eyes on him, he followed her out.

When he and Kate stood together under the sagging shingled roof of the porch, George asked, "Why did mentioning the Ghost Dance upset people?"

"It only bothers some of them, not all. But some people don't like being reminded that they were made to do something through magic."

"Magic? Come on now, Kate. I love Indian lore and tradition as much as the next person, but you can't really expect me to—"

"When things started to get really bad, Cloud-Being-Born was all but alone here," Kate interrupted smoothly. "Most of his family was scattered to the four winds. He had a daughter and a granddaughter and their husbands, that was about it. He wanted something more, so he worked with what he had. He taught the two men to dance the Ghost Dance. He danced it with them.

"It must have been very hard to make anything happen at first, with so few of them. But Cloud-Being-Born believed, and he made the others believe.

"The Ghost Dance is about communicating with the spirits of the ancestors. But Cloud-Being-Born used it to . . . to summon kindred spirits, I guess you'd say. Living kindred spirits. He used the magic of the Dance to reach out and call to Indians who'd left their ancestral homes and got lost in the white man's world.

"And it worked. People started coming to him here, seeking out this place. Two or three were his own relatives. The rest were just misplaced Indians. Like you, like me. Like Will and Harry and Slim and the rest. People who wandered in and didn't really know why they'd come.

"The old man turned some of them away. He never explained why. But the ones he wanted, he kept.

"A few weeks ago, when the radio broke past fixing, he told us we needed to dance the Ghost Dance again. I figured that with so many people dying, he wanted to save more while he could."

"Did you do it? Did you dance the Ghost Dance?"

Kate dropped her eyes. "The men did."

"What about you?"

"The Ghost Dance is for men. It uses their male power."

"Come on now! I'd say you're a pretty liberated woman, Comanche or not. Do you accept that six-steps-behind business?"

"No. But Cloud-Being-Born knows the Ghost Dance. I don't argue with him."

"If it ain't broke, don't fix it, eh?"

"Something like that," Kate said serenely. She gazed past him, sweeping her eyes across the drought-destroyed earth.

She looks at peace with this place and herself, George thought. Under the circumstances, that's damned near incredible. When did I last see anybody look that way?

Stacey for all her beauty had never looked at peace with herself. Like all their friends Out There, she had been charged with tension, anxious over her looks, her weight, her level of fitness, her achievements, her potential, even her ability to be multiorgasmic. Stacey had been many things, but never at peace with herself. Until she lay in her coffin, perhaps. But her family had kept the coffin closed at the funeral, so George would never know.

He dragged his thoughts back to the present. "So you're saying Cloud-Being-Born danced the Ghost Dance again, and I came as a result? Is that what you want me to believe?"

"Firstly, Cloud-Being-Born didn't do the dancing. He's too old. It must have been a terrific strain for him to do it that first time. Once he had a few more men gathered, he let them do the Dance under his supervision. But yes, you came as a result. I haven't a doubt."

"I do," George told her. "I certainly do. There's such a thing as free will, you know."

"I'm not denying that. I'm just telling you that some things override free will, or at least alter what we choose to do."

George was shaking his head. "I still can't buy it. And you haven't explained just how this Ghost Dance is done."

Kate crossed her legs and dropped effortlessly to a sitting position on the dusty porch. Mindful of splinters, George eased down less gracefully beside her.

"Since I didn't attend the Dance, I can't tell you the details," Kate told him. "But I do know there was fasting first and we built a sweat lodge out back. When the dancers were purified and ready, Cloud-Being-Born took them to a sacred place and had them go through the steps of a very ancient pattern, one his people have known for centuries. As I understand it, the pattern conforms to a pattern his tribe perceives in their own vision of the cosmos."

"Pattern." George screwed up his forehead. "You know, there was a time when I got interested in the Irish side of my family, just to irritate my mother, I suppose. I read a lot of books on Ireland. One of the things I remember was that the people used to do what they called 'a pattern' on religious feast days. It involved visiting some holy well, usually, and walking around it in a certain way."

Kate looked at him with light in her eyes. "Is the custom very old?"

"It predates Christianity, I think. The Christians just grafted their own saints and doctrines onto the pagan religion they found in Ireland. So the pattern may go back millennia, for all I know. There's been a civilization in Ireland for six thousand years."

"But in spite of an interest in Ireland, you chose to think of yourself as an Indian," she said. "Why, George?"

"Well, the way I look, for one thing. Black hair, bronze skin, features that aren't what you'd call Caucasian. But mostly I suppose I made that choice to irritate my mother even more than the Irish interest did."

"Did you dislike your mother so much?"

George considered the question. "Not dislike. I resented her because she resented me. It's a long story." He started to say, "I'll tell you some time," but then stopped. There might not be time for long stories. Time might have run out.

The sky was a hideous brassy color and the heat was intensifying. "Good thing we got your vegetables watered," he remarked.

"Yes." She smiled.

"But this Ghost Dance . . . what's the purpose of it, Kate? That's one thing you still haven't explained. You said old Cloud-Being-Born did it to draw people here, but why? Just to save them? And for what? It looks like we're all going to die anyway, of oxygen starvation if nothing else."

Kate's face sobered. "I honestly don't know. But I know the old man has a purpose. I have to be content with that."

There's her Indian passivity emerging, George thought. Then he checked himself. Are Indians passive? God knows I'm not. Are the Irish all drunkards? Of course not. When did we start accepting these stereotypes?

He thought again of Stacey, starving herself to be fashion-model lean because that was stereotypical beauty Out There.

Harry sauntered out onto the porch. "Well, old hoss, do you know all about the Ghost Dance now?" he asked George.

"Not really. It's still pretty much of a mystery."

"To all of us," Harry confided. "But the old man knows what he's doing. He's had a vision."

Suddenly George thought he understood. These people were sharing a common delusion brought on by stress. They were escaping an unbearable reality by putting their faith in the mystical visions of a senile old man. All over the planet, people were reacting to worldwide catastrophe in various ways. Plenty of them were losing themselves in religious mania, hyping up the adrenals, preparing to meet the end in a trance.

To meet the end. It all came back to that. To meet the end.

Why shouldn't American Indians prepare for the end by reverting to the faith of their fathers? It would do them no more or less good than any other.

George could not sit still any longer. He got up abruptly, clamped his Stetson more firmly on his head, and left the porch, seeking physical activity to ease his own tension.

Neither Kate nor Harry called after him to ask where he was going. They just placidly watched him leave.

He struck off aimlessly, not looking at anything in particular. Just moving. Using the body. Then he started watching the ground. The baked earth was scored with cracks caused by the heat, some of them wide enough for a man to put his foot into. They looked, to George's imagination, like mouths gaping for air.

Air. He looked up and saw the shimmer of a heat mirage in the distance. It floated, incorporeal, illusory, like a lake in the desert.

Desert, he thought sourly. The earth's turned into a desert.

The mirage sparkled ahead of him, as out of reach as a rainbow.

How long has it been since I saw a rainbow? George asked himself.

He could not remember.

He walked on, eyes fixed on the mirage. The sun beat down on his Stetson. He could smell his white cotton T-shirt, his sweat, his baking skin. I should have taken a couple of aspirin before I came outside, he thought tardily.

The sky was, as it had been for months, a flat-looking sheet of light with the blue long since leached out of it. It appeared to have no depth, no dimension. Yet when George looked at it more closely he discovered that the air was filled with tiny little squiggles, darts and flashes of color against that flat backdrop, minute figures liked coiled hairs wriggling and twisting in empty space.

What I'm seeing, George reminded himself, is really the imperfection of the human eye. Scratches on the eyeball, glitches in the optic nerve. Everyone has them.

Yet he kept on watching, with mounting curiosity. The longer he stared, the more convinced he became that he was seeing something of substance.

Dust motes?

Life forms?

Whoa, boy, the sun's getting to you! he cautioned himself.

But he was intrigued. The air looked alive.

It's full of angels, he thought fancifully.

That was the moment when he decided to turn back. Obviously the sun was getting to him.

When he reversed course he was startled to see how far away the buildings of the reservation were. They were only tiny dots in the distance. He extended his stride, anxious to be back in the shade again.

But the busy air kept pace with him, the tiny darting spiraling figures accompanying him, monopolizing his vision. It was like swimming through a school of . . . of . . . beings?

George stopped abruptly. He had a compelling sense that he was not alone. He turned around slowly, but in whatever direction he looked, he saw no human, no animal. Only the tiny images in the air. When he blinked his eyes, they were still there. Not on his eyeballs. Beyond. Outside. Around him.

Watching him.

An irrational fear overtook him and he began to run.

He pounded up onto the porch of the store, panting hard and dripping with sweat. The porch was empty. He stopped for only a moment, then went inside.

Cloud-Being-Born had come out of his corner. He was sitting on a stool just inside the door. He looked up as George entered.

"Come to me," the old Indian said.

George stood in front of him, still panting, feeling slightly foolish. What had he been running away from? *Air?*

"Let me look in your eyes," Cloud-Being-Born commanded.

George bent down. The old Indian's eyes met his for a long, searching look. Then the ancient man nodded, satisfied.

"This is the one," he said.

Straightening up, George looked beyond Cloud-Being-Born to the others in the store. Only half a dozen were there at the moment, the rest, presumably, being in their own quarters, in the barracks or the stifling tin-roofed shacks. There were no women in the store, George noted, automatically looking for Kate. But Harry Delahunt was there, and Two Fingers. And Jerry Swimming Ducks, and Slim Sapling, and the one called Westervelt whose first name George had forgotten, since it was not as memorable as an Indian name.

"What's he talking about?" George asked the men. "What does he mean, I'm the one?"

"He's been talking about doing another Dance," Harry said.

"Another Ghost Dance?" Maybe I'll learn what it is, George thought.

"Not this time," Two Fingers said. He was a short, swarthy man with only two fingers on each hand, obviously not the result of an accident but of some peculiarity of birth. "This one's going to be a new Dance. One we haven't done before."

"We were waiting for you," Cloud-Being-Born said.

George tensed. I don't want to be part of this, he thought. It's one thing to be an Indian, it's another to buy into all this religious ecstasy nonsense. I don't believe in it. I want a clear head when I go, it's going to be the last great adventure and I don't want to miss it.

"Count me out," he said to Cloud-Being-Born. Then he smiled, trying to mitigate the refusal. "I have two left feet when it comes to dancing," he added.

"It is not your feet we need," the old man replied.

George looked at the other men. Their faces were studiedly impassive. But he had an uncomfortable feeling that if he tried to make a break for it, they would stop him.

And where would he go anyway? Where was there, except this ratty, rundown reservation with its odd assortment of people loosely linked by heritage?

Very loosely linked, George thought.

"I'm only half Indian," he said lamely.

"You need not be Indian at all," Cloud-Being-Born replied to his surprise. "What we need is not your blood."

"Nor my feet?"

"Nor your feet."

"Then what?"

But Cloud-Being-Born said nothing else. The old man seemed to go off somewhere inside himself. Deep within the seams of his wrinkled face, his eyes filmed over. George was dismissed. The store and the other men in it were dismissed.

George stood, shifting from one foot to the other, feeling increasingly uncertain, until Jerry said kindly, "It's okay, he doesn't hear you anymore."

"Is there going to be another Dance?"

"Looks like it."

"What kind of Dance? When?"

"He hasn't told us yet. He will, when the time comes." Jerry seemed as oddly passive as the rest of them, accepting.

George felt a flash of anger. I can't do that, he thought.

But what choice do I have? I bought into this when I came here. He was annoyed with himself.

He spun on his heel and left the store.

Since there was no place else to go, he headed for his shack. He kept his eyes on the ground, deliberately not looking at whatever might be swimming in the air.

Pollutant particles, he said to himself, trying to believe it.

The door of the shack was open, but the heat collected beneath the tin roof struck him in the face like a blow. He could not go in.

Turning aside, he headed for the only other possible sanctuary, the two rows of barracks. At least they were roofed with asphalt shingles, though in very bad repair. They should be marginally cooler.

As he approached the buildings he heard voices coming from inside. Someone was singing. He stopped for a moment to listen, recognizing Kate's voice.

She had been well named, Kate-Who-Sings-Songs. Her voice was a pure, clear contralto, deep and sweet as well water. She was singing a ballad George did not know, a song of loss and regret.

He opened the door and slipped inside.

Kate was standing in the center of the long room, singing with her eyes closed. All those who were not gathered in the store, including the children, were sitting in a circle around her.

A row of cots alternating with rusted iron beds ran down one wall. A few broken chairs were pushed against the other. At the end of the room was a single porcelain sink, with a run of rust down its backsplash, below the faucet. In one corner, a faded shower curtain half shielded a seatless toilet.

This is what they gave us to live in, George thought, an old anger rising in him. The people who seized our land and raped it for profit.

For a moment he forgot the other half of his family, the white half. Seeing the destitution of the reservation, he was pure Indian, as he had been pure Irish when he read the histories of colonial atrocities perpetrated on that race.

Kate finished the song she was singing and opened her eyes. She looked directly at him. "Hello," she said over the heads of the others.

"Hello," he replied with the same soft-spoken gravity.

She smiled then. "We have music every day," she explained. "Would you like to join us?"

Bert Brigham, who was seated nearest the door, moved over, beckoning to George to take the place beside him.

They were all sitting on the floor. No one was using the broken chairs.

George sat down. The air in the room was hot and still, but not as bad as it had been in his shack. And at least there was a roof to keep out the sun, though a few relentless rays made their way through the broken shingles and rotten boards beneath to illuminate dust motes dancing in the air.

George wanted to believe they were dust motes.

Someone suggested another song, another one George did not know, and Kate closed her eyes again and sang. George closed his eyes too, losing himself in the listening. Then the song ended and he heard her say, "This next one is for George."

Her smooth, supple contralto launched into a love song he had heard only once or twice in his life, in Irish pubs in Boston. "My Lagan Love." A song from Northern Ireland, incredibly difficult to sing. As he listened, George realized Kate must have been a professional singer . . . Out There.

He would ask her. He wanted to know more about her.
He wanted to know all about her.
But there was no point. They would soon die.
The ballad flowed to its final, ineffably poignant lines:

> ". . . and hums in sad, sweet undertone
>   The song of heart's desire."

George opened his eyes to find Kate looking at him. For a moment they were quite alone in the room.

Not now, George thought. Not now, at the end of the world.

He dropped his eyes, breaking the connection.

Someone else began to sing then, and one of the younger men produced a guitar and played an accompaniment. Kate moved from the center of the room to sit down with the others, though not by George. She listened with apparent keen interest, not looking in his direction again, and he felt a pang of regret.

The music session lasted for an hour or so. There were songs, some of them undeniably what George considered "Indian" music, others speaking of different cultures. Kate sang again after a while, this time a smoky rendition of "Walk on the Wild Side" in the best New Orleans tradition, affirming George's opinion that she had been a professional singer. He could just see her leaning against a piano in a top-dollar jazz club, carrying them away on the magical river of her voice.

By unspoken agreement, the group broke up after Kate's last song and began drifting away. Some of the women busied themselves sweeping the barracks and trying to make a presentable home of a place that could never be presentable. The children, denied the pleasure of playing outdoors, used the broken chairs to create a fort for themselves and began a rowdy game of Cowboys and Indians.

To George's amusement, it seemed they all wanted to be Cowboys.

"No takers for the role of Indian," he remarked to Kate as she walked past him.

She stopped. "Not exotic enough. Kids never want to be what they are."

"Did you?" he asked. Then, mildly embarrassed, he added, "We talked about me but not about you. I don't know anything about you, except that your husband died in New Orleans. Were you singing in a club down there?"

Her eyes twinkled with amusement. "You didn't have to be a genius to figure that out."

"Did you always want to be a singer?" he persisted.

Kate turned to face him squarely. "No," she said. "When I was a kid I wanted only one thing: to be rich. To have fancy clothes and more jewelry than any Indian woman ever possessed.

"So I grew up to become the highest-paid call girl in Tulsa."

24

George's jaw dropped. "Excuse me?"

"You heard me. I was the highest-paid call girl

in Tulsa." Kate said the words matter-of-factly, as

someone else might say they had been a housewife—

or a meteorologist.

"But . . . I thought you were a singer . . . I mean . . ." George fumbled, wishing he had never opened this particular can of worms. At the end of the world, why bother anyway?

Kate smiled. "I was a singer. Eventually. I made enough money on my back to buy some but not all the things I wanted. But I learned enough to realize I would have to change my life to get them. So I saved enough money to take myself off to Chicago and get a formal education, a bit of polish, so I could snag a rich husband who would give me the rest of the equation. The highest-priced hooker going can't afford to buy herself Rolls-Royces and villas in the Mediterranean."

"That's what you wanted?" George asked in amazement, gazing at her serene face, her smooth, plain hair, her simple slacks and shirt.

"It's what I thought I wanted. What the magazines and the TV had taught me to want ever since I was a little kid. In Chicago I got married, all right, but not to a millionaire. Like a fool, I fell in love with a saxophone player. Really fell hard, so hard I couldn't bring myself to tell him about my past. Until the day he died, Phil thought I was just a nice girl from the Southwest.

"He was the one who discovered I had a voice. He began calling me Kate-Who-Sings-Songs, using the Indian connection to make something unusual so he could get bookings for me.

"It turned out I was more successful than he was," she said softly. Sadly. "My career took off, his went downhill. We drifted apart, and then one day I learned he had died of an overdose of designer drugs. Designer drugs," she repeated with a world of contempt in her voice.

"You can't blame yourself for that," George said.

"I don't. Honestly. I did for a while, but then I realized everyone is ultimately responsible for themselves. And I had better start being responsible for myself. I cleaned up my act, you might say.

"Just in time to realize—" She broke off and shook her head as if she was angry.

"What?" George took hold of her elbow. "To realize what? Tell me."

Kate looked past him, toward the children. "Just in time to realize it was all too late. I was never going to be able to have . . . What's wrong with her?" she asked abruptly.

George followed her gaze. The tiny, big-eyed daughter of Mary Ox-and-a-Burro had stopped playing and was standing swaying, rubbing her forehead.

Her face was glazed with sweat.

Kate hurried to the child and crouched down beside her. George followed. "What's wrong, honey?" Kate was asking. "Don't you feel well?"

The little girl whimpered, "Hot. Hot."

Kate put her hand on the child's forehead and frowned. "Too hot. That feels like fever."

"I have some aspirin," George volunteered, but Kate was not listening. She gathered the child into her arms and called out to the room at large, "Does anyone know where Two Fingers is?"

"In the store," George said. "At least, he was."

Kate gave a brisk nod and headed for the door. Mary Ox-and-a-Burro bustled across the room to join her. "What's wrong with my baby?"

"I don't know," Kate said. "I think she has a fever."

Mary gasped. "Not . . . ?"

"I don't know," Kate said. "Don't start worrying before anything happens. We'll take her to Two Fingers."

"Is he a doctor?" George wanted to know.

"Better than that," said Kate. "He's a healer. It's his gift."

"How can a healer be better than a real doctor?" George wanted to know. He was having to trot to keep up with Kate who, with Mary at her shoulder, was sprinting across the open ground toward the store. But Kate did not answer him. All her attention was focused on the child, who was now very flushed.

Fortunately, Two Fingers was still in the store with Harry and the others. The two women took the child straight to him. "She's sick," Kate said, holding out the little girl.

But Two Fingers did not take her into his arms. Instead he gestured to Kate to put her on the floor. Kate and Mary sank down together, almost as one, with the child between them.

From his stool, Cloud-Being-Born watched.

Two Fingers held the palms of his deformed hands above the little girl's head, moving them slowly back and forth, as if he was smoothing a blanket. His face assumed a remote, listening expression.

The rest of the community came flooding in the door, talking worriedly among themselves. When they saw what Two Fingers was doing they fell silent and ranged around the walls, watching.

Two Fingers began to chant. The sound was eerie, hackle-raising, an echo from another time. The repetitive syllables sounded like gibberish, but he repeated them insistently, with rising and falling volume making a sort of music.

"You," said a voice behind George. "You, Burningfeather. No tobacco?"

George turned. Cloud-Being-Born was sitting right behind him.

"No, I'm sorry. I didn't bring any."

"Too bad," the old man said wistfully. "Tobacco draws evil spirits. Evil spirits like tobacco. Circle of tobacco would draw illness out of child."

Two Fingers continued to chant. His outstretched hands never touched the child. He reached out with one foot, however, and nudged the two women, urging them to move away from her. Kate complied at once but the girl's mother had to be nudged a second time.

When space was cleared around the child Two Fingers began to move in a circle around her, keeping his palms downward a precise distance above her head. As he circled he sometimes bent forward, sometimes straightened up, but he never lost the rhythm of the chant nor varied the distance of his hands from her head.

George was painfully reminded of the people he had seen contract disease and die. It often began like this, with a sudden fever. The deadly viruses announced their presence like a rattle-snake rattling, but they had already struck, and there was no antidote.

If the child's illness was the precursor of one of the viral diseases invading the reservation at last, the slim hope of some genetic immunity would die with her; with the rest of them.

I don't suppose it matters, George told himself. The whole planet's sick, it won't support us anymore anyway.

Then, as he watched with hopelessness spreading through him, he saw the flush fade from the child's face.

She smiled up at Two Fingers.

"You and you and you," Cloud-Being-Born said, stabbing the air with his fingers as he pointed at three of the men, "go build a medicine wheel. Quickly."

The three ran from the store.

Two Fingers kept on dancing and chanting.

The little girl sighed, curled herself into a ball on the floor, pillowed her cheek on her arm, and slept. To keep his hands the same distance from her head Two Fingers had to circle her in a crouch, but he never lost his rhythm.

The three men soon returned. "It's ready."

Two Fingers picked up the sleeping girl and carried her outside gently, so as not to awaken her. The rest of them followed. Even Cloud-Being-Born arose from his stool and paced after them, to George's astonishment. He had not imagined such an old man walking. Yet he not only walked, he walked with a relatively straight back, like a much younger person.

On the baked earth in front of the store was a circular arrangement of stones, resembling a wheel with spokes and a hub. Hastily assembled, it consisted of no more than the absolute minimum number of small rocks and pebbles to give the shape required, yet George counted a full twenty-eight spokes. Out of curiosity, he took the compass that was hooked to his belt and checked the alignment. As he had somehow known, one pair of spokes was perfectly aligned east-west, and another north-south. Perfectly. Yet none of the three men who had made the wheel was carrying a compass.

At George's shoulder, Harry Delahunt said, "Twenty-eight spokes for the days of the lunar month. We don't count the day when the moon is dark."

Carrying the little girl, Two Fingers stepped into the first wedge between the spokes, did an intricate little shuffle of his feet, stepped into the next wedge, and so on around the circle, still chanting. As he stepped over each spoke he lifted the child toward the sky, then lowered her to a comfortable carrying position again.

As he danced, the women, but not the men, stepped into the circle and followed him around the wheel. The men took up the chant, but the women repeated Two Finger's steps between the spokes.

"So women do dance," George muttered under his breath.

Harry Delahunt glanced at him. "Men do one thing, women do something else. Not the same thing at the same time, that'd be a waste of energy."

When the circle was completed and the last woman stepped outside the wheel, Two Fingers put the child back in her mother's arms.

George could not help himself. He stepped forward and touched the little girl's forehead.

It was no hotter than his own, and absolutely dry.

The people drifted away, most of them seeking the shade of the store. When Kate turned toward the barracks, however, George hurried after her and caught her by the arm.

"Is that child actually cured?"

"We hope so," she replied with equanimity.

"What is it? Laying on of hands, something like that?"

"Two Fingers is a healer, as I told you. A medicine man. More than that, he's a Sioux. The Sioux are best at using the medicine wheel."

"And Cloud-Being-Born, what is he? The chief?"

Kate paused and looked up at him, frowning slightly. "No. He's a, a sort of a medicine man too. But more than that. He's a . . . a . . . a shaman," she said, hitting on the word with relief.

"You mean a sorcerer?"

"A shaman," Kate reiterated firmly. "That's what aboriginal people called them, isn't it? Their holy men? People who could use earth magic and sky magic?"

"I don't know, I suppose so. I'm just a meteorologist. You'd have to have an anthropologist to explain all that."

"I don't have to have any of your modern scientists at all," Kate corrected him. "I have . . . we have . . . this." She extended her hands as if to indicate the reservation and everything it contained.

Sunbaked soil, dying trees, dilapidated buildings. Two Fingers. Cloud-Being-Born. And what else?

"What do you mean by 'this'?" George demanded to know.

Kate began walking again, hurrying toward the shelter of the barracks. The sun beat down on them like a fist. George kept step with her, subconsciously aware of the flex and swing of her legs in the cheap cotton slacks she wore.

She did not answer him until they were inside the building. Then, with a sigh of relief, she pulled a handkerchief out of her pocket and mopped her face and throat. When she handed it to him for the same purpose George noticed it was a handkerchief made of cotton, rather than a tissue of pulped paper.

"Now tell me," he said as he gave the damp cloth back to her. "Just what were you talking about out there?"

She sat down on the edge of a cot and looked up at him. "The people Cloud-Being-Born has gathered here are a very special group, George. No one told me that, it's just something I've observed for myself since I've been here. Each of us has a gift. No two have the same gift. Two Fingers is a healer, for example. I sing. Sandy is a Navajo and, though you'd never guess it to look at him, an exceptional artist. Mary is a water diviner. Don't smile; she can really find water anywhere. Each of us can do something. Cloud-Being-Born organizes us into various groups to achieve various results. You saw a Healing Dance just now. When we planted the vegetables we did a different Dance. And it worked. They came up."

"Vegetables do that. They come up."

"Do they? Are you so sure? The average temperature here is a lot hotter than it used to be just a few years ago. That's changed the growth habits of every plant. Just look at the trees, they're dying. But our vegetables are thriving."

"You give them a lot of tender loving care."

"We give them more than that, George. There's no way they should be alive under that sun out there. Nothing else is, even the mesquite trees are dying."

"Yeah. Well." George scratched his head, trying to think of some explanation his scientific mind could accept.

"Do you know of anyone else who can do what we're doing here?" Kate challenged.

"No," he said ruefully. "The radical change in the planetary climate was one of our biggest worries, for a while, because of crop failure on an international scale. We were predicting worldwide famine. But before that actually became a problem, it was overcome by even bigger problems. I doubt if anyone out there is obsessing about worldwide famine anymore.

"You know, Kate, it's like an old dog I read about someplace years ago. His owner said he died of everything at once. That's what's happening to this planet. It's dying of everything at once.

"No single factor is killing the planet, you understand. The ecology is being overwhelmed by dozens of assaults. The hole in the ozone layer is just one example. We didn't worry a helluva lot about that one, for a while. It was just a problem to the Australians, who had to start closing down their beaches during the hottest part of the day because too many people were getting skin cancers.

"But the problem didn't stay in Australia. Like the cancers themselves, it spread. Everything seemed to be connected to everything else in ways we hadn't fully perceived.

"Take Kazakhstan and Uzbekistan. Those countries needed a crop to boost their economies. So they diverted their major watercourses to irrigate fields and grow cotton on huge cotton plantations. They didn't realize they'd created a disaster until their climate was changed and drought set in. To combat the drought, they diverted rivers from Siberia, which in turn destroyed another ecosystem. Climatic change was spreading.

"That's symptomatic of what happened all over the globe. Famine in Ethiopia, rain forests destroyed in Brazil . . . in every case, someone was raping the land for the sake of jobs and profits and the balance of payments. All perfectly justifiable. We have to have jobs. And a man's entitled to a profit. And God knows we have to redress the balance of payments!

"But what we didn't seriously take into account was the amount of damage we were doing to the planet. Of course, along the way we've destroyed ourselves, because we've made the atmosphere unbreathable. But I suppose on the cosmic scale the destruction of earth's air-breathers is pretty small potatoes compared to the murder of a planet."

"Is that what's happening?" Kate asked. She shivered in spite of the heat. "The murder of this planet?"

"You might call it that. Oh, it isn't going to be blown up in an atomic explosion the way people feared fifty years ago. It'll still be here, circling the sun. But there won't be any life on it. Perhaps there'll only be water. The polar ice caps are melting as they've never melted before. If that doesn't stop—and we have no reason to think it will—then the continents as we know them will be inundated.

"Eventually the earth will cool again—far too late to do us any good, needless to say. Then the ice will come back. A great glittering ball of ice. Sterile. Dead."

"Everything that is, is alive," Kate said.

"Where'd you hear that?"

"It's a saying Cloud-Being-Born uses a lot."

"Meaning ice too? Well, maybe, according to his way of thinking. But as far as I'm concerned, a world covered in ice is totally damned dead." George's pent-up anger resonated in his voice.

Looking at him, Kate saw that his fists were clenched. "Did you know all this when you came here?" she asked him.

"Of course."

"Did you ever think of killing yourself?"

"Sure. Lots of people preferred suicide to sitting around waiting for the end. But somehow I couldn't do it."

"So you came to a reservation instead."

"Yeah. Home to die. Metaphorically speaking. It's what I get for being romantic about my Indian heritage. Funny thing about Indians, Kate. People did tend to romanticize them, same as they did the Irish. I've got Indian and Irish in me, so I guess that makes me doubly romantic, eh?" He essayed a halfhearted grin, trying to lighten the mood.

Kate replied seriously. "There's nothing wrong with being romantic. Maybe the Indians and the Irish still knew that when the rest of us forgot. Human beings have a real need to put a shine on things, to give them glow and glory.

"Why do you think I was so successful as a call girl? I'm no great beauty. But I could give my clients romance. I could give them soft music and low lights and intelligent conversation. I could even give them buckskin and beads and a real live Indian princess, if that's what they wanted. And they did. They loved it. The men who came to me were starved for some sort of romance.

"You and I grew up in an age that glorified what it called 'reality.' Ugliness was the fashion, everything else was sentimental crap. Garbage was art and noise was music. People's souls were starving, George, long before worldwide famine could kill them.

"No wonder our world turned so ugly. We made it that way. Maybe we all deserved to die."

"But you didn't kill yourself either," George reminded her. "You came here."

"Yes. I know now that Cloud-Being-Born called me here."

"You really believe that?"

She looked at him with enviable composure. "I know it," she said.

"Why?"

Instead of answering, Kate said, "Perhaps you should ask yourself why he called you here, George."

25

During the days that followed,

George felt more and more a part of the community.

Sharing their isolated existence, he was able to forget

for hours, sometimes for half a day, the lurking

catastrophe.

The Indians did not discuss it among themselves. Their only acknowledgment was to comment on the heat.

It was impossible to ignore the relentlessly increasing heat.

But they focused on other things, on the rituals of survival. Working together, they tended the vegetables and carried water from the well and milked the goats and made the repairs necessary to keep the dilapidated buildings from falling down. The men and women worked together. There was little division of labor according to gender. Everyone turned their hand at whatever needed to be done, according to their abilities. Mary Ox-and-a-Burro was the best carpenter on the reservation. Bert Brigham was the best cook.

George, somewhat to his surprise, discovered an unsuspected talent with needle and thread and was soon responsible for mending clothing in addition to his other chores.

Heat, sweat, dust, shabby things getting shabbier.

How strange it is, George thought, that a woman like Kate who sold her body to buy herself a better lifestyle is willing to settle for this. Indian fatalism, perhaps? He was not sure.

The influence Cloud-Being-Born exerted on the others was an ongoing source of fascination to George. The old man did not seem to do much of anything but sit around the store. Yet everyone deferred to him. On the rare occasions when he spoke, people held their breaths to listen.

Not that he said much. Mostly he just sat, dozing or ruminating, it was hard to tell which. Of all of them, Cloud-Being-Born was the only one who gave the impression of just . . . waiting.

George made several unsuccessful efforts to engage the old man in conversation. Finally Harry said, "I'd leave the old man alone, if I were you. When he has something important to say, he says it. Otherwise, he don't waste time in palaver."

Harry was beginning to get on George's nerves. There was the same arrogant I'm-in-charge-here-and-don't-you-forget-it air about him that T. J. Dosterschill had possessed. The irritant lay not so much in what they said, as in the way they said it. Both spoke as if contradiction was unthinkable.

"I'll talk to him if I want to," George replied. Only after the words were spoken did he realize he sounded like a sullen little boy talking back to his mother.

Harry shrugged. "Suit yourself. But it won't get you anywhere. Remember, I told you not to bother."

"Who put you in charge?"

Harry grinned. "Me? I ain't in charge, old hoss."

"Then what's your specific role here?"

" 'Specific role,' " Harry mimicked, still grinning. "My my, what fawncy language we do speak."

George snapped, "Cut the crap. You're no more an ignorant reservation Indian than I am."

"Mighty perceptive of you, old hoss. Point of fact, I used to be a supervisor for Con Ed, back East. Had practically the whole Long Island grid at one time."

"What tribe are you?"

"Mohawk. My dad was one of those structural steel workers who went up on the skyscrapers and walked around on exposed beams with nothing to lean against but the wind. That was phased out, though, by the time I came along. I had to find some other line of work."

"Until Cloud-Being-Born summoned you."

"Yeah. Now, he is a reservation Indian. But he sure as hell ain't ignorant, he's the smartest person here. Mescalero Apache, he is. He and my father had something in common. The Mescaleros used to say they 'lived in the sky.' All their rituals revolved around solar and lunar alignments, things like that. Very complicated people."

"I thought they were from the mountains in New Mexico," George said.

"Most of them. Cloud-Being-Born's people wound up here for some reason, on the flattest piece of desert for miles around. But at least he has a great view of the sky at night," Henry added. "When the rest of us are asleep, did you know he just sits on the porch steps and stares up at the stars? Don't even seem to sleep. Just sits there, staring up. Damndest thing you ever saw, old man like that."

Cloud-Being-Born and I have something in common too, George thought to himself. We're both displaced mountain men. The Mescaleros came from the White Mountains of New Mexico; my father came from the White Mountains of New Hampshire.

And here we are. In this godforsaken desert.

Here we are.

As he lay on his cot that night, with the door of his shack open in a vain effort to fight the heat, George could not sleep. He thought about the old Indian staring at the stars.

Then his thoughts slid sideways and circled around Kate. He folded his arms behind his head and thought about her until he could not stand it anymore, then got up and slipped on his cut-off Levi's and slipped out of the shack.

There were no lights on in the barracks. The community had a few kerosene lanterns and there were boxes of candles in the store, but generally daylight was the only illumination they sought.

In spite of the darkness, however, George felt sure Kate was awake too. He could sense it, as if the air between them was vibrating.

How to call her outside without looking like a fool? He stood lost in thought for a few moments, then the idea came to him.

Very softly, he began whistling "My Lagan Love."

As he had known she would, Kate came to him.

She was dressed in a thin cotton shift. Even in the light of a waning moon, he could see her body clearly through the fabric. She was barefoot, her glossy hair lying in a thick plait across one shoulder. She walked toward him without shyness, moving with a straightforward and sinuous grace.

No wonder the johns thought she was an Indian princess, George thought.

She is.

She stopped when she was so close to him he could reach out and put a hand behind her head and pull her mouth to his.

But he did not.

Not yet.

Instead he said something foolish, as people do. "How did you know it was me?"

She smiled. Even if the night had been pitch-black, he would have heard the smile in her voice. "Oh, George."

Suddenly it was George who was shy. "You don't have any other . . . I mean, there's no special man . . . ?"

"I know what you mean. And no, there's no man in my life now," Kate said calmly. "Have you anyone? Now?"

George made a gesture that took in the entire world beyond the reservation. "There isn't anyone," he said. "Almost literally."

"A few."

"Yes. A few. But none of them that care for me, or that I care about. That's an awful feeling at a time like this, Kate. I know we live and die alone in the strictest sense, but when you're faced with the end of the world, you should at least have someone to put your arms around, someone to cry with."

"Are you the kind of man who can cry?"

He had never given it much thought. But now, trying to be honest, he said, "Yes. yes, I guess I am." And to his surprise felt the tears just beneath the surface, burning in his throat.

The end of the world. All those people . . . all those lovely little things he had taken for granted . . . the laughter of children running across a schoolyard . . . the perfume of a strange woman lingering in an elevator . . . the roar of the crowd at a baseball game . . .

She knew. Kate felt the twist of agony in him, and knew. With one step she closed the distance between them and put her arms around him.

"Don't," she whispered, pressing her lips to the exact place at the base of his throat that was aching with the need to cry. "Ah, don't." Her lips moved on his skin. Moved slowly away from his throat, down his bare chest, brushing across his stiffened nipples, circling back up, up, seeking his mouth.

For just one terrible and shaming moment, he wondered if she was healthy. Then he almost laughed aloud. Irrelevant, irrelevant! He gathered her into his arms. She was a strong, solid woman, but he lifted her easily and carried her back to his shack; carried the captive princess home.

Neither of them was aware of the old man sitting on the steps of the porch in front of the store, watching them in the faint moonlight.

George had left his door open. He hated taking Kate into that small, stifling room, but it was better than lying her down on the rock-hard earth outside. At least he had a cot with a mattress on it.

He even had flowers. Since the first day, there had always been flowers in the pitcher on the dresser.

George did not put them there. But they were always there. Fresh ones every day.

He laid Kate on the bed and bent over her, wondering what were the appropriate words to say in such a situation. What phrases did you use with the highest-priced call girl in town?

The unbidden thought made him angry. He did not want to think of her that way. Indeed, it was impossible for him to imagine. She was Kate-Who-Sings-Songs, a lovely, grave Indian woman of grace and dignity. That was the true person. The call girl she had mentioned was an alien. He did not believe in her.

There was no room for her in what was left of the world.

If this is going to be the last time, George thought, let it be be beautiful.

They were gentle with each other, at first. Their shared hunger made them gentle, eager to prolong the pleasure. Kate had a superb sense of timing, George discovered. Whatever he needed, she kept him waiting until one heartbeat before unbearable, then she gave him more than he could have hoped. Her hands knew what his skin wanted.

"You're beautiful," he whispered to her, knowing the trite old words to be inadequate.

"So are you," she whispered back.

No one had ever called George Clement Burningfeather beautiful. It had never occurred to him that the term might be applied to a man. Yet he recognized it for what it was: a high honor. That clean, simple word, without all the euphemisms and evasions, was an accolade. A salute.

As her hands explored him he felt the male's ancient moment of concern, of insufficiency. Then its counterpoint, a sudden sure pride. He took her strongly, knowing himself capable and powerful.

"Yes!" cried Kate-Who-Sings-Songs.

Sitting on the splintery steps, looking at the stars, Cloud-Being-Born heard that cry. It was soft and low and muffled by the walls of the shack, yet he heard it. His keen ears would have heard if it had been much softer and much farther away.

He had been waiting for that sound.

The old man nodded to himself. Slowly, giving his ancient joints plenty of time, he got to his feet. He cast one more look at the stars.

Then, done with waiting at last, he went into the store and lay down contentedly on the pile of blankets in the corner that was his only bed.

Cloud-Being-Born had everything he needed now.

Before dawn, George and Kate lay pressed together on the narrow cot that smelled of sweat and love, and listened to the beating of their hearts. At last Kate made a move as if to get up, but he held her back.

"Where are you going?"

"Back to my own bed, before the others wake up."

"Don't you want them to know about this?"

"It isn't anyone else's business."

"Isn't it?" George wondered. "We're a mighty small group here. What one does could affect all. Stay with me, Kate. Let people see us together."

With a smile in her voice, she asked, "You want to boast?"

"Maybe," he admitted.

She snuggled against him.

They did not leave the shack until the red sun had begun to peep over the horizon. The sun was always red now, night and morning. It glared at the earth through an omnipresent dust haze. There seemed no moisture left in the world except the blood in their bodies. And that, too, would overheat, boil away, evaporate as the planet roasted and shriveled.

But there was a little life left. George resolved to enjoy what they had. He took Kate's hand in his own and gave it an encouraging squeeze.

"I don't suppose old Cloud-Being-Born is empowered to marry people," he said.

Kate glanced at him. "What?"

"Marry. You remember. Join for life, et cetera. I don't have that much to offer, I know. Slim prospects, you might say. But . . ."

She turned to face him. Her eyes were large and very solemn in the lurid dawn light. "I marry you," she said. "Here. Now. I, Kate, take thee, George."

"I, George, take thee, Kate," he responded, equally solemn.

The great hush of dawn lay around them. The dying land was witness.

The old man standing just inside the door of the general store, gazing out, was witness too. He said over his shoulder to Harry Delahunt, "Gather everyone. Here. Now."

The rising sun was a red and baleful eye.

Harry went first to the barracks, then to the individual shacks.

Some people had opted for communal life in the barracks but others had preferred to be alone, at least for part of the time. The community accommodated both.

Everyone was awake. Mary Ox-and-a-Burro's little girl was playing happily, the picture of health. Mary picked her up, gave her a loving hug, and followed Harry Delahunt outside.

The atmosphere was sultry and oppressive. Walking from their sleeping quarters to the store was enough to set people's lungs to laboring and their hearts to pounding. The little girl's good humor evaporated. She clung tightly to her mother's hand, with the thumb of her other hand firmly fixed in her mouth.

Harry did not need to summon George and Kate. To George it seemed somehow appropriate that they go to the hub of the reservation, following their exchange of vows. He felt a need to be at the center of the community; at the center of what life remained.

When they entered the store they found Cloud-Being-Born on his feet. The old man stood facing the door. He peered intently at the face of each person who entered, then gave a nod as if checking them off against a mental list.

George went up to him. The occasion required a formal announcement. "Kate and I . . . we've decided to marry," he said, feeling suddenly shy.

But Cloud-Being-Born hardly seemed to notice. He gave one of his brief nods, grunted, and looked past George to see who was entering the store next.

George went over to Kate, who was standing by the counter. "Bit of an anticlimax," he reported. "The old chief doesn't seem impressed by our marriage."

"Did you think he would be?"

"I thought he'd do something. Say something. Disapprove, maybe, I don't know. But I expected a reaction."

Kate patted his arm consolingly. "It doesn't matter. This only concerns us, really."

To her surprise, Cloud-Being-Born turned and looked straight at her, as if he had heard her words, though she had spoken very softly. Even more surprisingly, he smiled.

Then he raised his arms. "Strength of man, strength of woman, are joined!" he announced in a clear voice that belied his years. "It is a sign!"

The assembling group looked at him blankly.

"When everyone is here, we go outside," Cloud-Being-Born said. "Harry. You go, look. Be certain no one is left out." With an imperious gesture, he sent Harry out the door for one final head check. Then he just stood quietly, waiting.

"What's this all about?" George said out of the corner of his mouth to Will Westervelt.

"Beats me. Prayer meeting before breakfast?"

"I don't think so. You see anybody preparing food?"

Will glanced around. "I don't see anybody doing anything. Think I'll sit down." He started toward the nearest chair.

"Stay where you are." Cloud-Being-Born's voice cut the already overheated air like a stab of lightning.

Harry returned. "Got 'em all," he announced, shepherding the last of the group, a yawning Sandy Parkins, ahead of him.

"Good. We go now." Cloud-Being-Born headed for the door, obviously expecting everyone to follow him.

"Hey!" Anne Swimming Ducks protested. "No cup of coffee?"

"No time," said the old man.

Harry Delahunt advised, "We better go with him. That's what he wants."

"But the sun's up and it's already very hot outside," said Mary. "I don't want to take my child out again if I don't have to."

Harry shook his head. "You have to."

"Is that an order?"

"I guess so, yeah."

"By whose authority?" Will Westervelt wanted to know.

"His, of course." Harry pointed a thumb toward the old Indian, who by this time was out on the porch and on his slow, methodical way down the steps. "Someone go catch him and give him an arm to lean on," Harry added. He did not do it himself, however. He stayed in the store, bullying and cajoling to get the others out.

The teenaged boy caught up with Cloud-Being-Born and walked beside him, but the old man did not lean on the young one. He marched straight and sure across the dying earth with his head up.

The others, mystified, followed.

They were all too aware of the gathering heat; the baleful sun.

Cloud-Being-Born led his strange little parade for some hundred yards or so, to a withered clump of mesquite trees that slumped dejectedly at the edge of the rutted road.

The road led east.

Toward the sun.

Cloud-Being-Born stopped walking and drew a deep breath. For a moment he swayed; then he put one hand on the boy's shoulder and steadied himself.

When he spoke his voice was strong, however. "This place must do," he said. "We must do. We must hope there are others to do, also. You." He looked meaningfully at George. "You said there are others? Still alive?"

"Some, yes," George replied, puzzled.

"Like us?"

"I don't know what you . . . yes. Like us. At least there were. Amerindians, Maoris, Inuit, some African tribes . . ." George felt a growing sense of understanding.

"Ah." The old man took another deep breath. "Let us hope they know. Know what is needed. Know how to do." Cloud-Being-Born closed his eyes briefly, communing with himself. Then he opened them and looked toward each of his people in turn.

"You stand there," he began, beckoning to Harry and pointing to a bit of ground that seemed like any other bit of ground. Harry went over to it. "No," said Cloud-Being-Born. "One step back. There.

"Now you." He gestured to Mary Ox-and-a-Burro. "You, there."

But when Mary started forward holding her child's hand, the old man ordered, "Leave child! She has her own place."

Kate swiftly crouched down beside the little girl and comforted her as she watched her mother walk away from her.

Why don't any of them disobey him? George wondered. Or at least ask more questions?

But when his own turn came and the old man assigned him to a particular spot of earth, George felt his feet carrying him without hesitation.

It took a long time to get everyone arranged to Cloud-Being-Born's satisfaction. Meanwhile, the sun pounded on their heads. Not everyone was wearing a hat. Most of the women had straw hats, and the little girl was wearing a strange and faded garment that appeared to have once been a cotton sunbonnet. But the young boy was bareheaded, as was the old Indian's adult granddaughter.

Nor did Cloud-Being-Born himself have any kind of protection from the sun. It beat down mercilessly on his uncovered grey head.

George curiously studied the arrangement the old man had made using his people. There were thirty of them altogether, including himself and the children. They were spaced at irregular intervals to form a rough star shape with four points. The youngest children were at the outer edges. Cloud-Being-Born was at the center. He had very deliberately placed George and Kate on either side of him, so that they faced one another.

"Now," the old man said.

"Now we dance the Healing Dance."

"But there isn't a medicine wheel," George said.

Cloud-Being-Born replied, "Medicine wheel is not like medicine doctors give. Means something else. Means the moon. Means the seasons. Today we need to make medicine with the sky. Different."

He closed his eyes and began to chant.

The others stood, glancing uncertainly at one another. Are we supposed to do something? George wondered. If it's a dance, shouldn't we be moving around?

But no one else was moving. They had not been told to move. They stood. And waited.

The old Indian chanted.

Then Harry Delahunt began to move. His feet shuffled; his body began to turn in a series of abrupt, jerky movements. When he faced toward George, George could see that his eyes were open but were not looking at anything in particular. He held out one arm, however, rigid forefinger pointing.

At Two Fingers.

Something seemed to jump between them, like a spark of electricity. Two Fingers' body responded with the same sort of jerky movement that was animating Harry's. He began his own chant, almost sotto voce, very different from that of Cloud-Being-Born. As he rotated in place he held his hands palm upward, toward the sky.

Harry pointed at Kate.

Kate began to sing. A soft, wordless, plaintive air, rising and falling, strangely reminiscent of the sound of wind soughing in pines.

Harry continued to single out each member of the group in turn, as if he were turning on the power points of a . . .

. . . of a grid.

George felt gooseflesh rising on his shoulders.

Each person, when called upon, responded intuitively with something unique to that person. Their special gift. Their contribution to the dance.

The old man's granddaughter was a weaver, and when her turn came she began tracing patterns in the air with flying fingers, as if she were drawing invisible threads together.

Slim Sapling had been, in his former life and long ago, a professional boxer. When his time came he doubled his fists and began a simulated attack on the blazing sun, pummeling it furiously, darting and ducking, bobbing and weaving, defending the earth against its unshielded rays.

What will I do when my turn comes? George wondered. How will I know? How do *they* know?

The faces of the performers were trancelike. Perhaps they did not know what they were doing, or why.

Suddenly George realized that questioning was not relevant. Not appropriate. The thought processes of the human mind were not involved here. Each person in turn was submitting to the control of the old man's chanting, which in its turn was an intuitive response to something else.

Cloud-Being-Born wore the same trancelike expression as the others. The syllables he was chanting were not coming from him, but through him.

In the moment when George realized this, Harry Delahunt's finger pointed at him.

He felt a very definite electrical jolt. The sensation was unsettling but not unpleasant; curiously like the jolt of Cloud-Being-Born's firewater.

A tingling ran through his body. Harry's pointing finger moved on, seemingly making selections at random. Yet George felt that the connection remained, and as each new person was singled out, he was aware of an added force being joined to his own.

He was not unconscious. He did not even think he was in a trance. He was perfectly aware of who he was and where he was; he was also aware of a most curious phenomenon inside his skull. As if they were ranged around the perimeter of his brain, he could see the glowing computer banks and the charts showing wind currents and barometric readings, the plethora of scientific fact from which a meteorologist made his assessments.

George found himself studying them as if he were sitting in his air-conditioned office, forehead wrinkled in thought, fingers flying over the keyboard of his word processor as he made his notes. This and this and that, yes. Major depression here. Anticyclonic winds accelerating there. Yes. All in his head, clear to his inner eye.

Then something else came into his head. He became aware that he was listening to Cloud-Being-Born chant, but he was no longer hearing meaningless syllables. The old man was speaking directly to him, and the words made sense.

"Show me," said Cloud-Being-Born. "Show me where we are. Now."

And George scanned the maps and charts and pinpointed the exact location. "Here," he said in his head.

"And what is this?"

"That's an area of high pressure."

"What does it do?"

George tried to frame a simplistic explanation, but it was not necessary. He had only to open the door to his hard-won knowledge and the old man walked in.

He heard Cloud-Being-Born's distinctive grunt. "If high pressure moves this way, what happens?"

Again, George thought the answer—and the Indian knew it at once. In his head, standing with him in his head, surveying the technological miracles he could never in a thousand years have understood.

George had no way of measuring the amount of time that passed as Cloud-Being-Born sucked him dry of knowledge. He could feel that knowledge being disseminated through the group; through the network Harry had linked. Each person was receiving as much of it as they needed to incorporate with their own abilities.

Two Fingers ceased making smoothing motions with his palms toward the sky and began making great sweeping gestures with his arms.

Kate's song became less gentle and more insistent, as if a drum were beating in her, establishing a compelling rhythm.

The weaver bowed and bent and pulled and tugged, seizing invisible strands and crossing them over one another in an intricate pattern.

The boxer redoubled his symbolic attack on the sun.

Sandy Parkins, crouched on his haunches, was drawing designs in the sand.

Mary Ox-and-a-Burro, who could divine water, was rocking back and forth on her heels, turning her head from side to side like a blind person, sniffing the scorching air.

The teenaged boy began pulling hairs from his uncovered head. Wearing the communal entranced expression he began arranging the hairs on his bare chest, attaching each to his skin with a bit of saliva. When his mouth was too dry to furnish spit he paused, worked his lips, gnawed on his tongue, then at last found another drop of moisture and continued.

Everyone had something specific to do.

All the while the old man chanted.

All the while the sun blazed in the cloudless, killing sky.

All the while Cloud-Being-Born continued to demand access to the contents of George's head.

Through the Dance, George felt the others. He recognized the distinctive flavor of each mind; he observed and understood what they were doing. He knew, without having to think about it, why an awkward thirteen-year-old boy who knew nothing of metaphysics had precisely arranged a pattern of hairs on his skin to correspond to ley lines. He knew why Mary was searching for water. He knew why Bart Brigham was stamping his feet in an irregular rhythm.

A seemingly random assortment of human beings were performing together an incredibly intricate series of apparently unrelated actions that would make no sense at all to anyone else.

But it did make sense.

George felt the exact moment when the first faint sense of control touched the group. They all felt it simultaneously.

Control.

It was like the unforgettable moment when a child trying to learn to ride a bicycle wobbles, upright and unsupported, for a few revolutions of the wheels.

The balance was quickly lost but they tried again, tried harder, concentrated more.

The sense of being able to control returned.

Sweat poured from their bodies.

George was increasingly sensitive, in some new way, to the others. Kate in particular he perceived as he had never perceived a woman before. He felt her weaknesses, aspects of her persona that were incomplete, or misdirected, or in the process of being shed as a snake sheds its skin.

He felt her strengths, and knew what they had cost her.

He found the deep, calm pool at her center, and knew she had gone through an excruciating period of self-questioning and self-blame, to arrive at last at total, clear-eyed honesty.

He saw himself as Kate was seeing him. A man with the child still alive behind his eyes. A man who could cry, who could be romantic about being an Indian, even when he saw the reality of the reservation. A dichotomous human being . . .

Dichotomous . . . divided in two . . . consisting of two parts that need to be joined together again . . .

Joining.

Healing.

Cloud-Being-Born's voice rose above the sounds many of the others were making, a clarion command.

"Look!" he cried.

"Look up!"

26

They could not stop the Dance.

They would not be allowed to stop the Dance until it

succeeded in whatever its purpose might be—or

until it killed them.

But they were allowed enough autonomy to look up.

They were exhausted. George could feel it in himself and knew it must be worse for many of the others. Human flesh and blood could not sustain so intense an effort, in such terrible heat, for long. They needed a transfusion of motivation.

They were allowed to look up.

"Oh!" said a voice. The littlest girl, whose task had been to perform a pantomime with her own shadow, continued her pantomime but threw back her head and stared at the sky with huge eyes.

The blazing, brassy sky.

The yellow, superheated, poisoned sky that was burning away life.

For months that sky had been cloudless.

Now something interrupted its glaring expanse.

A tiny thread appeared, halfway between horizon and zenith. It could almost have been a hair on the eyeball.

But it was not.

As they watched, it grew. It drew unto itself, out of apparent nothingness, a visible wisp of matter as delicate as a feather. George had to squint to be certain he was seeing it. The heat and glare made his eyes water.

All the time the old man was in his head, busy.

The delicate tracery in the sky grew minimally larger. A tenuous swirl of vapor resolved itself into a tiny scrap of cloud.

In the mountains of New Hampshire, George had once watched as a mountain drew to its summit the moisture evaporating from the pine forests on its flanks. The moisture had coalesced into a silvery banner that blew from the highest peak, waiting for a montane wind to dislodge it and blow it across the land in the form of cloud.

Now he was seeing the same phenomenon take place above the desert. No trees. No mountains. Just polluted sky and pitiless sun. And the Dance.

"Damn," George said in an awestruck whisper.

Inside his head, the old man was working himself into a fever pitch. Like the conductor of a symphony he was trying to keep all the instruments in perfect harmony while building them toward an inevitable climax. George could feel the frenzy in him, and knew he could not continue for much longer. He was a very old man.

The cloud was expanding.

It grew from a wisp the apparent size of a fingernail to a mass the size of a half-dollar. Then the size of a bus. Then it multiplied itself into the sails of a galleon, full and billowing in breathtaking purity against the backdrop of dirty sky.

The clouds did not look polluted. They were as clean and white as fresh snow.

The armada set sail. It cast cool shadows on the land beneath as it headed for the northern horizon. There the clouds thickened, deepened, darkened. Became black-purple.

The first breath of cool air swept southward.

Cloud-Being-Born redoubled his efforts. Vision faded; George was not using human eyes any longer. He was being forced to a level of concentration he would not have thought possible, drawing on inherited gifts of strength and intuition and sensitivity.

At the old man's command he stretched his awareness. It was seized and woven by the Dancers into a net of consciousness that was then flung beyond the limits of the reservation and cast across the continent, seeking.

"Go farther!" cried the old man in George's head.

George had an impression of ocean, of water and weight.

Then he was deliciously buoyant, floating upward to follow the air currents he had once studied. Entering familiar territory seen from a new perspective, he began to examine the abused fabric of the atmosphere and guide the Healing Dance to its wounds.

He came to a vast gaping hole, like an immense burn. Its scorched, decaying edges extended for thousands of miles. The hole sickened him. It was a loathsome disease, a terrifyingly large ulcer that had somehow become malignant.

"Here!" George called to the Dance, summoning. "Here!"

Healing began to flow from earth to sky. George felt waves of comfort channeled through himself. The Dancers were mending the ozone layer. But the hole resisted. Its edges tore again.

"We need more help!" Cloud-Being-Born cried. "Can you find any others like us?"

George was totally consumed with his own efforts. He could not stretch any farther. But Kate responded.

Her song altered. Its syllables were incorporated into the structure of the Dance. Her song was no longer audible to human ears, but, amplified by the Dance, was radiating outward in sound waves capable of covering vast distances in microseconds.

Kate's song began reaching other minds. Elsewhere.

From such far-flung corners of the earth as the depths of the Amazonian jungle and the mountain peaks of Tibet, the response came. It came as a searing whiplash of energy that scorched through the Dance.

Harry Delahunt writhed, screaming with pain and clutching his head.

But the Dance must not stop.

Cloud-Being-Born was driving George mercilessly. George's knowledge was the guide. An increasing number were following the charts in his head. He could sense them joining in as Kate's song reached pockets of survivors in Australia. Alaska. A village in Wales. A community in Mongolia.

People who had never forgotten they were an integral part of the living planet.

Their mental strength was added to the Dance. Each had something unique to contribute as a result of that person's assortment of genes and experiences. No two were alike. Each was invaluable.

Summoned to the Dance, the last children of earth gathered into one consciousness. They had no sense of self.

There was only the Dance. The Dance, succeeding!

The Dance, cleansing and healing.

The Dance as an act of creation, making the earth whole again.

Feeding on powerful energies, the Dance was taking on a life of its own—and emotions of its own.

All the damage could not be corrected at once. Toxic wastes could not be made to vanish. They would have to be absorbed and purified, which in some cases would take eons.

Pollutants must be neutralized. They would have to be taken apart through natural action and reassembled into the basic, harmless substances from which man had constructed them. This, too, would take time.

Trees would have to grow from seedlings to replace the murdered forests.

Many generations would be required to restore the ecological balance of the seas.

The planet would be a long time healing.

The Dance had done all it could. The rest was up to the ages. But the Dance was not satisfied to wait; the freshening air began to crackle with the very human emotion of frustration.

Lightning laced the sky.

Thunder boomed its response.

Lightning stalked around the horizon on forked legs.

Thunder roared and rolled, reverberating like the cry of an angry god.

Lightning flamed in a dazzling sheet across the heavens, illuminating masses of boiling black cloud like dark armies on the march.

The air crackled and sizzled with anger.

Anger and energy and desire!

A minute fraction of George's commandeered consciousness sensed the gathering storm and recognized danger. He fought to clear his thoughts. He called out in his head to Cloud-Being-Born, "We've gone too far! We've unleashed forces we can't handle!"

He was trying to communicate with the old man, but instead he caught, just for an instant, the flavor of Kate's gentle irony, and heard her saying in his mind, "How like us."

Then she was gone. A massive storm howled around them, engulfing Dance and Dancers.

George felt the last shreds of their control being torn from them.

Ocean of air was convulsed by tidal wave of storm. Rain fell with murderous force, pelting down on the parched earth faster than it could be absorbed. Hurricanes roared into being, battering land and sea. Tornadoes spun out of nowhere in a deadly dance of their own, whirling cones of death darting down from the blackened sky.

The wind rose to an unbearable shriek.

George had an impression of incalculably mighty forces rushing in to fill a void. Their pressure kept building until he felt as if he was at the bottom of the sea, with its entire weight crushing down upon him. He fought desperately to keep his lungs working.

The old man in his head was silent.

But there was no other silence.

Above the tumult of storms that raked her from pole to pole, the earth screamed.

27

George came back to himself very

slowly.

He felt as if every bone in his body was broken.

He lay without moving. Gradually he became

aware that he was lying in mud.

Rain was pouring down on him with the force of a deluge.

The storm had passed, however.

He remembered the storm.

He remembered the terror of the storm.

But it was over. There was only rain. Cold rain falling from cold air.

George drew a deep but shaky breath. The air tasted sweet on his tongue.

His open eyes looked up into a sky banked with clouds. The clouds were no longer black, but a soft grey. Even as he looked they began to break up slightly. The deluge eased, became only a moderate downpour.

He sat up. His bones were not broken, but his entire body was bruised. His brain felt even more bruised. The inside of his skull was sore.

The old man!

He blinked rainwater out of his eyes and looked around.

He was sitting in the center of a circle of bodies. Sodden figures lay all about him in the mud, unmoving.

"Kate!"

She was some distance away. She lay flattened on the earth as if all the life had been pounded out of her. George threw himself toward her in a lurching, crawling run.

He cradled her head in his arms. Her eyes were closed. He could detect no sign of breathing.

He tried desperately to force his bruised brain to remember how to do mouth-to-mouth resuscitation.

Keep calm. Pinch the nostrils closed. Force air into the lungs through the mouth. Establish a rhythm. Keep calm!

Her jaw surrendered slackly to his probing fingers. Her mouth gaped open. George covered it with his own and began trying to blow life into her body.

There was no response.

In with the good, out with the bad, keep calm. Blow into her mouth, press down on her chest, maintain the rhythm. "Breathe, dammit!" Make her breathe.

Make her breathe!

Taking great gulps of cool, sweet air, he forced them deep into Kate's lungs.

After a frighteningly long time, her eyelids fluttered.

When she was actually able to open her eyes and look up at him, George felt weak with relief. "Hi there," he said inanely.

With an effort, she focused on his face. "You look awful. Water's dripping off your nose," she said in a faint voice.

"It's raining."

"Raining?" Her voice grew stronger.

"Yeah. And it's cool. Can you feel it?"

"Cool. Yes. Yes! I feel it!"

"You'll get a chill. We'll have to wrap you in something to keep you warm." George looked around, thinking vaguely that he might borrow a shirt from one of the others.

The others!

Puddles of people were scattered on the drenched earth. One was moving, feebly.

George got up and ran over to him. "Will! You okay? Say something!"

Will Westervelt groaned. "I don't have to get up until seven," he said clearly, eyes screwed shut.

"You have to get up right now, dammit. Get up and help me."

Will's eyes opened. "What happened?"

"We did it! We did something. I don't know exactly. But everyone's stunned. Or . . . get up, help me with them. We've got to get these people out of the rain. It's getting colder every minute."

"Colder?" said Will in astonishment. He scrambled to his feet and stood, swaying.

George went back to Kate and helped her to her own feet. "Move around," he advised, "warm yourself up."

"I'll be all right. What about the children?"

George found the little girl lying half under the body of Jerry Swimming Ducks. The child was awake and just starting to cry. George eased her out from under Jerry's unconscious form and looked around for her mother.

Mary Ox-and-a-Burro lay a few yards away. Dead.

Her body was not only lifeless but dessicated, as if every drop of moisture had been sucked out of it.

George stared down at her in horror. Then he turned and carried the child to Kate. "Look after her, and don't let her go anywhere near Mary if you can help it."

Harry Delahunt was dead too, his body blackened and burned, almost unrecognizable.

The young boy was alive. Dazed, almost incoherent at first, he responded when Will began talking to him and was soon on his feet. Will put him into Kate's care and went on, with George, separating the living from the dead.

Almost half of the Dancers were dead. Their resources had been totally exhausted.

Out of the corner of his eye, George kept glancing toward the silent form he knew was Cloud-Being-Born. He knew the old man must be dead. He had probably been the first to die. But he did not want to go to him and confirm the fact. It was as if the old Indian held a magic that would be broken once he was accepted as dead.

George still felt the influence of the magic. He saw its power in the falling rain and heard its voice in the north wind.

At last he could not put it off any longer. He went over to the old man's body and crouched down beside it.

Cloud-Being-Born lay on his back. His face was turned toward the sky. His dead eyes were open.

The sky was reflected in them.

George stared down.

As he watched, the clouds mirrored in the old man's eyes sped before the force of the wind. As they moved, they revealed the sky behind them.

The blue sky.

George twisted his neck and looked up.

The sky between the gaps in the cloud was azure-blue.

George blinked, then let the tears come.

It took a long time to get everyone, the living and the dead, back to the store. The dead were laid in a row on the porch, covered with blankets. The living huddled inside, wrapped in more blankets.

The cold was increasing.

Of the living, Two Fingers was the weakest. Even he did not seem to know if he would survive. Anne Swimming Ducks used the last of the coffee, liberally laced with firewater, to try to give him some strength. Then the straight firewater went the rounds. They drank it down like water. It seemed to have no effect.

Gazing out the door at the bodies on the porch, Slim Sapling remarked, "We need Cloud-Being-Born to conduct the burial ritual."

The teenaged boy spoke up. "I think we'll know what to do when the time comes."

"He's right," someone else agreed. "When it stops raining, we'll just know."

In spite of the patches of blue sky occasionally visible, there were still clouds and rain. No one was anxious to see the rain end, and the burying begin.

They waited.

While they waited, they talked among themselves.

There was a surprising lack of speculation about the Dance and its results. What one knew, everyone knew, though their minds were no longer linked in the Dance.

Their questions were about the future.

They felt confident there would be a future, now.

"Just think of it," said Will Westervelt. "Little groups of survivors like us scattered all across the globe. It's sort of like natural selection, when you think about it."

Kate knew what he meant. "It's as if," she said softly, "the planet left enough of us alive to save herself."

They sat in the cold and considered the thought.

Someone asked, "Think we should try to join up with the others?"

George shook his head. "Logistically impossible. There was an almost total breakdown of travel by the time I came here. I'd say it's worse now. Hopeless, internationally. No, it's better if we stay here and make the best of what we have. Get things going again in our little corner."

Kate managed a faint chuckle. "The announcement of the end of the world was slightly premature."

George grinned at her. "It was." He reached out and took her hand. Her fingers twined through his.

"It's not going to be easy," he warned. "The effects of what happened are going to be a long time working through the ecosystem. We'll have to face that and find ways to live with it. I suspect there will be a continued, and massive, climatic change on a planetary basis until some sort of natural balance is reestablished."

"What sort of change?" Jerry Swimming Ducks wanted to know. His speech was still slightly slurred, but he was otherwise recovered from a long period of unconsciousness.

George thought before answering. He felt the stirring of a powerful intuition. It might have been a remnant of his recent expanded awareness.

It might have been a genetic gift surfacing.

"The planet's had many recurring cycles of glaciation and warming," George told the others. "That's been the natural course of events. Something tells me we have another ice age coming now. A monster, I'd predict. To finish cleansing the surface and get the earth back into sync."

"Surely we won't live to see it?" someone said nervously.

"Probably not," George agreed. "Our descendants will, though. They'll have to learn how to survive it."

A tinge of coral crept into Kate's cheeks. Her fingers tightened on George's and squeezed hard. "Our descendants," she murmured, savoring the word. "Let's hope they appreciate what they inherit."

Keeping an optimistic smile on his face, George returned Kate's squeeze.

He did not say what he was thinking.

We might have it all to do again someday.

Humans are an arrogant species.

When the ice cap melted, the seas rose.

When the ice cap melted, the seas rose.